Unwelcome Audience

Martin Russell

Walker and Company
New York

First published in the United States of America
in 1986 by the Walker Publishing Company, Inc.

Library of Congress Cataloging-in-Publication Data

Russell, Martin James, 1934–
    Unwelcome audience.

    Reprint. Originally published: A dangerous place
to dwell. London : Collins, c1978.
    I. Title.
PR6068.U86D36   1986   823'.914   86-11072
ISBN 0-8027-5652-2

Printed in the United States of America

10 9 8 7 6 5 4 3 2 1

CHAPTER I

I'M LOOKING AHEAD, SAYS THE GIRL FROM WEST HAM

Biting uninhibitedly into a cream-stuffed pastry, my tea-time companion eyed me with candour across the table.

'The past year or so,' said Anjelica Browne, her clear voice still betraying more of the influence of East London than of California, 'has taught me a lot.'

Contemplating the residue of the confection as if regretting not having helped herself to a couple while she was at it, she went on:

'The thing I've come to realize is that I can be *stretched*. And what's more, that I must be. I want to show people that I'm not just a saucer-eyed creature who happens to be quite good at stepping out of her clothes. I want them to see that I can *perform*.'

My acquiescent noises must have rung hollow. With a touch on her magnetism accelerator, the luminous Miss Browne drew me closer to her in the tea lounge of London's plush Cosmopole Hotel facing the spring daffodils of Hyde Park. I had the distinct feeling that, on full throttle, she could comfortably have shifted the Rockefeller Building a yard to the right.

'Corny it may sound to you,' she said severely (*No, no*), 'but it's still a fact – the spreading of wings is vital in this business. Unless, that is, one doesn't mind being pinned to the same card for life. Which I do.'

I found myself wondering which of the Herb Joseph myth-makers had primed their prodigy with this one; but dismissed the thought as unworthy. Our biggest home-produced screen name in three decades possesses enough gumption, one senses, to create her own metaphor.

She seemed to read my mind. Challengingly she added: 'And I haven't been got at over this. In fact, there are plenty who've said I should stick to what I do best. But then, I daresay people like – like Florence Nightingale, for example, had the same advice. The world's full of cautionary voices. There comes a time when it's best to ignore them.'

But Miss Browne, I murmured, was scarcely bracketing herself with the Florence Nightingales or Nurse Cavells of this planet?

The smile that rewarded this had the penetration of a tropical sun. I began to get an inkling of how it was that one of Hollywood's tungsten-capped motion picture tycoons had cheerfully separated himself from half a million dollars and a three per cent share of the gross in exchange for Anjelica's relatively modest (in duration, that is) services on behalf of *The Fantasies of Flora Smythe*, currently on global release and reportedly well on the way already to recouping the awesome loss sustained by the erratic Herb Joseph from his previous cinematic venture, the ill-fated *Rusty Tarrant* (which, as it happens, did *not* feature our Anjie).

'One hopes,' she said winsomely, 'not to be bracketed with anyone in particular. As far as I'm concerned, I'm just me, Anjelica Browne, with or without the final "e" – the girl from Eastern Gardens who was lucky enough to be noticed in the crowd. Okay, the *Miss Cosmos* title wasn't exactly a handicap. I've never said it was. But you know, don't you, what became of most of the previous winners? Things just happened to work out better for me, that's all. Now, with luck, they'll improve still further.' A beam came at me. 'That's my immediate future in a nut-shell. Which is what you met me to ask about, isn't it?'

I hastened to agree. A down-to-earth young woman, Miss Anjelica Browne, elder daughter of a West Ham printing technician and his ex-typist wife from Barking. I experienced the awakening of a certain sympathy for the Herb Josephs of the Golden West, mere cardboard targets for the optical tracer-bullets that were now pinning me to my heavily-upholstered chair. The future, I managed to croak. This, certainly, was what fascinated most of us. After *Furnace of the Mind* – what then?

'Just now,' she retorted, 'I'm not looking beyond *Furnace*. It's only just emerging from the planning stage, after all. And seeing that it's the most exciting project I've been in on since I started out in films, I'm giving it my whole attention. For the moment, anything else can take care of itself.'

Was she, I probed delicately, looking forward to working with a director of the calibre of Roger Mayhew, whose dearest friend – if he has one – would hesitate before ascribing Christian benevolence to his make-up?

'I'm sure Mr Mayhew and I will get along fine.' Nothing if not diplomatic, the stunning Miss Browne . . . when she feels it to be necessary. Was there the slightest tightening of that seraphic mouth, the faintest lift of the gold-topped head? If it came to a mid-scene personality clash, I for one should not care to take bets on the outcome. Neither, one is aware, would she: though for different reasons. The essential innocence of Anjelica's screen caperings – the quality that undoubtedly accounts for the universality of their appeal – seems merely a reflection of her real-life character, in which nothing so questionable as a gambling streak, by any impartial reckoning, would stand a snowball's chance in hell of survival.

Resolute, I persisted. 'Just suppose some kind of difference arose between you. A question of interpretation . . .'

Again the smile. 'We'll cross that bridge if we come to it.'

How true was it to say that Miriam Hargill, tormented heroine of *Furnace of the Mind*, represented the kind of part that Miss Browne, actress, would prefer to concentrate upon from now on?

Munching the final morsel, she thought about it. Others in the tea lounge – of both sexes – were lobbing glances our way; I had the feeling that few of them were alighting on me. With the kind of glow she radiates, Anjelica Browne could light and heat a cathedral. Without trying.

'I wouldn't mind,' she confessed, 'tackling some of the major roles. Hedda Gabler, for instance. Later, when I was more . . . mature. Honestly, I think I've got potential. I'm crossing my fingers that *Furnace* will prove it.'

I said I was certain it would. Then took my audacity in both hands.

'The past few months,' I said cautiously, 'from all accounts can't have been easy for you in your private life. Anything you'd care to say about that?'

I expected a flash of anger and I got one: but it was brief. Depositing her fork carefully on the plate, she slid it aside. Her voice when she answered was quiet, controlled.

'My private life, I've always said, is just that. A lot's been written and talked about it – this is something I can do nothing about. When you're widely known, you have to accept it. Right now, all I want to say is that the past is past, and the future is what counts. That's the way I'm looking – ahead, not back.'

One last attempt. Was there, I asked warily, the slimmest possibility of a reconciliation with Terry O'Malley at any time in this future she was keeping her eyes upon?

This time, instead of wrath I got a glint of humour.

'Earth's a small place these days,' she observed. 'Why don't you jump a jet out to Santa Barbara and ask him?'

'My God,' I said.

Allowing the *Sunday World* to drop to the carpet, I kept my feet up on the deep-sprung settee for a while, thinking it over. Presently I retrieved the newspaper and re-read the article. Eventually, I started to laugh.

The hilarity did no harm. It stopped me picking up the telephone and dialling the *Sunday World*'s number. Nobody would have been there, anyhow. I did pick up the telephone, but the number I asked for was one in Mayfair, and the voice that belatedly replied was sleep-suffused, California-accented and disgruntled. Though not for long.

'Herbie? Did I get you out of bed?'

'Hi, honey. Nope, you didn't. I'm still there.'

'You haven't seen the *World*, then?'

'I've not what?'

By the time we had this sorted out, Herbie was awake. 'So, you grabbed a page to yourself? That's my Angel. He have some nice things to say about you?'

'He had some things.'

'Yeah?' Herbie's voice took on a serrated edge. 'Like what?'

I fed him a quote or two. For a space there was digestive silence from the distant bed. Then his voice returned, stronger, more incisive.

'We'll be in touch with this joker. What's his name? Nigel *What*? Moorforth? Okay, I've made a note of that. I'll have Wally Parsons put in a call – '

'No, Herbie.'

'Huh?'

'He hasn't written anything I didn't say. That is, all he's done is string it together so as to make me sound like a cross between Monroe and Garbo with a splash of the Taylors, and you like Howard Hughes with a touch of the Sam Goldwyns . . . and when you read it a second time, you find the effect isn't that bad. Even if it's not quite the one we were after. I don't see there's anything we can do.'

'There's always something we can do.'

'Only to make it worse. Shouldn't we shrug it off and chalk it up to publicity? Which it is, after all. It needn't do *Furnace* a scrap of harm.'

'It'd better not.' He spoke like a boy threatened with an attack upon his pet dog. 'But I tell you what, Angel. Next request we have for an interview, we check it out, all the way back to source – right?'

'You can't gag the British Press, you know. Start being

obstructive, they're liable to get shirty and cause a lot of – '

'Who's causing obstruction? It's merely a matter of pre-empting an undesirable . . . Forget it. You're right, we need the media as badly as they need us. How's it feel, honey, to be back in your home town?'

'My home town is West Ham.'

'You don't dig the apartment?'

'The hotel's fine, Herbie. No complaints. Super view across Hyde Park. I think even Nigel Moorforth was impressed.'

Herbie growled something unmannerly about Nigel Moorforth. 'What do you aim to do with yourself today, Angel? There's nothing fixed. Press shindig isn't till Thursday, and I thought maybe – '

'I'd like to call on my family.'

I could hear him swallowing. 'You did say you figured you might do that.'

'D'you mind?'

'No, honey, why would I mind? I'll call for you around eleven, eleven-thirty. We can take in your folks, and after that – '

'I'd prefer really to go by myself. I've not seen them for close on two years. You understand, don't you, Herbie?'

Although my mind was made up, I felt contrite. His disappointment was evident in his silence. This first Sunday of ours in England, I knew, he had pictured as a twelve-hour idyll, just the two of us, I showing him London and he showing me off: a placid prelude to the razz-amatazz that was to follow. Armour-plated though he might be in Nigel Moorforth's estimation, Herbie, I was reasonably sure, had fallen for me in a thunder of echoes, and I was both pleased about it and sorry. The pleasurable part was that a top Hollywood producer who itched to make a prestige movie of a modern classic should be under my spell. The sorrow stemmed from my inability to respond. Investigating my emotions, I had long since concluded that what I felt for Herbie was the tolerant fondness of a niece for a slightly absurd uncle whose expansive generosity was concurrently helpful and an embarrassment. Certain people might have said I was using him. Nigel Moorforth, for one. But it wasn't like that. A bond did exist between us, and there seemed no sense in scissoring it to no purpose.

With a somewhat louder briskness he said, 'Hell, yes, I understand. Naturally you want to see them alone. Maybe we'll get together later in the day, huh?'

Because I was fond of him, I said, 'I'd like that. How about dinner with me here this evening?'

His voice toned down and cheered up. 'It's a date. Tell you what – don't go eating too much of your mother's blackberry pie. We want you in good shape for the next three months.'

'After which,' I said with a laugh, 'I can just let myself go? Don't worry, Herbie. I detest blackberries. So does Mum, for that matter. See you around seven? That'll give us time for a cocktail.'

When he had hung up, boyishly bolstered and exuberant, I ran myself a bath of considerable warmth and depth and occupied it for forty minutes, thinking dreamily about the script.

With one degree of intensity or another, I had been doing this for the past seven months. Since the moment, in fact, when Herbie had called me in to tell me the part was mine. Anjelica Browne as Miriam Hargill. The words still made sweet music. To my ears, at any rate, if not to those of a sceptical world. Nigel Moorforth was simply a microcosm of the universal attitude. The hand across the curled mouth. Anjelica Browne, as Miriam? It was a joke. A derisive handflap from a foundering tycoon. Joseph Films couldn't be serious.

I, who had devoured the book and identified with its heroine well before it became unexpectedly a world bestseller, knew differently. Herbie was committed. He craved to do screen justice to *Furnace of the Mind*. Also he believed that I had it in me to give Miriam the qualities that she demanded. And I happened to consider that he was right.

I was still in my bathrobe when the suite attendant returned for my breakfast tray.

'Good long piece about you, Miss Browne, in the *World* this morning.'

He was a lean, saturnine youth of Italian extraction, with impertinent eyes. My murmured response seemed to leave him dissatisfied. He hovered. 'I suppose you have to put up with a lot of that.'

'Publicity? Yes.'

Still he lingered. I turned from the wall-mirror to face him. 'Was there something else?'

'I had a bet,' he said nonchalantly, 'with the boys downstairs.'

Stifling panic, I said calmly, 'A bet? What about?'

'They said I wouldn't dare ask if you minded . . . you know, when you make these films, whether you minded – '

'Taking my clothes off?'

He smiled. It wasn't a nice smile.

I said, 'You can tell the boys that I'm like someone else they may have heard of. I cry about it all the way to the bank.'

His nose twitched. 'I'll tell 'em.'

When he had gone I dressed slowly, using elements of the outfit in which I had arrived at Heathrow. Suddenly I felt depressed.

CHAPTER II

ON MY LAST visit home, Ted's sweetshop had still jostled the Tube exit. Now, there was an Eiger Face of glass and plastics. The Metropolitan Assurance and Security Service. MASS.

'You'll notice a change or two, love,' Mum had said

on the telephone. 'Streamlined, we're getting. Another five years, you won't know the old place.'

The bus stop, at least, was where it had always been. Crossing the street to the tubular-steel shelter, I saw myself, twenty feet high, partially disrobed in hurtful colour on a hoarding. Flora Smythe's *Fantasies* had found their way to E.15. It was as though they had trailed me across the Atlantic and swarmed nimbly into position to extend a mocking welcome. Inside the shelter, two other people were waiting for a bus. A man, holding the *Sunday Mirror*; and a coloured girl. Neither of them glanced away from their thoughts.

After sixteen minutes the bus arrived. The Sunday schedule. I made for a front seat on the upper deck. From this pitching viewpoint I stared down into people's back-yards and mean kitchens and 'best rooms'; across concrete forecourts strewn with Massey-Ferguson plant; over bridge parapets at rail tracks and sidings. Five years? A romantic, that was Mum, with an ancestry rooted in Irish peat. Here and there, however, I did spot something fresh: a new supermarket, a manicured amenity garden, bingo instead of a double-feature at the Orion Cinema. In the main, it was still my home patch. With a Sunday-morning look about it. And, rounding the acute bend that took us into the approach to Eastern Gardens, the bus lurched as drunkenly as ever into and out of the sunken manhole that the drivers could never avoid.

Walking from the request stop towards the house, I could see from a distance that the paintwork of the shallow bay window stood in desperate need of radical surgery. Dad never noticed things like that. In the end, Mum would daub some undercoat over it herself. If I gave her money to call in the professionals, she would be hurt. 'We've always managed our own decorating, love. You keep your cash. You might be needing it.' Practical help she would have accepted. Anjelica Browne in cover-alls up a stepladder, using blowlamp and scraper. A gem for publicity. If I mentioned it to Wally Parsons, maybe we could set it up.

A figure leapt the three steps to the pavement. Peeping my way, it commenced a hesitant walk. I waved. The walk became decisive. I called out, 'Hi there, Liz.'

We met at the pillar-box. Liz looked smart in a red jersey-suit that bore a marked resemblance, I noted with amusement, to one that I had worn – briefly – for an early scene in *Flora*. She said shyly, 'Wasn't sure if it was you. We thought you'd be coming by car.'

'And miss a ride on a London bus?' We were holding hands. She kissed me; then impulsively wrapped me inside a bear-hug. I gasped.

'Hey – take it easy. I come expensive, you know. Heavy insurance on breakages.'

She stood off, examining me. Either she had lost her freckles or she had discovered remarkable skill with cosmetics. Whatever the means, the outcome was more than fetching. She said breathlessly, 'That awful scarf! Take it off, Anjie. Let's get a proper look at you.'

'Now I'm here, I can.' I tugged it loose. 'The real me,' I said dramatically, shaking out some hair. 'That better?'

'Not half.' In rising excitement, Liz began skipping up and down as we approached the house. 'I suppose you *have* to disguise yourself all the time?'

'Saves trouble. How's Mum?'

'Trying to dig out a packet of biscuits,' Liz said with a gurgle. 'MacFarlane Assorted. She *knows* she put them in the right-hand cupboard . . . only they're not there. They'll turn up on top of the freezer. Now you look fabulous, Anjie.'

'You too. Dad all right?'

'Sunk in the back room with the papers. Pretending he doesn't know you're coming.'

The street door of number 17 stood open, exposing the pale pink and turquoise flowered wallpaper that the three of us – Mum and myself, absently assisted by Dad – had hung in the course of several evenings at a time when Los Angeles, as far as any of us were concerned, was a name that cropped up now and then in newspaper showbiz columns. Liz had been seven. Eight years ago. Deceitfully, without warning, the lump formed in my throat. I hoped Mum would delay her emergence from the kitchen. Then, perversely, as I trod along the passage with Liz at my heels, I wondered why she hadn't appeared. At the kitchen doorway I halted. A rear view of Mum, semi-interred in a cupboard beneath the sink, shattered my remaining defences. In a strangled voice I said, 'Buttered crackers would do, you know . . .'

She hit her head on the cupboard door. Crawling backwards, she wobbled upright, turned in her tracks and released a wail which I echoed wholeheartedly as the laryngeal lump became too much for me. For several minutes we sobbed over one another while Liz embraced the pair of us, setting the seal on the scene's suitability for inclusion in the fifth reel of a screen epic set in the Deep South during the American Civil War. Herbie would have approved. Finally I tore myself clear.

'It's only been twenty-three months!'

Mum mopped at her eyes. 'And two weeks. Cup of coffee?' she asked tearfully. 'I've got Maxwell House.'

'Tea,' I said firmly.

Relief illuminated her face. 'Just switch the kettle on . . .' Doing so with one hand, she blew her nose with a handkerchief in the other. Then managed a smile. 'My, Anjie. You look . . . you look . . .'

'Expensive,' supplied Liz.

'Million dollars.' Mum was regaining poise. She popped teabags by the half-dozen into the pot, inspecting me. 'Did you see your posters?'

'Couldn't miss.' I pulled a face. 'Whatever will the neighbours think?'

'They've all been to see it,' Liz announced. 'Everyone thinks it's great.'

'Have you seen it, Liz?'

'You bet.'

'According to the poster I saw, it has an "X" rating.'

Scorn seized her features. 'I've been getting to see "X" films since I was eleven. Anyway there's nothing in *Flora*.'

'Bit of wife-swapping,' I agreed. 'An orgy or two. Nudity by the acre. Can't think what all the fuss is about.'

'I've seen lots worse on the box.'

'Have you, my girl?' Mum was hurling milk into cups. 'When, might I ask?'

'After you and Dad have gone to bed.' Liz wriggled, looking flushed and pretty and adorable: I could see why she was admitted to 'X' films. Our eyes met; we exchanged winks. Snorting unconvincingly, Mum set the milk jug down with a clap.

'Pop in and say hello to Dad, Anjie. You know where you'll find him.'

'Too much to expect him to poke his head out,' Liz said tolerantly.

I opened the door to the back parlour. A faint rustle came from the *Sunday People* in the cushioned rocker in the farthermost corner; there was no other movement. Tiptoeing across the stained Axminster, I flicked the newsprint lightly with a forefinger.

'Fancy meeting you.'

He came up with an exaggerated start. 'Hul-lo, my dear. No one told me you'd arrived. Good to see you.'

He stood up to receive my kiss. His cheeks, as ever, were smooth and gleaming from soap and razor. He wore his hair longer than when I had last seen him; the strands were directed in fuzzy streaks across his scalp. The lapels of his brown woollen waistcoat sagged from the neck. 'Take the weight off your feet,' he advised, folding the *People* into a careful tablet and sliding it under the rocker cushion, 'and tell us what you've been doing.'

'Dad! You *know* what she's been doing.' Liz had pursued me in. 'Why pretend you've not been taking an interest?'

'All I know,' he rejoined mildly, 'is what I hear you and your mother talking about from time to time.'

I handed him the digital watch I had bought in San Francisco. Rendered incoherent, he attached it gingerly to a wrist while Liz and Mum took similar action with their bracelets of chased silver. Mum's face was mutely eloquent. Liz, less inhibited, whooped her pleasure and delivered a smacking kiss to my left cheek before carrying her arm to the window to examine the markings. Meanwhile a 'Coo-ee!' came from the passage.

'Stand by,' I said ruefully. 'Here we go.' After a tactful opening twenty minutes, Eastern Gardens was about to close in.

'When are you going to get me a screen test, Anjie?' demanded Liz, devouring a third chunk of American candy.

'When you're finished with school exams,' I told her.

She sent me a scowl. Shuffling my colour transparencies back into order, Dad passed them across. 'This new film,' he said, carefully removing his glasses and restoring them to their pouch. 'Why's it being shot here in England?'

'The book,' I explained, 'is set mainly in this country. Also, Herb Joseph reckoned it would cost less here, and he's a bit budget-conscious at the moment.'

'He's not the only one,' observed Mum.

'Another thing is that the author, Jon Templar, is supposed to be acting as some kind of script consultant, and apparently he'd have found it difficult to go to the States. So, all in all, it seemed the obvious thing.'

'How long will it take, my dear?'

'Shooting? Three months is the estimate.'

'Meaning a year,' Liz said knowingly.

'It can't. For tax reasons. By the way, I'll try and arrange for you all to come down to the studios one day and see us at work. If you'd like to.'

'Lovely,' gasped Mum. 'Where are they?'

'We're taking over the ones used by British Unicorn before they folded. Near Winchester.'

'That'll be a nice day out.' Mum got to her feet with the preoccupied look that I remembered vividly. 'I might try reading the book first, give us an idea what it's all about. Feel like giving us a hand with the coffee, Anjie?'

I followed her out to the kitchen. She closed the door firmly. 'What d'you reckon,' she said, igniting a jet of the gas cooker, 'about Lizzie?'

'Film-wise, you mean?'

'Yes. Think she's got what it takes?'

'As far as looks go – and that's quite a way – she certainly has. But it's early days.'

'Mad keen, she is.' Mum passed me a tray.

'I might get Herbie to work her into a crowd scene. But I'm not promising anything. And you're not to breathe a word to her about it.'

'I won't,' she said earnestly.

I began stacking crockery on the tray. 'Regarding this movie, I'm a bit like a child myself just now. Can't wait to get started.'

Unscrewing the cap of the coffee jar, Mum regarded me obliquely. 'I can see that. And I'm glad. You need something to occupy your mind, like, after all that – '

'You mustn't believe,' I said lightly, 'all that gets into the newspapers. It wasn't so traumatic. In fact, now I'm on my own, I haven't felt so lighthearted in a long while.'

Mum surveyed me gravely for a few moments, before standing on tiptoe to give me a peck on the forehead. 'Welcome home, love. We've all missed you.'

CHAPTER III

HERBIE WAS in good form at dinner.

'Contacted Templar this morning,' he told me through a mouthful of curried chicken. 'We agreed he'll show up at the studios twice a week. Rest of the time, he'll be available the other end of the phone.'

I nodded. 'Sounds sensible. What's he like to talk to?'

'Sounded wrapped up in some other world of his own – as I guess he probably was. Kind of remote.'

'You're sure he grasped what was being arranged?'

'It was he that suggested it. Said he'd fix it so's he did his current stint of writing at home, which I gather is in . . .' Herbie squinted ferociously at a mystified waiter. 'Peter-Something or other . . .'

'Petersfield?' An elderly cousin of Mum's had once lived there.

'That's the place. Seems it's not too far from BUC so it won't be that much of a sweat for him to get along there. Sounds okay, huh?'

I surveyed him sternly. 'You'll take *some* notice of what he says?'

Herbie registered surprise. 'Why, sure, honey. Otherwise what's the point?'

Penitence overtook me. 'I was just thinking of all those Hollywood legends. You know. The sensitive writers who finished up as alcoholics. I'd hate anything like that to happen to Jon Templar.'

Herbie drank convulsively from a tumbler of iced water.

'This man's work,' he said earnestly, 'I respect. That's the reason I'm making the movie.'

'I know. I wasn't serious.'

For a mouthful or two we ate in silence. We were early: the Cosmopole's Grill Room, a pillared and carpeted version of an airship hangar, was barely a quarter full. After Mum's substantial fatted calf at lunchtime I felt disinclined to do more than pick at my Dover sole; but in a quiet way I was enjoying the meal. When Herbie was at peace with himself, which was much of the time, he was restful company. It was an attribute that I had come to appreciate during my worst times in the States. He had something of a gift for divining whether or not people wished him to talk, and, if so, in what vein. Possibly this accounted for his string of largely amiable collaborations with an assortment of volatile directors. While I was thinking this, Herbie proceeded quietly and efficiently to demolish its validity with his next remark.

'Terry's here in London. Did you know that?'

I managed to grab at my fork before it clattered into the plate.

'I didn't, but it doesn't astonish me. He flits around.'

Herbie eyed me shrewdly. 'From what he said, he flitted into Heathrow not so long after us. Coincidence?'

'Of course, naturally.' I squeezed lemon over some fishy remnants before glancing up again. 'What he *said*?'

'He called me. Right before I came out. Exiles abroad, how's it going, Herbie, and all that jazz. Asked how you were liking this place.'

'How did he know I was here? Oh! The *Sunday World*. Bless its tiny italic paragraphs. I'm beginning to dislike Nigel Moorforth.'

'Most other newspapers carried pieces about our arrival,' Herbie pointed out with a touch of smugness. 'Wasn't exactly the mystery of the year. Let's face up to it, Angel: if it's peace and seclusion you're after, we'd best scrap the entire project, pack our bags and get back to LA, right?'

I sighed. 'Right.' After a moment I added, 'I don't expect to be treated like a nun. I'd be mortified if I was. Some sisterhood! But . . . oh God, Herbie, why can't he accept the situation and bow out? Does he have to keep plugging away?'

Shrugging massively, Herbie precipitated a morsel of messy chicken across the table-linen, leaving a sepia trail which he concealed with his serviette.

'Seems it's gotten to be a habit with him.' He leaned forward. 'Listen, honey, I'd not have mentioned it, only he said something about being in touch with you, so . . . Well, forewarned is forearmed. I didn't want you taken by surprise.'

'Where Terry's concerned, nothing he did would surprise me any more. Except drop dead. And that wouldn't be a shock. More like mortal gladness. I wish he'd die, Herbie. I honestly wish he would.'

His eyes, slightly glazed, were turned upwards and bulging. I looked up to find the waiter motionless at my elbow. Herbie coughed.

'I guess we're through with this course. Want something to follow, Angel?'

'Just coffee.'

'Suits me too. Hell, no – bring me a strawberry ice.' He thumped his waistline. 'The damage is past repair.'

The waiter smiled thinly, collected the plates, glided off.

Herbie scratched his left temple. 'We can always say,' he observed, 'you were mugging up on your lines.'

'You'd better arrange to have them written into the script.' Suddenly I giggled. 'Miriam would never have said a thing like that.'

'Nope. She'd have just gone out and done it.'

As though conscious that he had introduced a jarring note, Herbie steered the conversation into new channels relating to the shooting schedule. He was having, he confided, a touch of difficulty in luring the chief cameraman he wanted from a lucrative floating association with several TV companies, but was hopeful of winning him in the end. Meanwhile, I was to stay in London and pick up all the Press coverage I could get. My leading man was arriving in two days' time from Malmö in southern Sweden, where he had been making a TV film: we should show ourselves in partnership at a Press reception at the Savoy on Thursday, before travelling to Winchester to get settled in by the weekend. Work at the studios would start in earnest the following Monday.

'I seem to have heard that before,' I said cynically. 'Haven't you forgotten something?'

'What's that?' he asked apprehensively.

'Air and sea services out of Sweden are going to be at a standstill from tomorrow, for two weeks. Industrial trouble.'

'I'd not heard that,' Herbie exclaimed, gripping the table-corners. 'Jesus, that does it. We'll have to charter a special flight . . .' His voice trailed away as he met my innocent gaze. 'Aw, come on, honey. Don't do this to me. Not even in fun. I'm having to watch the cheque-stubs as it is.'

'Sorry, Herbie.'

'You're getting to be some actress. Had me fooled there for the minute.'

'I just wanted to see your face.'

A grin spread across it. 'How's this?' He tugged it back into its natural lugubrious folds as his ice-cream arrived, liberally adorned with a mud-coloured sauce. 'What's this?' he demanded. But the waiter was already out of earshot. Herbie heaved a despairing shrug. 'That's one more sleepless night. Soon I'll be in line for complaints from the folks downstairs: twanging bedsprings. They already figure I'm some dropout who's moved in on a squat while Edgar's out of town. I have to watch my step.'

Edgar Pattison was head of the British end of Herbie's film empire. Currently he was on a trip to Frankfurt and Munich, and Herbie had taken over his office and flat in Mayfair.

I said, 'The bailiffs are quite considerate, you'll find. They let you keep the clothes you're wearing, plus a couple of ballpens.' I placed a hand on the arm that was not conveying sauce-drenched ice-cream to his mouth. 'Think of all that's going well. You've got a shooting script and you've got the author. You've got studios and a location. You've got a co-operative leading lady: soon you'll have a male star who's a byword for rubbing along with anybody. And you've a title that ought to sell any movie by itself. That's not so bad for a start, is it?'

Herbie's grin this time remained in place.

'Angel,' he said contentedly, 'you'll have to stick around. Someone like you I need at my right ear.'

My reference to the leading man was, I hoped, accurate. Although neither of us had personal knowledge of Denholm Baxter, his malleability was acknowledged by those whose opinions were supposed to count. By this yardstick, he was among the top dozen cast-iron reliables in the screen business. Having served a lengthy apprenticeship as one of those nameless, faceless supporting players in numerous second features and TV serials – frequently inside dense period costume which tended to apply the ultimate blanket of obscurity – he had found himself, practically overnight, blinking in the glare of an acclaimed television production of an Edwardian saga which, apparently against the odds, had found an instant and immense market in the States, establishing him as someone to watch. That was six years ago. Since then, his career had prospered in a solid, dedicated way. He pursued a policy of discrimination over parts, and in each one he improved. If he was not yet inside the superstar bracket, one had the feeling that it was only because such a category had never been designed to accommodate a performer of his style. His choice for the role of Neville Grant, opposite that of Miriam, had been my suggestion. I was keeping fingers crossed about him.

I said, 'Have you warned Denholm about the Press reception?'

Herbie looked puzzled. 'Why? He allergic to 'em or something?'

'Oh . . . I think he'd appreciate the need for a certain amount of exposure,' I said optimistically. 'It's just that it's the day after he arrives back in England. He might be feeling threadbare.'

Herbie shoved away the melted remains of his confection. 'Honey, if he is, I'm relying on you to get him sewn up again.'

After bidding Herbie good night in the hotel lobby, I took a lift to the penthouse floor. My suite greeted me with the alien frigidity of all lodgings; but by now I was seasoned enough to shrug off the weight of my surroundings, and besides there wasn't time to mope. My copy of the *Furnace* script, curling at the corners, emerged from its suitcase in the bedroom like a faithful if demanding old friend. Dumping it on the bed, I got out of my dress and into working trousers.

If someone had said to me, 'Page forty-seven' and asked me to quote what was on it, I could have obliged with the same readiness as with any other number, without faltering. I knew it forwards, backwards, edgewise; misprints and all, its symbols were etched into my brain. My memory had always been excellent. Retention of lines was no problem. In my worst moments I reminded myself of this, and it did me no good at all.

Such dialogue as had occurred in my previous pictures had been minimal in extent, besides falling some way short of literary refulgence. Apart from which, it had tended to be subordinate to the action: notably the action involving myself. If a phrase got twisted, nobody had cared too much. I had sometimes wondered whether a couple of ideas were tapped into a computer and later extruded as, so to speak, tapescript: functional, reliable, hygienically sterile, capable of sustaining celluloid life without risk of cross-infection. *Flora* was the supreme example. We could have spoken the lines from right to left and no one would have noticed.

Furnace was something else.

It was a venture that I felt deeply about at two levels. For its own sake I wanted it to be a triumph; and on behalf of my career I was resolved to excel. If an inspired performance rested upon mastery of the spoken word, I was prepared if necessary to undergo cerebral branding, syllable by syllable, with white-hot irons. The carcass of the book had been minced initially by its author, Jon Templar, and subsequently rehashed by one of Herbie's more dependable screenplay mechanics, a cheerful, unassuming old pro called Vic Roach, who had achieved considerable success in his limited objective of rubbing down or rasping out what had manifestly been seen as the eccentricities of Templar's verbal prose, without sprouting additional grey hairs over the question of whether or not its underlying quality had been irretrievably mislaid. Notwithstanding his efforts, there remained dialogue phrases that lurked like landmines: they could blow up in your face. By now I had a vivid mental chart of their locations; even so, my confidence was far from total. I wanted to be sure.

Taking the photo-copied stapled sheets through to the studio couch in the main room, I punched the spare cushions into a nest and sank into them. I turned to page eight.

The light was poor. I looked for a nearby wall-lamp: there wasn't one. On the dressing-table in the bedroom, I remembered, stood a brass lamp, an eighteen-inch scrolled monstrosity with yards of surplus cord coiled at its base. Someone at the Cosmopole had hankered after a touch of tradition. Bringing it through, I fixed it precariously on the back of the couch so that its unshaded candle-bulb shone directly upon the script. For the second time I put my feet up. Found page eight again. Sighed deeply, to relax.

A double rap hit the outside door.

'Damn,' I said, quietly but viciously. I raised my voice. 'Who is it?'

'The Manager, Miss Browne. May I please have a quick word?'

The voice was muffled. Wearily quitting the couch, I crossed to the door. 'What's the trouble?'

No reply. It was below the dignity of hotel managers to bawl through woodwork. Superstars were less fussy. However, resignedly I twisted the lock, moulding my features into the tolerant sweetness that was least harmful to my image. As I released the door it shot inwards, striking my left big toe. While I was gasping with pain, my ex-husband stepped through the gap into the room.

'Nothing changes.' He adopted a masculine stance, feet apart, hands pocketed, in the dead centre of the available floor. 'Last time we were together, you looked to have just chewed a mouthful of sour fruit. That's the way you look now.'

'You hurt my foot.'

'You hurt my entire life.' The opening was exploited with vintage deftness.

'Oh God,' I said. 'Are we jumping straight into the melodramatics?'

'Why don't we close the door?' he suggested. 'That way, we avoid jumping into tomorrow's scandal sheets. If the thought bothers you.'

We stood inspecting one another. He looked reasonably sober, although it was sometimes hard to be certain. He wore a thigh-length, tailored topcoat over a dinner jacket; as ever, his raven hair mantled his scalp in tight, wiry spriglets, uniform all round. Once, I had been spellbound by his hair and how it never got ruffled in a gale. Good as my memory was, an effort was now needed to recapture, even dispassionately, the essence of that infatuation. After a moment's consideration I closed the door.

'I heard you were here.'

'I read that you were. So it seemed polite to pay my respects.'

'Wouldn't it have been better manners to stay clear?'

His face puckered. 'You don't have to say a thing like that, Anjie.'

'Don't I?'

He looked around. 'Cosy set-up you have here. Herbie taking good care of you?'

'My employers,' I said, 'do their best for me. In return, I work hard for them. I was trying to work when you burst in. I've no wish to be unkind, Terry, but it's important I have some time to myself.'

He nodded with an appearance of abstraction. 'Always was, I seem to recall.'

I mastered my breathing. 'I don't intend getting involved in backchat. You've called on me: we've talked: there's nothing more to say. It's getting late and I'd like you to leave. Plain enough for you?'

'More than plain,' he said. 'Ugly.'

He made no move. I went to the telephone. 'Want me to call the manager? The genuine one?'

'To have me thrown out? Not so good for your image, Anjie. The new, serious, dedicated persona. *Screen Goddess in Hotel Brawl*. Can't see Herbie going for that brand of promotion. If he was making another *Flora*, maybe. Not for *Furnace*.'

'I'm glad,' I said acidly, 'you're able to discriminate.' My fingers were on the receiver but it remained on its hook.

My hesitancy was not lost on him. His manner underwent a subtle gear-switch. An element of schoolboy gawkiness stood out in his diffident progress towards the couch.

'Where you're concerned, Anjie,' he said thickly, 'I can discriminate like hell.'

He sat heavily, head nursed in hands. 'Don't have me bounced out just yet.' He was speaking to the carpet. 'I'll go in a little while. That's a promise. All I want first is five minutes' civilized conversation. An exchange of real, human talk. Then maybe – maybe I'll feel different about the whole thing.' He looked up. His face was creased, ravaged. He looked ninety. 'That's not much to ask, is it?'

The familiar helplessness engulfed me. I stood watching him, wanting to call the manager but knowing I wouldn't, a prey to a set of emotions of such diversity . . . frustration, pity, remorse, anger . . . that for the moment a course of considered action was beyond my powers. With a sense of incredulity I heard myself say, 'Five minutes, then – no more. And then you must get out. For good.'

I felt myself move away from the telephone, over to a brocaded armchair at some distance from the couch, but facing it. *Fool*. The word was being hissed at me by some other person, someone deep inside, whose opinion I respected but pig-headedly was sitting upon, aware that later I should be forced to eat humble pie and make my peace. Balanced on the chair-edge, I surveyed the love of my life with what I hoped was a healthy cynicism.

'So what did you want to talk about?'

His expression again had altered. It now transmitted a boyishly self-deprecating charm. He did it well. I had forgotten how well.

'Us,' he said.

'It's all been said.'

'Nothing's been said. A few things have been stated. At second hand: lawyer to lawyer. God in heaven, Anjie . . .' He sat forward. 'You know something? I'd no idea we were divorced till I got that kind of printed circular from your legal outfit, notifying me of the occurrence. Can you imagine the way I felt? It was like someone had hacked off my own shadow at the heels, hidden it some place . . .'

'I wish you'd cut out the B-movie dialogue, Terry. The divorce may have been a quickie but it was perfectly valid and you were a party to it from the beginning. It was done with consent on both sides. Don't try to make out otherwise.'

'But my point, honey, is this. What we agreed to right at the start was a trial separation: okay? If it didn't work out we were to meet up again, discuss it some more. Set some divorce wheels in motion – maybe. Nice and gradual. That way, there were chances of retraction all along the line. Hell, Anjie, what happened to the schedule? Before I knew it, you were calling up the Press boys from – '

'Nothing,' I said tiredly, 'went wrong. There was never any question of reconciliation. That was entirely in your own mind. The reason I suggested a trial separation was so as not to hurt . . . to sort of ease us closer to the final break. I knew darn well we wouldn't be getting back together. I thought you did. It seemed clear enough.' I plucked at the upholstery. 'As for contacting the Press, I did nothing of the kind. Word got to them, that's all. It always does. Of course they clamoured, so finally we had to issue a statement. I made it as neutral as I humanly could. I was sure you'd understand.'

'She was sure I'd understand,' he mimicked. 'I'll tell you how you could have been more positive. You could have written me a letter.'

'And started the whole thing up again?'

'Or come to see me. There I was, alone in Santa B, waiting, wondering. Sick to my stomach with it all. People asking questions. Smirking behind my back. "We're both hoping it'll work out" . . . How many times did I repeat that crummy formula?' Self-pity throbbed in his throat. 'I was still saying it, three days after you'd signed that miserable scrap of Mexican paper. I've not clapped eyes on you since.'

'Did you expect to? Where would have been the point?'

'Human decency. Consideration for my feelings.'

I restrained a laugh. 'You'll forgive my saying so, Terry, but I didn't feel under a special obligation in that respect.'

His face darkened. There was a pause before he went on.

'For eight months I've not worked. Can't hold the lines any more. Studios won't touch me. Career-wise, I've reached a break in the trail . . .'

'I'm sorry about your career. Is it me you're blaming?'

'Before, I was doing well. You know that. Fifty grand a picture. Auditions for the *Prisoner of Zenda* re-make. So what happens? My wife walks out on me. My mind goes to bits. Wham, pow, scuttled amidships. I've not surfaced yet. The studios – '

I rose from the armchair. 'The auditions came well before we split. You didn't fluff it because of me. You blew your chance because you were stoned out of your mind.'

'And why was that?' he shouted.

'Search me,' I yelled back from the far side of the room. 'Maybe you were always an alcoholic. Don't ask me to plumb the origins. A miserable childhood, you once said. I wouldn't know. I tried to help. Once I realized what I'd married, I did my best to live with it, hoist you out of the pit – but what was the use? You're beyond aid. I can sympathize to an extent, but I can't wreck my whole life trying to retrieve the impossible. I'm sorry, Terry, but that's how it is.'

I stood breathing hard, gazing not at him but at the opened script lying next to him on the couch: the sight of it seemed to provide a sorely-needed anchor. More quietly I said, 'Now do you understand?'

He was silent, staring across at the door. Its design seemed to arrest him. His neck had sagged into his shoulders; his hands were clenched on his knees, as though he was in a certain amount of physical pain. With this one, I was not unfamiliar. I had witnessed the pose innumerable times. And yet, weirdly, it still had the power to unsettle me, to make me feel that the one fundamentally at fault was myself; to transfer the blame. The words I had just uttered, irrefutable at their moment of genesis, marched about the walls like jackboots in quest of a victim. I wished he would speak. The hurt, whipped look in his pupils was intolerable. I willed him to react. He just sat. After some moments I returned to the arm-chair, awkwardly resumed my place, folded my arms, regarded him with what was intended as compassionate understanding but felt more like despair.

At last I repeated myself. 'I'm *sorry*. What more can I say?'

The silence stretched to snapping point. He gave a very slight shake of the head.

'There's nothing more,' he murmured. 'That says it all.'

I was being played for an idiot, and there was no visible counter. At this, he was a master. Set up the scene: lure in the opposition: slaughter them where they stood. He would always win, because the charade to him was not a means to an end, it was the end in itself. Knowing the peril, I had offered myself once more on a slab. I made a feeble attempt to crawl off.

'In that case, you'd better go. You've had your five minutes – pointless to spin it out. We're not related any more.' Futilely, I paused. 'Are you leaving?'

An expression of tender melancholy had taken command of his face. Leaning back, he crooned to the ceiling.

'Ask her about it. That's what I told myself. Ask her if there was some mistake. There had to be. She's the one I'm close to, the one that understands.'

'Terry, look. It's no use – '

'So it's not easy to believe what I'm hearing. But I have to believe it. Face up to things. The brutal truth.' Descending, his gaze brushed past me, halted at the *Sunday World* which the room-maid had picked up and placed tidily on the writing-table. 'They didn't make it up, that trash they printed. She said it. Past is past, here's to the future. She actually said it. O'Malley? Sweep him out, with the rest of the garbage. A ball of dirt picked up along the way – that's all need be said about *him*.'

'You're simply torturing yourself. Nobody else. The more you harp, the worse you'll feel. You've got to snap out of it, Terry. Somehow.'

With sudden meekness he said, 'I know I do.'

I looked at him sharply. He had the air of a man crawling away from a flogging. My heart gave a wrench.

'You're totally correct, Anjelica.' He was holding his left shoulder with his right hand as though to quell an ache. 'Packed tight with commonsense. Always were. You should get on. You sure deserve to.'

He got slowly to his feet. I held my breath. Taking three paces towards the door, he halted, swayed, met my eyes. 'I'd like to wish you all the luck in this thing you're doing. I sincerely mean that.'

I passed fingers through my hair. 'Thanks, Terry. I appreciate it.'

'Means a lot to you, I guess?'

'*Furnace*? It's the biggest . . .' I caught myself. 'A great opening for me,' I said soberly, 'and I mean to do the best I can. That's all any of us can do.'

'You're so right.' A pace more. Again I was willing him on, but he came to a fresh halt. 'All do our utmost with what we have.' The twisted, wistful smile gleamed and died. 'What would you say, Anjie, are my special gifts?'

Something about this conversation wasn't dead on key. But I wasn't going to analyse: with luck, in thirty seconds he would be out of the suite, and once gone he wouldn't be coming back. So I humoured him.

'Several things,' I said lightly. 'Charm. You can captivate people. That's an asset a good many would give their right arms for. You could make better use of it.'

He gave his slow, reflective nod. 'Maybe I shall,' he agreed.

He stood thinking it over. I said encouragingly, 'Have a quiet drink downstairs – a soft one. Do some planning. You'll be surprised how things fall into – '

'Now don't rush me. I can plan right here. Also I can let you know what I decide. I owe you that.' The magical smile played over me.

Nervous tension caught up. I felt jelly-kneed, slightly dizzy. My own smile was becoming harder and harder to sustain. My brain declined to produce further trivialities. Politely he added, 'Fact of the matter is, I've reached a conclusion already. We're getting together again, Anjie. You and me.'

'Now wait a minute – '

'Oh yes. Otherwise this prestige motion-picture of yours and Herbie's, this vehicle for all the talents . . . it's a non-starter. It's not going to happen.'

The chair-springs bounced beneath me. I hadn't been aware of sitting. I could hear a voice. It sounded like my own.

'What are you blabbing on about, Terry? You're talking nonsense.'

'Now don't get me wrong. When I say it wouldn't

happen . . . well, Herbie and his crowd could still go right ahead and make it, I guess. But not with top movie star Anjelica Browne. They'd need to think again on that.'

'Just what are you trying to say?'

'I'm saying it,' he pointed out mildly. 'You only have to listen. *Furnace of the Mind* . . . it's the stuff of a classic. A quality product. A one-off cultural winner for Joseph Films. And, brother, they need it. Skin-flick candyfloss like *Flora* – that's not going to last. It's ephemeral. To stay in business, Herbie has to come up with the genuine goods. *Furnace* is the way he plans to do it. So he's collecting the big names. And he can't afford mistakes.'

A stab of anger helped me override my bodily inertia. 'You're suggesting my choice as Miriam is a mistake?'

'A mistake?' He mused. 'It could be. Supposing a certain bunch of film negatives were to become public property, Herbie might decide – who knows? – he might figure you were just that little bit hot to keep his fingers on.'

'You can't hold that sort of threat over me.'

Terry looked pained. 'Who said anything about threats? All we're doing is discussing the existence of a few photographic records that nobody outside of the two of us need ever . . .'

At the telephone, I picked up the receiver. 'Herbie should be back at his flat by now. I'll get him over here right away and you can tell him about it. Man to man. I'm sure you'll welcome the chance to do that.'

'Why hassle Herbie at this stage? I mean, you're contracted for the part. If he dropped you now, he could find himself at the wrong end of a lawsuit. Why not think it over first?'

I replaced the receiver. My mind was operating in a series of surges.

'I won't disturb him now. There's no need. You're right about this film, Mr Terence Patrick O'Malley. A lot is riding on it. Herbie's reputation: maybe the future of Joseph Films . . . I don't know. Certainly my acceptance as a screen actress. But if it comes to a choice between that and keeping you out of my life, then I'm afraid it's no contest.'

For an instant the mask slipped. I saw the desolation and the terror. Even at this moment he seemed to me a pathetic figure for whom somebody should do something, as long as it was not myself. I had tried and failed.

He shrugged. 'Suit yourself.'

'Terry . . .'

On his way to the door, he paused without turning. I said, 'Be sensible. You might hurt all sorts of people but you'll achieve nothing for yourself. Where's the good in that?'

His face came round. 'Where've you been, Anjie? Missing out on life. Didn't you know? Hurting people can be fun.' He lifted an arm. 'See you again.' He opened the door.

My voice was shriller than I had intended. 'You cause any trouble and you'll be sorry. I'm warning you.'

He vanished, leaving the door wide open.

Going across to shut it, I met the courteous, insolent gaze of the young Italian waiter who had taken a bet over me. He was standing beside a trolley outside the door of the adjoining suite, rearranging bottles on a tray.

'Something I can do for you, Miss Browne?'

Instinctively I heaved a smile on to the appropriate hooks. 'No, thank you,' I said brightly. 'Everything's just great.' I threw a cheery wave at the lift doors, which were closing behind Terry. 'Good night,' I beamed, stepping back and closing the door.

It was my finest performance to date. Returning to the couch, I stood staring down at the script, trying to remember what it was all about. Except that it looked scruffy, it meant nothing to me at all.

CHAPTER IV

AT MID-MORNING of the following day I gave an interview to *Modern Madam.*

The magazine's emissary was a small, dark-eyed woman with cropped hair and darting movements. She was keen for my views on sex equality, so at short notice I manufactured a few. They seemed to please her. Less pleasing, to judge from her demeanour, was the account I gave her of my antecedents, embracing schooldays at a West Ham comprehensive, my seven-week career as a West End salesgirl, and my admittance to filmland via the *Miss Cosmos* title. At mention of this contest, she twitched her small shiny nose.

'Did you enjoy being paraded?'

'Enjoyment hardly came into it. I hoped it might lead somewhere. Which it did.'

'The Lorna Doone role?'

'Yes . . . though in fact that film was never made. But when *Nightshades* came along . . .'

Nightshades had been the shocker of the mid-70s: a violent chiller given a streak of critical acceptance by the touch of a director whose reputation and capabilities happened to be riding high at the time. One of the parts was a strong one of a prostitute, and I had been usefully on hand for the purpose.

The woman from *Modern Madam* changed position carefully. 'Did you resent having to gain recognition by the back door in that way?'

'I didn't regard it as the back door. I remember it as quite an exciting picture. Possibly I wouldn't think so now.'

'But,' she persisted, 'it would hardly compare with, for example, something like *Furnace of the Mind*?'

'Of course not.'

'In other words, Miss Browne, this represents a new dimension for you, does it not? Miriam Hargill – such a figure of challenge, is she not? Can I ask how you see her, yourself?'

I took a breath. 'She's a woman,' I said slowly, 'whose whole life has been disastrously channelled. She knows she's not fitted for marriage or motherhood. Deep inside, she resents having been pressed into both by the over-powering conventionality of her family. She feels she has potential in other spheres, but she's tied by domestic commitments . . .'

My interviewer's battery-powered tape-recorder whirled hotly, consuming my words. To my own ears, they were sounding less and less like the perceptive dissection they were meant to be, more and more like a glib restatement of values already tarnished by over-exposure, missing by a mile the point of Jon Templar's new-minted, glittering revelations about the human condition. But the woman from *Modern Madam* was enchanted. Or, if she wasn't, she was a better actress than I could ever aspire to become. She listened, nodding at intervals, until I ran out of things to say; then thanked me warmly.

'So nice,' she said, packing her electronics, 'to meet a screen celebrity of intelligence. I do hope *Furnace* goes well.' Her nose twitched. 'After *Flora*, you should find *Miriam* quite a stimulus.'

The afternoon I spent shopping.

At one stage, I was within fifty yards of Herbie's Mayfair headquarters and had in fact turned towards the building before changing my mind and retracing my steps to Oxford Street, where I took a bus to Knightsbridge. It was raining, which simplified matters for me. A low-brimmed rain-hat and buttoned collar were, with the help of thick-rimmed glasses, sufficient to bury my identity. I removed the hat but retained everything else while I sat sipping tea in Harrods. I stayed there for more than an hour, thinking.

A number of questions needed pondering.

In the first place, how many – if any – prints or negatives did Terry still possess?

In the second, what use would he be prepared to make of them?

After a four-year marriage, facets of his character were still hidden from me. Threats in a hotel suite were some way removed from practical action. Terry might pine to have me back, but he couldn't be that desperate? If I held out, what would it gain him to rub my name in the slime?

The answer to that last one was disturbingly prompt. Terry had the deficiency of all weak personalities: the urge to drag others down to his level. If he couldn't climb, why shouldn't the rest fall? It was sterile, it was child-like, and it was the best possible reason for my taking him seriously. To count upon his better nature was a perilous snare.

The practicalities of the matter were more debatable. As I recalled, the merchandise concerned was of a nature that precluded its publication, even these days, through the more reputable channels of the media. On the other hand, there was nothing to prevent my ex-husband from showing samples to some avidly muck-raking newsman on one of the seamier Sunday nationals – even such as Nigel Moorforth on the *World* – and clearing the way to a course of character-assassination that would leave my hopes and ambitions strewn in raw lumps along the route.

The filmgoing public was tolerant. It expected – indeed wanted – a certain moral laxity in the deities it worshipped. But the limit was clearly defined.

Herbie had expounded on this. 'Honey,' he had told me once, 'get married eighteen times – they'll love it. Have yourself seen in nightspots with other dames' husbands – they'll click their tongues and storm to see your next movie. But there's a thing they won't take, and that's dirt. Real dirt. It wrecks your basic credibility, and if it's a worthwhile career you're after . . . that's death.'

Coming from a maker of movies which some might have described as medium-erotic, this was perhaps a shade disingenuous; but Herbie had been thoroughly in earnest, and I did see what he meant. Every instinct in me agreed with him. Which was why I had come to drink tea at Harrods instead of calling on him to ask his advice.

I was scared. Petrified by the possibility that, if I confided in him, he would be fatherly and sympathetic and understanding . . . and leave me out of the cast when *Furnace* started shooting. If he had, I couldn't have blamed him. He had an investment to protect. A dubious Miriam was something that he simply could not afford.

Those negatives. Shutting my eyes, I saw them again, in vivid colour.

At nineteen, one does things which at twenty-four one doesn't necessarily wish to be reminded of. On my arrival in Hollywood I was greener than new grass. *Nightshades* had given me ideas about myself that were not merely inflated but pumped to bursting-point. The suggestion by a Los Angeles-based outfit specializing in the production of 90-minute TV thrillers that I should fly out for 'evaluation' had landed me on the first available jet, with my handful of British commitments tumbling unheeded in my wake. I was on the way. It was only when I had been in Los Angeles a week that it started to dawn upon me that there might be more than myth to the Hollywood legend; that the road to fame ran perilously close to the scrapheap. This was after my one and only audition, a sketchy affair squeezed in among a number of others, at the conclusion of which I was told bluntly that the requirements of the corporation's existing programme failed to tally with my specific projection . . . they actually employed such language, like thick cottonwool padding around a jagged missile. I felt half-indignant, half-winded as I went away to find an agent.

The books of the one I engaged were not short of replica Anjelica Browns. He warned me of this, adding that most of them had armed themselves with names like Dawn

Cristal and Sunny Gloe and didn't I think I should do the same? Something stubborn inside me made me adamant that people could have me as Anjelica Brown or not at all (the final 'e' came later). He didn't argue, but his shrug was eloquent.

By nature I was not assertive. As a raw teenager at the gates of a mansion with the shutters fastened, I lacked the siege-guns needed to blast them apart and gain a berth at the fireside. At the same time, insecurity perhaps gave me a defensive, prickly look. Whatever the reason, I made no friends. Such other girls as I encountered seemed to me young tigresses, their claws permanently unsheathed in the stealthy hunt for game. The males with whom I came into contact were so blatantly on the prowl that I recoiled, and eventually retreated. For the most part, I stayed inside the modest but costly 'apartment' I had rented, waited for a phone call, and tried not to watch the dollar equivalent of my sterling capital melting remorselessly away in the Californian kiln.

But I wasn't going to fly home. Not yet. After all the counsel, the cautions, the finger-wagging I had received from my British sponsors, pride prevented me from crawling back with a bloodied nose before I really had to. I was going to stand my ground.

Within a month, my cash situation was desperate. On the same evening that I had finally decided, sick at stomach, to invest my remaining dollars in a flight home the following day, my agent called.

A producer, he said, wanted to see me. He happened to have seen *Nightmares* – I didn't bother with a correction – and he was interested. No, he wasn't that widely known, as a madda of fact. The agent had only vaguely heard of him. Far as he knew, the guy was into some kind of situation comedy series that was syndicated out to the TV stations. It could lead to something. Was I available?

I said yes, I could probably manage to get along to talk to him.

The building at which I arrived the following afternoon

was outwardly substantial, inwardly stunning. From what had been hinted at by the agent, I had prepared myself for a seedy set-up in a downtown locality: not for rich carpeting, Space-age furnishings, a sleek female reception clerk who spoke softly into an invisible intercom before installing me in an ergonomically-designed padded seat beneath potted palms next to a miniature tinkling waterfall. To wait there in air-conditioned serenity for forty minutes was scarcely the hardship for which the clerk kept apologizing. I was almost rebellious at being hauled away, shown through to the equally opulent sanctum of a youngish, bright-eyed man in a sharply-tailored lightweight suit who came out from behind his steel and chromium desk to clasp me warmly by the hand and propel forward in the same movement a fat, moulded chair that received me with an almost human caress. After the opening pleasantries he talked at an even, confident pace, as though the principle of my adoption by the corporation had already been established and all that remained to be eased into shape were a few trifling details. He asked about my 'alternative commitments'.

'At the moment,' I said cryptically, 'I'm reasonably free.'

'Fine.' He surveyed me with benevolence. 'We'd want you on exclusive contract, Miss Brown: this is the way we operate. So we wouldn't be happy to run foul of any prior arrangement you might be a party to elsewhere . . .'

I slung caution aside. 'There's nothing else,' I assured him. 'Nothing whatever.'

He nodded, eyeing me narrowly for an instant before the benevolence seeped back. He put a few questions about my British achievements; seemed actually to have seen and remembered *Nightshades*, which he, too, referred to as *Nightmares* (it was not until much later that I discovered that the title had in fact been adjusted for the US market); made a complimentary reference or two to my performance and 'screen persona'; and by dint of a laconic instruction into another invisible intercom arranged an audition for me in two days' time. He accompanied me back to the reception area and waved goodbye from the waterfall.

Returning in a breathless state to my apartment, I took the irreversible step of breaking into the sum of dollars I had set aside for the flight home and paying out another week's rent. I was burning my boats. But Hiram Mildendorf Junior, as his card described him, had seemed taken with me: something told me that I had scored a hit, although nothing had been said about the brand of TV series the Mildendorf Corporation turned out, nor even whether I was envisaged as an addition to its cast-list. Discussion of such matters, I guessed, would come later.

The audition took place in a well-equipped studio at the rear of the Mildendorf building. I was asked to read aloud an extract from a brilliant American novel, just published. Then told to move into camera-range, say 'What the hell is all this? I'm getting out, and I'm taking little Christy along with me', turn on my heel and sweep off. This I did with, I thought, a good deal of aplomb. After that, the man in charge conferred briefly with the cameraman before turning deferentially back to me.

'D'you mind a natural shot or two, Miss Brown?'

I was perplexed. 'How do you mean?'

'I mean in a state of ... ah ... undress. *Au naturelle.*' He smiled winningly. 'It's part of our habitual programme. But of course, if you've any objection ...'

Nightshades had included two scenes in which nudity had been asked of me. I hadn't objected. I saw no reason to object now. The cameraman looked bored, indifferent; the man in charge was manifestly worldly and professional. I said, 'No, I don't mind – within reason.' What I meant by this I had no idea, but it seemed prudent to slip it in, and he gave a grave nod of acknowledgement.

'Change behind the screen there,' he said tactfully. 'Then give us a walk and a pirouette, will you? After that we can all relax and have coffee.'

I did what he asked. We then drank coffee out of a

dispenser, and I was invited to call Mr Mildendorf Junior in a day or so to 'finalize the situation'.

Which seemed a welcome variation upon 'Don't call us, we'll call you.' I gave it one full day, and phoned on the second morning. Someone calling herself Mr Mildendorf's personal assistant said, 'He'll be glad to see you, Miss Brown, if you can find the time to step around. Could you make this afternoon?'

My involuntary gulp probably amused her. Half-stifled, I replied that I thought I might, and waited for her to name a time. She merely added, 'Okay, fine. See you then, honey,' and disconnected, as though I were a seasoned acquaintance who had been invited at the customary hour for cocktails.

This odd informality, I decided, was part of the organization's charm. Timing my arrival for just before three, I was permitted only six minutes beside the waterfall before a young man – younger than Mr Mildendorf but just as impeccably attired – came bustling through and noticed me, pausing to deliver a quick smile and a moment's appraisal.

'Anyone seeing to you?'

I was there, I told him, to see Mr Mildendorf Junior. The thought ran through my head that he, himself, might be a still more junior Mildendorf, a nephew perhaps; the entire company, for all I knew, comprised a pyramid of Mildendorfs; but all he said, placidly, was that Mr Mildendorf was currently in conference for a half-hour or so, and in the meantime I was to come through, if I would be so kind. I pursued him into another office, fitted out with a discreet plushness, to be presented with coffee out of a dispenser and a short address of greeting.

Dazed, I said, 'You mean there's a job for me here?'

He laughed musically. 'If Mr Mildendorf wants to see you again, I guess you can say he has something in mind. Tell me about yourself.'

That particular four-word phrase can normally be relied upon as a conversation-freezer. In this instance, the thaw was immediate. There was something totally disarming about Mike, as he asked me to call him. He had a way of looking relaxed, peaceable, and yet alertly gripped by what was being told him, as though at that moment it was what he most wanted to hear. A month or so of reclusive existence, solitary, in an alien environment, sick with apprehension about an apparently void future, had brought me to a condition in which, to put it mildly, I was not unsusceptible to such an approach. My garrulity seemed to entertain him. Later, he took me to dinner.

This was after I had been seen by Hiram Mildendorf Junior and told they had me in mind for the plum role in a new series they were presently casting. Much remained to be fixed, and he wanted me meanwhile to place myself in Mike's hands, learn all I could about shooting schedules and associated technicalities – he sounded engagingly vague about them – and, while a contract was being drawn up, to accept an interim salary of six hundred dollars a month. Was this agreeable to me?

I dined with Mike in a happy haze. Much as I should have liked to talk about the series there and then, I didn't mind when he brushed it aside for the evening, saying it could keep until 'the technical boys' were around. His job, he explained, lay more in the field of public relations. He was the guy who would be expected to 'sell' me, as and when my face began to come into focus on TV screens, coast to coast.

He sounded relaxed about it. I could see him as a publicity man, getting on with everybody, taking it all in his stride. I liked him enormously. I had the impression that the feeling was mutual. At the end of the evening he seemed as interested in me as he had at the start. He took me back to my apartment and I said good night with bugles blowing in my brain.

A week elapsed.

Sit at home, I had been instructed, and wait for Mike to call. He did, a couple of times. On the second occasion, it was to say that a minor problem or two had arisen over the series, but they expected to have them ironed out before too long: meantime, I was to keep myself looking gorgeous for when I was needed.

I said, 'Mike – it's all right, isn't it? Mr Mildendorf isn't having second thoughts about me?'

'Honey, Mr Mildendorf wasn't taught about second thoughts. You're on our books now. Relax.'

I hung up feeling better. And felt better still, the following morning, when a cheque for six hundred dollars arrived in the mail. Had I been doing anything to earn it, I should have felt on top of the world. Indisputably, however, the money imparted a healthier tint to the colour of my bank account; and I consoled myself with the reflection that, when the time came to justify the advance, I should not be found wanting.

Half of the next week slipped by without a word from anyone.

On the brink of telephoning Mike, I had a call from him on the Wednesday evening to say that a serious hitch had come up. Mr Mildendorf's biggest financial backer had suddenly withdrawn, leaving the projected series and a couple of existing ones severely starved of funds. Unless a new backer could be found, the entire thing was in the melting-pot.

I said dismally, 'Oh, Mike.'

'Now honey, you're not to panic. We're not licked yet. We've a line or two being cast. There's this one guy in particular . . . he could come up with the goods, only we have to work on him. It's just a matter of time.'

I stared blankly at the wall. My stomach felt as though it had been filled with molten zinc which was now cooling. I said, 'I see.'

'Point of fact,' Mike added, 'there's a way you could possibly help to speed things up.'

'Me?'

'Sure. We're having this character along for cocktails tomorrow – kind of a softening-up touch, if you get me.

How's about you joining the party? He's a sucker for a pretty face.'

'But he's also a bullet-headed businessman, presumably?'

'Anjelica baby, no one's *that* hard.'

'I don't mind,' I said, feeling obscurely more hopeful. 'If you think it'll do the slightest good.'

'Worth a try,' he said breezily, and told me he would pick me up. 'I want you to perform a real good PR job on him. You could tip the scales for us.'

'I'll do my best.'

The party took place in the penthouse suite of the Mildendorf building. The only other woman there was a middle-aged, paralysingly smart matron-figure who was taking a leading role in the distribution of drinks and verbal lubrication; she treated me with the same brisk affability as she did the rest, who seemed to be mainly executives of the middle rank, apart from a dusting of older men who either were of greatly superior status or had never made it. One or two of these were members of the group into which I was introduced. It included Hiram Mildendorf Junior, who threw me a confidential grin; and a tall, stringy man of about fifty with a domed forehead, a cleft chin and a stoop. He was the centre of deferential attention.

'Governor,' said Mike, 'I'd like you to meet Miss Anjelica Brown from London, England. Miss Brown is hopefully the star of our new show. We're expecting big things of her.'

The stringy man stooped lower to embrace my fingers. His eyes protruded at me. I put on my most dimpled smile: I was fighting for my career. 'Delighted to meet you,' I said, conscious of the Englishness of my accent.

It seemed to strike him just as forcibly. He looked expansively around the group.

'Now that's the way I like to hear somebody talk. Queen's English, I guess you'd call it . . . is that right?'

I nodded, observing that Mike looked happy. 'Queen's Cockney, anyhow. I haven't quite shaken East London out of my larynx, as yet.'

Putting his head back, he roared briefly. 'And is this what you aim to do?'

I said pertly, 'Don't you think I should?'

Suddenly solemn, he enfolded me in a masterful arm. 'You cling right on to your London blood, Miss Brown. You're from prime stock. Kind we need in this lousy twentieth-century trashbag we're creating . . . right, boys?' There was a dutiful assenting chorus. The Governor applied slight extra pressure to my rib cage. 'I'm what I guess you'd call an Anglophile . . . for the correct reasons, I hope. Because I admire your guts. The way you come back. If we're to combat this mish-mash of liberalism that's swamping in from all sides, we're going to want the support of all you fine Britishers – and we may need it sooner than we think.'

The group looked suitably impressed. Having allowed an orator's pause, timed to the split second, he propelled me to one side. 'Now I'd like you, Miss Brown, to fill me in on a thing or two in regard to your native country that I'm curious about. Will you do that?'

'I'll try,' I said, fighting the urge to duck out of his stale-tobacco precincts. 'But you've come to the wrong place, you know. Anything to do with ourselves, us Britishers are always the last to know.'

'Now there you have – ' He broke off to guffaw. 'You do have a point,' he informed me, manoeuvring me into a corner from which I could see that Mike had smoothly re-formed the group without us and was recharging glasses. 'Except it's by no means confined to one nationality. We all need outsiders, maybe, to tell us where we're deviating. Sort of a nanny-figure, you might call it. But don't worry. Chiefly what I want to know is, about the customs and habits of the citizens in your neck of the woods . . .'

To the utmost of my capacity I coped with his questioning while bearing with his evident predilection for standing closely alongside and staring at my feet. He drank steadily between puffs at a pungent cigar. I was, I had to keep reminding myself, doing a job. His enquiries about Britain were, in fact, penetrating: I collected an impression of astuteness coupled with a forcefulness of personality that, I could easily see, might well add up to a potent political armoury. Also, presumably, he had money. A formidable amalgam. It was almost disenchanting when, after an hour, he demonstrated a degree of human fallibility by having to excuse himself to visit the men's room.

'Don't run off,' he instructed.

'I'll be here,' I said, demurely. I had hung on to my first drink and my wits.

Mike detached himself from a ruck and wandered across. His proximity was bracing. I muttered, 'How am I doing?'

'Swell, honey. Just keep on as you are.'

'I haven't much choice. Who is he? Governor of California?'

Mike shook his head. 'One of the smaller mid-West States. He's here on vacation. As you've probably gathered, he's the guy we have to cultivate.'

'Can a State Governor back a TV show like this?'

'He can do what he likes with his own money. Anyway it can be done on the slant . . . no call for him to be directly involved.' Mike replenished my glass. 'So happens,' he went on, 'he's a TV serial addict. Also very partial to the English brand of femininity. Something about an accent like yours gets him every time.'

'You don't have to tell me,' I said ruefully. 'I can see why you wanted me along. What's his name, again?'

'Mason. But call him Governor. He'll like that.'

Discreetly, Mike melted from view at the Governor's reappearance. For another hour we were left to ourselves. At that stage I noticed that the party had dwindled. The female matron, among others, had vanished, and there was no longer any sign of Hiram Mildendorf Junior. The

Governor had drunk quite a lot. With an arm across my bare shoulders, he had progressed to talking in maudlin terms about the burdens of office, the need for a man to wind down, reactivate his batteries. Exhausted as I was, I kept up my façade of interest and sympathy, hoping my smile was less taut than it felt. From a distance Mike sent an encouraging gesture or two.

I prayed for him once more to come over, relieve the pressure. By now the Governor had stopped talking. He simply stood against me, fingers prodding my flesh, his gaze alternately sweeping the room and returning to loiter on my face, as though there were something he had in mind to say but couldn't identify. My brain had long since withdrawn from the struggle. The rest of me stood dumbly, awaiting demobilization. At last, Mike wandered across.

'Governor, could you spare Mr Weinburg a couple of seconds of your time? Something he'd appreciate a word with you about.'

Reluctantly the Governor relinquished my neck. 'I'll just be a minute,' he assured me. Getting himself together, he set off carefully in the direction Mike was pointing. The moment he was out of range, I puffed and sagged.

'Thanks. I don't think I could have stood a minute more.'

'You're doing some terrific job, Anjelica honey. Listen: we think we might have him just about hooked. He's showing a lot of interest . . . especially in you as a person.'

'You can say that again.'

'But he still has to be landed. Just wants a tiny heave, I guess. Will you do that for us?'

I looked back at him. 'What sort of a heave?'

Mike came confidentially closer. After the Governor, his wholesome adjacency was a joy. I realized how fond of him I was getting. He spoke in a lowered voice.

'What he'd most like, right now, is a little time with you to himself. Alone. To pour out his heart, I imagine.

And listen to that cute little English voice. How about it, Anjie?'

I uttered a moan. 'You mean now?'

'There's a room downstairs. Cosy and quiet. Take him there. Make him some coffee – be nice to him.'

Pensively I placed my glass on a nearby table. I turned back to look Mike full in the eyes.

'How nice?'

He didn't look away. 'As nice as you have to be.' He gave me his easy grin. 'It's for the series, remember.'

It was late morning of the following day before I got back to my apartment. The first thing I did was to take a shower.

After that I prepared a meal of sorts. I wasn't hungry, but I needed something to help settle a queasy stomach. The queasiness was in no way due to what I had drunk the night before.

I tried not to think about the night before.

My hope that Mike would call me was not fulfilled. Towards the end of the afternoon I rang his number, to be told he was out of the office for the day. I went to bed early, and barely slept.

The next morning I spent indoors, awaiting Mike's call. By now, I thought, he should have some concrete news about the series. Doubtless it was the reason for his absence from the Mildendorf building the previous day: he had been attending conferences with the Governor, finalizing details of the funding agreement. The less I dwelt upon the Governor the better. I tried to focus my mind upon the prospects of a TV comedy slot . . . although this, again, was not easy, since no one had ever outlined to me the form it might take or the species of role it might offer. My questions to Mike had been countered airily.

'We specialize in the family show, honey. The weekly squabble, the weekly kiss-and-make-up. You know the kind of thing.'

I did, hazily; but this was no help in grooming myself mentally for the work. What I should have liked was to read a script, meet the others involved, get to grips with the project. Now that I had been actively and squalidly brought in on the financing side, it seemed to me that I was entitled to more consultation all round.

Nobody called to consult me. Before lunch I telephoned Mike again; on being told that he was 'non-available at this time' I asked to be put through to Mr Mildendorf. The switchboard girl said she was sorry but Mr Mildendorf was not to be disturbed at this time. I said, 'Would you please tell him it's Anjelica Brown.'

She said, 'Honey, if I told him you were the Archangel Gabriel it wouldn't cut any ice at this time.' And she severed the connection.

After lunch – coffee and a couple of crackers – I waited a little longer in case Mike should call; and then I went out. Daylight hit me violently between the eyes: it was the first I had encountered for about forty-eight hours. My head ached savagely. I walked for half an hour until the pain had dulled to a throb; then I took a cab to the Mildendorf building.

Before reaching the entrance I came to a halt. Suddenly I couldn't go inside. I couldn't face anyone: most of all, I couldn't face Mike. Switching course, I walked on past the glass doors and along to an intersection, where in a kind of trance I crossed the street and started roaming the sidewalks, as I had learned to call the pavements, gazing unseeingly at the shop displays and telling myself I was too impatient. Business matters took time. Why should anyone bother to brief me on progress, or the lack of it, at this stage?

I failed to delude myself. All being well, Mike should have been in touch: after what I had done for him, it was the very least I could have expected. Lumps formed in my throat, were got rid of, formed again as I trudged. I felt lost and alone, and very scared. At one point I turned back, filled with renewed determination to march into the

Mildendorf emporium and demand enlightenment. After a few steps my nerve failed. I veered instead into a plaza encircled by low buildings; it was flagged underfoot, and in one corner tables were set out under palms. Flopping into a seat, I ordered an iced orange juice to keep me looking occupied while I pondered the bleak immediate past and the blacker future.

A man who was strolling past stopped, turned, gave me a second look. He came back. Braced for defensive action, I pulled resolutely at my orange juice with my gaze upon the glass. It didn't prevent him speaking.

'Miss Brown, isn't it?'

Startled, I glanced up. 'Right,' I said uncaringly. 'Have we met?'

'Couple of nights back.' With a wide beam, he extended a hand. 'You won't remember, but we were introduced at a party. Weinburg. Walter Weinburg.'

'I remember.' I did, just. He had been one of the group of which initially the Governor and Hiram Mildendorf Junior had been components; we had exchanged a few words, and after that I hadn't seen him again. But I did recall that, towards the finish, it was Weinburg to whom Mike had sent the Governor off to speak.

'Mind if I sit down?' he asked.

'Please – join me.' He looked good-natured, and if there was one quality I needed near me at this moment it was kindliness. 'Can I get you something?'

With an efficient snap of chubby fingers he ordered himself a beer. 'Well now, this is nice,' he declared, leaning back and surveying the plaza in the manner of a student of good living before giving me his whole attention. Short and stubby, he wore a cotton suit of a generous cut, an open neck and no hat. His brownish, very neat, rather thick hair was not, I estimated, his own. 'Taking it easy,' he enquired, 'between studio sessions?'

'You might say that.'

'Only I'd be wrong?' he added, after a contemplative pause.

'You'd be half-right. Certainly I'm doing my best to take it easy.'

His beer arrived. Taking a quick swig, he said tentatively, 'Forgive me if I'm in error, Miss Brown . . . but I understood you to be a very busy young actress out of England, making some kind of a TV – '

'I'm an actress out of England. End of story. I thought I was lined up for TV work. Now, I'm not sure.'

'You mean you're not in the middle of a series?'

'I'm in the middle of a crisis. I've a feeling I shall be flying home quite shortly.'

Solemnly he rearranged himself to gain the shade of a palm-frond. 'Care to tell me about it?'

I gave him an edited version to which he listened intently. Having considered for a while, he consumed some more beer.

'The way you figure it, if something had been fixed you'd have heard by now?'

'It's only a day or two,' I conceded. 'Probably I'm being absurd in expecting to be – '

'One way or another, Mr Mildendorf should've been in touch.' He spoke as though his opinion of Mr Mildendorf was not worth airing. He mused. 'You're not under contract to him, then?'

'I . . . No, at present I'm not.'

Again Mr Weinburg leaned back. 'That's interesting.'

I forbore to ask why it was interesting. Presently he swung his body forward once more, pushed aside the beer-glass and looked earnestly into my face.

'I don't exactly know how to put this to you, Miss Brown. What I mean, you sound like you've had some kind of a raw deal already, and you could be rightly suspicious . . . Let me phrase it this way. If I told you I belong to a motion picture corporation that happens to be on the lookout for someone remarkably like yourself – that is, a young English person, not too well-known in the States but with acting experience and a fresh personality, if I can put it that way – to possibly take over a part that's been causing us a few headaches . . . how would you describe your reaction?'

I gazed back at him steadily. 'Cautious.'

He nodded. 'Understandable. But maybe I can do this: maybe I can persuade you at least to come along some time and talk to us. What would you have to lose?'

My introduction to the Herb Joseph film empire, and to Herbie himself, followed swiftly.

It was, in the corniest Hollywood tradition, like a dream. Talent scout plucks new star from sidewalk café. It was many months before I could stop reminding myself that such things no longer happened, if they ever had; that it was a stimulating episode, no more, to be chalked up to experience. Something to tell the people back home. It still seemed likely that, sooner rather than later, I should be forced to return.

Herbie liked me on sight. I was screen-tested, placed under contract, and cast almost immediately for a minor role in his new sex frolic, *Truck Stop*. Soft porn with a classy edge, it had a screenplay of some wit by a Hollywood name in the genre and was directed with a touch of style. In the distributed version, my tiny part had shrunk practically out of sight: Herbie himself, however, took the trouble to call me in, assure me that I had done well, that there was no danger of my being released from my contract, and that bigger things for me were contemplated. It was during the making of *Truck Stop* that I met Terry O'Malley.

The person I didn't meet was Mike. I never saw him again: neither did I renew acquaintance with Hiram Mildendorf Junior or anyone else associated with his set-up. I did, though, have a confrontation with the Los Angeles police.

They came one morning to my new apartment in Malibu. A lieutenant and his deputy: slim, polite men who first asked me about myself, then showed me photographs of Mildendorf and some of the others and wanted to know if I could identify them. After I had done so, I was 'invited' down to police headquarters and interviewed alone by the Chief of Detectives, a heavy-featured individual named Jansen, with close-set eyes and a manner that contrived simultaneously to be ingratiating and offhand. His questioning was casual.

'You've not been in the States too long, Miss Brown?'

'About three months,' I said anxiously. 'Is there some trouble about my work permit? I understand – '

'No problem.' He lifted a meaty hand. 'Or if there is, it's nothing I know about.' His smile exposed some discoloured teeth. 'Or want to. What interests me is the contact you had, a few weeks back, with the Mildendorf Corporation.' Pausing, he studied me in a fatherly way, then shot a question. 'Were you ever on their payroll?'

I hesitated. 'Not exactly. I never signed a contract, if that's what you mean.'

'But you had money from them?'

'One amount of six hundred dollars. I was supposed to be in line for a TV part.'

A muscle twitched in his face. 'It didn't come to anything?'

'I never heard any more about it.' I stared at him uneasily. 'Are they claiming the money back?'

He didn't answer this. Taking a folder out of his desk drawer, he sat with a hand upon it: his facial expression would have suited a computer that had undergone sudden inexpert conversion to synthetic flesh and blood. 'Tell me,' he said, 'about the last time you saw Mildendorf.'

'It was at a party . . .'

'When?'

With an effort of memory I named the evening. He nodded, contentedly. 'What was it in aid of – so far as you were concerned?'

'I was told it was being given for some people who might help to finance this TV series.'

'Did you meet any of these people?'

'One or two. At least, that's who I assumed they were.'

'Did you learn their names?'

'We were introduced. If I heard any of them, I've forgotten.'

'Were you given a hint as to their . . . capacities?'

'Not really.'

He had been examining the folder. Now he cast me a look. 'Not sure I entirely follow you there, Miss Brown. You mean you had no indication of any kind?'

Unwillingly I said, 'I was given to understand that one of them was a State Governor.'

He nodded, as though finally satisfied. Opening the folder, he turned it and slid it across. 'Recognize anybody?'

Recognition was no problem. The room of the Mildendorf building in which I had been nice to the stringy Governor from a distant State had evidently not lacked the finest of photographic equipment, effectively camouflaged. When I looked up from the colour prints, I had no idea how long I had been staring at them; for all I knew, it could have been an hour. The Chief's unchanged posture, however, seemed to contradict this. He was studying me in the manner of a doctor mildly gratified by signs that the patient he had been treating unsuccessfully for a month was responding. I closed the folder, compressing its leaves, as though by doing so I could somehow obliterate its contents. I shut my eyes.

'They told me I could help . . . persuade him.'

'Persuade him to do what, Miss Brown?' Chief Jansen's voice was like buttermilk.

'Finance the series.'

'*That's* what they told you?'

Involuntarily my eyes reopened. His brows were lifted in a quizzical way that didn't suit him. I said wretchedly, 'I'd never have gone into that room with him otherwise.'

'You knew about these?' He touched the folder.

'*Knew* about them?' I glared. 'What do you take me for – some kind of twisted exhibitionist?'

I wanted to get out of his office, beyond range of his slobbering paternalism. I felt I needed to be sick.

'So, if you didn't know about them, equally you were unaware of the use they were intended for?'

'Don't tell me. Hard-porn movies?'

'Nothing so innocent. These, Miss Brown, were employed recently in an attempt at blackmail.'

'Oh my God.' I gripped the desk-edge.

'An abortive attempt, I might add. The, uh, prominent political figure involved had the intelligence to come to us – that is, to me – with the result that the Mildendorf Corporation . . .' Chief Jansen brandished a paw. 'Let's just say that one hell of a lucrative racket has been bust wide open.'

I got some breath back. 'Who . . . I mean, how many –'

'Mildendorf and his bunch weren't choosey. Correction: they were *very* choosey. The ones they picked on were the vulnerable ones who couldn't afford exposure and could afford to pay: and did. People like – oh, State Governors with clean-cut images and trusting wives and families.' After an interval, during which he gently relieved me of the folder and shut it back into the drawer, he added: 'Will you testify for us, Miss Brown?'

A hammer struck my stomach.

I managed a gasp. 'Do I have to?'

He said consideringly, 'It would help a lot.'

I seized upon the absence of finality from his voice. 'I'm in a very, very awkward situation. I've just been given a film contract – in fact, I'm in the midst of making a film. It's a reputable company – Herb Joseph, you know? – and if they got to hear that I'd . . . I mean, if I gave evidence in public they'd have to know, wouldn't they? Couldn't I sign a sworn statement or something? Have my name kept out?'

The computer-face remained impassive. Desperately I plunged on. 'It's not as if I knew what . . . what was

happening. Believe me, I'd no idea. I thought it was just –
you know, an extra bit of encouragement . . . a bonus for
someone who might help us to . . .'

My voice trailed off.

Every syllable that emerged seemed to add itself to the
wreckage. In utter misery I stared helplessly at the Chief,
certain that he would now rise to his feet with an official
phrase requiring me to attend court on a specific day to
present my evidence and answer questions. I could hear
Herbie's sad bass/baritone. 'You do appreciate our position, honey? I'm sorry about it, but a blackmailing
rap . . .'

My world once more lay in ruins. This time there
seemed no possible way clear.

Chief Jansen stayed seated. He sucked in his lower lip,
creating a sound between a bubbling and a hiss. Everything that he did or said was repellent. For all this, he was
my sole hope. Looking back with total objectivity, I think
my appearance would have plucked at most heartstrings,
and it was one that had needed no rehearsal. At the time,
I was unaware that such heartstrings as the Chief possessed
were made of piano-wire, and loose in the frame.

'I guess,' he said slowly, 'we've enough testimony as it is
to put this mob away . . .'

My pulse started to race. I gazed at him dumbly.

His eyes roamed the room. 'Your career means a lot to
you?'

'It means *everything*. Honestly, if I were to – '

'Enough for you to make sacrifices?'

'What kind of sacrifices?'

'Financial. Shall we say.'

'Oh – well . . . Money means nothing if I'm to – '

'Look at it my way, Miss Brown.' Now he stood,
rounded the desk, lowered himself upon it to bring his
face within a yard of mine. 'I've a useful case: only it's not
complete. What you could tell a federal jury in corrobora-
tion of what those prints inside there – ' he jerked his
head ' – could show them, would wrap it up pretty

nicely. But I'm not saying I couldn't get by without either. I'm not saying this.'

As he seemed to expect some comment, I said faintly: 'So what *are* you saying?'

His face loomed nearer.

'I pride myself,' he said confidentially, 'on being an adaptable sort of a guy. I try to keep an open mind. For example, in a case like this, if someone were to offer me any kind of a deal . . .'

Terry heard the story in silence, getting through most of two cigarettes in the course of my stumbling recital as we sat looking out through his Pontiac's curved windscreen at the blue Pacific. Stubbing the second butt into the ash receptacle, he put an arm about me and exerted a slight but enduring squeeze.

'My poor Anjie,' he said huskily. 'They really played you for a sucker.'

'How could I have *been* such a fool?'

'That,' he said with a trace of humour, 'you'll have to try to figure out for yourself.'

He was at his best: warm, quickly sympathetic, human in every way. Shooting on *Truck Stop* had gone well that day and he had stayed off the bottle. We had done a scene together. The success of the operation seemed to have had the effect of welding some final connection between us. Although I knew about his drinking, at this time it amounted to no more than a somewhat endearing frailty.

'Terry, what am I going to do?'

'What you can't do,' he said positively, 'is get mixed up in an exposure of this kind. It's going to make headlines from here to Washington.'

'But unless I – '

'How much did Jansen say he wanted?'

'Ten thousand dollars.' My voice reflected the despair that I felt.

'To keep your name right out of it?'

'Mine and the Governor's. I imagine he's making a

separate deal with him.'

Terry said unemotionally, 'How about the prints?'

'He didn't say. I suppose he'll either keep them or sell them back to the Governor, or . . .'

'No dice, honey. We'll pay him an extra ten grand for prints and negatives. Then we can have the pleasure of destroying them ourselves.'

I twisted slowly to look at him. 'What did you say?'

'I said, Please marry me, Anjie. Didn't you cotton on the first time?'

He took me into a kiss that left me breathless. Breaking away, I said, 'Terry, you can't pay out that kind of money for me. I can't let you.'

'Luckily for me,' he said, 'you can't stop me.'

He kissed me again, tenderly, upon the forehead.

'For you,' he added in his best C-movie style, and yet with an apparent sincerity that knocked my scruples aside, 'there isn't a lot I'd jib at doing. Least of all investing hard cash.'

In excess of what Terry had predicted, the blackmail racket scandal swept the world.

Heads rolled in most States. Venerated heads, with hitherto spotless records. For weeks, television stations, Press and radio were kept joyfully vociferous as one scrofulous revelation followed another. The carnal propensities of the nation's leaders on their nights off were an eye-opener. While the hubbub was at its height I existed in a state of terror, scarcely daring to read each fresh edition or watch the latest newscast in case the worst should have occurred.

Miraculously, the weeks stretched into months, without catastrophe. Terry had paid out. So, presumably, had the Governor; and Chief Jansen kept to his part of the bargain. His case rested upon the testimony of other victims, other showgirls and would-be starlets who had given their pathetic services as bait. Neither my own name nor that of the Governor was whispered. For a time it seemed im-

probable to me that nothing whatever concerning either
of us would be mentioned in court by Mildendorf or one
of his associates: and yet nothing was. Evidently they saw
no reason to add gratuitously to their troubles. As Terry
pointed out, while Chief Jansen kept his silence they would
remain in the dark as to just who among their prey had
jerked the rug from under them, and so they would have
no particular motive for a cheap revenge. To them,
Governor Mason was just one more in an extended line.

Before marrying, Terry and I waited until the dust had
fully settled.

Our film-set romance made some useful publicity for
Truck Stop, by then on release. This did little to prevent
Herbie – who seemed to take a personal interest in my
future – from displaying scant enthusiasm for the event.
He even went so far as to administer a transverse caution
beforehand.

'I want to be glad for you, honey. You know that.
You're sure marriage is for you at this particular moment
in time?'

I tugged my chair a little closer to his. We were talking
alone on the set after the day's shooting.

'What you're really saying, Herbie,' I told him,
straightening his cravat, 'is: am I sure this particular
husband is for me?'

'That,' he hedged, 'is something every moonstruck
bride has to ask herself.'

'And you're afraid I haven't?'

'I know you're a level-headed girl, Anjie. In practical
terms, you could have a great screen future. No fooling.
I'd just hate to see it – '

'Herbie, we're madly in love.'

'That's not what I'm enquiring about. We assume that.
What I'm asking – '

'I'll be pushing on with my career. Terry understands
that. He wants it. We'll be a working partnership.'

'Terrific,' said Herbie with unconvincing heartiness.
He gave my hand a squeeze. 'Never mind the old man,

honey. He worries too much. Maybe he's seen a couple of Hollywood hitch-ups too many. No reason yours shouldn't work out.'

I kissed the top of his head. 'No reason at all.'

The madness of my love for Terry was at that time indisputable. The converse was another matter. Certainly he wanted me, in the sense that a small boy might crave a model car and give nobody any rest until he gets it. Basically, Terry was in love with himself and his wishes; and yet his route to fulfilment could be littered with the traces of acts that were easy to confuse with generosity. Like the small boy and the car, he desired me so strongly – whether as sex object, prestige symbol, or counter to his own insecurity, I was never able to determine – that if I had mentioned a passing fancy for Herbie's head on a clapperboard he would probably have taken a hatchet to the studio next morning. Far from feeling repugnance at the Mildendorf episode, he had, I believe, positively welcomed the chance it gave him. The scenario was made to measure: application of pressure in the guise of knight-erranthood.

At the time, I had no inkling of this. I was merely consumed with loving gratitude at his masterly disposal of the matter. I left it entirely to him. He dealt directly with Chief Jansen, and the subject was referred to between us only once again, a week before the wedding, when I mustered courage to ask whether 'everything was all right'. His nod and grin were rallying.

'You'll hear no more, Anjie. Nobody will. It's okay, sugar. That was money well spent.'

I swallowed hard. 'The photos . . .?'

'He handed them over. Prints and negatives. I had a small private bonfire in my backyard. It's finished, honey. You've nothing more to worry about.'

CHAPTER V

AN ATTENDANT cleared my table, leaving me with an uncomfortably barren expanse across which to meditate. Taking the hint, I left Harrods and walked over to Kensington Gardens.

The rain had become drizzle, just unpleasant enough to keep the footpaths clear for those walking with a purpose. At this time of afternoon there were not many purposeful Londoners around. Setting course for Park Lane, I picked up the threads of my recollection.

Nothing to worry about?

It could still be true. Terry might in fact have destroyed every particle of evidence and now, in altered circumstances, was using my uncertainty in a bid to haul me back.

Equally, he might have kept at least some of the prints; either because they excited him or because, even then, their possible usefulness in the future had not escaped him. Knowing as much about him as I now did, I felt each of the latter alternatives to be valid.

Again I applied myself to the question. Assuming that he had kept them, what harm could they now do?

On the most modest level, as I had already surmised, they could give rise to some nasty innuendo which would do me no good at all, professionally or otherwise.

At worst, they could drag out and reopen the entire scandal. Five years had elapsed since the story broke. Many things had changed. But not human nature. If there had been a lessening of the universal appetite for slime, I hadn't noticed.

The risk was too extreme. Passing the Serpentine's Lido, I acknowledged the decision that had formed itself at the outset. Terry and I would be having another talk.

*

The man who opened the door to us remained attached to the handle, as though it was the only support he could trust. Fatigue flattened his voice.

'Mr Joseph? And Miss Anjelica Browne, of course. Do please tramp in.'

The flat, on the seventh floor of a careworn block near Victoria, had seen better days and was still mourning them. People like Denholm Baxter, who occupied it for brief periods between tours, were said to appreciate the shreds of the neighbourhood's bohemianism: looking at him, I could believe it. Leaning upon the door to shut it, my prospective leading man straightened up cautiously and seemed to reach out for various anatomical parts, to reassemble himself. He cantilevered a hand.

'Delighted to meet you both. Like your pictures, Mr Joseph. It's an honour to be working with you.'

Herbie gave a relieved grin. Flattery of the most sledgehammer kind was capable of bringing sunshine into his life; he was worse than any woman. Conversely, a verbal slight could wreck his sleep for a week.

'Did you have a good trip to Sweden?'

'Profitable, but cold.' Baxter trundled a couple of threadbare armchairs into the vicinity of the gas-fire, which was emitting obscene popping noises as though some fuel had disagreed with it. 'Also somewhat taxing. Sherry for both of you?'

While he poured, I studied him. Auburn hair in disarray about a lean, amused face, careless corduroy trousers and a lumpy sweater added up to an effect which in someone less patently regardless might have seemed mannered. He looked a youthful forty-eight: I knew him to be a battered thirty-four. His eyes were hooded, a little sleepy.

He handed us glasses. 'Here's to a white-hot *Furnace*.'

'Amen to that,' Herbie said piously. He paused, apprehensive. 'What's your estimation of the script, Mr Baxter?'

'Denny. The script? Pretty good, I'd say, by and large.'

Herbie relaxed. 'We had a guy by the name of – '

'There are one or two places which might benefit from a spot of attention.'

Herbie pitched a little. I said hurriedly, 'Probably what I've already mentioned. It's a good effort, but just here and there it seems to miss the book's flavour, somehow.' I glanced at Denny. 'Is that how you see it?'

He nodded. 'I've taken the liberty of pencilling in a few suggested alterations . . . Mind if I show you?'

'Sure, why not?' Back on an even keel, Herbie spoke with heroic restraint. Whatever his faults, the head of Joseph Films was a professional who didn't lack vision, and Denny's proposed adjustments, discussion of which occupied the next half-hour, turned out to be thoughtful and, in my view, practical. Once or twice I caught a look of reserve upon Herbie's face, as if he sensed collusion between the pair of us. Giving provisional approval to the bulk of the refinements, he added a caution.

'You have to remember, I'm not the guy who's directing this motion picture. Roger Mayhew could possibly have ideas of his own.'

'I should hope so,' I remarked.

Herbie came massively to his feet. 'We have to be going. Glad to've made your acquaintance, Denny. Look forward to having you with us.' He eyed him appraisingly. 'Braced for the Press jamboree this evening? Savoy, six o'clock.'

'I'll be there. But it's Anjie they'll want to mob.'

'I'd like you in the front line. You have the cultural status we need,' said Herbie with the engaging candour that formed part of his stock-in-trade, 'to convince those hyenas we're not aiming at some kind of slushy romp masquerading as a cinematic landmark. We want them to know, this is one screen version that's for real.'

'I'll accept that,' Denny said solemnly, 'as a compliment. Until six, then. Tomorrow we travel down to Winchester, is that right?'

'You've your own transport?'

'I don't drive. I'll be going by train.'

'Come with us,' I suggested.

'Sure. There's room in the car.'

'Well, thanks. That'll be fun.'

Driving me back to the Cosmopole, Herbie intruded upon an extended silence.

'Looks like you and Denny Baxter are going to get along, honey.'

'Looks like it,' I assented.

He flipped me a glance. 'You don't sound that delirious.'

'Oh, but I am. He's so ideal . . . it's almost too good to be safe. I just want nothing to go wrong.'

'Any reason it should?'

'No. No reason.'

Having completed the navigation of Hyde Park Corner, Herbie retrieved a fragment of concentration with which to give further utterance. 'You seem kind of . . . subdued, Anjie, this morning. Nothing bothering you, is there?'

'Bothering me?' I smiled at his profile. 'Of course not. Everything's kosher.'

CHAPTER VI

THE TELEPHONE BLEEPED as I was applying eye-shadow.

'Your parents are in the lobby, Miss Browne.'

'Thank you. I'll be right there.'

The glass told me I had done all that was practicable. The result was hardly radiance, but it might pass muster after a glass or two of wine. Putting on a fur wrap, I left the room and took the lift down.

'Hi.' Liz's greeting was hushed, although she was doing her best not to seem overawed by her surroundings. 'Do I look all right?' she demanded.

'Peachy.'

She had overdone it marginally, but was youthful and delectable enough to carry it off. Her halter-neck dress was a rich emerald chiffon; her blonde hair, piled high on the crown, descended in a cascade behind. There was a sparkle in her eyes. Giving her warm cheek a kiss, I murmured, 'Who's granting the interviews tonight – me or you?'

'They can fight over us. Tell Mum she looks fabulous. She won't believe me.'

'You look fabulous.' I stooped to hug her. 'I always did like that gown. The pearls set it off nicely. Hi, Dad. Managed to get away, then?'

'I had a half-day owing.' Engulfed in a very dark suit which appeared to have been tailored for someone four sizes larger for some other occasion, he was standing stiffly with his back to the reception area, as though intent on teaching the regardless staff a severe lesson. He gave me a solicitous survey. 'Been hard at work, my dear, mugging up your lines?'

'Blotting out a few. The ones hatching my face. Here's Herbie.'

Resplendent in pale grey, Herbie was at his most patriarchal, inclining himself over the hand of each of the ladies, greeting Dad man to man. 'An honour,' he informed them, 'to finally make the acquaintance of Anjelica's family.'

Liz, speechless, gazed up at him. 'When it comes to looks,' he added, turning his full presence upon her, 'Anjie's not the exception, I can see that. My compliments, ma'am, sir, on a remarkably fine pair of daughters.'

He led the way out to the car. Trotting beside me, Mum filled the lobby with a carrying hiss. 'You never told us, love, what a gentleman he is, this Herbie of yours.'

Informal in belted jacket and checked trousers, my leading man greeted me with a kiss on each cheek. I said, 'Denny, I'd like you to meet my family.'

He shook hands gravely all round. 'I saw you,' Liz

announced, 'in *Pewter Idol*. Thought you were fantastic.'

'But, as you see, I'm not. I'm an ordinary guy in socks. Aiming to follow your sister into films, Liz?'

'Hoping to.'

'You shouldn't have too much of a problem.'

Pride battled with reserve in Mum's demeanour. 'Liz, stop preening yourself. You'll fracture an eyelash.'

Herbie came back with a tray of alcohol. 'Angel, would you mind stepping across and joining Wally Parsons? He has Melvyn Somerby with him. *Movie Monthly*. He can do us some good.'

'This,' I told the family, 'is where I start work. Enjoy yourselves.'

Melvyn Somerby was a sleek but shrewd young man. His questions were deceptively throwaway. Forced to think about my answers, I lost touch with the room for twenty minutes until Denny rejoined us and gallantly took up the running. Herbie materialized at my side.

'Angel, they'd like you for some shots.'

I did some posing against a blank wall. My all-accommodating smile was a cover for the genuine discomfort that I felt: it was less the impatience of the celebrity with the tiresome junketing involved, than an increasingly acute awareness of its essential hollowness by any standard. Whether published or not, the two-dimensional images now being recorded would never amount to more than ephemera . . . a worthless addition to a mounting journalistic junkheap. Was that too harsh? The process constituted, after all, a means to the end of propagating the product in which I passionately believed; who was I to feel contempt?

Staring back at the cameras, flanked by dispassionate, bored or ingratiating faces, I found myself re-living another occasion. Five years in the past, and yet suddenly as immediate, as menacing, as though it had occurred yesterday. The outcome of that, too, had been images upon celluloid; just as flat; but ephemeral . . .?

Countering questions of a personal nature from the film

critic of *The Clarion*, I experienced a choking sensation.
The Regency Room's oxygen supply seemed to have been
cut off. The active lips of the *Clarion* man remained
visible to me, in immense close-up; but although I could
still hear his voice its cadences no longer conveyed meaning; my responses sprang from no identifiable source.
From his expression, I couldn't deduce whether I was
continuing to make sense of an acceptal le kind. He
glanced away, and I concluded that he had reached a
stage of ultimate bafflement; but he was merely selecting
a drink from a hovering tray. I seized the chance to look
around for Herbie. Catching my eye, he hurried across.

'Making out, Angel? When you've a moment, I want
you to meet – '

'Herbie, I'm not feeling so good.'

'You what, honey? You'd best lie down a while. I'll
get 'em to – '

'I don't want to lie down. I want to make a phone call.'

Discretion froze the obvious question on Herbie's lips.
His head jerked this way and that. 'You can phone from
the lobby. Why not fade out for ten minutes? Wally
Parsons and I'll keep 'em happy. Denny's looking after
your folks.'

'Come with me, Herbie?'

He eyed me narrowly. Sidling away, he muttered
briefly with Parsons: both of them peered across the room,
then back at me. Encircled by tall heads, I could see
nothing. Cleaving a way back, Herbie shepherded me in
silence through the crush to the door. One or two inquisitive glances pursued us. Outside, he steered me
efficiently to the right, around a couple of corners, as far
as a broad and lofty inner vestibule where lounging
basket-chairs were arranged between screens of plastic
trellis offering a home to swarming foliage anchored in
troughs. Lowering me into a chair, he dragged up another
and sat on it, chin upon hands, studying me.

'Phone call?' he queried presently.

I shook my head. 'I don't even know the number.'

'My line's available.'

'I know. Thanks.'

After an interval I added, 'You wouldn't happen to know where I can contact Terry?'

His reply was delayed. 'I can tell you that, sure.'

I glanced at him sharply. 'You know where he's staying?'

'I know where he is, right this minute.' Herbie hesitated, before jerking his chin. 'You didn't see him? He's back there.'

Shock pinned me against the cushions. I gazed at him in silence.

'We figured you'd noticed,' he said apologetically. 'Wally and I, that is. The way you reacted, seemed to us you wanted out till the guy took off for home. Wherever that is.'

'I was hemmed in. Never saw him arrive.' I thought swiftly. 'How did he know about this? An advance paragraph in one of the papers?'

'I guess. Want me to have him thrown out?'

'No, Herbie!' I grabbed his wrist. 'That would be . . . Anyhow I do want to see him. We've . . . something to discuss.'

He looked disturbed. 'Changed your mind about alimony?'

'Nothing like that.' I made a cautious selection of words. 'He came to see me, Sunday night. At the hotel. He wants us to get back together.'

Herbie nodded like a venerable owl. 'And is this what you want?'

'For God's sake!'

'So tell him to get lost.'

'It's not as easy as that.'

'You bet it is. I don't mind telling him for you.'

'I'd much sooner you didn't.' Mechanically, with my left hand, I remoulded a tress of hair. 'It's all a bit delicate.'

'Okay, honey. You know best. But listen: you wander

back into that room and meet up with him now, you're
liable to set the lines buzzing from here to Tokyo. You
want this?'

'You know I don't.'

'On the other hand, say we had him out to join you . . .'

'There'd be more hum than ever. Hobson's choice,
Herbie. I'll have to face him openly and play it cool.
Anyone who's curious can ask, and I can tell them. Re-
marriage plans are strictly a non-event.'

'But what'll Terry tell 'em?'

'That's up to him.' I paused. 'I'll still have to talk
seriously with him, in private, later. But first, we go
through the motions.'

Herbie spread his hands. 'Okay, Angel. Whatever you
say.'

Our reappearance among the newsmen was the signal
for some subtle shifts in the interrogative pressure. Confronting a semi-circle of avid faces, I found myself in
contention once more with Nigel Moorforth of the *Sunday
World*, evidently a late arrival, who in a courteous but un-
yielding way desired to know whether the unheralded
presence of a former husband meant that either or both
of us might be thinking in terms of reconciliation, or
whether conceivably Mr O'Malley, ex-swashbuckler of
the screen, was under consideration for a more cerebral
role in *Furnace*, or whether possibly . . .

With what blandness I could summon, I replied that
Mr O'Malley was in attendance purely as an old friend.
We had no plans of a joint nature. In no circumstances
was there any question of his addition to the cast-list. We
might, I added, meet for a drink and a chat over old times,
as former partners were wont to do. Nigel Moorforth
looked courteously disbelieving.

'Would either of you object,' he asked, 'to being
photographed together?'

I shrugged. '*I* shan't object. Hadn't you better put it to
Mr O'Malley?'

A drift occurred in Terry's direction. With renewed

shock, I observed that he was in conversation in a corner with Mum, Dad and Liz; their exchanges were apparently absorbing him to the exclusion of all else. As the Pressmen closed in about him, Herbie growled at my side: 'Hope you know what you're doing, honey.'

'I'm trying to play it by ear.' I moved forward. The Press parted with alacrity to give me access, and my arrival at Mum's side was effected without difficulty, as was the flippancy of my greeting to Terry. 'For some reason that I can't fathom, they want shots of the two of us. In tandem. Any serious objection?'

I could see that he was two-thirds inebriated. Habit was holding him together, but only just. He looked incredibly handsome. Mum looked bright-eyed and intrigued; Liz was practically hanging on to his sleeve. On the perimeter stood Dad, a small aloof figure. Pivoting carefully, Terry gave me his half-smiling attention.

'In tandem,' he repeated. His articulation was clear. 'Sounds like the appropriate formation. Say where you want us, fellahs.'

Arranging us against the blank wall, they took us shoulder to shoulder, each with glass in hand, each of us smiling away from the other. When one of the cameramen suggested that we entwine arms, I rebelled and moved off. Rejoining the family, I heard Terry answering questions.

'Right now I'm here in London to relax, look around. Plans? I'd rather not talk about those just now. I customarily have a few in mind. That's one you should put to Anjelica. Sure our relationship's amicable. We've met up. Draw your own conclusions. You guys will anyway. No, it's the first time I've met her folks, and I want to say they seem like one pippin of a family. I'm hoping we'll get to be real good friends . . .'

With suppressed excitement, Liz said, 'Anjie, he's great! Talked to us just as if he was from the next street.'

'Oh, Terry can be matey.' Across the room I could see Herbie in anxious consultation with the distracted Wally Parsons, who was appraising the new centre of interest as though seeking a way to break it up without bringing the occasion to a premature halt in a shudder of vibrations. Terry's voice could still be heard clearly. He was now extolling the cinematic potential of *Furnace of the Mind*, which I was moderately certain he could never have read. I turned my back upon his vicinity. 'Dad – can I get you another drink?'

'Thank you, my dear, I'm doing nicely with this one.'

'*Will* you be seeing him again?' demanded Liz.

'No personal questions, love.' Mum placed a cautionary finger to her lips.

Rather hastily I swallowed a sweet martini. 'Now that you've met him, Mum, what do you think?'

She pursed her lips. 'Seems pleasant enough.'

'What was he gassing to you about?'

'Oh . . . this and that. How much he still thinks of you.' She gave me a coy glance. 'He seems mighty keen to . . . You know.'

'Put the past where it belongs?'

'He's still fond of you, Anjie, I reckon.'

I studied her for a moment. 'Made a good impression, didn't he?'

Embarrassment was not a weakness of Mum's. 'You can only go by what you see of people. See and hear. I expect you had your reasons for splitting up.'

'I expect we did.'

'He says I'd be a bombshell,' Liz told me, 'for the movies.'

'Discerning of him.'

'Says he can get me a screen test. What do you think, Anjie?'

'I think he's had rather a lot to drink. Don't count on him remembering about it in the morning.'

'He doesn't look pickled to me. Don't you *want* me to have a chance?'

The brightness of her pupils outdid Mum's; her mouth quivered. On screen it would have added up to a performance. Liz wasn't performing: she was genuinely puzzled by my reaction. I slipped an arm across her shoulders.

'I want you to go all the way, Lizzie. To the top. But you won't do it on Terry O'Malley's back – take my word for it. I'm only telling you for your own good.'

A look of obstinacy entered her face. Wriggling out of my reach, she snatched her wineglass from a corner-shelf and gulped its contents. Dad said rebukingly, 'That's enough, Elizabeth. We don't want you making an exhibition of yourself.'

'*You* don't want me doing *anything*.' With a flamboyant gesture she stalked off, heading for Terry's group. Mum and I exchanged looks. I shook my head.

'What made me say that last bit? It'll just make her more stubborn.'

'She'll get over it,' Mum said confidently. 'All up in the stars tonight, she is, imagining things. By tomorrow she'll be two feet on the ground again. She's a sensible girl.'

'But she's fifteen,' I observed. 'And screenstruck. Certain people know how to cash in on combinations like that.'

Mum subjected me to one of her scrutinies.

'You're quite positive, Anjie, there's nothing Terry could do for her? I mean, after all, he's a big name . . .'

'He's a big has-been,' I said bluntly. 'That's not being catty. He's brought it on himself. No producer will look at him now – so as far as professional influence is concerned you can forget it, and so can Liz. He's nothing.'

'I'll tell her what you said.'

Mum spoke absently. She was gazing sidelong at the clamorous throng now surrounding Terry and her younger daughter, radiant in the flare of flash; and I became sickeningly aware that she attached no weight to a word I was saying. At home in West Ham, marshalling saucepans, Mrs Ruby Brown, née McConnell, could give a persuasive impression of solid sense: here in the Regency Room of the Savoy, amid glitter and bombast, she was ready to dance right back into the bog and peat with the leprechauns. My eyes met Dad's. He went on quietly sipping at his scotch and water, four inches of surplus shirt-cuff flapping at his skinny wrist. Neither of us spoke; I felt, however, that a certain rueful understanding had stationed itself between us.

CHAPTER VII

'READY, HONEY?'

'I'm not leaving just yet, Herbie. Terry and I have some unfinished business. I'll call you, first thing to-morrow.'

Hunched inside a fur-collared coat against the wind chewing in from the Strand, Herbie removed his hand from the car door. 'If you're seen talking – '

'The damage is done. We're going to be written about, so what does it matter?'

His scalp came in for some scratching. 'Something in that, I guess,' he conceded finally. 'Take it easy, though, huh? No scenes.'

'Any scenes of mine,' I assured him, 'are reserved for where they belong.'

Herbie squirmed himself behind the wheel. Wherever he was, he always insisted upon driving his own vehicle. 'Pleasure meeting your folks,' he shouted through the window. 'Tell 'em they're welcome on set, any time.'

I delivered a good-night tap to the intervening glass. With a salute, he purred off.

Slowly I returned to the hotel lobby.

Fatigue was starting to crowd me. An hour previously, the last of the Pressmen had left for Fleet Street or wherever else they were due. Half an hour after that, we had packed Mum, Dad and Liz into a taxi and despatched them home. Then Herbie and I, with Denny Baxter, Wally Parsons and a couple of others, had discussed arrangements for the following day over a last drink. Now I was by myself.

Or would have been, had Terry not been waiting within. Joining him, I said curtly, 'Where shall we go?'

'Why don't I take you home?'

'To my hotel room, you mean? No thanks. Let's take a walk.'

'It's cold,' he protested.

'You're wearing plenty. I'll see if I can scrounge an extra wrap.'

A reception clerk obliged with a shapeless mass of tweed which he said was used sometimes by female staff who wanted to slip out to a news stand or the chemist. As Terry and I were leaving, a flash lit the night. At the opposite kerbside, a man clutching a camera ducked into a taxi, like a rabbit diving to earth. The taxi took off, turning right into the Strand. I said resignedly, 'By morning, as far as the general public's concerned, we'll be on our second honeymoon. Terry, I'm warning you. Whatever you might read, don't let it give you ideas.'

'I do run to a few of my own,' he said humbly.

When Terry was being humble he was at his least predictable. I directed our steps down towards the Embankment. Docilely he kept pace, remaining scrupulously out of bodily contact as though deferring to a wish I had expressed aloud. Gusts chopped across the Thames. Their cutting edges were stropped as only those of early April can be; but the evening was dry, at least. I walked with pocketed hands. There were holes in the borrowed coat's lining. Terry gazed interestedly across river at the South Bank, where the National Theatre and Festival Hall complex blazed its existence.

'Quite a shrine,' he remarked. 'If you happen to idolize concrete. Any plans for playing Lady Macbeth on the brand-new stage, Anjie? Or didn't they ask you?'

'I'm in work at the moment. Unlike some people.'

'That wasn't too diplomatic,' he said after a moment.

'It wasn't meant to be.'

'In our profession, there's a fixed limit to the amount of – '

'Climb off it, Terry. It's me you're talking to, not one of your fantasy-figures. When did you last earn anything?'

He lifted his gaze meditatively to the street lamps. 'Last thing I seem to recall earning was a gratuitous insult from my ex-wife.'

I said coldly, 'If you invite insults you must expect to get them. Look: we're not here to carry on the war – are we? I want to help you, Terry. Purely for old times' sake; nothing else. For God's sake be clear on that. I know you've not worked for a year or more, and I know why you haven't, and I'm not sure there's anything I can do but I'm willing to try. I don't relish seeing you make a display of yourself as you did tonight.'

He said inconsequentially: 'Real nice folks, your ma and pa.'

'If I speak to Herbie, I know he'll put in a word for you with Supreme Pictures or Astral when he gets back to the States . . .'

Terry began to hum. Irritated, I said, 'I suppose you think you're above needing a helping hand? You may have been a big name once, but what you have to realize – '

'Did I ask for professional help?'

I was silent for a while. The wind clawed at my neck. At the base of Cleopatra's Needle I halted to lean on the stone balustrade, staring out at the lights of a launch scuttering down-river towards Westminster. At a yard's distance, he did the same. I felt the chill of the stonework seeping through the protective layers into my flesh.

'If I write you a cheque tonight for twenty thousand pounds, will you catch a flight home tomorrow and promise we shan't meet again?'

The launch-lights had vanished beneath Westminster Bridge before he spoke.

'Trying for it on the cheap, aren't we, Anjie? I paid

nearly as much for you, several years back.'

'Thirty thousand.'

He made elaborate calculations. 'Getting on for sixty grand. Well, that starts to take care of inflation. Don't forget interest, though. Plus depreciation.'

'I'm not the Federal Bank. You have to be reasonable, Terry.'

'I'm a reasonable guy.'

'Well, then. How much will you settle for?'

'Oh . . . let's see. How much would you say you can lay hands on?'

I released a breath. 'I've no idea. A lot of it's tied up, I don't understand the . . . You'd have to give me a few days.'

'No need to go to all that trouble. I'll accept payment in kind.'

'What do you mean?'

'You know darn well.'

My head wanted to sag. I propped it with the palm of a hand. 'Terry, we're finished. Can't you assimilate that? I'm not getting involved with you again, not ever.'

'But honey, you are involved.'

A note of low triumph had teamed up with the spitefulness in his throat. I tried to estimate the depth of assurance lurking behind it. For all my hard-won knowledge of his nature, it was an impossible exercise. I knew only that my approach had taken the wrong course and that an adjustment was now out of the question: the initiative was his, as usual. Thrusting myself clear of the balustrade, I resumed the walk, wretchedly aware that he had fallen in alongside like an unsolicited tugboat intent upon extracting harbour-dues from a liner.

'You've shown me no proof of that.'

'Then why are you offering cash?'

Fair question. I kept my voice down. 'I'm trying to settle things on a harmonious basis. I want you to have a future, Terry. Standing on your own feet.'

'That'll be easy. With an arm to lean on.'

We were back, once more, in the clutches of the script-writer's patter. Every conversation we had seemed to degenerate into this mechanized exchange. I raised the collar of the tweed coat to my chin.

'No deal.' Apart from matching the mood, the phrase had the merit of brevity.

'Your career comes first?'

'If you like.'

'So you wouldn't want anyone doing anything to jeopardize that?'

'I don't believe you would.'

'Don't try me, honey.'

'If you still have any of those damn prints or negatives, why not show me?'

'Why don't you just assume I haven't? Then you could shrug me off, like you will that coat you're wearing. Like you did before.'

'Will you show me?'

He slanted me a half-smile. And said nothing.

'I don't believe you kept a single one.'

'You're entitled to your beliefs.'

'I think I'll say good night now.'

'Night, Anjie. May I say, in my own view you'd have made a top-grade Miriam in a marvellous picture. I mean that sincerely.'

In the act of walking away from him, I felt my feet drag. It was as though they were unattached to me by nerve or sinew, and yet bringing me by some kind of osmosis to a standstill. A man swathed in mackintosh and scarf trudged heedlessly by in the direction of Blackfriars. I waited while he passed beyond earshot. Then I turned.

'Whatever else you are, Terry, I don't believe you're vicious. I can't believe anyone could be as vindictive as that.'

In the glow from an overhead lamp he simulated mild astonishment.

'Who said anything about vindictiveness? Utilization of assets is sound business practice.'

I returned a few paces. 'Assets? What assets? It may interest you to learn that I've already acquainted Herbie with the details of my scarlet past. The works. As far as he's concerned it's immaterial, so how about that?'

His laughter was soft, controlled.

'This why you were willing to come up with sixty grand?'

'That was a friendly offer. The supporting arm you were talking about . . .'

'Nice try, Anjie. Anyhow there's a world of difference, you'll find, between sympathetic noises and harsh reality. If it came to the crunch – which I'm convinced it won't – I've a feeling Herbie would find a way to sympathetically throw you out on your cute little ear.'

My last throw had been tossed back. I had nothing left. As I stood in the paralysis of despair, Terry advanced to place a hand on each of my upper arms. His head tilted. He spoke kindly.

'But why are we talking in this vein? You're not going to force me to take any action that would lead to unpleasantness. What's the point? All I'm asking is that we skip back a little, to happier times – '

'Happier?'

He blinked. Releasing me, he stepped back. His voice hardened.

'For one of us, at least. And there's a couple of small things you might bear in mind, Mrs Anjie O'Malley. But for me, you'd have been in no position to follow your precious screen career five years back: you'd have been discredited, or in jail. You could remember that. You could also acknowledge that I'm not asking you to give it all up. You're a star. You can stay right on up there, part of the firmament. All I'm asking – '

'You make it sound so easy,' I said scornfully. 'The answer's no, Terry. Understand? A flat negative. The kind you say, not the type you unwrap and show to people. If that's what you're itching to do, then go ahead and do it. I'd sooner that, than feel I belonged to you again.'

His voice, low-pitched but distinct, pursued me on the breeze.

'*Screen Goddess was Prime Mover in Sex Blackmail Racket.* How does that grab you, Anjie, as a sample headline?'

The down-to-earth normality of Herbie's amiable rasp was the equivalent of a week's course of vitamins.

'Sure thing, Angel. Come on round. I'll get busy on the coffee. Take it easy, I'll be here.'

When I arrived, he was: all fourteen and a half companionable, comforting stone of him. It seemed the natural thing to sob into his lapels. Herbie had dealt with too many studio tantrums not to have developed a technique. First he remained still, gently patting my spine, until I had finished dampening his lapels; then he guided me into a receptive easy-chair near the electric heater; then he brought in the coffee pot while I attended to the facial damage. Whistling to himself, he rattled crockery around, raising the pot's lid at intervals to assure himself that things were happening as they ought.

'Black would set you up . . . but I know you'll insist on cream. Heathen habit. There . . . we . . . are. Figured I'd seen the last of you for tonight. No such luck. By the way, did I mention how well you handled the news vultures earlier on?'

'Better than I did my personal affairs, I hope.' Returning my compact to my bag, I took a sip of coffee and smiled wearily across at the solid bulk of him, wedged unsuitably into a narrow rocker with wooden arms. 'Trouble is, one can't rehearse those.'

'They're apt to depart from the script,' he agreed. His glance was uncertain. 'Want to tell me about it?'

I absorbed a deep breath, a second mouthful of coffee, another breath. 'Terry's threatening me.'

The rocker plunged as though in a heavy swell. 'The hell he is!'

'Wait a second, Herbie. Before you do him or yourself a mischief. It's nothing physical. I wish to God it was.

That I could deal with.'

Herbie fell back. 'Moral blackmail?'

After some hesitation I said, 'That describes it, more or less. Apologies, Herbie, and all that . . . but I'd rather not say just what's involved. I . . . I can't, somehow. Can you understand?'

'Sure, honey, sure. Everyone has things they want kept under plain wrappers.' Taking a burbling pull at his black, unsweetened fluid, he contemplated the cup for a few moments before setting it down. 'I take it he has something on you?'

'Right.'

'That could hurt you?'

'Badly.'

'In a professional context?'

'In every way. Me, and others.'

The rocker embarked upon a series of undulations, seemingly independent of motive power from its occupant. Herbie was thinking deeply, and very fast.

'What is it you're saying, Anjie?'

'Really, I'm asking. Can you envisage any circumstances in which you *wouldn't* want me as Miriam in *Furnace*?'

His head shook with ferocious emphasis.

'None at all?' I persisted.

'Jesus, honey, what is this? Masochism? If the wheels of a London bus put you in the mortuary, I might just hesitate before wiring you up to go through the action: aside from which, the answer's no. That satisfy you?'

'Yes, Herbie. Thank you. It does.'

Seated opposite him in the intimate warmth of his Mayfair nest, it was hard to withstand the shock-waves of his fervour. If a wrinkle of doubt remained, for the moment I stamped it flat. I shone him a smile which, from experience, I knew would render him inarticulate for a number of seconds. While he recovered, I made a show of drinking some more of his awful coffee and draping my fur wrap more tidily over the back of the chair: the

borrowed tweed I had returned to the Savoy before
getting a taxi. Reverting to coherence, Herbie gave me
his Dutch-uncle look.

'Feel better about it now?'

'I'm darned hungry.'

'You poor kid.' He shot from the rocker, leaving it acti-
vated. 'Why didn't you say?'

'I just did.'

I followed him into a small, glittering kitchen, infested
with consoles and dials like the flight deck of a jumbo jet.
He stood in the centre, looking helpless.

'Been feeding out,' he muttered. 'See the left-hand
heater there? I can actuate that. Haven't dared touch
anything else, case it snapped back. You figure there's
food around?'

'Take that end,' I directed. 'I'll cover this.'

Between us we opened a lot of cupboards, producing a
plastic-wrapped sliced loaf and a tin of chopped ham. I
tracked down a manual tin-opener, because neither of us
could make out how to operate the electric one plugged
to the wall. The refrigerator yielded butter, with which I
plastered the slices: Herbie slapped in the meat. We ate
sitting side by side on a worktop. Nothing – Mum's
welcome-home lunch included – had tasted so good to me
since my first meal after finally walking out on Terry in
Miami; I had the same sensation of flavours rediscovered,
of alimentary delight renewed. It was my first intake of
solid food for ten hours. Annihilating his third sandwich,
Herbie heaved a gusty sigh.

'Remember how we used to do this in Pine Mountains?'

I nodded. 'Making *Flora*. That was a wonderful spot.'

'You've some pretty nice scenery in Hampshire, they
tell me.' He swung his legs like a schoolboy. 'Come
summer.'

'Time for a picnic or two.'

'Sure, why not? Now and then we'll have to get clear
of the studios. Ease the stresses.'

I said gently, 'Is there going to be a lot of stress?'

He elevated a freckled hand. 'Tell us a work of art that's not taken it out of someone.'

I turned towards him. 'This picture, Herbie . . . means a lot to you, doesn't it?'

'Means everything.'

'Artistically?'

'In every way. My shirt's riding on it, Anjie.' He spoke with the simplicity of absolute commitment. 'See, honey, you might call it my passport back to respectability.' He paused. 'You wouldn't know about this, but when I started out I was the new Eisenstein, the fresh white hope of Hollywood. Way before your time. One or two movies I was responsible for . . . they hoisted me into the ratings, the critical hemisphere. I was the name to watch. I packed a lot of effort, a lot of thought into those pictures – they were *good*.'

'I bet they were.'

He reflected, thick fingers tapping the sandwich plate. 'The approach I used then got results. Maybe I should've stuck with it.'

'Why didn't you?'

'I developed. Shifted with the times. Updated myself. Always some such damned excuse. Know what I was really doing? Coining the fast buck. Yep: as original as that. Joseph Films. The spreading of empire. All I could think about. To hell with quality.'

'You've made some good films since.'

'Some frothy entertainment. Know how I regard *Flora*? I think of it as the ultimate rehash of a mixture that's been stewing for a decade or more and is running low on flavour. Tastes change, Anjie. With society headed the way it is, jocular titillation is out. You have to go the whole way, and that's a barren trip to a dead end. Or else you have to turn and hike back. Re-explore the basic values.'

This, to me, was a new Herbie. His words should have sounded pompous; but there was something compelling about his deliverance of every syllable as though it was the result of a great deal of thought.

'This is what I'm doing now,' he added. 'Returning to investigate. Something tells me that unless I do, it's curtains.'

I said uncertainly, 'For yourself? Or Joseph Films?'

'Comes down to the same thing, I guess.' He gave me his big, warm, sudden smile. 'No cause to flip, honey. *Furnace* is going to deliver, for all of us . . . I can feel it. There's a great movie on its way, and you're going to make Garbo look like trash.'

'If Terry allows it,' I couldn't help saying.

Swinging himself off the table, he stood confronting me, frowning. 'He really does have you steamed up, doesn't he? Why not go to the cops?'

'No, Herbie.'

'If it's blackmail, they can – '

'He hasn't demanded money. All he wants is for me to go back to him. They can't run him in for that.'

'But if he's threatening you . . .'

'What he's threatening is something they can't get him for unless he actually does it. Not even then, probably. The Los Angeles police might take an interest in him – but they'd take a damn sight more interest in me.'

Herbie looked bemused.

'Sure you don't want to tell us about it? It's kind of difficult to advise unless I'm in on the detail.'

For an instant I was powerfully tempted. He looked the epitome of dependability, worldliness. A strand of reserve held me back.

'Mind if I sleep on it, Herbie? I might burden you for no reason.'

'It's more of a burden,' he pointed out, 'not knowing.'

'Sorry. But I could be taking Terry more seriously than he warrants. I'll work something out.'

'From tomorrow,' he observed, 'you'll be in Hampshire. Where's Terry going to be?'

'New Hampshire, for preference,' I said flippantly. The electric digital wall-clock caught my eye. 'Hey, we're in time for the late news, I think. Let's see if we've made the videotape.'

Leading the way with alacrity back to the living-room, Herbie switched on the colour television. The newscast was in progress. A deadpan political commentator was speculating upon the likely consequence of some procedural contortion in the Commons. Herbie listened earnestly. At the end of the summary he shook his head.

'Guess I'm not quite tuned in to your legislative set-up, Angel. Seems to me, what he's saying – '

I flapped him into silence.

'On a lighter note,' the newscaster was saying with a quirk of the lips, 'speculation was renewed tonight over another enigma – this time in the world of showbusiness. At a London reception, Anjelica Browne, who's here in England to make the film of Jon Templar's best-selling novel, *Furnace of the Mind*, told newsmen that, contrary to reports, she and her former husband, American screen star Terry O'Malley, had NO plans to remarry. However, from Mr O'Malley, who was also at the reception, came a somewhat different comment. *We may have something to announce*, he said, *quite shortly*. He advised photographers: *Stick around and keep those lenses demisted*. Miss Browne told correspondents she had nothing further to say. Shooting of the film,' the newscaster added whimsically, returning into view in place of the head-and-shoulders of myself that had been occupying the screen, 'starts next week at the former BUC Studios. Miss Browne's leading man is Denholm Baxter. And that's all the news for tonight. The weather tomorrow . . .'

I doused the set.

'For the moment,' I said flatly, 'he's got what he wants.'

'The spotlight.'

I collected my handbag and wrap. 'All publicity for *Furnace*, I suppose.'

'We don't want it at your expense.' Herbie looked and sounded restive. 'If that dipso ex-husband of yours is just out to make a nuisance of himself – '

'It's my problem. Sorry I saddled you with it this evening. It's just that I was upset after what he said, and tired, and hungry . . .'

'And you needed some place to go.' Herbie spoke hoarsely. In sudden mild alarm, I consulted my watch with an extravagant gesture.

'Must be away. Tomorrow . . .' I broadened my accent. '. . . we head South.'

His mood wasn't going to allow him to leave it there. The rate of his advance caused him to trip on the edge of a rug, but he recovered to station himself between me and the door as a preliminary to planting a pair of wide palms upon my shoulders and peering intently into my face.

'Y'know, honey . . . you don't have to scuttle.'

'Yes, I do. Sleep to catch up on.'

In a half-strangled voice he said, 'Sure. How about a good-night kiss for Herbie?'

I brushed his forehead briefly with my lips. Before I could withdraw, his grasp had tightened and he was coming back at me with stabs of the mouth against my right cheek. Faintly ludicrous as it was, I didn't object strongly enough to make an especially firm stand. My familiarity with Herbie was long-established. I knew him as a clean-living man of decent principles, and this was not the first time we had kissed; it was merely the first time it had signified anything beyond routine affection on either side. I wanted neither to hurt him, nor to imply any promise that didn't exist. Tonight of all nights was the very last occasion upon which to make him feel rejected: so much that concerned me depended on him.

My calculating streak appalled me to the extent that, fleetingly, I tried to whistle up an answering surge of emotion, to convince myself that a Herbie-figure was what I needed; that I had only to drop my guard to allow an emotional attachment to add itself to the respect and confidence that were already entrenched. His mouth moved against mine, and I knew at once the impossibility of the concept. I stayed rigid.

Almost immediately he gave up. His hands dropped to his sides.

'Sleep tight, honey.'

'Thanks, Herbie. You're sweet.'

'Yeah.' He spoke harshly. 'Sweet and sticky. Everything I adhere to gets mussed up.' He forced a grin. 'At least I'm in good company. Even the O'Malleys of this planet can't hold you for long.'

'Herbie, he's not even in your league. Never will be.' Opening the door, I manufactured a gesture, something between a wave and a blessing. 'Don't rush me,' I added, throwing him a useless sop, and hurried off downstairs, despising myself.

CHAPTER VIII

ALTHOUGH ON THE cramped side by Hollywood standards, the Hampshire studios were in Roger Mayhew's opinion good enough for our purpose.

He had arrived two days previously to assess their potential and to meet the author. At dinner on the day we joined him, he gave us a staccato rundown of the building's assets and liabilities, pursuing this with an outline of the sequence in which he proposed to tackle the early scenes. All on-set shooting out of the way first, was his programme; location work later, when the weather improved. Herbie nodded slowly.

'Reservations?' Mayhew enquired sensitively.

He was a tubby, balding man in his middle fifties, with snub nose and double chin. In appearance he was light-years from his professional reputation, but I had learned not to be swayed too much by façades. Herbie transmuted the nod into a shake.

'Only that I've always inclined to the chronological approach myself. It's entirely a personal fad. Your way sounds sensible.'

With a shiver, he peered around the dining-room. 'Anything that keeps us between heated walls for the rest of April has my total support.'

'May can be pretty savage,' said Mayhew with the serenity of the prophet in his own land.

Denny Baxter, seated next to me inside a cashmere sweater that hugged his neck to the level of his ear-lobes, said stoically through a mouthful of soup: 'I'm never going to feel warm again. Not until I retire to Florida.'

Herbie said, 'They get the odd hurricane. Speaking of a rush of air . . . can we prevail upon Mrs Emmerson to have the heating jacked up in the bedrooms? I barely had the courage to switch jackets just now, never mind change my shirt. How about you, Anjie?'

'I don't wear shirts. But I must admit, I practically had to shake the ice-crystals out of my sweater before I could drag it on.' I lowered my voice. 'If she's after a surcharge for re-setting the thermostat, count me in for my share.'

'I'll talk to her,' Mayhew growled.

On a ten-week composite tariff, we had taken over The Beeches, a 'country house hotel' managed by a Mrs Cynthia Emmerson, her voiceless husband, and a staff of assorted relatives who crept about the groaning stair-cases and across the rending floorboards with all the vigour of crippled sidesmen taking the collection in chapel. Superbly sited at the head of a shallow valley, in its own grounds with a rhododendron-lined driveway and a hard-surfaced tennis court whose crop of spring weeds would have kept a botanist happily absorbed for a month, the place was handily close to the studios without, as near as I could estimate upon the strength of a few hours' ac-quaintance, offering a single subsidiary amenity that could not have been found in an adequately-equipped cattle shed. The 'heating' to which Herbie had alluded was the same in every room: an entanglement of pipes and hissing cylinders, crudely bracketed to the papered

walls and releasing into the washbasins a trickle of tepid
moisture of a repellently amber complexion, as though
the duty of one of the sluglike relatives was to clamber
periodically into the loft and pour quantities of rusty nuts
and bolts into the water-tank. The sounds occurring at
intervals behind the wallpaper seemed to confirm this
hypothesis.

Notwithstanding the hubbub, the rooms themselves
remained stubbornly at a temperature nudging zero. They
were not rendered more agreeable by ill-fitting sash
windows that declined either to climb or to drop the
ultimate inch. A sense of chauvinism inhibited me from
conceding to Herbie just how dire The Beeches was by
any yardstick of civilized accommodation; but I saw no
reason for withholding my support for such action as could
be enforced to alleviate the rigours.

Herbie pushed away his lentil soup, half-finished.
Champing upon a piece of chalk-white, arid bread to
which the aroma of plastic wrapping still adhered, he
said, 'What's your impression of Templar?'

Mayhew's lips puckered. 'Withdrawn.'

'Oh my God.'

'I don't say we're going to have trouble with him. He's
a little remote to talk to . . . but then we may not need to
do much talking. I can't see him paying frequent visits
to the studios.'

'Happy to leave it to us?'

'Day to day, I would think so. He'll want to see the
rushes from time to time, and of course he reserves his
contractual rights to have a say in things . . . but I doubt
if he'll bother us too much. He's well into his next opus.'

Herbie caught my eye.

'Regarding the script,' he said gingerly, 'Anjie and
Denny and myself have indulged in a small editing
session . . .'

'Oh yes?' Mayhew's tone was neutral.

'In our view – that is, they consider, and I go some way
along with them – that although Vic Roach did a great

job, here and there he possibly overdid the condensation a little. Drowned out the overtones. Nothing serious, just a matter of – '

'I thought the whole thing was first-rate.'

'In general terms, we don't quarrel with that. There's merely a handful of specific . . .'

The tone of the ensuing discussion, which took us through to the end of the meal, did nothing to modify my view that we were in for a stimulating two or three months. Although I slipped in the occasional word, for the most part I was content to leave the immediate debate to the others. Its liveliness came as a relief.

Since the previous night, the relationship between Herbie and myself had undergone the subtlest of variations. There was nothing I could have pin-pointed. On the surface, everything was exactly the same, if one discounted a slightly more boisterous note to our exchanges, a marginal tendency on each side to over-react to every wisecrack. In the course of the drive from London, Herbie's manner had been characteristically bluff and kind. And yet, for all this, something that had been hovering in the intervening airspace, awaiting identification, had been shot down. Crippled: possibly destroyed. It was a weird, disturbing feeling. I wished desperately that there was something I could do to put the clock back thirty-six hours. Without Denny's company inside the car during the journey, I might have asked Herbie to pull in somewhere quiet and tried to sort things out; as it was, we had covered the distance in one jump in a couple of brisk hours, and the literal frigidity of our reception at The Beeches had not contributed to the kind of atmosphere desirable for such an exercise.

In addition to the four of us, several others were to make Mrs Emmerson's ice-palace their headquarters for the duration. Charlie Penhurst, the coveted chief cameraman. Dilys Meridew, Herbie's continuity girl with a supplementary talent for administration. Graham Forde, straight from repertory to play husband to my Miriam. And Roger

Mayhew's assistant, a young man with the improbable name of Adrian Allister – another unknown quantity as far as Herbie was concerned, but understood to have distinguished himself recently in the field of award-winning documentaries. Mayhew had asked for him, and Herbie had raised no objection. The balance of the cast and the technical team were being housed in Winchester hotels, and were to be ferried to and from the studios daily by chartered bus.

Over the anaemic coffee that brought Mrs Emmerson's dinner to a flatulent conclusion, Mayhew said, 'When do Charlie and the others arrive?'

'Tomorrow,' replied Herbie, belching stealthily.

Denny sighed. 'Poor bastards. Slumming it in those nasty hot rooms in the centre of town.'

'Can we have them all at the studios on Saturday morning? Get 'em briefed.'

'Sure,' said Herbie. 'Sooner the better.'

Roger Mayhew, it seemed, didn't smile much. I was startled, if gratified, when he turned a neat row of top teeth upon me. 'I imagine, Miss Browne, you've given a good deal of thought to the character of Miriam. May I ask what conclusions you've reached?'

I glanced at Herbie. 'Seems to me it's wise not to commit oneself too heavily beforehand. I'm keeping my options open.'

He kept his codlike gaze upon me. 'I see.'

It was difficult to say whether my reply had been totally the right one, or disastrously wrong.

Over the telephone, Mum's voice sounded more metallic than it did normally. 'Settled in, love, are you?'

'Still chipping away the ice. Where are you calling from?'

'The box on the corner. I reversed the charges, like you said.'

'Good. When do you want to visit the studios?'

'Lizzie'll be off from school, end of next week. They're

doing the heating. How about Thursday?'

'Thursday it is. Hire a car from Jacobson's, door to door. How's Liz? Got over her sulks of last night?'

'Chirpier than ever. After tonight.'

'What happened tonight?'

'We'd a visitor. Guess who.'

'Uncle Reg? The Parker boys?'

'Nobody like that,' Mum scoffed. 'It was Terry.'

'Terry Who?'

'Your Terry, of course. Only one I know of.'

For a moment I gaped at the receiver. 'He came to the *house*?'

'Why shouldn't he?'

'He's got a damn . . . How did he find the address?'

'Liz must've told him, I reckon. At the do last night.'

Biting back the words crowding my lips, I substituted others. 'I don't think he should descend on people like that. Not with things as they are. What's he trying to prove?'

'I don't think he was trying to *prove* anything, love. He was just interested to see where we lived. He'd heard such a lot about it from you.'

'I don't remember telling him that much. If I had, it wouldn't have sunk in.' I hesitated. 'I'm not keen on this, Mum. He shouldn't be poking his nose in.'

'I don't know as I'd call it that.' Mum sounded hurt. 'More of a courtesy visit, like. Ever so nice he was, Anjie. Brought me flowers. Cigars for Dad.'

'He would.' I said it under my breath. A weight had toppled into my stomach and was lying motionless at the base. Aloud I said, 'I've never had occasion to question his charm. Don't let it fool you.'

'People can't charm me.' Mum sincerely believed this. She always had. 'Know what I think? I think he felt lonesome, by himself in a strange country . . . wanted to be reminded of you. That's why he called on us.'

I struggled for words that might express what I wanted to tell her. *He's using you.* To have said so, outright, would have sounded shrill, unconvincing; anything more oblique would have missed target. Mum, I could tell, had been a walkover. The clean-cut, boyish, all-American approach had crushed her like a tank. Liz had already been flattened. That left Dad. I wondered about Dad.

'Did he say what his plans were?'

'He's stopping on in England for a bit.' Mum's inflexion suggested that such a decision was only right and proper. 'Wants to have a look around, like.'

'Don't let him pester you. He could, you know. Give him an inch – '

'Aren't you being rather unfair to him, Anjie? It's harder for you, I know. We wouldn't want to interfere in your . . . private life and that. After all, that's your business. But I couldn't feel right if we was to make him think we was turning our backs on him just because of what went wrong between the two of you in America. See my point?'

I sagged against the wall. In this vein, I knew, Mum was perfectly capable of talking in ever-widening circles for the next hour. I said carefully, 'Yes, I see yours . . . but mine will have to keep till you get here. Thursday, then? A car direct to the studios, don't forget. Make it early. We'll have dinner at Winchester afterwards.'

'Lovely. I'd better get off now, there's two people waiting outside.'

'Bye now. Love to Dad.'

Prompt on cue, Mrs Emmerson drifted on an arctic current into the entrance hall as I hung up. I played a beam over her.

'I think I must have exceeded my stake. Take another pound, Mrs Emmerson, will you? I've no way of checking.'

'Shocking price, calls, nowadays.' In four words she contrived to condemn comprehensively the iniquities of government, the profligacy of visitors and the rigours of hotel management as she folded the pound note into the pocket of her georgette blouse. It had short sleeves. Her arms were a mottled mauve. 'Breakfast at eight?' she queried, writhing pencilled eyebrows at me.

'If that's possible.'

'The difficulty is staff.' When she smiled, it was worse than when she didn't. 'We'll do our best. I know what it is for people like you. I've a little theatrical experience myself.'

I said cheerfully, 'How nice.' And, before she could press her case: 'I'll say good night, then. Bed's the cosiest place, don't you think?'

She didn't turn a hair. The famished smile dogged me up the staircase.

Somebody had turned back the covers of my bed, exposing sheets that either were spotted with a fungoid deposit or had already begun to be attacked by frost. From a shop in the nearby village I had succeeded in obtaining a hot-water bottle, which I now held to the washbasin tap. It hiccuped twice, splashed some liquid rust over my wrist, hiccuped again, gulped, and was silent. The momentary flow ceased. After waiting several minutes, during which there were hints of a low murmuring on the far side of the wall, unaccompanied by further precipitation, I threw the hot-water bottle into a corner, tore off my garments and flung myself between the bedclothes. The shock was violent. For a while I lay gasping, massaging one foot against the other. Presently I was able to breathe.

I switched off the light.

Ever so nice he was. I think he felt lonesome.

Mum's voice, clattering about my skull. Refusing to lie down. After a while, for all that the piercing draughts from the window could do, I started to sweat.

CHAPTER IX

'MR TEMPLAR, I'd like you to meet Miriam.'

The author and I shook hands. With slight breathlessness I said, 'I warn you, I'm not literary. But I do love the
book.'

He blinked at me. 'That's cheering. You must come and
tell my wife. She inspired most of it.'

Herbie said respectfully, 'Behind every great man . . .
huh?'

'Is she here?' I asked.

'No, I came by myself this morning. Guessed things
might be a little chaotic.'

Herbie chuckled. 'If you call this chaos, Mr Templar,
you should come back next week when we really get
started. Right, Anjie? You're looking a little pale. Feel
okay?'

'Raring to go.'

Jon Templar had continued to brood upon me. He said
diffidently, 'I meant that, you know. My wife would love
to meet you. When can you spare the time?'

'When can I spare the time, Herbie?'

'Between now and Monday. That's when the schedule
grabs a hold of us,' he explained to the author, a short,
stocky man with sparse, silvering hair, deep-set eyes, and
a mouth that seemed to have skirted the perimeter of
cynicism before settling into folds of resigned acceptance.
Success had reached him relatively late: I judged his age
to be around sixty. In an odd, controlled way, he looked
nervous.

'Hardly your scene, all this?' I suggested, indicating
the surroundings.

'I find it rather exciting. I adore the cinema. Though
I'm a complete ignoramus as to the mechanics of it all.'
He peered at Herbie. 'Shall I be in the way if I poke

around for a while?'

'Be our guest,' Herbie said expansively.

I took Templar's arm. 'Like me to show you over?'

'I'm sure you must have more important things to do.'

'Not needed, Herbie, am I?'

"'Course not, honey. Who'd need you?' We both laughed.

'Nobody really knows the mechanics of it, Mr Templar,' I told him, leading him off. 'Generally we just muddle through. It just happens.'

He nodded. 'Writers have the identical experience.'

We paused to watch Roger Mayhew arguing something out with Charlie Penhurst in front of Stage Three, a shabby kitchen. It looked almost ready. By Monday it would have to be, since it was here that shooting was programmed to commence. Templar gazed at the edifice in evident fascination.

'Your book,' I remarked, 'said an awful lot to me, Mr Templar. Now, to meet the author . . . Well, you know. It's an experience.'

'That's rather funny,' he said mildly.

'What is?'

'I was just thinking what an experience it is to meet Anjelica Browne.'

'A depressing one, I'd have thought.'

'Why?'

'After the glossy posters, I must look so *ordinary*.'

He examined me gravely. 'We've seen most of your films. My wife and I, that is. We've often said: I wonder if closer acquaintance would explode the illusion . . .'

'Don't tell me,' I pleaded. 'I'd sooner not know.'

'But you don't mind if it's favourable?'

'Nobody minds that. Actresses least of all.'

'I'm very keen that you should meet Celia. That's my wife. When she heard you'd been cast as Miriam, she said immediately: Perfect! No hesitation. It surprised me rather, because I have to admit, I didn't see it myself.'

'I don't wonder.'

Gazing spellbound at the testing of camera-booms and associated equipment above our heads, he said, 'Don't run away with the idea that I, um, disapproved of your screen image. Quite the contrary. I just didn't see you as the tormented creature I'd tried to represent.'

'Do you now?'

His eyes returned to me. 'I'm re-examining my ideas,' he said honestly.

I swung to face him. 'If it's any help – I think I feel as deeply about Miriam as anyone could. I want to do her proud.'

'I think you might. What's through there?'

'Stage Five. The hideout. The shack in the woods, you know, where Miriam and Neville Grant – '

'Yes; I'm familiar with the story.' I blushed, and we both laughed. 'Can we take a look?'

A lone carpenter was roaming Stage Five, applying desultory taps with a mallet. On the pretext of stationing ourselves at a good viewpoint, I repossessed Templar's arm. Its solidity was a reassurance. His remarks concerning me, qualified though they were, had been bracing, coming at a time when the ice encircling me was showing signs of fissuring. Also I liked him. We watched the carpenter launch a sudden destructive assault upon a section of weatherboarding that seemed to have offended his craftsman's eye. 'I suppose,' I murmured, 'that's the kind of thing you find yourself having to do.'

He caught on instantly. 'If something's not right, then you must hammer at it. Drives you mad, at times. But it's the only way. A post out of line can spoil the whole fence.'

I nodded towards the set. 'Hope nothing's wrong there.'

He squinted. 'It's a shade on the big side. And the position of the window doesn't seem quite right in relation to the door. If you recall, the layout of the place has a bearing on the story. There doesn't – '

'I'll mention it right away.'

'No, no! You're not to think of it.'

'That's why you're here – to vet and advise.'

'But not to carp.'

'You simply must assert yourself, if it's necessary. We want to do Miriam justice.'

His glance showed amusement. 'I'm beginning to think you're more passionate about her than I am. Now, when are you coming to see us? Manage dinner tonight?'

'Won't your wife – '

'The food,' he added with innocent candour, 'comes straight out of the freezer. Don't let that bother you. Bring a friend and be along as early as you like. Seven-ish? I'll let you have our address . . .'

'Willow Cottage, Park End, Petersfield.'

Surprise crossed his face. 'You've done your homework.'

'Us theatrical folk,' I told him, guiding him back, 'rarely do anything else.'

After his briefing and pep-talk to the assembled crew, Roger Mayhew called Denny Baxter and me aside.

'A word about the script. I feel it's okay as it stands.'

One of Denny's eyebrows twitched in my direction.

'So do we. Very largely.'

'I think it's important,' Mayhew said smoothly, 'for each working part of a machine to perform its own job.'

'We have to say the lines.'

'Which the experts write. I'm not making an issue of it,' Mayhew said with breathtaking insincerity, 'but I feel there should be some mutual tolerance. As I see it, once you start allowing all and sundry to have a nibble at the tissue, you're on the way to ending up with a corpse.'

'We had in mind about a dozen trivial adjustments,' Denny said mildly.

Mayhew sniffed. 'So Graham follows up with another dozen. Then Myrtle has a go. After that, it's the turn of Charlie Penhurst to pronounce that none of you is photogenic and he wants a fresh cast. Pretty soon – '

'I think you're exaggerating rather.'

'I'm simply outlining the possible repercussions.'

'Herbie doesn't object to our suggestions,' said Denny, still mild.

'I'm objecting,' said Mayhew, still smooth.

I spoke up. 'Does that mean you want them all scrubbed?'

'It means I'd appreciate a certain amount of forbearance.'

'In that case,' I said, 'you won't want me to mention anything about the hideout set.'

Mayhew stiffened. 'What about it?'

'It's all up the creek.'

'Who says so?'

'The author of the book. But you won't want to know about that.' I turned to Denny. 'Coming to lunch? I'm starved.'

'Seems an appropriate moment,' he grinned.

Outside the building, a dark-haired woman was standing in meditative posture on the edge of the concreted approach, hands pocketed inside a belted leather jacket. With it she wore a pleated plaid skirt and knee-length buckled boots. Her gaze was fixed upwards as though she were assessing both the likelihood and the desirability of an appearance by King Kong over the nearest roof. I said, 'Hi, Dilys. Finally made it, then? Herbie was starting to champ.'

'I missed the train out of Waterloo.' Dilys Meridew had not reached the age of thirty without having acquired the knack of accepting such an occurrence as a matter of course. On set, she brought to her job of continuity the kind of minute attention to detail that had made her indispensable to Herbie for eight years; in the real world outside, it seemed, her guard dropped. She was always arriving late. When she did show up, it was not unlikely that she would be nursing a scorched finger from a cooker, or a wrenched knee from tripping on the stairs. Personal mishaps were a part of her culture. It made more engaging a personality which in any case was one of the gems of Joseph Films. To date, she had worked on all my pictures. Sometimes I wondered how it was that she had contrived to remain on the other side of the cameras: there was more rampant sexiness, I considered, in a single wide stare from her faintly dark-circled green eyes than in the entire range of artifices I had picked up or been taught. But she seemed to have no interest in self-projection. Her job suited her. She motored through life on a snorting mixture of cool efficiency and vague scattiness. She was Dilys. The mere sight of her hoisted my spirits. I introduced her to Denny, who eyed her with amiable interest.

'We were just heading out for lunch,' I told her. 'Join us?'

'Okay,' she said agreeably, turning with a squeak of boot-leather upon concrete. 'Where's Herbie?'

'Tied up with some admin. He told us to go on.'

'Suits me. I'm pretty famished after that rail excursion. The compartment was so *cold*, Anjie. I had to exercise to keep myself alive. And you know what I did? Banged my fist on the baggage rack – brought it right up.' Hauling off a glove, she displayed a faint discoloration of the back of a well-shaped hand. Denny gave it a solemn inspection.

'Shattered carpus, I'd say. No cocktail-shaking for the next three weeks.'

'If you heated your trains, I'd be right as rain.'

'Been to the hotel yet?' I asked her.

'No: took a cab straight here. It's waiting in the parking lot. Got all my stuff inside.'

'You did right,' remarked Denny. 'By comparison with The Beeches, this place corresponds to a solarium at midday in a hot July.'

'He's kidding?' Dilys said anxiously.

I shook my head. 'We're working on the manageress, but so far all she's done is to plant a one-bar electric fire at the head of the upstairs corridor so that we kick it as we go past. A candle or two would be more effective.'

Dilys digested this. 'Best thing I can do, after I've

checked in, is immerse myself in a hot tub. That gets me into a glow.'

'Great idea,' applauded Denny. 'Mrs Emmerson, for a small fee, brings up the first kettleful herself: after that you have to – '

'Shut up, Denny. You'll have Dilys taking the next train back. Let's find a real hotspot for lunch.'

'There's an inn in the village,' he told us, 'that does a three-course nosh for about ninepence, according to my information. Which stems, admittedly, from no more infallible a source than the elderly female cybernaut who clanked in with the early-morning tea six minutes before breakfast this morning, crushing my right shoe with her crankshaft en route. "Central 'eating an' all, they've got there," she throbbed, spitting aviation-fuel into my hair. To which I was about to retort, "Has it never occurred to your own switch-operator – ".'

'Let's go,' Dilys said decisively, leading the way to her taxi.

The main attraction of The Hunter's Arms proved to be a log fire of a magnitude and ferocity that reduced the three of us to a condition of near-insensibility over plates of roast turkey. We stayed two hours. At moments of consciousness, we discussed the script and the director and the probability or otherwise of a major clash somewhere along the line. Denny opined that it was no more than a little sabre-rattling on Mayhew's part. I predicted trouble. Dilys suggested that script-differences were as old as the cinema, and just about as unimportant. 'Get some words on to that soundtrack – any words. Long as they make some kind of sense.'

'But,' I argued, 'if the architect of the original is on hand to object . . .'

'Does he?'

'He might. Anyway he should. Incidentally, I'm having dinner with him tonight.'

'With Templar? No fooling?'

'He's dying for me to meet his wife.'

Dilys snorted. 'I should be so lucky. The men I've known, they were killing themselves to keep me clear of theirs.'

'Known the wrong men,' Denny said sleepily.

'The right men – in the wrong situations.'

I looked at her with affection. 'You've never had an illicit relationship, Dilly. You're not the type.'

'If I haven't, it's not for want of trying.'

'You can't expect us to believe that. Why not come along with me tonight? He said to bring someone.'

'Okay. Fine.'

'Think of us,' Denny said sourly, 'wrapped in eider-downs in the Great Hall of The Beeches, chipping the ice off the celery soup. I might get into another dust-up with Mayhew, if only to assist circulation.'

While I was changing shudderingly into a long dress, there was a knock upon my door. 'Spare us a second, honey?'

I struggled with the zip. It caught midway: leaving it, I unbolted the door. Instead of marching straight in, as normally he would have, Herbie remained in a stance of slight enquiry on the threshold, one hand against the frame. 'Pass on a message to Templar for me?'

'Of course I will. Come inside, Herbie.'

He stepped past me carefully, avoiding contact. Closing the door, I followed him to the centre of the room, where I turned my back on him.

'Just the man I wanted to see. Drag the zip past my fourth spinal disc, will you?'

He began simultaneously tugging and talking. 'Tell him, we'll be glad to see him any time he feels like drop-ping in. Also, next time he does, we'd appreciate if he'd take another look at the hideout set, let us know what's wrong. We're anxious to make any necessary changes. Do that?'

The zip ran up to my nape. Stepping away, I turned with a smile, pursuing the scene to its trite conclusion. 'If you want me to. He did say he wasn't – '

'If it's inaccurate, we have to put it right.'

'I'll tell him. Anything else?'

The phrases emerged more pertly than I had intended. I saw Herbie flinch.

'I guess not . . . You might mention that we'll be respecting his vision in every way possible. Kind of an added reassurance.'

'Including the script?' I enquired.

'Script included.'

'With adjustments?'

Herbie started patting at pockets as though in quest of something.

'You did agree the alterations,' I reminded him, 'with Denny and me.'

'Sure, Anjie, I know. That was before – '

'Before Roger Mayhew asserted himself?'

He concentrated on an inside pocket. 'He does occupy the director's chair.'

'You occupy the producer's.'

'Mayhew's a smart guy. I wouldn't want him – '

'Upset?'

'Hell, honey, what's the point? For the sake of a few minor . . .'

'Don't my views, and the leading man's, count for anything?'

I hadn't mapped out this line: it seemed to have drawn itself as we went along. I was putting Herbie needlessly on the spot, and I wondered why. But it was a little late for withdrawal. Already he was giving my query the earnest consideration that it didn't merit, doubling himself backwards to be fair to all parties.

'Naturally they do. They count for a lot. You're our Miriam and you're going to carry the picture and you've the right to a big say in the matter. On the other hand, there are certain things we have to safeguard. Fidelity to the storyline is one thing: practical dialogue's another. All I'm saying – '

'Herbie, the odd phrase-alteration here and there isn't going to bring Vic Roach across the Atlantic with a shotgun.'

Finding a cigar at last, he stood tapping it on the palm of a hand, frowning at it. 'You're talking as if you know better than Vic *or* Templar.'

'I wouldn't mind betting I know more about it than Roger Mayhew.'

Tap-tap-tap, went the cigar. Herbie was flummoxed. I could see lights pulsing, dials registering as he pondered his response. When eventually one emerged, it was accompanied by an odd politeness.

'In regard to that, you're entitled to your opinion. You've made a study of the book: I know that. You feel strongly for it. Shouldn't we pay Mayhew the compliment of supposing he's done similar? And that he sees the entire thing in cinematic terms, as a director should?' Herbie's giant, soothe-all grin arrived with difficulty, stayed under protest. 'In other words, honey, that he knows his job.'

'Meaning I don't.'

'Now did I say that? Did I imply it, even?'

'What you implied is that I'm to knuckle under everything Mayhew tells me. Is that what you want?'

'Within reason,' he said quietly.

'Who decides what's reasonable?'

'I do.'

'So you're ordering me to play it Mayhew's way . . . come what might?'

The cigar dropped to the floor. As Herbie stooped to retrieve, I glimpsed the bald patch on the crown of his head and felt a sudden guilt-ridden pang at my own recalcitrance; by now, however, I was into the rhythm of the quarrel, powerless to break step. In ten minutes' time I should regret the whole absurdity. The thing prodding me on was the conviction, built up over a period, that Jon Templar's *magnum opus* had somehow been dedicated to me and that I was now the guardian of its values. That morning I had met the author and we had hit it off.

In an hour's time I was dining with him. If clinching evidence of an affinity had been needed, this, in my present mood, would have sufficed.

Over and above this, there was irritation with Herbie. For his apparent truckling to Mayhew's autocracy; and for his clumsy unbalancing of our personal relationship. Why couldn't he have left well enough alone? A middle-aged, balding great-uncle, scrabbling in front of me for a dropped cigar . . . He should have known better. Conveniently, for the moment, I forgot that I had scuttled to his Mayfair retreat for comfort. I forgot many things.

Uncoiling himself, Herbie tucked the cigar back into the inside pocket, using the interval for thought, as a pipe-smoker will gain a respite by packing the bowl.

'I'm asking you, Anjie. Bearing in mind what you've picked up concerning the director/cast affiliation, I'm confident you'll give this part all you've got . . . under expert guidance. You'll be a great team. This I know. It has potential that's not worth ruining for the sake of some cockeyed disagreement over a side-issue.'

'To me, it's fundamental. I want you to put it to Jon Templar.'

'Nope.' He shook his head. 'I'm not asking him to . . . adjudicate on a matter between two of my principles.'

'We just leave him out of it, then? The creator of the entire thing. The one man who should be – '

'Will you pack it in?' he asked angrily. Jolted, I stopped. Shaking himself briefly, like a splashed dog, Herbie came closer to peer into my face. 'What's with you, honey? This isn't Anjie Browne. It's a different person. Something wrong?' His eyes narrowed. 'O'Malley? He's not been bothering you again?'

'What does Terry have to do with it?' I demanded. 'We're discussing scripts, I thought, not ex-husbands.'

The concern died from his eyes. Herbie had taken real offence. Backing a pace, he collided with the foot of the bed.

'My apologies,' he said stiffly, stepping out of its way.

'Guess I was labouring under the impression you'd things on your mind about him. Can't imagine what gave me the idea. Sorry, doll.' He paused at the door. 'I'll acquaint Mr Mayhew with your views. I'm certain he'll take them into account. Good night. Give my kind regards to the author.'

I stepped forward. 'Herbie . . .'

The door closed behind him.

CHAPTER X

DILYS NOTICED that something was wrong.

She said nothing until we were inside the taxi from the village, under sedate propulsion towards Petersfield by an elderly taciturn helmsman to whom screen goddesses, I suspected, were merely a tiresome addition to the day's overtime. After a mile or so, leaning back into her corner of the upholstery, she gave me a quizzical look.

'What is it, Anjie? Hypothermia?'

I smiled wanly. 'The spiritual sort.'

'Stemming from what?'

'I've just had the silliest dust-up with Herbie over nothing at all.'

Dilys was a good listener. She made no comment while I outlined the trouble; then she thought it over for a few moments before delivering a judgement.

'Herbie doesn't bear malice. Come morning, you'll say sorry, and he'll say what the heck, and the script will go back to what you want, and he'll have a quiet word with Roger M. telling him to cool it.'

'I wish it were that easy.'

'It is, honey, believe me. Unless there's something you've not told me.'

Her perceptiveness was alarming. For an instant, I teetered on the very brink of blurting out to her the full story and gaining the benefit of some sound and available feminine counsel. I held myself from toppling. A secret once divulged, no matter to whom, was a secret no longer. Already I had let slip to Herbie more than seemed prudent in retrospect. With an attempt at nonchalance I said, 'You're probably right. I'm a bit strung-up just now. Pre-shooting jitters. I'll grovel to Herbie tomorrow.'

'No need to grovel. You've a right to your point of view. A mild expression of penitence'll be enough, I'd say.' She relapsed into silence. Presently, with apparent inconsequence, she added, 'Your cabs are a deal warmer than your trains.'

'I think you were just unlucky this morning.'

'I sure hope so.' She flexed her bruised hand. 'Maybe a few more travellers would have helped. Sitting alone in those wide open spaces . . . oh my. I actually got to wishing somebody would enter the compartment and molest me, so I could have felt his hot breath.'

Despite my inner desolation I had to laugh. 'Wasn't there anyone?'

'Not inside a mile of where I was sitting. Like I had the plague or something. When we reached Winchester, though, a few other ice-chunks did detach themselves farther along the train. And you know the funniest thing?'

Her glance contained an element of speculation. Still superficially amused, I said, 'No, I don't. Tell me.'

'From the rear elevation, one of them looked kind of familiar to me. If I hadn't known better, I'd have said it was Terry. Your ex. But of course it couldn't possibly have been. He's way back in Santa Barbara, isn't he?'

'Far as I know,' I said. 'Must have been a local with a similar walk.'

In physique, contrary to my expectation, Celia Templar was even less solid than her husband; but behind the velvet I detected steel. After one sherry she delivered an opinion on me.

'I told Jon you'd be perfect for Miriam. And now that we've met, my dear, I haven't revised my view.'

I thanked her. From the drinks table, the author sent me a confidential smile. Within the setting of Willow Cottage, a raftered relic of the sixteenth century, he looked the literary lion that he now was. I liked them both. Briefly I had been engulfed by the atmosphere to the point of relaxation; but already the underlying chill was seeping back and there was nothing I could do to seal it out.

Terry was not giving up. This was now horribly certain. A person of acute observation such as Dilys could not have been mistaken: if she thought she had seen Terry, then he was in Hampshire. She knew him almost as well as I did; had worked on films with us both.

Why had he come? Not to take the country air, that was for sure. To watch the on-set shooting? That was a hoot. The only studio work in which Terry had ever taken the smallest interest was his own. And, as far as he was concerned, screen roles were a thing of the past.

With a single exception. At this moment, he had star billing in one particular charade. And if he was intent upon playing it to the limit, where did that leave me?

I became aware of three pairs of eyes fixed upon mine. I had been asked a question.

'Sorry. My mind drifted . . . Could you repeat that?'

Jon Templar chuckled. 'I think you've probably answered it. My wife was wondering whether you found your work demanding.' His sunken eyes twinkled. 'From the look on your face, I'd guess you were mugging up your lines at that very moment.'

'Your lines,' I corrected him. I hesitated. The chance seemed a good one, but before I could snatch it his wife interposed. Leaning across, she patted my wrist.

'We musn't keep at you about films and filming. You're here to relax. Sit back and enjoy your drink while I ask your friend Dilys about American politics. Do you follow them, my dear?'

Dilys smiled tolerantly into her glass. 'Follow them, sure. Understand them . . . maybe. Sometimes.'

'That's a consolation. We do try to keep abreast, but . . .' Celia Templar flipped a hand in well-bred despair. 'These Republican nominations, for instance. A short while ago it looked as if Senator Conway was the man. Now, it's all Governor Mason. And no one seems to know much about either of them. How are the electors to judge?'

'Same as the voters in your country, I guess. To an extent, you have to take politicians on trust, wherever you are.' Dilys paused. 'Maybe,' she added, 'I'm the wrong person to ask. I have to declare an interest.'

'Oh, really?'

'My father happens to be pretty active in the Washington ambit. And like a dutiful daughter, only it's my independent viewpoint also, I go along with his line of thinking . . . that we need someone fairly tough, un-compromising, up there in the White House right now.'

Our hostess gave this some consideration.

'It's a tough world,' she allowed. 'And of the two we've mentioned, which do you think – '

'Mason's our man,' Dilys said promptly. 'No question.'

'Is he what they call a hawk?'

Dilys laughed. 'To his political opponents, he comes more in the shape of a vulture. Which needn't be such a tragic thing for the West, in the current situation.'

Celia Templar regarded her with apparent amusement. 'You feel fervently about it.'

'Sure. It's our survival at stake.'

Our hostess turned to me. 'What about you, Anjelica? Do you find yourself more involved with United States affairs these days – or does Britain stay at number one?'

I said, 'We're all in it together now, aren't we? No country can go ahead in isolation any more.'

'Right,' said Dilys.

Celia Templar's head went to one side, whether in assent, denial, or contemplation, it was hard to judge.

Presently she began: 'But what I don't grasp . . .'

She rose suddenly. 'I must go and see what Barbara's

up to with the vegetables. Dilys, my dear, if you'd like to follow me out to the kitchen, perhaps you can put me right on one other thing. Bring your drink. Now what I want to know . . .'

Her voice receded as Dilys, with a comical look at us, pursued her from the room. Templar, who had been listening to us with his own brand of attentive abstraction, remarked to me, 'Barbara comes in from the farm along the lane. Just now and then, to help out. Gives Celia a break. It's one of the many things I'm pleased to be able to afford now.'

For the first time in minutes, I relaxed in my chair. My nerves had been tightening to snapping-point: the departure of the others had occurred not an instant too soon. Fearful that Templar might revert to the topic of their debate, I threw in a diversion.

'A place like this, though, must be almost a pleasure to keep smart. Marvellous to work in.'

'Ye-es. Though it can become a prison, of course. Which is why I rather welcome the descent of you and your gang, if you'll forgive the expression. Gives me a prime excuse for a drive out to the studios twice a week.' His face brightened. 'I daresay the petrol's tax-deductible.'

'You'll be showing up regularly, then?'

'I don't say that.' He answered hurriedly, as though under the impression that I had been charged with the task of vetting him on the point. 'I shan't poke my nose in, unless – '

'But you must,' I told him. 'Any time. We mean that.'

He studied me thoughtfully. Before momentum was lost, I added, 'There are things you should be in on. The script, for one. Are you happy with it?'

Slightly flapping an arm, he said nothing.

'You know that one of Herbie's screen-writers did a spot of . . . adapting?'

He nodded. 'Mm.'

'In fact, a great deal. Dialogue, especially.' I stared at

him hopefully. 'I don't know how you feel about it . . .'

Templar took a peck at his gin-and-tonic.

'The view I take is that the movie-makers know their trade. I'm the novice, remember.'

'But you provided the raw material. Also a script of your own. What's the point, if someone else – '

'I was very tactfully asked,' he said gently, 'to suggest a treatment and have a bash at cobbling together some sort of apology for a screenplay. Handsomely paid too, I might add. But really, it's not my forte. Your professional chap – Roach? – did a superb renovation job on my bit of wreckage: I'd be a fool not to recognize the fact. What right have I got now to demand this and that?'

'The right of the author . . .' I began feebly.

'The author's had his hour. Now it's up to you lot. Different field entirely, and you're the experts. I'm nobody. Whatever methods you adopt, I'm sure the end product is going to be a winner.'

I was silent.

The ground had been dug from beneath my feet. With a rebellious Templar at my elbow, I could have confronted Roger Mayhew, taken pleasure in cutting him down to size. Instead, my impotence was complete. Because of a silly miscalculation, I had placed myself in bad odour with both Mayhew and Herbie, and in present circumstances it was not the wisest thing to have done. Tomorrow, somehow, I should have to make it up with Herbie: the earlier, the better. If we were back in time, I could do it tonight.

Plans for a conciliatory approach started buzzing through my head, deafening me again to Templar's remarks. It took the return of his wife and Dilys, carrying a vegetable dish and looking as though she was enjoying this burst of domesticity coupled with the chance to talk politics, to haul me back from the immediate future. I was glad that I had asked Dilys along. To a considerable extent, she would have to carry me for the rest of the evening.

'Well, now,' said Celia Templar, beaming, 'I've had it all explained to me about the Presidential nominations, and I'm none the wiser. Shall we all sit at the table, and in return I'll tell Dilys everything I know about cricket.'

'Boy,' said Dilys sleepily. 'Good thing tomorrow's Sunday. If we were due on set at nine, I'd be done for.'

'What time is it now?'

'Turned eleven-thirty.'

Too late, probably, to nail Herbie before he retired for the night. My heart sank. Half an inch lower, I thought wretchedly, and it would be alongside the lump already immutably installed in my abdomen. The thick, short neck of the driver was an outline in the gloom. Disliking the silence, I said, 'They made us welcome.'

'It was a nice evening.'

For the past three miles, I had been awaiting Dilys's query. 'What got into you, honey? Not that I mind hogging the conversation, but . . .' By nature she was direct: the fact that no such question had emerged was a tribute, I hoped, to the performance I had contrived. Although she seemed disinclined to talk, a reluctance to face my own thoughts kept me trying. Perversely, like a youngster picking at a scab, I said, 'You certainly made a hit with his wife – clueing her up like that. Never knew you took such an interest in politics.'

'I told you, my old man's part of the circus.' She gave vent to an immense and prolonged yawn, showed symptoms of settling limply into her corner.

'Does he know Governor Mason?'

'Personally, you mean? Oh sure.'

'You?'

'I've met him.' After a space she added on a livelier note, 'He's a great guy. Type we need at the wheel.'

'What sort of reputation does he have?'

'Rock-solid,' Dilys said on the edge of another yawn, 'in every way.'

She was close to sleep. For something to do, I fumbled

in my bag for the door-key allocated to us by Mrs Emmerson upon learning that our return might exceed the hour of 10 p.m., beyond which, she had given us to understand, the lubricated mechanism that maintained The Beeches at top revs was customarily silenced for the night. By the time I had found it, the car was hopping from one rut to the next on the approach to the hotel, which appeared to be in darkness from ground-level to roof. Dilys stirred.

'Guess we missed out on the cabaret.'

'There's always midnight Mass.' I paid off the driver, who uttered his fifth word of the evening before taking his bucking vehicle back between the rhododendrons to vanish from sight and earshot, leaving us in a black still-ness which the brooding hulk of the Emmerson establish-ment did nothing to alleviate. 'Before I crawl into that bed,' I remarked as we scrunched across the gravel, 'I'm dosing up with a swig of the Templars' brandy.'

'Great idea. And use the empty bottle to slug the icicles off the sheets.'

Surprisingly, the key worked. Pink light, from a bulb of minimum wattage positioned on the opposite wall, rescued the entrance hall from total blackness; but it was a near thing. While I refastened the door, Dilys groped ahead.

'Watch out for the furniture, Anjie. There's a chair sticking out to your left, and I've just stubbed my – '

The sentence ended in a gasp. Thinking she had done it again, I moved forward with caution: then realized that I was seeing things more distinctly. Among the things I was seeing was a figure at a doorway, backed by the stronger radiance which abruptly had improved visibility in the entrance hall. For a fanciful moment I took it for that of Mrs Emmerson in trousers, waiting up for us in a condition of concentrated fury. The voice, however, was easy, masculine, and unmistakable.

'Need some illumination, girls? No charge for the additional service.'

'My,' said Dilys severely. 'You gave us a turn.' She came

back to join me, standing comfortingly close. 'It *was* you I saw, then? At the station this morning?'

'It's possible.' Terry left the doorway, allowing more light to spill through. 'Hi there again, Anjie. Settling in nicely, I hope.'

'I was.'

'Want me to stick around, honey?' Dilys's glance was searching. I shook my head.

'It's all right, thanks. You get off to bed. Terry and I are due for a little talk.'

'I don't mind staying.'

'I know. But I'll be fine.'

With a shrug, she headed for the stairs. Terry said, ' 'Night, Dilys.' She ignored him. When she was out of view, I gestured towards the room he had left.

'In there?'

'Why not?' he said amiably. 'It's well above freezing point. I think.'

A sniff as I passed him told me that he hadn't been at the bottle. A good sign – or an ominous one? Making for the most upright chair I could see, I arranged myself upon it and waited while he secured the door and sauntered back to the dent which he or somebody had made in the cushions of an ancient divan. Filled ashtrays and a used glass here and there suggested that Herbie and the others had been in occupation earlier: this room was, Mrs Emmerson had announced, the Residents' Lounge, and at a distant end there stood a two-bar electric fire to prove it. One of the bars functioned. I could have moved closer, but all the seats encircling the miserable glow were practically on a level with the floor. I stayed where I was, opposite an auxiliary door to the entrance hall that was kept locked. With a shiver, I pulled my coat about me.

'When did you get here?'

He consulted his wrist. 'Around nine. The others had just finished dinner.'

'I trust they were pleased to see you.'

'We chatted. Mayhew impressed me. Sound views on the

cinema. He was telling me – '

'Your opinion of Roger Mayhew doesn't fascinate me. What are you after, Terry?'

He began to whistle softly. Wanting to scream, I kept my voice even. 'Does Mrs Emmerson know you've stayed on?'

'Mrs Emmerson entirely understood that a husband and wife would want a chance to talk. After being . . . separated.'

'You're talking drivel, as usual. What did Herbie have to say?'

'Not a lot.'

Less than he would have had, perhaps, if events earlier had been different. Consciousness of my utter stupidity gnawed at me like some tiny, vicious beast. As steadily as I could, I went on: 'What did you mean by calling on my family like that?'

'Like what?'

'You knew it would embarrass me. What are you trying to prove? That you can still do as you like, even though I've scrubbed my hands of you? You wouldn't be trying to ingratiate yourself with them, by any chance?'

'They're nice folk,' he said reflectively. 'Decent people.'

'You didn't wait here till nearly midnight to tell me that.'

'I didn't? Then it must be something else.' He frowned at the floor.

My shivering now was due only partially to the room temperature. I waited until I could be reasonably certain that my voice would emerge without a wobble.

'This farce isn't funny any more. If you don't stop pestering, I'll have no hesitation in calling the police.'

Surprise crossed his face. Sitting back, he spread both arms along the cushion-tops.

'You're not obliged to speak to me. Want to get to bed? Away you go.'

When I made no movement, he flipped a hand. 'Seems you prefer to stick around. Who's pestering who?'

'My reason for waiting,' I said tightly, 'is to see you gone from the premises, with an assurance that you'll be flying back to the States tomorrow. I just want to know you've *left*.'

'But I'm here on vacation. Why would I hurry home? There's lots I aim to see.'

I stood. 'Where are you staying?'

'Here.'

'You can't!'

'Your Mrs Emmerson seems to think otherwise. To the extent that she's already allotted me a room.' Extracting a key from a pocket, he held it up. 'Seventeen. My lucky digits.'

'She told us she was full.'

He smiled. 'Very susceptible lady, Mrs Emmerson. Sensitive to the crackle of banknotes . . . brings her out in a rash of improvisation. It may not be five-star – '

'All right.' I sat again. 'You've wormed your way in; you're here. Now what?'

'Now you start taking a leaf out of her book. Come up with a little . . . accommodation.'

A clamp tightened itself about my chest and throat.

'Is that a threat?'

'It's a request.'

'Terry, you know the position.'

'No. Tell me.'

'I don't want you around.'

'That's not the full position, as I see it.'

'I think you're seeing it wrong.'

He examined his fingernails. 'What is it you've doubts about?'

'Your ability to put into effect . . . what you're hinting at.'

He put on a puzzled air. 'Not sure that I . . . Oh, by the way, honey. Something I meant to show you.'

His right hand moved to an inside pocket of his snappily-tailored jacket. 'Home movies bore you, I know,' he apologized. 'Here's a little something, though, that you might find more than usually absorbing.'

Barely a glance was needed. The blown-up version displayed to me by Chief Jansen in his office had been four times as large; but the detail in Terry's offering was sharper. The colour was as vivid as I remembered it. Unkind as it was to the blotches upon Governor Mason's middle-aged skin tissue, it did full justice to the contrasting bloom of my own. Tearing the print into six pieces, I carried them to the electric fire. Holding each fragment in turn against the solitary live element, I dusted away the result, trod the flakes into the threadbare carpet. When all traces had been obliterated, I switched off the fire and returned to my chair. I remained standing beside it.

Terry had been watching with interest. He met my gaze serenely.

'Understandable reaction. The one I anticipated, in fact: which is the reason I brought an expendable specimen. The others are real eye-openers.' He allowed an intermission. 'Had any second thoughts,' he ventured presently, 'on that accommodation I was speaking about a few moments ago?'

'It won't wash, Terry.' I was short-winded but resolute. 'You can't mend a non-existent relationship. Certainly not that way. It's ludicrous.'

'I can have you back.'

'The shell of me.'

'At least it's a start.'

'You're just deluding yourself. I was no good to you before, any more than you were to me. You're in love with two things, Terry: yourself and the bottle. There's no room for anyone else.'

'For you,' he said huskily, 'there's always room.'

'Stop dramatizing.'

'You're coming back to me, Anjie.'

Something in his tone of voice made me sit again, abruptly. I said nothing.

'Take me seriously, honey. It'll pay you to. Those

prints are available: I've proved that. If necessary, I'll use them. I hope I shan't have to. I'm giving you one week. By the end of that time, if you're sensible, we'll be back together and the newspapers will have carried the story. Also, you'll have worked a part for your reconciled husband in this prestige production you're obsessed with. You can fix it. I'm only asking,' he added reasonably, 'for what's my due. We belong side by side. If you'd not walked out on me, I wouldn't be back on the bottle and I'd still be getting the parts.'

Ignoring the outrageous distortion of the facts, I said steadily: 'And if I'm not sensible?'

'Then next Saturday, as a regrettable preliminary, your influential pal Herbie will be shown a bunch of photos and told a story. One that wasn't scripted by one of his hacks. One he won't like.'

A cranial roar drowned his next words, addressed to me from the door. One of his hands was raised, and he was smiling. I was on my feet, jelly-legged but under propulsion, pursuing him into the entrance hall. He was starting to mount the stairs. To disperse the roar, I shook my head with violence.

'You wouldn't dare!'

In leisurely fashion he turned. 'I wouldn't dare?' he asked, stressing the personal pronoun.

'If you imagine Herbie would take the least bit of notice, you're insane.'

He shrugged. 'In which case, you've nothing to worry about.'

'Come back here!'

He resumed the ascent. Catching up, I grabbed him by the waist, tried to drag him down while he held the banister rail. Frustrated, I beat at him with my fists. 'You can't do this. I'll kill you first . . .'

The face of Dilys came between us. She was hauling me off. For a second or two I resented it enough to try to thrust her aside, get at him again; but she was physically strong, and suddenly I was the victim of a debilitating feebleness. I let her hold me away. With fussy movements Terry adjusted the hang of his jacket, patted his immaculate curls, handed Dilys the corrugated grin that in his palmier days had seen him through many a fraught scene on celluloid. He spoke coolly.

'Anjie's a little overwrought. Needs to rest, I guess. See she gets to bed, will you?'

Climbing the remainder of the staircase, he bade a casual 'Good night, fellah' to Denny, whose startled face had appeared above the landing balustrade, before vanishing into the corridor that gave access to the bedrooms. A clang resounded from Mrs Emmerson's portable electric fire as he kicked it in passing.

Leaning against the staircase wall, I gave Dilys, who was only partly undressed, the tautest of smiles conveying the very antithesis of mirth.

'He gets me that way,' I informed her, and broke into ungovernable sobs.

I was distantly aware of a pat on the shoulder and a word or two from Denny, who then faded out. Dilys took me into her bedroom where, with on-set efficiency, she whipped eau-de-cologne from her washbasin shelf, seated me on the bed and dabbed at me with paper tissues. Chokingly I tried to launch some kind of explanation which she halted at the head of the slipway. 'Later, honey. If you still want to. Maybe you should sleep here with me tonight? No? Okay, but take one of my pills with you: they're dynamite. Have a long, long kip. We'll see you at breakfast, gorgeous as ever. Don't think about him. He's just a guy, and they're all kids.'

'You see, all I want is to be shot of him, and all he wants – '

'It'll work out. For tonight, forget it. It's Sunday already, for Pete's sake. Sleep tight, sugar.'

I did exactly that. After undressing in my own room, I uncapped the miniature bottle of cognac pressed upon me by the Templars as we were leaving, and swallowed the lot. Recklessly with the final gulp I sent down Dilys's sugared depth-charge, wondering, without really caring, whether the combination would prove lethal. There was no time to dwell upon the matter.

CHAPTER XI

'NOT LIKE THAT.'

Roger Mayhew spoke with a kind of peremptory patience, his own odd brand of mingled ferocity and forbearance. He prowled forward from his chair. 'We don't want you draped across the cooker, looking like a commercial for Oven-Pads. You're a proud woman. Semi-crushed, but you haven't slung in the towel. Your shoulders stay back: it's the voice that betrays the tension. Understand what I'm getting at?'

I said, 'Wouldn't my hands be revealing something, too? Missing the saucepan-handle the first time – that sort of thing?'

'Let *us* worry about the saucepans, Miss Browne.' His punctilious usage of salutation and surname gave me an inner buckling sensation. 'Concentrate on voice, posture. The power, ripe for unleashing. The stifled volcano. All this has to be suggested, not semaphored. Miriam in the early stages is an enigma, not just to her husband and the others around her but to herself, so that when eventually . . .'

Withdrawing quietly to the perimeter of the set, Graham Forde groped in a pocket. I saw him convey to his mouth yet another square from the chocolate bar with which he had been sustaining himself since the lunch-break. Tall, lean and young, he had an obviously good opinion of his own abilities and a poor one, unsuccessfully disguised, of mine. After a morning's toil, a twenty-second scene was in the can, and the morsel of dialogue that it included was exclusively his. He had got it right; it was on film and soundtrack; now he was waiting, all of them were waiting, for a comparable effort from the leading lady.

'Try it again, Miss Browne. We're not shooting. Just run through the words.'

I rearranged myself at the cooker, drew breath. 'I've no objection, if that's what you want. How could I have? The choice has always been yours.'

Mayhew sat silent in his chair. Most of the film crew were watching him; the rest were ostentatiously busy upon technical adjustments. There was a hunched look about his shoulders that I was fast coming to dislike.

'Again, please. Lots of inner torment.'

'I've no objection, if that's what you want. How – '

'*Torment*, Miss Browne. You're not discussing the state of the Common Market.'

A mutter of amusement travelled the studio. I looked for a friendly face. Dilys was in low-voiced conversation with a wardrobe assistant; Denny, who made no appearance in the opening scenes, was nowhere in sight. Herbie was there, and Herbie was watching. Ordinarily I could have appealed to him; but the circumstances were not ordinary. The previous day, I had patched things up with him, and on the surface we were back somewhere near our old footing. Beneath it, we were feeling around.

'I've no objection, if that's what you want . . .'

Concerning the midnight rumpus on the stairs, nothing had been said. Herbie's silence on the matter, and on the presence of Terry among us, had not been hard to interpret. Wounded, he had opted out. For the time being, at least, he was giving Roger Mayhew his head, showing me who was boss. This, plus the after-effects of a night's stupor induced by drink and drugs, had undermined my confidence. The instability showed in my voice.

'How could I have? The choice . . . Should the emphasis be on "always", Mr Mayhew, or on "yours"? It's not clear from the next line.'

'The tonal shading, I'd have thought, is largely up to you. What I'm listening for are the undercurrents.'

'I'm putting as much feeling into it as I can.'

'I trust you're wrong.'

Twisting in the seat, he had a whispered consultation with his assistant, Adrian Allister, a quiet, intense-looking younger man by whom at this moment I should much have preferred to be directed. He looked considerate. For a few moments they murmured together while Graham Forde disposed of the last of his chocolate, flicked the compressed wrapping across a shoulder and transmitted what might have been intended as a rallying grin but reached me as a reproof.

I tried some long, slow breathing. Like any miserable amateur, I had been rushing to get the phrases out, robbed of vocal stamina by mental unrest and Mayhew's strictures and the unblinking survey of Terry from the back of the studio. He had arrived mid-morning, disappeared during lunch, re-materialized afterwards to resume his vigil. At present he was not in sight, but his absence came as no relief. It was not, I guessed, of a permanent nature.

Mayhew turned back. 'We'll make this one a take, Miss Browne. See if the whirr of the cameras has a galvanizing effect.'

The fractional broadening of his lips was, I assumed, his contribution towards lightening the atmosphere. Appreciating the intention if not its utter failure, I braced myself at the cooker. Returning to the set, Graham Forde took up station alongside the open toolbox on the kitchen table, resting his right hand upon the electric drill in readiness for squinting into its interior as I spoke. For this scene, the main camera was located behind the cooker and focused upon Graham beyond me, so that my profile was in close-up but blurred.

'Everybody ready?'

The usual hush clasped the studio.

'Scene Four, Take One . . .'

Absolute stillness. A swift glance showed me a vista of

observant faces in the penumbra behind the lights. Among them, over to the right and some way back, that of Terry was discernible. His jaw looked slack. The way it had looked on occasions during our marriage, at times when the bottle had been handiest.

'*Action.*'

I began instantly. The lines came without difficulty. They seemed to be out and gone in a flash: I found myself wishing there had been more. Instead of calling for the cut, Mayhew allowed the action to fizzle out. Charlie Penhurst, an old hand, shut down of his own accord, and turned his attention to unwrapping a pellet of chewing-gum. The studio's outer lights went up.

Graham, who had been looking at me, removed his gaze and let it roam. Nobody spoke.

Uneasily, I walked a few paces nearer to where Mayhew sat. He was scanning the script in his lap. Allister gave me a quick smile.

I said, 'Shall we try it again?'

Without lifting his gaze from the sheets, Mayhew said, 'Tomorrow. Adrian, what d'you think about this?'

He indicated something in the script. Allister leaned across and they went into a huddle. The studio relaxed. On set, Graham replaced the drill with a clank. Herbie approached, gave me a neutral lift of the eyebrows, joined the discussion. It was being conducted in undertones.

I stood a little apart, feeling more of a novice than I had when making my first picture. Presently I walked across to the refreshment trolley. The urn-lady addressed me with brisk kindness.

'Nice and creamy, Miss Browne?'

The smile I gave her was my best and biggest. 'Black. Lots of sugar. I seem to need a kick.'

'Not many of us as don't,' she said comfortably, 'from time to time.'

She devoted attention to the pouring. I wondered whether she felt she had left anything unsaid. Her name

was Miss Chappell: she went, it seemed, with the studios.
She gave an impression of having seen it all. And cared
about remarkably little. Accepting the plastic carton she
passed over, I sampled its tongue-singeing contents while
staring deliberately around, ready to meet people's eyes
but colliding with none. Nobody seemed inclined for a
chat. Dilys had been summoned to the conference at the
director's chair. One other person was available. By
means of a circuitous route, I kept clear of his orbit in
the course of my return to the group, the constituents of
which remained in close communion, their murmurings
unintelligible to me. Suddenly irritated, I elbowed in.

'Why not try the scene again? There's an hour to go.'

Herbie was among those who glanced round. With an
attempt at his old manner he said: 'We're wrapping it up,
honey, for the moment. Get to it fresh in the morning.'

'I'll be starting from cold. Can't we knock it into shape
while I'm coasting?'

Dilys looked embarrassed. Herbie said diplomatically,
'We figured you were looking a mite sleepy. A night's
rest – '

'Herbie, for God's sake. Don't treat me like a child.
What's tiredness got to do with it? No one's let it bother
them before.'

He scratched his neck. 'Matter of adjustment. For a
relaxed attitude . . .'

'How can I relax? With him staring from the sidelines?'

That grabbed their attention. My voice had carried.
Heads turned. Noting the direction of my stabbing finger,
they turned again, settling their owners' scrutinies upon
the lolling figure of Terry, who met them with an air of
fuddled serenity before hoisting himself to a posture
approximately upright and giving a general wave. He
took a lurch towards some sound equipment. Its cus-
todian raised alert arms to fend him off. Coming to rest,
Terry bowed from the waist, first to the left, then to the
right, finally to the centre.

Mayhew muttered something. With an appearance of

restraint, Herbie said, 'He's doing no harm.'

'I want him out of here.'

Coffee from the carton had spattered my dress. Mechanically I brushed at the stain, the colour of which closely matched the material's. I no longer cared who heard what I said. 'While he's standing there, I can't act. You should know that.'

'We can't be expected to know things,' Mayhew said tiredly, 'unless we're told.'

'I'm telling. Until he's out of it, I'm not going to carry on making an idiot of myself on set. Is that clear?'

'Honey, no one said – '

'They didn't have to say.'

I glared from face to face. Adrian Allister's was the one that looked most acutely uncomfortable. Mayhew made a dismissive gesture. Dilys placed a hand on my arm; in my wrath I shook her off.

After some hesitation Herbie said, 'Why don't we all come back here tomorrow and start over. Most of us, that is,' he added meaningfully.

Dilys nodded. Mayhew shrugged. In the background, Terry drew himself erect and sent us a military salute. Somebody sniggered.

I was wondering how to terminate the farce when a member of the studios' permanent staff entered from an outside door. 'Telephone call,' he announced, 'for Miss Browne.'

The voice on the line was male and silken. 'Apologies, Miss Browne, for disturbing the schedule. Leonard Bagnall, *The Clarion*.'

'Oh yes,' I said brightly. 'I see your column. It's very good.'

'How kind of you. Miss Browne, we hear on the grapevine that there's now a strong possibility of a reconciliation between yourself and your former husband, Terry O'Malley. Would you care to comment?'

'No,' I said after an interval. 'I wouldn't.'

'You're neither confirming nor denying it?'

'I'm making absolutely no statement. Where did you pick up the rumour?'

'Um, a spokesman for Mr O'Malley has been in touch with us.'

'I wasn't aware he had one. Do you mean Terry himself?'

Disregarding the question, he said, 'So I can say you're not contemplating remarriage at the present time?'

'You can say . . .'

I pulled myself up. My brain was racing on. 'I'm afraid it has to be no comment. I'm fully occupied, as you know, making this picture at BUC Studios. It's taking up all my time at the moment. *Furnace of the Mind*,' I added helpfully.

'Perhaps you can tell me: are you seeing Mr O'Malley?'

'Our paths cross from time to time. I see a good many people from the film world.'

'Anyone in particular? Might there possibly be a new Mr Anjelica Browne – if I can put it that way – in the offing?'

I said sweetly, 'I'm not peering too hard into the future just now.'

A sigh reached me.

'How goes the filming?' He sounded less than frantic to know. 'You're starring opposite Denholm Baxter, of course.' Animation renewed itself. 'May I ask how you're finding the experience?'

The unspoken questions jutted through the creases in his voice. An admonition of Wally Parsons nudged my mind. 'Always keep the Press on your side, Anjelica. Don't antagonize them. They hold most of the aces.' I gave my answering intonation a fluting quality.

'We've not done a scene together yet. But I find Mr Baxter a charming colleague to work with, and I'm really hoping our screen partnership will please everybody.' I was not displeased with this sentence. Before its effect could be dissipated, I added, 'Thank you so much, Mr Bagnall, for calling. Lovely to talk to you. If you'll excuse me, I'm being called back on set. Never a dull moment. Thanks again. Bye.' Inserting considerable mateyness into the final syllable, I hung up.

Ducking out from beneath the telephone's bubble hood, I stood irresolute for a while.

Fear, anger, indecision . . . I was experiencing them all. Miriam would have sympathized. Presently, instead of returning to the studio I walked across to the vestibule entrance, manned by a pensioner in a peaked cap whose stertorous breathing over Teach Yourself handbooks seemed to betoken a desire for self-improvement that was laudable if belated. 'Brian,' I said, thinking once again how absurdly the name sat upon his gnarled personality, 'do you think you could whistle up some transport for me, quickly?'

CHAPTER XII

REMOVING MY ROOM-KEY from the pegboard, I hesitated briefly.

The Beeches reclined in late-afternoon torpor. Of the Emmersons or any member of their shuffling retinue, there was no sign. My hand went to the pegboard. In a casual movement I detached the key to room 17.

The hotel remained still and silent. Slipping the second key into my bag, I made for the stairs.

Terry's room lay at the far end of the first-floor corridor, beyond a linen-closet. To judge from appearances, it had been pressed hastily into use: if haste was not too extravagant a term to employ in relation to any particle of the establishment's body-domestic. In one corner were stacked a number of rolled rugs and carpet off-cuts, indicating the room's normal function. What degree of munificence, I wondered, had been required of Terry to persuade Mrs Emmerson that his addition to the guest-list was worthwhile? It seemed likely that whatever she asked he had been prepared to pay. Just as he had not cavilled at hiring a self-drive car in Winchester for his personal use; nor at putting in costly telephone calls to London newspapers. If the dregs of his cash resources were dissolving in this crusade, what of it? He was counting upon a high-yield return.

Carefully reclosing the door, I considered locking it from the inside. This, however, seemed imprudent. If interrupted, I could say I had returned to collect something for Mr O'Malley. The statement would not have been wildly untrue.

I began with his suitcase. Fastened but not locked, it contained a change of underwear, socks, a roll-necked sweater in a shade of green, and a bound copy of the screenplay of my first film that I remembered giving him. Momentarily this threw me off balance. The discovery that he had kept it, carried it about with him, was one that I should have preferred not to make. I turned my attention to the chest of drawers, each of which was lined with grubby tissue, but otherwise void. The wardrobe door grated like the long-abandoned entrance to a mine-shaft. Inside were a pair of shoes and a jacket on a hook, three buckled wire hangers, and a sheet of yellow newsprint dated 6th March 1968, detailing some activities of the Greater Barndean branch of the Rotary Club of Great Britain.

The mattress was a sprung one, and heavy. I managed to raise it on both sides. Underneath was a flattened copy of an ancient *Titbits*, open at the cartoon page.

Smoothing the bedclothes back into shape, I stood contemplating the stacked rugs.

Terry could scarcely have foreseen his occupancy of a room containing such extras. Listlessly I went across, tugged out the one nearest to me. Heavily foam-backed, it had fused damply into a mass and could not be unravelled without tearing. Heaving it aside, I tried the next. This was corded, and unrolled readily in billows of dust which set me coughing. From its recesses emerged a gigantic spider. My involuntary faint shriek accompanied the release of the rug to the floor, where it stretched itself in a series of writhing movements while I leapt backwards on to the bed, which skidded beneath me and struck a chair.

The silence that ensued was disturbed by a creaking floorboard.

Scrambling off the bed, I thrust it back into line. The chair, which had been tilted by the headboard, lost its support and fell against the wall. Simultaneously, the foam-backed rug that I had first disturbed toppled forward to land with a slap across the blue-tiled fireplace that was a fixture of each of the bedrooms at The Beeches, although the grate recess in every case had been meticulously boarded up. In its descent, the tip of the rug caught squarely on its black head a vast china cat squatting on the tiled area, causing it to roll noisily in a far from feline way until it collided with a gas-tap on the opposite side. I was back on the bed, covering my ears, when the door opened.

'Somehow figured you might be here, honey.'

Herbie spoke softly, having first scrupulously refastened the door and then listened with an ear to the woodwork. Trying hard to come back with a smart retort, I found myself instead, for the third time in a few days and the fourth in six years, indulging myself in what Dilys was wont to describe as 'a damn good bawl'. They were tears largely of pure frustration. I felt like a small girl, caught out in her tenth transgression of the week and wondering how she had lost her touch. Herbie, as ever, was understanding. Standing with pocketed hands before the disordered rugs, he gazed down at them with an assumption of the keenest interest, as though they were all he had come to see. I spoke chokingly to his back.

'They're not there.'

He peered round. One eyebrow was comically higher

than its twin. 'What aren't?'

I dabbed at my eye-corners. 'The things I was looking for.' After a pause I added, 'How did you – '

His right hand went up. 'It's a nice night for a drive, Anjie. Let's get the hell out of here.'

After a twisted mile or two between grassed banks and naked oaks, the lane expired in a compacted expanse facing a field. Inside the field, white-painted horse-jumps were laid out upon a circuit. Beyond a clump of birches on the farther side could be discerned the roof and upper windows of a large house. Nothing else, human or animal, was in sight. Parking with the car's windscreen facing the circuit, Herbie switched off. For a few minutes we sat in silence, watching the pale sunlight fighting the onset of dusk. 'I'd guessed,' he said eventually, 'it had to be bad.'

'I did warn you.'

'Thanks for telling me.'

'You're welcome.'

Numbly, I was surveying the ruination of my career. Now that it had happened, did it matter so much? I couldn't decide. Miriam Hargill seemed a shadowy figure of small account, barely meriting the nervous energy I had expended upon her. In a way, it would be a relief to be free of her gaunt, looming influence, shot of the need to be credible and articulate to sceptical journalists.

I said dreamily, 'That phone call. The one from *The Clarion*. It was the final straw. Terry must have rung them while I was on set. Told them we were getting back together, then given them the studio's number so they could check with me.'

'Sounds feasible,' Herbie mumbled.

'I didn't know how to reply. What could I say?'

'Real problem.'

After a second or two I turned to face him. 'It's not, though. Is it? The answer's obvious.'

His head jerked as his attention came back. 'Huh?'

'We both know what it is. I wish you'd say it, Herbie. Get it over.'

'Give us a minute, honey. I'm thinking.'

Manifestly he was still adjusting. I let my eyes rove across the horse-jumps, imagining the weekend scene as the riders of the neighbourhood met to test their mounts. With Terry I had ridden a little in the States, and without him I should have enjoyed it. We had taken it up in a futile bid to wean him from the bottle. His first fall had confined him to bed for a fortnight, at the conclusion of which he was drinking harder than before.

'Whatever happens,' I ventured at last, 'I'm not going back to him.'

'The hell you are.'

'So long as I'm Miriam, he can louse things up. For all of us. So . . .' Lifting both arms, I slumped against the car door.

'If this thing blew,' Herbie said meditatively, 'we'd have to recast for *Furnace*. No question of that.'

'Unless I go back to him, it's going to blow. He'll see to that. And anything to do with that blackmail scandal in the States . . . As a serious actress, I'd be finished.'

'Damn right.'

'Well, let's not waste time. The longer it's indefinite, the bigger the upheaval when you eventually have to find a new Miriam.'

'Hell, Anjie. I don't want a new Miriam. I want you.'

'After today's performance?'

'That wasn't Anjelica Browne there in front of the cameras. That was some scared young woman trying to say her lines with her blackmailer looking on with a fat grin spread across his face. If I'd had any idea – '

'Not your fault, Herbie. Mine, for being so touchy.'

'Touchy? In your position . . . Listen, don't take it to heart, whatever Mayhew said or hinted. You can show the guy. All of us. It's in you, Anjie, just waiting to come out. But it won't. Not with that incubus flapping around your head.'

His precise summary of the dilemma flooded me with an affectionate gratitude. Impulsively I threw myself forward, arms about his solid neck. He remained motionless. A not unpleasing aroma of cigar-leaf clung to him, reminding me nostalgically of smoky festive Christmases at home in Eastern Gardens, with a new, shiny, scented book to be devoured over a footstool; security inside the family fortress. Presently his face travelled round. He kissed the tip of my nose. I didn't draw back. The kiss transferred itself to my cheek. I made no objection. It was companionable; I needed company. When his attentions took on a new urgency it seemed churlish, and in any case too much trouble, to try to damp them down. The renewal of the old rapport between us was too great a relief to warrant interference. He kissed my lips with professionalism, not objectionably; and then I felt him hesitate.

He was debating whether or not to move on. His desire to do so, communicating itself to me in a variety of subtle ways, was urgent: against it was ranged his anxiety not to press his luck, to take things a step at a time, not to rush me. Recalling with shame the cheap phrase I had tossed him, like half a biscuit to a dog, I kept still, ready to let him persist if that was what he wanted; but his decision had been taken. His grasp relaxed. With a gasp, I sagged back.

'You've been practising. That was some clinch.'

'I don't have much chance to practise, Anjie.'

He sounded happy. I said cynically, 'Oh no?' Keeping the mood light. He shook his head.

'Know something? When some two-bit jerk with a straight profile walks into my office for assessment . . . son, I tell him – only not out loud – son, in a little while, assuming you get past the screen test, you're going to be paid plenty for the chore of embracing a string of the dishiest dolls in Hollywood; while the guy who's signing the cheques stops at home watching his old movies on tee-vee and trying not to notice the way his housekeeper's crossed eyes get in the way of her buck teeth. Where did I go wrong?'

I laughed, but I was puzzled. 'There's many a little starlet, Herbie, would be over the moon if you took her out to dinner.'

'Sure, sure. But then you see, honey, that's not for me. I happen to be choosey.'

I was silent. It could have been a glib compliment, but I knew it wasn't; and the knowledge wasn't a great help to me. Inch by inch, I was being nudged into a false position. Herbie's body shifted. My stomach tightened, but he was merely heaving himself into a more upright position.

'Question is,' he said, businesslike, 'what are we going to do about this problem of ours?'

Despair assailed me again. 'I've thought and thought. I've appealed to him, offered him money, tried calling his bluff. So far, I haven't caved in. I'm refusing to go back to him, or even hint to anyone that I might. And I'm making a start on *Furnace*. He's got the whip-hand, though. He knows he just has to keep prodding. All the while he does that, I'll be going to pieces.'

'We can ban him from the studios.'

'From the set, perhaps. I don't see how we can keep him off the premises. He's not making an outward nuisance of himself. You said so yourself.'

'They're private premises.'

'Technically. But if we tried to keep him out, we'd be playing into his hands. Can you imagine the publicity he'd whip up? Anyway, he'd still be there at the hotel when I got back.'

'We'll move you out. Fix you an apartment in Winchester . . .'

'He'd trace me in a day.'

Herbie's jaw had become set. 'Situation's impossible,' he muttered.

'He's doing his best to make it so. The longer I go on making *Furnace*, the more you've sunk into the project and

the bigger the disaster if eventually . . .' I took a breath.
'Let me drop out now, Herbie. Then I can fight him with
two hands.'

'No way, honey.' Obstinacy had hardened his voice.
'You quit now, you show him he's won and you're
finished.'

Having blotted out the house, the descending dusk was
pulling shrouds over the horse-jumps, obliterating the view
in the same way that a mantle seemed to be falling over my
future. I closed my eyes.

'I can't see a path through. Sleepless nights, camera-
fright, word-blindness . . . I've got the lot. No use fighting
it with half-measures. Five days. That's all I'm giving it.
If Terry hasn't called it off by then – he threatened to tell
you about it this coming Saturday, so maybe he sees that
as his last throw, maybe not – I'm leaving the cast.' I
reopened my eyes to look at him. 'Sorry, Herbie. There's
nothing else I can do.'

Abstractedly he gave my hand a squeeze. He said
quietly, 'We'll see about that.'

CHAPTER XIII

THE MORNING NEWSPAPERS arrived early at The Beeches.
In this, at least, it could lay claim to providing a service,
albeit exterior forces were largely responsible. Waiting
apathetically in the entrance hall for Herbie to come down
and shepherd us out to his car, I left the absorption of the
day's news to Dilys and Denny, both compulsive headline-
scanners. During the night a wind had got up. Rain was
blowing like washed gravel against the window-panes.
With sudden longing, I thought of the heat-haze of Los
Angeles.

Dilys touched my elbow. She had brought Denny
across with her.

'I want you two to meet,' she said solemnly. 'I'm

positive you'll hit it off swell.'

I gave her a dumb look. With a theatrical gesture she reopened her copy of *The Clarion* to display the gossip page. Beneath the Leonard Bagnall byline rambled a five-column announcement: *'Flora' tight-lipped on O'Malley re-run rumours but* . . . And underneath that, across three columns in bolder, fatter type: *Denny? He's a Real Charmer, Says Anjie.*

Denny blinked at the story, then at me. 'One aims to please,' he said mildly.

'Bagnall telephoned me yesterday,' I told them, running an eye down the text. 'Among other things, I said I found you a charming colleague to work with . . . here's his version. "Miss Browne, to whom the screening of *Furnace* supposedly represents a giant stride for womankind, appears nonetheless to nurse a feminine regard for her leading man on the studio set, none other than Denholm *(Elsie and The Earl)* Baxter, bastion of male chauvinism who happens to be 34 and unattached. Charming, was her uninhibited description of Mr Baxter when I spoke to her yesterday at BUC Studios where both are filming. The auspices for our Anjie's ex-spouse, work-starved and love-starved Terry O'Malley, look less than promising. By coincidence, no doubt, he is holidaying in the same area. A sanguine fellow, our one-time Hollywood hero. He tells me . . ." Sorry, Denny.' Refolding the *Clarion*, I handed it back. 'I should have known better. He asked me about Terry, then said how did I like working with you . . .'

'So you told him. And I take it most kindly.' Cheerfully he patted my shoulder. 'My charm, though legendary, doesn't always gain the recognition it deserves. Next time Leonard Bagnall phones, let me talk to him and I'll return the compliment.'

'Embrace,' drawled Dilys, 'and fadeout. Cut. That really gets to me, you know? Right here. That's really wunnerful. Now I want you both – '

'Do you want a clip round the ear?' Denny enquired.

'Not especially, but you might oblige Anjie by – '

'You'll both oblige me,' I interrupted, 'by dropping the subject. The Press may have its useful moments, but not many.'

After its poor start, Tuesday morning was an improvement upon Monday.

Roger Mayhew, in less acerbic mood, did his best to foster me along. Herbie, I supposed, had had a word with him. The supremely helpful factor, however, was the absence from the studio of Terry, who, with his hired Jaguar saloon, had not been seen since dinner the previous evening. Investigating before we left the hotel, Dilys had reported in true mystery-disappearance style that his bed appeared not to have been slept in. Hardly daring to allow myself to hope that he had called it off and departed for the States, I speculated instead upon the possibility of an alcoholic interlude which, on past form, could keep him out of circulation for anything up to a week or ten days. Freed, in any case, of his blighting presence, and cheered by the cementing of relations with Herbie – whose fond appraisal from the studio floor caused me nevertheless some underlying uneasiness – I surmounted the kitchen-scene hurdle with sufficient style to enable us to get a respectable footage into the can by the coffee break. The rushes of the first day's shooting, Herbie confided to me during the interval, indicated that Graham Forde had been a far from unhappy choice for the role of Miriam's husband; which perhaps accounted for the slackening of tension in Roger Mayhew's demeanour. Herbie's relief came off him in almost tangible waves.

'We're on the road to a great motion-picture here. Feel better about things today, honey?'

'A bit. A lot.'

'It'll work out. Maybe we should have a dozen crates of scotch delivered to O'Malley's door, if we knew where it was. Keep him quiet for a few months, before he kills himself right off. Come to think about it – '

'Let's not mention him, Herbie. I want to concentrate.'

'That's it. Forget him.'

Dilys, standing nearby with Adrian Allister, flickered an eyelid at me. Adrian's contribution was a friendly smile. He seemed good at those. The knots inside me loosened a little more. By comparison with the previous day, the studio atmosphere was transformed: consequently I was seeing everything in a brighter light. On Thursday, I reminded myself, Mum, Dad and Liz would be here to watch me at work. Eighteen hours ago, I had felt like cancelling their visit; now, it seemed a reasonable bet that it would not be entirely wasted. When Roger Mayhew, coffee-beaker in hand, approached me with the optical gleam which I was becoming aware meant a tactical briefing on the next scene to be shot, I was able to meet it with aplomb.

'Ready when you are, Roger.' My determination to get upon first-name terms with him had achieved, so far, the negative result of causing him to discard all modes of address and rely upon vocal intonation to catch my attention. I preferred this to Miss Browne, although a compromise Anjelica would not, I felt, have choked him. He was an odd fish.

'You've half an hour,' he proclaimed, 'to get yourself into Miriam's pinafore dress and floppy sandals, hair mussed about, scratch down your left cheek, expression of wildness mingled with exaltation . . . all right? Off you go, and I want you back here by eleven-thirty.'

Herbie said, 'Tackling the confrontation scene before lunch?'

'Why not?'

'No reason,' I said confidently. 'I'd appreciate an extra ten minutes, though, to work it up.'

'Do with a hand, honey?' asked Dilys.

She accompanied me to my dressing-room, a large, well-appointed but strangely bleak chamber leading off the main studio, from which the noise of preparation reached us as I got myself into physical and mental shape. Dilys, who was as familiar with the script as I was, pro-

duced the button-down print dress needed for the scene;
while I buttoned myself into it, she ran strong fingers
through the heavier tresses of my hair, separating the
strands in readiness for the total disorder that would be
achieved shortly by Pauline Hellaby, the tiny Texan make-
up artist who followed Herbie's productions around like a
baby rabbit incongruously in pursuit of a stoat. She had
signalled across the studio that she was on her way.

Giving a critical eye to her manufactured disarrange-
ment, Dilys remarked: 'It's none of my business, and I
know you don't want the subject raised, but if it was me,
and if my ex-husband was ranting to the Press about us
getting our names on a second marriage licence, and I'd
sooner throw myself under a Mississippi paddle-steamer
than come within a mile of the guy . . .'

'You forget, Dilly. I had practice in coping with
him.'

'Sure. He's just a noise.' She lowered her gaze from my
hair to my eyes. 'So why the hunted look?'

I forced a laugh. 'Miriam's, not mine. I'm not letting
Terry's ravings upset me.'

'Heaven forbid,' she said cynically. 'Just the same . . .
he could cause more trouble, couldn't he?'

'Of a sort,' I said, after a pause.

'So why not nip it in the bud?'

'How do you mean?'

She laid bunches of my hair experimentally at angles.
'The aim is to get him temporarily off your back – right?
For the duration of the picture. Where's the harm in
feeding him a line? Tell him you'll think seriously about a
reconciliation when shooting finishes. That keeps him at
tickover for a while. Then – '

'You don't know Terry as I do. Give him an inch, he'll
take five miles. One word like that from me and he'd be
making an announcement to the world.'

'He is anyhow.'

'Yes, but . . . I don't want to play it that way. Tem-
porizing, compromising . . . I've had it up to here with all

that. It's so *useless*. There's just one way to deal with Terry and that's knock him flat.'

Dilys nodded. 'If you have the muscle,' she observed. 'You think I haven't?'

'I think you're making slightly heavy weather of him, honey, this time round.'

She gave me a smile in the mirror. Her eyes betrayed concern. Again I had the feeling that she fathomed, or deduced, more than she was letting on; there was a motherly, let-me-help-you tone to her manner which I found hard to resist. One full confession, however, was enough to be going on with. Herbie and I could see it through. If not, there was little that anyone else could do. Returning the smile, I said with a modicum of breeziness, 'I'm not saying he's easy meat, but if I can't – '

Pauline Hellaby scuttled in. Standing back, Dilys watched as I was converted expertly into the haggard, abrased, semi-demented creature demanded by the screen-play. 'Stay that way,' she suggested, 'and you'll have no trouble from anybody. While you're getting mauled some more, I'll go check on the kitchen furniture.'

She withdrew, leaving Pauline and me in close com-munion as she added skilfully to the haunted effect of my pupils. I tugged the pinafore dress a little askew.

'Ever use any of this stuff on yourself, Pauline?'

'Ah'm a Helena Rubinstein girl myself, Miss Anjie,' she responded, exaggerating her Dallas drawl.

'But if you wanted to . . . adapt your image?'

She considered. 'Ah'd wear less make-up; not more.'

'I get you.' That was all right for her: the face she customarily wore came out of tubes, whereas an excess of additives did less than nothing for me, so that in my case the natural windswept look was both convenient and commercial. I added, 'There's always a wig, I suppose.'

Pauline frowned. 'You've gorgeous hair, Miss Anjie. Why bury it under junk?'

Whisking a brunette creation out of her case, she con-cealed my own hair beneath it and gestured into the glass.

'See? Does nuthin' for you. Who'd know it was Anjie Browne?'

'Autograph-hunters mightn't, with any luck.' I eyed myself speculatively. 'Can I keep this, Pauline, for a day or two? I might give it a trial.'

'Sure,' she said disapprovingly. 'Be my guest.'

Re-entering the studio, I felt the wind thumped out of me.

Slumped in a chair which was perched on a table near Miss Chappell's trolley, Terry was taking shallow sips from a coffee-carton and observing with apparent fixity the on-set bustle. He looked jaded, a little ill. To my incredulous disgust, I found that even yet I was not completely proof against the conglomeration of feelings, embracing everything from exasperation to guilt, that he had had the power to inspire in me from the start. My painfully-reacquired confidence melted like frost in the rain. Dilys's eyes met mine. She made no sign, but I saw that she was not deceived.

Terry ignored my arrival. I should have preferred him to take jaunty note, waft me an ironic kiss in his mood of the previous day. There was something unnerving about his stillness.

I managed a smile for Herbie. 'Ready for lift-off. Do I look lousy enough?'

'Pauline's done a great job.' His examination of me betrayed edginess. 'Everything's fixed, honey. Aside from a small re-think on the kitchen layout. Charlie figures on getting the pair of you kind of in silhouette against the dresser for the stand-up brawl . . . then back to the table for the stabbing episode. Means shifting the cooker a little. Coffee while we're waiting?'

'No thanks, Herbie.'

Neither of us glanced in the direction of the trolley. Having stood irresolute for a moment, he said quietly, 'Follow what Mayhew tells you, Angel, and this scene's a winner,' and wandered off.

I saw him take a chair next to Adrian Allister, with

whom he embarked upon an earnest conversation. On set, Roger Mayhew was conferring with Graham Forde, who was paying intensive heed with his gaze clamped unseeingly upon me. Mayhew beckoned me over.

'Happy about this scene?'

'Delirious.'

'Bear in mind,' he said sharply, 'it's the culmination of a traumatic period. I want it to come out in the phrases you spit at one another. And most of all, in your eyes. The point where Edgar goes on the defensive . . .'

We dissected the action for ten minutes until Charlie Penhurst voiced satisfaction with the arrangements and the lighting was switched to full power. The usual last-minute disorder ensued. Graham and I took our places in front of the kitchen dresser, hung with colourful china designed to crash about us when things got violent. Dilys sat broodingly in her special chair, staring at the set, occasionally making a note. Technicians ran about, picking up trailing cables, wheeling equipment beyond camera-range. Pauline Hellaby threw herself at me, undid another button of my dress and added to its creases. Somebody slid the kitchen table out of place. Unobtrusively, Adrian Allister strolled on set and slid it back.

I gave Graham a tight smile. 'Don't forget to pull your punches.'

'Don't forget to ride 'em,' he retorted.

I searched for something else to say. Anything to avoid looking into the shadows beyond the circle of radiance by which we were enclosed. Graham's eyes had gone opaque. He was gearing himself. I expelled a couple of deep breaths, like a tennis player taking in oxygen in readiness for serving at match-point.

'Everyone set?' Mayhew enquired calmly. 'This one's important. See if we can get it first time. There's a limit to our stock of china.'

'Quiet, please.'

Mayhew glanced around. 'Right. Let's have it.'

Graham's mouth opened in a sneer. 'Am I supposed not

to enquire where you've been?'

Extended pause. I waited a few seconds. *Close-up, left profile.* My lips began to part: too soon, I decided. With luck, the slight movement should emerge as a genuine false start. Graham's eyes urged me on. Capriciously I held the delay.

'How should I know? I've no one to advise me.'

'No one?'

'Unless you count the Rector. You can count, I take it?'

'I find flippancy a little tiresome.' *Pause.* 'How did your dress come to be torn?'

'Perhaps the Rector made a grab for me in the nave.'

'I'm warning you, Miriam. I'm in no mood to have things brushed off. I want to know where you've been for two hours.'

I sensed rather than saw the camera being slewed round by the grips, the lens focusing upon me from a new slant. We were carrying on then. Graham looked and sounded as I felt, braced for the directorial bark at any moment. His uncertainty re-infected me.

'The trouble with you, Edgar, is your insularity. You don't even know you're being Victorian. I think this is what I most dislike about you.'

'You're not implying – '

'If you did it on purpose . . . that I could grapple with. Obtuseness is another matter.'

'I'm sorry if you find my intellect at fault . . .'

'Your *what?*'

Sub-zero contempt in Miriam's voice. Edgar flinches as though he has been struck.

Still no intercession. Had I brought it off? Graham's wince seemed to me overdone.

A humming interval.

'Mutual respect is a vital ingredient of a marriage, I thought.'

'I've a certain respect for that breadknife. It does its job and it knows its place.'

'How apt. That you should reduce this discussion to the level of the cutlery.'

'It's a step or two above the gutter.'

'That's debatable. I'm starting to get a whiff of it in my nostrils.'

Miriam slaps him hard across the face.

My swing missed Graham completely. Off balance, I staggered sideways until brought up against his restraining arm. I tensed myself for the return swipe.

'Cut it, cut it. No point in wasting the crockery.'

The studio lights came on. Graham and I stood foolishly in mid-set, clutching one another like awkward lovers. There was a creak as Mayhew abandoned his chair and walked forward.

'We'll give it another shot after lunch. Two o'clock sharp, back here. Miss Browne – a quick word, if you wouldn't mind.'

Moving to one side, he waited for me to join him. I looked at him timidly.

'How substandard was it?'

'By any calculation,' he replied after a considered interval, 'it was quite awful.'

Herbie came over. His face was shrouded by the featureless haze that connoted inner stress. In dumb appeal I turned to him. He patted my arm.

'Kid wasn't given time to prepare, Roger. You slung her in at short notice.'

'Agreed,' Mayhew said briskly. 'Hence my decision to adjourn. During the break, Miss Browne can profitably devote some time to working herself, we must ardently hope, up to the appropriate pitch.'

'Now wait. What kind of a line is that to take? Anjie was trying her damndest – '

'That's precisely what bothers me. If she was, we might as well pack up and return to London.'

'You're over-reacting to the – '

'Shut up, Herbie.' By now I was articulate, and coldly angry. 'Mr Mayhew is perfectly right. I was terrible.'

'Honey, it wasn't that bad. Sure, you can do better. And you will. In a couple of hours' time – '

'Couple of hours, a couple of years . . . what difference?' My voice rang through the studio. 'As long as I'm expected to work in front of prying eyes, it doesn't matter if I'm trying to play Miriam Hargill or Big-Hearted Bertha from the Bronx – you won't get a performance worth a cent of anyone's money. Can't you see that?'

Mayhew turned to Herbie. 'What's she on about?'

For answer, Herbie swung about. He stumped across the floor towards the chair on its table, watched spellbound by those of the film crew who had not already dispersed. From the summit of the stack, Terry surveyed his approach. Halting at its base, Herbie folded his arms and stood massively, an impressive figure.

'Out, O'Malley,' he ordered. 'I want you gone.'

Terry flipped his empty coffee-carton across a shoulder. Bouncing tinnily on the floor-tiles, it rolled in erratic sweeps before coming to rest. Locking hands behind his head, he leaned back with eyes half-closed, whistling between his teeth.

'Hear me?' Herbie grated.

Terry said, 'The director, I take it, requires visitors to be excluded from the studio.'

'I'm producing this motion-picture. *I'm* telling you.'

Promptly, Terry swung himself by a lateral route to floor-level. On touchdown he reeled slightly, but recovered to adopt a casual posture.

'Word of the Producer is law. As a law-abiding American citizen . . . unlike a few I could name . . . I hereby obey his command.' Starting to walk off, he paused, turned his head. 'Funny thing. A lot of people would have tried *asking* first.'

At the crash of the outer door, Herbie relaxed.

'That's better. Now maybe we can all concentrate.'

Mayhew said stonily, 'Am I to understand that the departure of one seemingly harmless individual can be counted upon to transform the situation?'

'Wait,' said Herbie with an air of cunning, 'and see. By somewhere around two-thirty . . . Angel, baby, where are you going?'

'Outside.' As an exit line, it lacked everything except punch.

At first I thought I had missed him. Then I heard the clump of a car's door. The sound came from a parking area by the perimeter fence. I ran towards it. Terry's hired Jaguar pirouetted on the concrete, glided towards me. I stopped and waited. Abreast of me, its wheels locked. The nearside window slithered down.

'Nice performance of Herbie's. He should take a few walk-on parts himself.'

'You bastard,' I said.

He thought about it, before nodding. 'Legally indisputable,' he concurred.

'I'm not talking about your deprived childhood. I'm talking about the punk you've become.'

'That's an Americanism, Anjie. Doesn't suit you.'

'Do you know you're wrecking the chance of my entire career?'

'We both know where the remedy lies.'

'As long as you're around, I can't work. I can't focus, I can't *think*.' I beat upon the car's bodywork with my fists. 'Why don't you go away? Leave me alone.'

'What do you know about being alone?'

I kicked at the door panel, hurting my toe but cracking the paintwork. If I could, I would have reached inside, hammered his head against the windscreen.

'If you don't get out of my life, I'll kill you!'

'Out of your life, honey, I'm dead already.' He said it breathily. Leaning across, he shoved open the door. 'Come for a ride. Let's talk this through, once for all. We're both civilized people, we can – '

The thrust of my foot sent the door back faster than it had swung out; the retraction of his face was fractionally late. The bottom edge of the window-frame met the bridge of his nose. Falling back, he sat with both hands clamped to the spot. Blood began to flow.

My delight was fierce. At that moment I wanted him to bleed to death. Hurrying to the offside, I shouted through the window-opening: 'That's nothing to what you'll get if you stick around – I'm warning you! Now will you clear off?'

Leaving him there with the engine running, I rejoined Herbie, who with several others had emerged from the studio building in time to witness the incident. I seized his arm.

'Take me somewhere to lunch, for God's sake. Before I do something I might not regret.'

As we were leaving, an audible comment came from one of the group.

'Mayhew should have been here to see that. No attack, did somebody say?'

CHAPTER XIV

Blood Flows as Angry Anjie Hands Out Studio Rebuff was a typical headline the following morning. Several of the stories were front-page, enlivened by pictures of myself and Terry, juxtaposed in one or two instances to give an effect of confrontation. Somebody among the eyewitnesses, Dilys remarked, had evidently felt duty-bound to contribute to the record for posterity, to a degree which had overridden his natural aversion to financial reward.

Wally Parsons, summoned urgently from Winchester by Herbie, dealt lugubriously with the follow-up calls from Fleet Street, countering all enquiries with an anodyne statement and laying stress upon my personal non-availability for interviews.

My own reaction to the occurrence, in the sober light of dawn, was that I had made a public display of myself and lost sympathy. Also I felt grubby. The memory of Terry slumped in his driving seat, gory and with the breath knocked out of him, was one that I didn't care to dwell upon. I would have given a good deal to be able to reverse that impulsive kick of my right foot.

On other fronts, happily, there was progress.

A thrash-it-out conference between Herbie and Roger Mayhew had concluded in an agreement to defer the china-smashing scene until this morning, giving me the chance to prepare myself overnight and enabling two specific arrangements to be made. One was the exclusion from the set, during filming, of 'any person not actively associated with the production'. The other was a call to Jon Templar. His presence during shooting, I explained, would somehow be a help to me. Sounding faintly surprised, the author had agreed to be there.

With these things settled, I had been excused for the rest of the afternoon and had driven into Winchester with Herbie, who wanted to see the Cathedral and any other historic edifices that might be standing around. The sun had emerged; we had ended the day cosily over dinner at a timbered inn which had suggested itself to Herbie as a location for one of the later scenes in *Furnace*; and I had enjoyed the excursion in a subdued, post-climactic fashion, like somebody convalescing after weeks of debilitating disease. Back at The Beeches, over a nightcap in the breeze-torn Residents' Lounge, Denny told us that the evening had passed without the reappearance of Terry, whose hired Jaguar had been spotted by Dilys pulling out from the hotel drive as she was returning from the studios with Adrian Allister and Charlie Penhurst at about five o'clock. It had driven off in the direction of the main London road.

'Maybe he finally got the message,' said Herbie, kissing me good night just inside my bedroom door.

'There's a first time for everything.'

For a while I lay wakeful, listening for the sound of a car wrenching at the gravel outside. But eventually the sugar-coated capsule of high explosive that I had begged from Dilys took effect, and I slept heavily until daybreak. My first action on rising was to survey the car park from the window. The only vehicles in sight were Herbie's BMW, Charlie Penhurst's Princess, and Graham Forde's bright-green Fiat with its nose against the tennis court's rusted stop-netting.

Fortified by the discovery, I was able to take in my stride the Press stories confronting me at breakfast. Tactfully, the others steered off the topic. It was not until afterwards that Dilys took me aside. 'He's left a thing or two in his room, Anjie. I just took a look. But his hand-case is gone.'

'He may have abandoned the other stuff,' I said hopefully.

'What do you figure he's up to now?'

'About his ninth double.'

'How about when he sobers up?'

'Depends what mood he's in. Either my sock on the nose will have persuaded him he's wasting his time, or . . .'

'Or he'll turn mean.' Dilys sounded more anxious than I was presently feeling. I gave her a reassuring smile.

'I'm used to the O'Malley temperament.'

She continued to regard me with an air of maternal concern. 'But are you prepared for everything he might try to get back at you?'

A little shaken, I shrugged. 'That's a tall order.'

'If you did what I suggested,' she grumbled, 'and fobbed him off, you could be left in peace for the next couple of months.'

'That sort of peace would be worse than the war.'

'So you're determined to stand out?'

'I have to.'

'Crazy kid,' she said, shaking her head. 'Let's get along, then, while there's a respite. There's an epic at the studios, waiting to happen.'

The first retake of the scene was a flop, but Roger Mayhew kept his temper. Possibly he was inhibited by the presence of Jon Templar, small and humble against a back wall of the studio, radiating his mild influence. While replacement china was packed upon the kitchen dresser, I underwent further briefing; and then we shot the scene again. Mayhew said it would do, at a pinch, but he wanted a third try after lunch. At my urgent request, Templar stayed to partake of coffee and sandwiches at Miss Chappell's trolley, which as a special concession she had been persuaded to stock and man for the occasion.

'I want you here,' I told him, 'until I've got it right.'

'That last effort was fine, I thought.'

The comment was addressed on a note of enquiry to Mayhew, who delivered a smile that was only slightly rancid.

'Things are improving.'

I started to feel almost buoyant. I could even direct a benevolent look at Graham Forde as he pecked at a ham roll. The hold-up was none of his fault. He was good, and I was doing my best not merely to recognize his quality but to learn from him, despite the entire lack of affinity between us. Before long, I should have some scenes to do with Denny, who was waiting patiently for his first involvement in the action. Opposite him, I felt, I should find no difficulty in demonstrating to Mayhew that I was not, after all, an engine-shed diesel trying vainly to haul a crack express. Against Denny, the sparks would fly.

After lunch, perhaps sensing my increasing apprehension, Herbie allocated guards to the studios' outer doors with instructions to admit nobody without prior consultation. Secure inside the citadel thus created, I managed a performance that aroused from Mayhew no subsequent comment, derogatory or otherwise; there was, however, a tranquillity in his 'Shall we print that one?' to Charlie Penhurst which lifted the mood of the studios in its entirety and brought congratulations about my head. Dilys said, 'Great, kiddo.' Graham remarked, 'We even had some crockery over.' I gave him a kiss and a hug. Jon Templar patted my back and said he couldn't wait to tell Celia how it had gone. I thanked him warmly for being there. Adrian

Allister, hovering in his self-effacing way, gave me a quiet smile of approbation and said nothing.

Relief rose like steam from Herbie as he drove us back.

'I was speaking to Roger M. How'd you feel, honey, about tackling the first of the hideout scenes tomorrow?'

'Suits me.'

'While you're on the boil. Huh? You really took off this afternoon.' Sweeping us around a bend, he strummed a bar or two of a march between teeth and tongue before throwing me a swift glance. 'Same security system in the morning?'

I nodded. 'It helped. Oh – Mum and Dad will be here. And Liz. They're due to arrive about mid-morning. We'd better warn the sentries.'

'Also we'd better have something to show them. Your family, I mean. No question of their gimlet eyes cramping your style?'

I laughed. 'On the contrary. They'll spur me on.'

From the rear seat, Dilys said, 'Big sister has to be on her mettle.'

'Right,' I agreed. 'Liz will be expecting great things.'

As we scraped to a halt in front of The Beeches, Herbie was saying, 'I'll break the glad news to Denny about his scene tomorrow. It's been a – ' He broke off. 'Who's this character?'

A figure had emerged from the hotel entrance. Its bearing was familiar. I said, 'Oh, heavens.'

Dilys uttered a groan. 'Not more trouble?'

'Nigel Moorforth. The smoothie from the *Sunday World*. The one who did that piece when I first – '

'I've not forgotten,' Herbie said grimly. 'Been itching to come up against friend Nigel.'

'You won t say anything rash?'

He gave me a bland grin. 'I've respect for the gentlemen of the Press. Even when their home patch happens to be the sewer. Hm . . . suave-looking guy, but don't fancy his sideburns, they'd look better on an Afghan.' He wound down the window. 'Hi. You after somebody?'

'Mr Joseph? Nigel Moorforth of the – '

'Yeah, I'm informed. Pleased to make your acquaintance. Is it me you want, or my leading lady?'

'A fast word with Miss Browne, if it's not – '

'Come inside,' Herbie said affably. 'We'll get you a drink. Join us for dinner, how's that?'

'Most kind, but I have to be back in London. Twenty minutes of Miss Browne's time, is all that I – '

'You know what we've been telling you people all day? No interviews.'

'It's all right, Herbie,' I put in. 'I don't mind making an exception of Mr Moorforth.'

'Long as you don't make an example of him, honey.' Herbie guffawed a little wildly. 'You can have an end of the Residents' Lounge to yourselves.'

'I'll be glad of a private chat, Miss Browne.'

'We'll leave the pair of you alone.'

'Completely confidential.'

Herbie glared. 'What is this, some kind of – '

'I don't mind, Herbie. I'm sure Mrs Emmerson won't object if we make use of her dining-room for ten minutes.'

'We'll keep her occupied,' said Dilys. She linked her left arm with Herbie's right. 'Come on, Woolly Bear, I'll buy you a brandy.'

'See you for a quick one, maybe, before you take off,' Herbie said gruffly to the columnist.

'I'll look forward to that.' Moorforth followed me through the dining-room door, reclosing the glass-paned door with scrupulous care before taking stock of the environment. By tacit consent we both made for the only table unburdened with cutlery and serviettes: a square one in a corner by a window. I seated myself on the padded bench against the wall, conscious of Siberian currents about my head and neck.

'I'm afraid you need furs and foot-warmers for this place.'

He smiled thinly. He didn't look cold himself. Establishing himself in a chair opposite me, he positioned an elbow upon a table-mat, dead centre, while producing with the other hand a cigarette pack which he proffered. I shook my head. Returning the carton to a side pocket of his fleecy topcoat, he kept his hand there and seemed to set about an examination of the water-jug. Presently I made a movement.

'If it's about yesterday's little fracas outside the studios . . .'

'Your husband,' he said, 'came to see me today.'

The draught from the window acquired sudden additional frigidity. 'My *ex*-husband, you mean?'

'According to him, you're still legally man and wife in many parts of the world.'

'That's incorrect, Mr Moorforth, as I understand it. Anyhow it's immaterial. Mr O'Malley and I are certainly not getting together again, whatever he may say to you people.'

'Well, he didn't say that to me. Not exactly.'

'What did he say, then? Exactly?'

Moorforth's lateral scrutiny became a direct one, cool, appraising.

'He said he'd some items to show me. That I might find intriguing. Items concerning yourself.'

'Did he now? And what might those be?'

'He didn't enlarge. Not on the precise nature of the . . . articles. What he did indicate was that, in the event of his deciding to make them public, they would undoubtedly cause you very severe embarrassment.'

'That was the word he used?'

'Embarrassment? Actually it wasn't.' The thin smile stretched itself between his lip-ends. 'The phrase he employed was: "It would kill Anjie off as a star – it's that big." '

I met his gaze steadily. 'What did you say to this?'

'Naturally, I asked him what the articles consisted of.'

'Did he tell you?'

'He said he hadn't quite made up his mind about them. For some reason, he was keeping them back until Saturday. He didn't say why.'

'What was the point, then, in coming to you?'

'I imagine he wanted to prepare the ground. Gauge my reaction.'

'And what was your reaction?'

Moorforth's eyes didn't shift. 'Curiosity.'

'That I can understand.' My breathing was now under control. 'It's a typical Terry O'Malley gambit . . . full of apparent mystery and meaning absolutely nothing. What he's got, I expect, is some kind of glossary of Press clippings about my earlier films: knocking comments. He might think, if they were publicized now, they could harm my work on *Furnace* in some way.'

Moorforth inspected his fingers. 'Why would he want to do that?'

'I'd have thought yesterday's incident would tell you.'

'All it tells me, and a great many other people, is that the two of you are still slugging it out. If one knew what precisely lay behind it . . .'

'Is this what you came down here for?'

He looked up. 'I thought it fair to give you the opportunity of presenting your side of the story.'

'So you consider there's a story?'

'Miss Browne, the reading public isn't so naïve as you seem to think. When a famous screen star draws blood from her husb – her ex-husband in a studio brawl, they're not to be gulled with the information that the argument was about Government financial policy in the nineteen-sixties.'

'Why gull them with anything? I'm not interested in what people think or imagine. Mr O'Malley is a rather unhappy person who feels, mistakenly, that he'd be less miserable if he and I teamed up again: he's badgering me about it and I'm saying no. For what it's worth, that's the story.'

'There's nothing more to it?'

'Should there be, in your opinion?'

He gave a slight shrug. 'I don't go by opinions. I pursue facts. Mr O'Malley insinuated certain things to me today that I felt I should check on. Hence this conversation.'

'How were matters left?'

The door to the dining-room rasped open to admit the creeping figure of a female staff member, doubled beneath a tray of soup spoons and wineglasses. At sight of us she emitted a low buzz. I called brightly, 'Carry on, don't mind us. We'll be through in a moment.'

The old creature began clashing things on to tables. Moorforth stood.

'By my reckoning, we're about through now.'

'If you say so.' I rose also. 'But you didn't answer my last question.'

He paused to reflect.

'Mr O'Malley said he might be contacting me some time on Saturday . . . in time for most of Sunday's editions. Apparently it depends on developments between now and then.'

'Thank you,' I said. 'Very enigmatic, but then that's Terry to a T. I'll probably have another word with him, find out what on earth he's on about. In the meantime, I doubt whether there's anything more I can usefully say for the benefit of the *World*'s readership. Is there?'

He remained poker-faced. 'This is for you to decide.'

'Time for that drink?'

'Most grateful, but I must be on my way. I'm obliged to you, Miss Browne. For seeing me.'

I followed him to the door. 'What do you plan to do now?'

'Wait,' he said simply, 'until I hear from one of you. Or the other.'

Catching my eye, Herbie left his armchair to join me in the entrance hall. 'More trouble, honey?'

'Come upstairs.'

Seated on the edge of my bed, he listened attentively. When I had finished, he remained for a while in utter silence and stillness, as though in trance. I said tentatively, 'Herbie . . . are you all right?'

'Sure. Just exercising the little grey cells.'

'There's plenty to test their muscle. You think Terry's bluffing still?'

'Maybe he put Moorforth up to calling on you.'

'He's a busy man, our Nigel. He wouldn't take a trip out to Hampshire just to do Terry a favour.'

'If he was paid?'

I shook my head. 'Can't see it. I think whatever Terry said must have impressed him.'

'Question is . . . did O'Malley *show* him anything?'

'From the way Moorforth was probing, I doubt that.'

'Hell,' said Herbie explosively, 'we don't even know if the guy has anything left to show. We're guessing.' Abandoning the bed, he prowled the creaking carpet, smiting the washbasin regardlessly as he passed and re-passed.

I said, 'Seems we've got until Saturday, at least.'

Herbie stopped. In a hollow voice he said, 'Things went so swell today. We've a great movie on our hands. That creep can't wreck it for us.'

I went across, touched his arm. 'Till Saturday,' I reiterated.

'Three days.' Wrapping the arm about me, he drove wind out of my lungs. 'Trust me, Angel. I'll think of something, don't you fret.'

CHAPTER XV

' "DISHEVELLED AND WITHOUT make-up, but flushed and sparkling",' Pauline recited from the screenplay. 'Sure do their best, don't they, Miss Anjie, to screw things up for us.'

While she was conjuring the natural look out of a succession of bottles, I lay back in the chair before the mirror and tried to relax.

The night had been a bad one. Out of the darkness, the bland face of Nigel Moorforth had loomed repeatedly: on two or more occasions I had lurched into staring-eyed wakefulness at the sound of his voice beside my bed, announcing resonantly, 'It's up to you, Miss Browne . . .' Towards dawn, I had lain for what seemed a period of weeks in a condition of brittle alertness until the alarm snatched me from an encounter with a grinning Terry, crawling at me on all fours across the bedroom with a plain-wrapped parcel between his teeth while I fought to retreat to a non-existent door. The prongs of the nightmare had yet to be blunted.

Dilys looked in. 'How's it going? You're on call in ten minutes.'

'Practically there,' said Pauline with her easy good nature. What problems, I wondered, did she have? Everyone was supposed to have something. Some kind of yardstick would have been helpful, a sort of Richter Scale of emotional trauma for the classification of shock. 'As long as you're here, Miss Meridew, would you mind holding this hunk of hair the way I have it while I fetch some lacquer out of my bag?'

'Sure thing.' Obligingly Dilys obtained a grasp. 'Will you let Mr Mayhew know,' she called after Pauline, 'you'll be just a few minutes finishing Anjie off?'

'Okay.'

Via the mirror, Dilys sent me a grimace. 'Not feeling so perky, kid?'

'Does it show?'

'You weren't exactly chatty at breakfast. Come to that, you didn't eat any breakfast. This part of your sharpening-up regimen for a razor performance?'

'If it is,' I said limply, 'it doesn't work.'

'I can see that.' She regarded me contemplatively. 'More Terry trouble?' she asked.

'Sort of.'

She adjusted her grip. 'He's not been back, though. Has he?'

'Not so far as I know.'

'I checked again before we came out. His room's still as he left it. That's two nights he's not been around to cause a nuisance.'

'People don't have to be present,' I said after a space, 'to be a menace.'

Dilys nodded in solemn concession to the force of the proposition. She said thoughtfully, 'You know, it's pretty much the same in politics. You should listen to my old man. I told you he's active in the Washington hierarchy? He lets me in on one or two things, and honey, you wouldn't believe. Or maybe you would. In contact or at long range, the things politicians will do . . . It doesn't leave you with that many illusions.'

'I daresay. Mind if we don't talk about it, Dilly?'

'Sorry, kid. But there's just one thing I do want to mention. If you – '

Pauline returned with the lacquer. 'Sorry I was so long. Somebody dumped my bag in a closet. They're almost ready for you out there, Miss Anjie.' She took over my tresses from Dilys. 'Looking forward to doing a scene with Mr Baxter?'

'I was.'

Pauline and Dilys exchanged looks. 'You'll be mustard, honey,' said the latter, unconvincingly.

Awaiting me on the hideout set, Herbie studied me critically before wagging approval. 'That's lover-girl Miriam. Pauline's done a great job.'

'As always. Have I held things up?'

'There's some rumpus about the lighting. Coffee?'

Miss Chappell had a beaker filled and waiting for me. I put extra charm into my smile. 'I'm so sorry. I'd really prefer tea this morning.'

Philosophically she set the beaker aside. 'Got a thirst on, this time?'

'Dry mouth,' I said confidentially.

'Fetch it over here, Angel, will you?' said Herbie. 'There's a small script-alteration I want to tell you about.'

I joined him in a vacant corner. Opening his script copy at random, he spoke in a mutter.

'Been giving this business some more thought. My guess is, O'Malley's engaged in psychological warfare. So it's up to us to hit back. What d'you say?'

'Can't we forget it for now, Herbie?'

'No, doll. I understand what you mean, but we have to think positively or it's going to undermine us. You're not yourself. Behind that mask, you're fluttery. We have to keep a step ahead.'

'Show me a step and I'll take it.'

'Here's one for openers. What's O'Malley's ace card? Uncertainty. He knows that we don't know whether any of these damn prints still exist or not; nor whether he has them. Until we do, he figures, we daren't chance our arm. It's a good ace. So I aim to trump it.'

'How?'

'Tackle him head-on. Get him to myself for a half-hour, put the squeeze on him. Up to now he's had it easy. Bring him up against someone not directly involved . . . it could make a difference.'

'No rough stuff, Herbie. That'd be – '

'Who said anything about violence? Here's where it counts, honey.' He tapped the side of his head. 'Psychology – remember? Listen, I've worked out the basics of an approach and I think I can carry it through.'

'You don't know Terry.'

'Well, that's right. Not a tenth as much as you do . . . and maybe that's been the millstone round your neck? You're too close. Whereas with me . . . I guess it's worth a try.'

I sighed. 'Anything you could do, Herbie . . . But first, you've got to find him.'

'He must be in London. Obviously he was there yesterday – blabbing to Nigel. He's not been back at The

Beeches, so he's stopped on in the city. Planning to call you, tomorrow or Saturday, to hear what you've decided. Then he's nicely placed for a second visit to Fleet Street: if necessary.'

'All right. So what?'

'So I plan to drive up there myself, later on today. Track him down.'

'Just like that? London's not a village, Herbie. You'd need more than a – '

'Miss Browne, please.' Adrian Allister's harmonious voice floated from the set.

'You're on, Angel. Play this scene for what it's worth . . . leave the other action to me. I've dealt with worse than O'Malley in my time.'

There was a great deal I wanted to caution him about. Only there wasn't time. Roger Mayhew's voice contained the seeds of impatience. As I was making my way over to where Denny and the rest were waiting, one of the exceedingly large young men who had been assigned to the studios' outer doors intercepted me. 'Pardon me, Miss Browne, but your family have arrived.'

'Oh – that's early.' I felt a surge of relief and affection. It would be good to talk with Mum in the shelter of Dad's diffident solidity. 'We can get them settled in before we kick off. Where are they, in the vestibule?'

'Yes, only . . .'

'Don't leave them there, Howard. Wheel them in.'

'There's just one thing,' he said, looking troubled. 'They have someone else with them.'

My mind flew over the possibilities. The likeliest was Mrs Cornfeld from next door. 'Female?' I demanded. 'If so, we'd better – '

'It's not a lady, Miss Browne. It's Mr O'Malley.'

'I see,' I said, after a pause. 'Thanks, Howard. I'll look after it.'

I returned to Herbie, who was peacefully finishing his coffee. 'I don't think you'll need to take that trip to London, after all.'

'How's that, honey?'

'Terry's outside. With my family.'

His eyes bulged. Placing the beaker on the floor, he smoothed the flanks of his suit with both palms as he came to his feet. 'I'll handle this.'

'No fireworks,' I pleaded softly as we headed for the door to the vestibule.

'Take it easy. I'll have him clear of this place before you know it. Talk some sense into the guy.'

The four of them were seated on a long leather couch. At our appearance, Mum jumped up and hurried to meet us.

'Hallo, Anjie! Weren't we quick? Terry brought us. He'd hired a car, so he was able to drive us down here. Wasn't that lucky?'

'Terrific break.' I planted kisses on both of her chubby cheeks. 'In time to watch all the action.'

'My, aren't we looking forward to it! How are you, Mr Joseph?'

'I'm well, Ma'am. Good to see you again. Welcome to the Studios. If you'd care to step right inside, I guess we can fix you some refreshment.'

'Lovely. We could do with it. Dad's parched. We never stopped on the way.'

'When,' I asked, 'did Terry offer to bring you?'

'Yesterday, love. He came round in the afternoon. When he heard we was travelling down today – '

'He can't come inside the studios, Mum.'

'What?' She stared from me to Herbie, across her shoulder at the couch, then back to me. 'Whyever not? He said he might be able to get Liz a walk-on part while she was here.'

'He'd no right to say anything of the sort. That's for Herbie to decide.'

'Yes, naturally, but . . . Why d'you want him kept out?'

'Haven't you read the newspapers?'

'Oh, that. He explained about that. Accidental, like,

wasn't it? You never meant to hurt him.'

'I did mean to.'

She examined my face. After a moment she said cautiously, 'That wasn't very nice.'

'No. It wasn't.' I allowed another interval. 'He's not coming inside, Mum.'

Helplessness took possession of her. 'Well, I don't know . . .'

I walked over to where Dad was waiting by the couch, his grubby brown raincoat arguing slightly with shiny black shoes. He gave me a shy kiss.

'How are you, my dear? Hard at it?'

'Shall be, any minute now. Like to go with Mum and Herbie, Dad . . . see the studio? Liz and I will follow up.'

Liz said, 'Hi, Anjie.'

A touch of defiance lurked behind the defensiveness. My response was brisk.

'Hi, Lizzie. Say cheerio to Mr O'Malley and I'll give you your first glimpse of a film factory.'

Her chin lifted. 'Terry's coming too.'

'Sorry, kitten, but he's not.'

'Count me out, then.' She put a hand on his shoulder.

He continued to gaze calmly across the vestibule, as though in disregard of proceedings that barely concerned him. Except for a contusion across the bridge of his nose, he looked in good shape. The spectacle of Liz making physical contact with him hampered my thought-processes.

'Now that you're here, don't you want to watch the shooting?'

'Not without Terry.'

For the first time I looked at him directly. 'I hope you're proud of yourself. A kid of fifteen.'

He switched on his air of injured surprise. 'Liz and me are buddies. Right, honey?'

She nodded, watching for my reaction. I tried to give her none.

'Does Mum know you're not coming in?'

She shrugged. 'We thought Terry was going to be one of the party.'

'You thought wrong, Liz, I'm afraid.'

My heart was pounding, my stomach churning; all the assiduous focusing of theatrical energy was being cast to the winds. Dad had gone to join the others by the studio door; they were waiting, pretending not to watch. I walked over to them.

'She refuses to leave Terry. And we refuse to have him inside. What happens now?'

Dad looked wretched. Mum, with an appearance of do-or-die, cleared her throat.

'You don't think you're being a teeny bit unreasonable, Anjie love? It's not as if he wants to do any harm. All he wants – '

'Simply by being here, he does harm. Can't you see that?'

'No,' she said stubbornly. 'I can't. He seems to me a very nice man, and he's lonely. All he's after – '

'Mum, for God's sake! I don't want him near me – isn't that enough? Or has he conned you so thoroughly that . . . Dad, you can see through him, can't you?'

He fingered his neck. 'Well, my dear, the last thing we want is to cause you any pain or embarrassment . . .'

'At this moment,' I said bluntly, 'you're causing both.' He blinked, and I cursed inwardly but pressed on. 'Look, I couldn't be gladder to see you, and Mum, and Lizzie – but the way he's attached himself to the three of you is beyond words.' Desperately I hunted for some. 'He's operating to a plan. He is, really. He's just using you.'

Mum said gently, 'Remember, pet, we can see Terry as you can't. He only wants the best for you. He's told us that. Anyone can see it, with half an eye. He's potty about you. And we wouldn't want him to feel . . . I mean, for us to ditch him just because . . . Not right, would it be? Ever so kind to Lizzie, he's been. Given her no end of tips. They get on together like a house on fire. No harm in that, is there?'

I turned away to groan. 'What do I say? Herbie, what do I tell them?'

He gathered himself decisively. 'Take your parents inside, honey. You're wanted urgently on set. I'll talk with O'Malley and your sister.'

'That's it,' Mum said in relief. 'We'll leave it with Mr Joseph. Is this where we go? My, talk about Euston Station! This where you'll be making the whole picture?'

'Tell you about it later.' In mental turmoil I steered them to the chairs which Howard had considerately arranged in a corner, asked him to provide them with a beaker of strong tea and a cheese roll apiece from the trolley, told them they should be able to see everything, and adjured Mum to keep her voice down. She said reproachfully, 'As if I'd need telling,' on a note that carried to the ceiling and back. Dad made a circle of his index finger and thumb, which I took to be an expression of reassurance.

From the hideout entrance, Roger Mayhew remarked acidly, 'Delighted you could get to us, Miss Browne.'

'Sorry. My parents turned up.'

'Then shall we give them something to watch? Trial run, no cameras, up to and including the initial clinch. Is that,' he enquired sardonically, 'all right by you?'

'Fine.' I strove to collect the bits of myself, wedge them back into sequence. From his perch on the chopping-block outside the carefully rusticated shack, Denny threw me a comradely grin. Bitterly aware that in normal circumstances his friendly professionalism would have got me over almost any hump, I said to nobody in particular, 'Greeting my family has put me a little out of the mood. Make allowances, will you, for the first twenty minutes?'

Mayhew gave me a hard look. 'It's my custom to do so.'

At his signal, Denny took up position at the shack doorway, lounging with pocketed hands against the frame. Smoothing my hair mechancially, I remembered that it was supposed to be disordered, and ruffled it again while

I moved to the rim of the artificial clearing in which the hideout stood. Mayhew clapped hands.

'Quiet, please. Okay – dummy run. When you're ready.'

The familiar hush blanketed the studios. In their distant corner, I could see Mum and Dad munching and staring; I couldn't see the others, nor Herbie. Taking a massive breath, I walked forward.

A subtle rigidity overtook Denny's lolling body. His survey as I approached was poised simultaneously on several keys, suggestive of the examination that a disbeliever might devote to the undeniable manifestation of a phantom: so compelling was his reaction that I all but came to a halt, convinced there was something at fault. I was seeing an actor in full spate. Taking hold of myself, I moved on to within a couple of yards of the chopping-block.

'Please forgive the intrusion, Mr Grant . . .'

'Hold it.'

Mayhew's querulous voice cut in. I turned. 'What,' he asked, 'became of the pause?'

I repeated blankly, 'The pause?'

'You're supposed to stand there fifteen seconds in silence. Looking at him.'

'Sorry,' I said confusedly. 'I was thinking . . . I'll start again.'

I had forgotten the pause entirely. A drowning sensation engulfed me as I returned to the original spot, swung for a repeat advance. Denny quirked his lips at me. I was acutely conscious of the unblinking scrutiny of Dilys. On the job, there was something unnerving about the supremacy of her concentration. Gawkily I moved ahead once more. The journey seemed to take hours. Achieving the rendezvous for the second time, I began counting the seconds.

'Shoulders back, Miss Browne. More arrogance to the carriage.'

There was anxiety now in Denny's gaze. Had the pause

endured too long? I made an effort.

'Mr Grant, please forgive the instrusion. The only excuse – '

'For *Christ*'s sake.'

I turned my head to stare dumbly at Mayhew's contorted face. The face of a music critic in the agonies of hearing a classical symphony mauled by a school band. Next to him, Adrian Allister was looking down intently at his shooting script. Dilys, sitting back, was equally intent upon filing her nails. Other faces displayed a mixture of expressions: embarrassment seemed to predominate. In the background, Miss Chappell behind her coffee-urn was much too engrossed by a magazine. Close by her, Mum and Dad were seated comfortably in their canvas-backed chairs, watching interestedly, awaiting the action.

Of Herbie or Liz, there was still no sight. A humming note in my ears lasted for several seconds before cutting off, leaving me clear-headed, acutely aware of the smallest sound, the faintest shuffle; of which there were few. The most noticeable noise came from the scuff of my own shoes on the floor tiling as I walked off the set, over to where the director was crouched upon his chair. I stood before him.

'I'm sorry. I can't go on.'

'What?' His face came up.

'I said I can't do it.' My voice was a flat calm. 'Not fair on everyone else. You'll have to shoot another scene to-day.'

His eyebrows writhed. He fired a glance at his assistant, who now was watching me seriously. Everybody was watching me.

'Thank you, Miss Browne, for the directive. I confess to wondering what my programme should be for the next day or so. Thank you so much.'

Ignoring the weighty irony, I said with tiredness, 'If you want to bring in another Miriam, you'd better go ahead and find someone – quick. I shan't complain.'

For once he was at a loss. Mute or vociferous, he had

ceased to interest me: I just wanted to get out. Behind me, Denny said, 'Don't do anything on impulse, Anjie. Have a lie-down. Come back to it later.'

'What's the point?' I didn't turn. I made off for the door to the vestibule and nobody tried to stop me. It was the longest walk of my life, but at least I reached that oblong of grained timber, placed it between myself and the silence, stood dizzily on the other side while I mastered the sickness in my stomach, the singing inside my skull. When I was able to look around, I saw that the vestibule was empty.

Inside his entrance-cubicle, Brian the peak-capped doorman was drowsing over the back page of the *Sun*. I dealt him an unceremonious tap.

'Brian, do you know where Mr Joseph is?'

Jerked out of sleep, he bore no malice. 'Last I see of him, Miss, he was orff through them swing doors . . .'

'What about my sister? And the man with her?'

'They was already gorn.'

'Left, you mean?'

'Hear 'em take orff in that Jag of his, five minutes back.' His manner told me that he read the papers as closely as most. 'Was you wanting a word with 'em first?' he asked innocently.

'How long afterwards did Mr Joseph – '

Footfalls reached us from outside. The swing doors burst at the seam to admit Herbie, square-jawed and steely-eyed. I clutched him. 'They didn't give you the slip?'

With a glance at Brian, who made an unpersuasive show of returning to his newsprint, he led me across to the couch where Liz and Terry had been sitting. Swinging himself down beside me, he spoke in a low voice.

'Your kid sister seems to have it all figured out. She's with O'Malley. He's barred from the set. Therefore – '

'Where's he taken her?'

'Now that,' Herbie said carefully, 'is a slice of information he wasn't broadcasting. They didn't – '

'Couldn't you have stopped them?'

'Honey, I'm sorry. They pulled a fast one on me. Liz went off to the powder room: while she was gone, O'Malley said he'd something to collect from his car. So I hung on here, aiming for a quiet word with your sister when she came out. Only she didn't.'

'Then how – '

'There's a back entrance to that place. I just checked. She must've gone out that way, joined him in the parking lot, and they took off.'

'Perfect.'

'Time I twigged what had happened, they'd had several minutes' start. Some guy out there says he saw them leave, but he couldn't say which way they were headed.'

'Herbie, this is terrible. What's he going to do with Liz? Where will they – '

'Stay calm, Angel. Could be they'll make for Winchester. He'll show her around, take her to a movie, I guess.'

'We'll have to go after them.'

'Now wait a bit. We've a day's shooting . . .'

'Liz comes first. Anyhow I'm opting out.'

'You're what?'

'I've walked out of the picture.'

It was less difficult to say than it was, apparently, for Herbie to absorb. The sequence of his expressions added up to the epitome of the slow burn. His mouth opened and shut, opened and shut as his eyes glared into mine. The third time his lips parted, words struggled out.

'Let's go find her then, sugar. Sooner this is all cleared up, the sooner – '

'I'm serious. Miriam and I are through. We might as well face it: I'm useless. Come on, your car's outside.'

He stayed put. His face had whitened.

'I'm not shifting, Anjelica. Not till you take those words back.'

I said wildly, 'I'm taking nothing back. Roger Mayhew knows – the whole blasted studio knows. I'm finished. All

I've done from the start is let people down. I don't want any more of it. My mind's made up. Please, Herbie. Let's just go and find Liz.'

'Sit down!' he barked.

Jolted, I sat. He twisted to face me. For once, there was nothing remotely burlesque about his manner.

'Listen, honey. Listen good. Aren't you confusing mental distraction with professional incompetence? Not unnatural in the circumstances – but I'm damned if I'm going to stand by and just let it happen. You know, and I know, you can measure up to Miriam. We also know why, temporarily and unavoidably, you're finding her tough going at the moment. It's no reason for giving up. It's the more reason for fighting back, grabbing this thing by the throat, throttling the life out of it. Walk out on *Furnace* now and you're turning your back on existence. I've said it before. I'll keep on saying it, so long as you come up with these defeatist notions that seem to have gotten a hold on you.'

Herbie breathed hard. 'Who's this guy O'Malley? Some two-bit jerk who thinks he can take over your life? You're the kid from West Ham – remember? – where they pick themselves up off street corners and get back to the head of the gang. You've told me. I've believed you. And I don't figure on having to adjust my reaction. All I'm asking for, right now, is a little *spirit*.'

Presently I moved apologetically against him.

'Sorry, Herbie. One measure of ninety per cent proof, coming up.'

'That's my original Anjie! Now we go find Liz.'

I scrambled up. 'What about Mum and Dad?'

'Can't they stick around? We could be back before they know what's – '

'They'll be wondering what's happened. I'm not sure if they quite cottoned on to what I was telling Roger Mayhew, but if I don't show up again soon they'll be asking around and then coming in search of me.'

Herbie pondered. 'Have a talk with them,' he said

finally. 'Tell 'em about O'Malley.'

'Tell them!'

'Not the complete story, necessarily. Without dipping into detail, you can – '

From the studio door, Mum emerged, peering and perturbed. Herbie called to her.

'Mind stepping over here for a moment, Mrs Brown?'

With a squeeze of my hand, he rose and made off as she trotted across. 'What's going on, Anjie? Where's Liz and Terry?'

'Gone. We're just leaving to search for them.'

'*Gone?* Gone where? Whatever made them do that? Why did you walk out just then?' Bewilderment was not something that Mum tried to conceal: the questions tumbled like apples from a sack. 'What was you saying to that bloke in there? When do you – '

I put a hand over her mouth. 'Can't explain properly now. The point is: Liz has teamed up with Terry. And even if it's only for the day, that's too long – because there are things about him you don't know, and I think it's time you did.' Seeing the terror on her face, I said soothingly, 'I don't mean he's a sex maniac. I think he's simply using Lizzie as a lever. This is what I want to tell you about.' I hesitated. 'You see, Terry's blackmailing me.'

'Anjie . . .!'

'I realize the impression he's made on you all, and honestly I do understand. He can be horribly plausible. But no kidding, Mum, he's playing a dirty game. He wants me back, so he's using something he knows about me to force my hand. Now he's manipulating you three, into the bargain.'

'What is it he knows about you?'

Mum seemed reduced in size. I held her arms. 'Nothing too dreadful. Just a spot of bother I got mixed up in when I first went to the States . . . all forgotten now. But if it was raked up, it could be awkward. Now do you see why I hated the idea of you getting involved with him?'

She gave a feeble shake of the head. 'I'm in a flat spin

. . . I thought Mr Joseph was going to sort it all out.'

'Between us, we shall. Don't worry. But first we must get Liz away from Terry. While she's under his spell, we're in trouble.'

'But why does he need her with him?'

'Because he knows I'll be after him, and that's what he wants. He's obsessed. He'll pull any trick to get me back.'

Dragging a handkerchief from her handbag of imitation crocodile, Mum blew her nose. 'Seeing he's got this hold over you, why should he need Liz as well?' she persisted.

'That's just it. I'm – we're not certain how much of a hold it really is. I have to find out.'

The idea that had been incubating inside me for several days was administering small kicks. Giving heed to them, I lost touch with my surroundings until Dad's studiously non-anxious voice penetrated to my awareness. 'Something wrong?'

I turned. There was a suppressed urgency to his stance that made me bite my lip. With a glance at Mum, I said, 'Come over here a moment, Dad.'

He followed me to an immense window overlooking the main car park, now being dealt slanting hammer blows by a fierce April shower. His lips were compressed, indicating two things: he was pent-up, and he was scared of asking. I said cheerfully, 'It's just that Lizzie's being silly. She's gone off with Terry for a few hours.' I studied his face. 'I'd better explain.'

I told him as much as I had divulged to Mum. He listened with silent concentration, the sole sign of stress being the heightened colour on each cheekbone. When I had finished, he nodded several times. 'So what do you plan to do?'

'Herbie's going to look for them.'

'But you, yourself? You can't – '

'I'll probably go with him. I think it's best if you and Mum stay on here. No sense in all of us charging about the countryside. Besides, they might come back. I'll get

Dilys Meridew – she's a friend of mine – to take you to lunch. And then later on, if Lizzie's not back . . . well, you'll have to sort that out between you. I might have to be away more than a few hours. A day or two, perhaps.'

'Might you, my dear?'

'Sorry, Dad. It's essential.'

He looked hard through the window, as though in hope that the thrashing downpour might tell him something. 'You know best. What about the police?'

'Early days yet. I'm sure we shan't need to bring them in.'

I conned him a little worriedly. His facial skin was yellower than I had ever seen it: in his light blue pupils was a suggestion of the glitter that had always disturbed me when, as a child, I had somehow driven him to the outside limits of forbearance. I had never seen him lose control; but Liz claimed to have done so. On an occasion in the local park, he had been waiting for her by the boating pond while she visited the public convenience: she was eight at the time. Emerging, she was accosted by a middle-aged man. In fright, she scampered back to Dad, whose coverage of the ground, she told me, would have earned him a gold medal in the Olympic hundred metres, while his treatment of the molester when he got to him would have taken him comfortably to the boxing final, welter-weight division. When he returned to her, she declared, having permitted the man to make a halting escape across the railings, his demeanour would have put the breeze up Muhammad Ali.

I had treated her story lightly. To me, he had remained the small, reticent counterpart to Mum: the provider of funds; the occasional presence who was mysteriously 'in the print' somewhere near Ludgate Circus and knew people who wrote articles for *Cycling News* and *Two-Wheeler Weekly*. Looking at him now, I wondered whether I had been a little blind.

Uneasily I added, 'Leave everything to us, Dad. There's nothing for you to worry about.'

His head gave a tiny jerk. 'All right, my dear. You do as you think fit. We'll look after things this end.'

'All squared with Roger M.,' announced Herbie, hoisting a monster umbrella over the two of us before we left the shelter of the vestibule porch. 'He's written you off till next week – okay? Gives us time to attend to matters. Now listen, honey. When we get to Winchester we'll try all the restaurants and bars. If that gets us no place – '

'You try, Herbie. I'll be heading for London.'

With the key in the doorlock of his car, he paused to stare at me across the roof. 'You figure they're back in Town already?'

'I've no idea. I shan't be looking for them.'

'Huh?'

'That's what he wants, don't you see? Anjie Browne scurrying in his wake. Well, I'm not going to fall for it. I'll be on a plane. This evening's flight from Heathrow to LA.'

He sagged against the bodywork. 'Anjie, honey, you're not quitting? That's ridiculous. What happened to – '

'You don't imagine I'd simply walk out on the situation? I'm taking the action I should have taken a week ago. While you were fixing things inside there, I phoned through to Heathrow and got a booking. It's the only way, Herbie.'

'What is?'

'Get us inside and I'll tell you.'

As we were fixing seat-belts, a face under a plastic rain-hat appeared at my window. I lowered it. 'What's the trouble, Dilys?'

'Herbie asked me to look after your folks, Anjie. That's okay, I'll see to it: but they'll want to know when you'll be back. What do I say?'

'By the weekend,' I told her. 'Can't be more specific. Make reassuring noises, Dilly, will you? Only don't let on where I've gone.'

'Fat chance,' she snorted, 'when I don't know myself.'

I hesitated. 'Back to LA. But keep it under your hat. It's business.'

'As the tycoon said to the typist. Well, so long. Have a nice trip.' Her dripping face registered perplexity. 'See you soon – with a fresh suntan?'

'I'm not going back for the climate. Tell you what, Dilly. If things pan out that my parents want to stay down here, they can use my room at the hotel. It's got twin beds. If Liz shows up, though, they might want to go home tonight.'

She gestured baffled assent. Engaging the clutch with a roar, Herbie drove at hair-prickling speed for the main gate.

'Now, Angel,' he said, wrenching us on to the Winchester road, 'you can explain to a very puzzled man just what you have in mind.'

CHAPTER XVI

AFTER THE snaking lanes of rural England, the freeway into Los Angeles from the airport was less than narcotic. I had dozed patchily during the flight. Now, I felt keyed-up, eager to be getting somewhere, tempted to spur the hired Oldsmobile above the limit; but held back by the fear of being booked for a speeding offence that would blow my cover. Above the Atlantic and at both ends, the brunette wig had done a good job. Some glances had strayed my way, but no more than might have been expected by any unattached female in a departure lounge or aboard a Boeing 747. Passport officials had been helpfully discreet. While I was sipping coffee after touchdown, waiting for the Oldsmobile to be brought round, a young man who could have been an agency reporter had appraised me thoughtfully more than once, but finally had been diverted by the appearance of a top Congressman who, an early edition informed me, was flying out to make an on-the-spot assessment of the Middle East situation: after that, the only individual to take any notice of me was the hire-car representative, who had shown no tendency to give a start of recognition and edge towards a phone.

Anjie Browne Shock. Anjie Storms Off Set . . . The words on the news placards as I was leaving London still haunted me. By now, the media in all quarters would be on the alert.

Relying almost totally upon the wig, I had decided against darkened glasses: they drew attention. Driving through the haze of a Californian morning – the peak-hour pandemonium had yet to build up in earnest – I wondered whether Herbie, five thousand miles away, had succeeded yet in tracing Liz and Terry; whether, if not, he was managing to dissuade Mum and Dad from notifying the police; whether Dilys was looking after them; whether Roger Mayhew and his underlings had packed up in disgust. A sense of unreality had settled over me like damp muslin. It was not until I was within the city limits, and having to concentrate, that I started to shake it off. Parts of Los Angeles I knew to some extent: steering a course through them was another matter. By the time I came upon the area I was most familiar with, a headache of jungle dimensions was crouched at the base of my skull, poised to pounce. Stress, sleeplessness, scratch meals, jet-lag . . . Think of a cause, I was showing the symptoms. Before making for my final objective, I called in at the Peridale Hotel, just off Olvera Street, and did my best to freshen up in that establishment's decadently opulent washroom. I had been there once previously, for a promotional jamboree, and remembered it as a place where no one took a lot of notice of anyone else. My memory was not at fault. The only jolt I received was on seeing my reflection in the washroom mirror: under the wig, my face was pale and strained, the eyes inclined to stare. I needn't worry, I told myself listlessly. Nobody would recognize Anjie Browne. Leaving, I gave the attendant a dollar. She palmed it sadly away. 'You on a visit, honey? Take in the tour at Universal. That truly is something. Universal. Don't miss it.'

Thanking her, I returned to the car and drove to police headquarters.

Stomping down the broad steps, a uniformed patrolman swung me a glance. I returned a couple of rows of helpless teeth. He paused in mid-step.

I said, 'How do I get to see somebody in authority?'

'You could try raiding a bank, lady. Have someone special in mind?'

'The Chief of Detectives.'

He gave me a wary look. His speculation was visible: paranoiac female or well-heeled connection? He decided to distribute the risk.

'Tell you what.' He pointed up the steps. 'Why don't you step right through those swing doors, take the first opening to your right, have a word with the detective you'll find on duty at the nearest desk? He'll be happy to assist you in any way he can. My pleasure, ma'am.' Giving a push to his peaked headwear, he stood back, watched me to the top; turning, I thanked him again with a wave. He made a movement with his chin. Then he sauntered across to a prowl car in which a colleague waited in studied boredom at the wheel. When I glanced back from the swing doors, both of them were watching me.

I was glad to get inside the building. And then the years fell away, dumping me back into the pit of panic that I had first experienced as a raw kid of nineteen, fresh to the Golden West and its minefields. I forced myself to bear right. From some distance along a corridor came a sub-dued rattle of mechanized activity, the buzzing of tele-phones, occasional clashes and sliding noises that I identified as file cabinets being opened and shut. Human frailties, encapsulated in metal. Legalized time-bombs, ticking away . . . With a confident tread I marched into the office, smiled appealingly at the first face to gravitate towards me.

It belonged to an extremely young man, lean, fresh-faced, in plain clothes, who was picking out characters on an electric typewriter at a pace which seemed to be causing him some dissatisfaction, to judge from the frown-lines that loitered just above the bridge of his tilted nose as his gaze rested broodingly upon mine. I kept the smile in position. Its impact upon him was not manifest.

Tentatively, I said, 'I was told to come in here . . .'

He remained statuesque. It dawned upon me that he was looking, not at me, but at the outline phrase within his head that he was struggling to chisel into shape. Glaring abruptly at the keyboard, he selected some finger positions and began stabbing, harder than was necessary. At the conclusion of the burst he lifted the sheet and read back. With a faint sigh, he let it drop. Then he swivelled his chair.

'Help you at all?'

'Maybe.' I had my East Coast accent ready-sharpened. 'Is it possible to speak with the head guy? Y'know. The Chief.'

'Anybody can talk to the Chief.' He spoke crisply, neither obstructive nor falling over himself. 'That's assuming they have something significant to say. What's it about?'

'Actually, it's a confidential matter.'

His second sigh was less faint. 'Everything we handle here is confidential. The Chief's a busy man. Which is why us lesser mortals are dug in here, taking the heat off him. Give us a rundown on what's bothering you and we can possibly – '

'I couldn't do that. It's very delicate.'

Trying not to betray my breathlessness, I fell back upon my world-renowned, winsome, small-girl, mute scrutiny. He met it dispassionately. Presently, rolling back his chair, he climbed lazily to his feet, lounged across to the counter-flap, employed an elbow as a prop, and contemplated my handbag. 'Delicacy,' he volunteered, 'happens to be another of our specialities. How about a word with the Lieutenant? Nice, understanding guy, lots of experience . . .'

'Look,' I interrupted. 'When I ask to speak with the Chief, it doesn't mean I'm interested in deputy assistant intermediaries. This is important.'

Doubt flickered in the young detective's eyes. I followed up instantly. 'Five minutes. That's all I'm asking. I'm a very succinct lady. I've no time of my own to chuck around, and I don't make a habit of wasting other people's.'

'Is it a felony you want to report?'

I closed one eye. 'Could amount to more than that.'

'Reservation of information's an indictable – '

'Who's hiding anything? I'm requesting to be permitted to tell the Chief.'

He blinked. 'Hold it a second, will you?'

He went and whispered to a colleague. The pair of them considered me. Rising, the second man crossed the room to an inner office with tinted windows, emerging shortly to resume his seat and his coffee-intake. Before long, a stocky individual of about fifty followed him out, drifted my way, stationed himself at the flap and gave me a tired but seemingly genuine half-grin.

'Lieutenant Podolski. Hear you've some information for us?'

'For the Chief of Detectives,' I said firmly.

He exchanged glances with his lean subordinate, lolling nearby. 'It'll get right to him.'

'Sure it will. Direct from me.'

He said patiently, 'Know how many people we get in here? Dozens in a morning. If we let everyone talk to the Chief – '

'I'm one person. Putting in a special request.'

'If you could give me an idea what it's about . . .

'Yeah. That'd be nice. Too bad I can't.'

In a faintly hysterical way I was starting to enjoy it.

The persona of an obdurate brunette was taking me over. I was almost disappointed when he uncoiled, said mildly, 'I'll see what I can manage,' and returned in a stealthy leonine lope to his tinted office. The young detective edged closer.

'Will you at least give me your name, Miss . . .?'

'Jameson. *Mrs* Martha Jameson.'

'Address?'

I gave him a fictitious one in the district where I had first occupied an apartment. He noted it carefully on a jottings block.

'You're getting five-star treatment already, you know that? The Lieutenant's pretty busy himself.'

'I want to save him trouble, don't I?'

'Chief Meredith's practically never available. We have to – '

'Who?'

His head jerked at my tone. 'I'm talking about the Chief. Normally he's not – '

'What did you say his name is?'

'Meredith.'

'It's Chief Jansen I want to see.'

'He retired,' he said simply.

'Oh God.' It was no longer necessary to act. 'How long back?'

'Six months. Seven, maybe.' His eyes narrowed. 'This a personal matter?'

'You could say that.' I thought frantically. 'Any idea where he is now?'

'Taking things easy some place, I guess. Look, Mrs Jameson, if you have information that's relevant to our operations, I have to point out to you – '

'I never said it was.' A note of Englishness had nudged its way into my voice; he gave me a keen look. I hardened my accent and manner. 'Candidly, it's no concern of anyone's outside of him and me . . . and it isn't what you're thinking, either, so you can scrape that look off your face.'

'I was just paying attention,' he objected.

'I bet. Well anyhow, this successor of his, this Meredith – he's no use to me. I needn't bother him. How do I go about finding Chief Jansen's current whereabouts?'

At this moment Lieutenant Podolski returned, arms hanging slackly. He said, 'Before the Chief'll see you, he has to know – '

The young detective interceded. 'Lady's changed her mind, Lieutenant. It's the Chief's predecessor she wants. Jansen.'

'Uh-huh?' The Lieutenant's survey was like the scratch of razor-blades. There was a pause. 'So this in your opinion does not rank as a current police matter, Miss...?'

'*Mrs* Jameson. I was saying, it's private business. I just want to contact him, that's all. How do I do that?'

The expression of Lieutenant Podolski was transparent. Jansen . . . Jameson . . . he was coupling the names, estimating their possible significance. Picking his phrases, he said, 'I wouldn't want to intrude on anyone's privacy, but you have to appreciate my position, Mrs . . . ah . . . Jameson. The ex-Chief of Detectives is now in retirement at – at his home. And I guess he has the right to select his callers. Unless you can – '

'His home. Is it here in LA?'

'It's within the area,' he conceded.

'Then I can trace him anyhow. Eventually. It would save me a heap of trouble if you could give me his address. Or phone number.'

The Lieutenant inflated his cheeks. 'Guess there'd be no harm in me calling him . . .'

'I'd rather do that myself.'

His head shook. 'Sorry.'

'Afraid I might be setting him up for something?'

'It's a thing I have to take into account,' he said calmly. 'Cops make enemies while they're in office: it's inevitable. Which is why they don't exactly scamper to have their phone numbers listed.'

He looked and sounded immovable. He was my one hope: I had to compromise. I flapped a hand.

'Okay. If you could talk to him on my behalf, I'd surely appreciate it. A brief word with him – that's all I want. Tell him . . .' I flogged my brain. 'Tell him it's a lady about a film part and a twenty-thousand-dollar offer.'

His eyebrows lifted. He seemed inclined to say something else, but instead turned and headed back towards his sanctum. The young detective eyed me with frank interest.

'Sounds intriguing, Mrs Jameson.'

'It was meant to.'

After a moment he returned to his desk. Extracting the paper from his machine, he scanned what he had typed. I waited, wondering whether Chief Jansen would be acute enough, long-memoried enough to make the connection; and fascinated enough to follow it up. Five years was half a decade. The name Mrs Jameson would mean nothing to him. Twenty thousand dollars, I hoped, might. The chance was slim, bordering on emaciation: but nothing fleshier lay to hand. Of all the eventualities I had tried to foresee, the possibility that the post of Chief might have changed hands had not occurred to me.

The youngster glanced across. 'Care for some coffee while you're waiting?'

Suddenly too weary to muster an ounce of common politeness, I shook my head. He took no offence. Probably he was used to a great deal worse. Drunks, junkies, psychopaths . . . he must see it all. I gazed around. From the far side of the room, a coloured detective was observing me thoughtfully; as our eyes clashed he didn't look away but remained in contemplation. Perhaps matching me with some mental file copy. Theoretically I was not on record anywhere, unless Jansen had played it both ways. The thought struck me that the coloured detective, having seen through my disguise to the Anjelica Browne that lay beneath, was awaiting the moment of maximum drama before publicizing his knowledge. With a casual movement I turned away.

Lieutenant Podolski came back. He said without pre-
amble, 'He'll talk to you, Mrs Jameson. Phone's right this
way.'

Dismayed, I said, 'Oh, but – '

He added patiently, 'You can have my office to yourself. I've plenty to see to out here.'

The coloured detective watched me broodingly into the
office. The Lieutenant shut the door from the outside. As
I picked up the receiver I saw him drag out a file cabinet
drawer near the glazed partition, pick out a document,
start to peruse it, leaning negligently against the wall in a
position from which the corner of his left eye could catch
every movement I made. Ostentatiously I perched myself against the edge of his desk with my free hand clasping my other arm. I spoke clearly, but softly.

'Mr Jansen?'

'Who's this?'

'I can't say much, but it's vital that I come to see
you . . .'

'Who is it?'

The voice was testy, somewhat weak. A prong of doubt
pierced me. Had I confused the names? In so short a
space of time, there could hardly have been two Chief
Jansens. I proceeded cautiously. 'The name I gave the
Lieutenant was Mrs Jameson, but actually . . . Does the
name Browne mean anything to you?' No reply.
'Anjelica Browne, then?'

I waited for him to say 'No, it doesn't' and hang up.
Waited for a circumspect 'It might . . . it all depends.' I
was unprepared for the words that ended the pause.

'The screen actress? Are you kidding? Am I speaking
to Miss Browne?'

'She'd like to talk to you,' I told him, purposely non-
committal.

'What d'you know?' It sounded as though he was
thinking about it. I could hear the sound of laboured
breathing. 'When?'

'Sooner the better.' I hesitated: it had to be asked. 'This is the Chief Jansen who was here about five years ago?'

A distant chuckle rolled into my ears. 'The same. And I may not be much, these days, but I do have a darn good memory.'

I inhaled deeply. 'Can you give me your address?'

Before collecting the Oldsmobile from the garage where I had stacked it, I found a hamburger stall and swallowed a few mouthfuls of food; not because I wanted it, but because commonsense informed me that without solid intake of some kind I should not keep going for more than another hour.

Enticingly close to the stall stood a callbox. The urge to put in a transatlantic call to Hampshire, to learn the latest developments, was hard to combat: but I won the fight. There wasn't time.

Although the Lieutenant had been obliging enough to lead me to a wall-chart, upon which I had traced the route that would take me to Jansen's retirement home in Beverley Hills, it was turned two o'clock before I had freed myself and the car from the stranglehold of the city centre and aimed us in the right direction. There had been one or two heart-stopping moments at intersections, but I had come through without a ticket. And, to the best of my judgement, without a tail. Curiosity had shown itself on the features of the young detective as I left. I pictured him and the Lieutenant getting together, discussing me, debating the wisdom of keeping tabs on this mystery brunette with an apparent hold over an ex-Chief of Detectives; having my progress logged. How would they go about it? In such matters I was less than a novice. The drama of an old-fashioned chase was one they would doubtless wish to avoid. In real life, car pursuits tended to work out less neatly than they did on screen: it was a favourite wry observation of Herbie's.

The district I wanted was plainly signposted, as the

Lieutenant had declared it would be. Here, the highway broadened and quietened; the residential properties laid themselves back behind screens of giant palms and eucalyptus and banks of vivid blooms. Anyone who made it to this place hadn't done badly for himself. Oddly, it was my first visit. At an early stage of our marriage, Terry and I had given vague consideration to the idea of buying ourselves a base in the area, superstar-style; but nothing had ever come of it.

Hilltop Boulevard. Fifth house along. Single-storey, with a full-width veranda and roof-tiles of a dull orange, it sprawled beyond clumps of exotic shrubs and an expanse of lawn, upon which two sprinklers were in docile rotation. On the driveway sat a silver-grey Buick with a soft top, its prow nuzzling a garage door. Nudging the Oldsmobile against the kerb, I switched off and climbed out stiffly.

Solid stone steps took me up to the veranda. I pressed the buzzer. From here, the sheer peaceful luxuriance of the locality could be taken in, marvelled at: if sunlight battling through foliage in a healing stillness was one's notion of ultimate attainment, there was no need to travel farther. Even the door-handles were made anti-rattle. I was not aware that my buzz had been answered until the woman coughed.

'You'll be Mrs Jameson. He's expecting you. Will you step right inside?'

She was the mother-image from Stage Nine, even to the steel-wire hair parted down the centre and swept behind her ears. There was a kind of half-whimsical severity about the look she fastened upon me as I followed her into a spacious, modernistically-furnished living-room dominated by a built-in TV screen of epic scale at one end, alongside a chromium cocktail bar that looked as unused as the day it had been installed. She said, 'Is there something I can fetch you? Coffee, maybe?'

My ill-digested hamburger rose to reply. 'I don't suppose it's possible to have some tea?'

'Sure.' Her whimsicality gained the upper hand. 'Cream or lemon?'

'Either would be fine. Pardon me, but you're Mrs Jansen?'

She exploded quietly into a chuckle. 'Not this lady, honey, the good Lord be thanked. I just . . . watch over him, you might say. The monthly salary cheques make it worth my while. More or less.' She led me across a snow-field of white carpeting to a distant door. 'Step right through, he's waiting. I'll be right back.'

I expected to walk into a study, strewn with documents, dictaphones whirring, memoirs being recorded. I didn't expect to find myself in a bedroom. It was large, furnished and decorated with the same grandiloquence as the living-room: the outer wall consisted entirely of glazed sliding doors commanding a view of palms and hibiscus. There was a loitering stench of tobacco-smoke. The man propped against pillows on the double-bed with a quilted head-board surveyed my hesitancy with an air of grim amuse-ment. His appearance awakened few echoes. While I could not positively have denied that he was the person I had last spoken to five years previously in a fifth-floor room of police headquarters, equally I could not have sworn that he was the same man.

'My apologies, Mrs Jameson, for receiving you from – what shall I say? – an unorthodox posture. Happens to be one of my less-oxygenated days. Take a seat, won't you.'

His voice had lifted slightly on the 'Mrs Jameson'. Poising myself on the brink of a low-slung chair at his bedside, I decided to waste no time.

'You know who I really am, of course.'

'Well, now. Could this be intended as some kind of a riddle?'

I glanced at the door. Swiftly removing the wig, I gave him a second or two to study me before replacing it. He made no comment. I rested my forearms along the sides of the chair.

'I don't know whether you follow the movies . . .'

'When you've difficulty in getting about,' he said gravely, 'you find they have to follow you.' He nodded towards another mammoth TV screen on the wall facing his bed. 'Load of crap, mostly – but they did show a couple of your early ones. Liked 'em both. Also I read the personality columns.'

'So you deduced it was me when I phoned?'

His mouth twisted. 'These days, people don't call me to offer – how was it again? – twenty grand for a walk-on part in a cops' commercial.'

'I'm sorry you're not well.'

He shrugged. 'At least I suffer in luxury. Did okay for myself while I had the chance. Now I'm paying for the questionable habits I picked up as a result.' He tapped his chest significantly. 'Oxygen cylinders help in the later stages, they tell me. I'm looking ahead to that. Something I can be doing for you, Miss Browne?'

'I'm hoping so. I've taken a quick flip over here from England, on the off-chance.'

'To see me?' he said ironically. 'Now that's nice. What do I have that other guys don't?'

'Some knowledge. About something terribly important to me . . . and others.'

He regarded me without expression.

'You want to know,' he said at last, 'if a certain Chief of Detectives ever flapped his great mouth in places where – '

The door bounced open to admit the mother-figure behind a small, oval, silver-plated tray bearing all the trappings of afternoon tea in the Cotswolds: milk and water jugs in stainless steel, a fat little floral teapot, a cup and saucer in bone china, a plate of assorted biscuits. Depositing it on the bed, my side, she said, 'Mind how you waggle your big feet, Chief,' flung me a woman-to-woman grimace, and departed, clumping the door with some finality into its frame behind her.

Rising, I said awkwardly, 'I thought she was just

bringing me a glass of something. There's only the one cup, but if you'd care to – '

'Thanks. Not for me.'

He gazed past me through the glass doors while I poured myself a little of the scented brew, discoloured it with cream, selected a shortcake biscuit. The names 'Huntley and Palmer' were etched into the texture. I sat back. Jansen went into a series of low coughs that rocked the mattress, spilling things into the tray. I felt shy of putting out a hand to steady it. When he was silent again, I carpeted the cup and saucer.

'I wasn't worried about you keeping your side of our bargain.'

He waited politely.

'You dealt, didn't you, with my husband-to-be? Terry O'Malley. He told me afterwards that he'd taken the – the material away and made a bonfire of it. I'd no reason to doubt him at the time.'

His face betrayed nothing. He seemed to be doing his best to suppress another bout of coughing.

'Thinking about it since . . .' I choked over a biscuit crumb. He seized the opportunity to cough himself. 'I've come to realize that it probably didn't happen just like that. I mean, it's hardly likely you'd have passed the stuff over to him for disposal. You'd have wanted to see to it yourself.'

I paused hopefully. His gaze was unblinking.

When he said nothing, I struggled on. 'What I'm wondering is, can you confirm that to me? It would be useful to know.'

The mattress heaved as he changed position. His hands went behind his head as he pondered the opposite wall. By comparison with when I had last seen him, his face was gaunt; what I could see of his body was similarly reduced. But elements remained of the official menace, the reek of corruption. Amalgamated with the vulnerability of a sick man, it added up to some weird chemistry.

Eventually he spoke. 'Mr O'Malley being bothersome?'

'I simply want to know – '

'Miss Browne. You're speaking to an ex-cop – remember?'

I bowed my head. 'Sorry. Yes, he's making a lot of trouble. That's why I'm asking.'

'I have my position to protect,' he remarked.

'It would take me a while to raise cash. But I can give you a cheque, and you have my word – '

'That's not what I mean to imply. I've made all I want . . . more than I can use. What's the good of it now?' He said it on a purely practical note. 'What I do value, however, is the freedom to be sick in my own way. I wouldn't brook any interference with that.'

'You can't possibly imagine I'd let slip a word about the wretched business? I'd be sinking us both.'

He nodded slowly. 'Logical. I'm glad you see it that way.'

Silence took hold of the room. Returning the cup and saucer to the tray, I lowered the whole outfit to the floor; then sat again. Jansen's lips were moving slightly, as though he was conducting a debate with himself. Presently he recaptured me in his sights.

'Naturally I wouldn't have left it to O'Malley to carry out the disposal. Not for twenty grand.'

A tremor coursed through me. 'So he *didn't* take them away to burn?'

'Nope.'

'You destroyed the evidence yourself?'

'I retained the evidence.'

'But Terry said – '

'The material stayed with me. On that occasion.'

I stared. 'What do you mean?'

He closed his eyes, evidently more from fatigue than from any wish to avoid mine. 'As I said, Miss Browne, I enjoyed those films of yours. You gave me a lot of pleasure. Me, and a billion others.'

'What does that have to do with anything?'

'Only that it makes me feel I'd like to help.' His eyes

remained shut. 'Listen, I'm past caring what in the hell anyone thinks of me. Some of that junk I stashed away here in my personal safe: the rest went back to Governor Mason. For a suitable fee. He was the coming man, even then. Scandal was something he couldn't afford not to spend his way out of. So I did okay. I also had the kudos for wrapping up the blackmailing racket. Bouquets all round.'

Jansen eased himself into a new position. 'Far as I was concerned, that was it. I'd had plenty out of it – I wasn't counting on more. Tell you the truth, after a while that trash left over in my safe out there kind of slid out of my mind. Until . . . oh, eight, nine months back, I guess it would be.'

'What happened then?'

'I had a second visit from your husband. As he still was at the time.'

I said steadily, 'What reason did he give for calling on you again?'

'He handed me this story. Said you appreciated – both of you – how I'd kept my trap shut on your behalf, only now that you were a big star you were anxious to plug any possible loopholes. He was authorized to make me a fresh offer for the remaining prints and negatives, so you could dispose of them yourself and know they were out of existence.'

'How much was he offering?'

'We settled on a hundred grand.'

I sat looking at him.

To my knowledge, Terry had not earned significant amounts for two years at least. And he had always spent as he had gone. I said, 'Did he have that kind of money?'

Jensen gestured. 'Cash on the nail.'

'You mean, you clinched the deal?'

Another shrug. 'I was coming up for premature retirement. Only paragons sniff at a fortune, and I never claimed to be one of them. As for the risk . . . I figured there wasn't much. After all, he was your husband. Even the gossip writers had you as the great loving twosome of all time. And his tale sounded plausible. You wanted things made tidy; you could afford to pay; why would I deny you that privilege?'

'I never knew a word about it.'

'So it now appears.' His eyes reopened to dart at me. 'That's all I can tell you. Any additional instalments, you'll have to get from him.'

'You know we're divorced?'

'I read that. It did get me wondering. Also I read about some recent shenanigans in London, when you and he clashed at a Press conference or some such. Frankly, I wasn't too startled to get your call today.'

He pulled himself higher in the bed. 'Okay, so I was a money-grabbing two-timer . . . but you know something? You make it too easy for us.'

CHAPTER XVII

DRIVING BACK TO the airport, I reviewed the state of the game.

The thing that stood out like a phosphorescent demon in a black forest was that Terry wasn't bluffing. He possessed the means to destroy me. The hypothesis I had come hoping to explode had instead been confirmed. The impact of the discovery had left me gasping, but at least I now knew where I stood. Uncertainty had never appealed to me. To hit back, one had to know the target.

The simple, obvious course was to do as Terry demanded and return to him. A cosmetic reconciliation, as mooted by Dilys, need not cause me irreparable harm. At best, it could provide a breathing space, an opportunity to provide some permanent alternative solution. A patch-up job was self-evidently the immediate answer.

Even while entertaining the possibility, I knew it wasn't on.

Terry was a malignancy I had cut out, got rid of. Who ever heard of a cancer victim inviting the tumour back?

A few miles from the airport, I observed a message chalked or painted on the blank wall of a factory building alongside the freeway. In monster letters it said *Conway's the Man*.

Only he wasn't, any more. The accepted view, just ahead of the Republican Convention, was that Conway had 'shown' three months too soon. His campaign had run out of steam. Governor Mason was the man. The Presidential white hope from the Middle West. Darling of the hawks. Bastion of family values. Stern; upright; incorruptible. The guy to stand up to the trendies. Weary of liberalism, the story went, the American people craved nothing more than the iron glove enclosing the brass fist. The Republicans considered they had one, uplifted and waiting.

By common consent, the Convention would amount to no more than a formality. Once nominated, Governor Mason need merely cruise gently to make harbour in the White House. Then – look out, Eastern Bloc! Watch your step, Third World! No more nonsense. A tight grip on the tiller. No deflexions from course. A foreign policy that put American and her allies first, carried through by a man in whom the common folk could place their trust. A family man. Guardian of the basic virtues. The guy the hatchet journalists had never been able to touch.

I was driving, I found, well above the limit. Unconsciously my foot had rammed down, taking me away at increasing speed from that sad, outdated slogan scripted by a Conway supporter. I eased back. With an eight-cylinder thrust beneath one's toe, resentment could be a killer. And I didn't want to kill. I wanted to get to a telephone and talk to Herbie.

'No trace of 'em, honey, as yet. I'll be back on the trail, first thing.'

'We're running short of time.'

'I know that. How'd you make out with Jansen?'

'Terry has the negatives.'

'Okay.' Herbie's response, delayed, seemed to come with an effort. 'So we know what we're up against. What time's your flight?'

'Eight-thirty. Which means I don't get in to Heathrow till about five tomorrow afternoon – London time. That's Saturday, isn't it?'

'Saturday's right. Stay cool, Angel. We've several – '

'I'm thinking about the deadline.'

'We'll beat O'Malley to it.'

'How? Only by finding him. And then either buying him off, somehow, or . . .'

'Or dealing direct with Moorforth.'

'Herbie, we can't. Even if Moorforth was open to a bribe, which I doubt, Terry would simply take the negatives elsewhere. He's got the whole of Fleet Street to choose from. He can just pick his time. There's only one final answer, and that's to get those negatives away from him. Once and for all.'

Across the Atlantic, there was a brief silence.

'You still don't want the cops brought in?'

'It's too chancy. The more people involved, the more risk of exposure. That's how I see it.' I leaned upon the telephone stand, wondering whether my curdled brain was producing sound sense or lunacy. Herbie made no comment. I added, 'Are my parents bearing up?'

'Pretty well.'

'They haven't mentioned the police again?'

'Your Mum keeps saying Liz is a sensible girl who can look after herself. That is, she was saying that, up until hitting the hay a few hours back with one of Dilys's tranquillizers. As for your Dad . . .' Herbie paused. 'Quiet sort of a guy, I guess you'd call him. Hasn't said a lot. Just stays put in an armchair right here in the lounge, case your sister shows up.'

'Dad never talks much.' I pictured his small figure,

embedded in cushions, waiting in the frigid environment
of The Beeches for the impetuous rush that would be Liz
returning. 'What time is it there, Herbie?'

'Three a.m. I got back from Winchester around midnight, then stood by for your call. Come daybreak, I'll be
off to London. Try a few places that occur to me. If your
parents want to come along, they're welcome.'

'I owe you so much . . .'

'Only thing you owe me, Angel, is your own peace of
mind. That'll do wonders for mine. Listen: whatever
transpires, I'll be at the airport to meet you off the plane.
Then our next step can be a joint one. Okay?'

'Herbie, you're a lamb. I'm so sorry. What a *mess*. I
can hardly think, I feel so done up . . .'

'Try to get some sleep on the flight. This is going to work
out. I've fought worse than O'Malley. He's nothing. If
he refuses to co-operate, he'll have to bear the conse-
quences.'

'Remind me to thank you properly some time. See you
tomorrow – Heathrow. Today, where you're concerned.
Is that right? I'm all confused. 'Bye for now.'

After hanging up, I headed for the airport restaurant.
The thought of food made my stomach turn, but without it,
I knew, my endurance would pass its limit. I was given
a table commanding a view of the main runway, and for
a while I sat there in a kind of dream – a daydream –
watching the ceaseless leaps and bellyflops of the jets,
remotely conscious of their unending screams. For the
moment, there was no hurry. My flight would not be
called for hours. I ordered haphazardly from the menu,
and was surprised to be brought soup. The process of
sipping it required a little attention, and it was then that
my telephone dialogue with Herbie began to play itself
back through my mind. His closing remark, in retrospect,
was cryptic. I wondered what, precisely, he had meant by
it.

CHAPTER XVIII

A MOTIONLESS but penetrative mist had Heathrow in its grasp. Our touchdown was a little early, and so I was not too perturbed at finding no Herbie awaiting me. Clearly he had been delayed. I hoped that it was by something constructive. I was badly in need of some good news.

Travellers came and went. On the far side of the arrivals hall a photographer was hovering, holding what was evidently a passenger list and scanning the passing faces. If my luck, and my wig, held firm, he would read nothing into Mrs Jameson of Reigate, Surrey; and I trusted the passport and immigration officials to maintain the inscrutability that had eased my anonymous passage in both directions so far. Waiting in a squeaky leather chair alongside a table upon which somebody had left, apparently the previous day, a cup brimful of coffee that was now pale-grey sludge, I took another codeine tablet. Its predecessors had had no effect upon the headache, a thing of steel hoops and clamps about my scalp: four or five at a gulp might have achieved something, but fear of a complete mental shutdown deterred me from experimenting.

At five-fifteen I was on my feet, pacing.

If Herbie for some reason had been unable to make it, surely he would have sent word? There had been no message, the Enquiries desk told me, for a Mrs Jameson. Nor for a Miss Browne. A tour of the concourse showed me a number of craggy heads with bald cranial patches: all belonged to strangers. Finding a vacant telephone, I dialled The Beeches, holding on until a wintry voice informed me that she was The Beeches.

'Is that Mrs Emmerson? Anjelica Browne speaking. Mr Joseph isn't there, by any chance?'

The ice thawed to frost. 'Mr Joseph hasn't been here all

day. He left early this morning and hasn't returned.'
'I see. Thank you. What about Dilys Meridew?'
'She isn't here either.'
I leaned on a directory. 'I'm awfully sorry to trouble you, Mrs Emmerson, but . . . would it be possible for me to talk to Mr Baxter? If he's around. It's rather important.'
The frost underwent a final reluctant transmutation into thin slush. 'I'll see if I can find him for you.'
Minutes elapsed. Cloudily I wondered what this trip, one way and another, was costing me. It didn't matter, but it was a way of passing the time. Denny's voice pulsed into my left ear. 'Anjie? What's the problem?'
'Where do you want me to start?' I clawed at the essentials. 'I'm at Heathrow, waiting for Herbie. He was supposed to meet me. He hasn't contacted you – or anybody?'
'Haven't seen him since yesterday. Rumour has it he left here with your parents at first light this morning and they were heading Londonwards. Actually I've only just got in myself. Had some calls to make. Any news of your sister?'
'Until I see Herbie, I shan't know. Thanks, Denny. How did shooting – '
'Get yourself organized, love. We can talk shop later. Best of luck.'
A fierce effort of memory failed to present me with the number of Mrs Cornfeld in Eastern Gardens. Directory Enquiries took four minutes to look it up. Having dialled it, I listened to the ringing tone for an eternity: at the instant I was hanging up, she answered. I said, 'Oh, Mrs Cornfeld – it's Anjie Browne. Sorry to be a nuisance, but do you think you could fetch Mum or Dad? If they're at home.'
'Certainly, pet. I think your Mum's in. How's tricks?'
'Fine.'
'Picture coming along all right?'
Strenuously I breathed in. 'Super.'

'That's good. Hang on, duck, I'll fetch her.'

At another time, I should probably have been relieved and amused that she still spoke to me as though I were the tomboy gangleader of West Ham. Waiting, I stared across the concourse in case the figure of Herbie should appear. By the look of it, four more jumbos had landed. The blur of faces was dizzying. Mum's voice came on, noticeably less metallic than usual.

'Anjie? Any news?'

'I was hoping you might have some. I've just got in . . .' I stopped myself. 'I was supposed to meet Herbie at five, but he hasn't turned up. Have you heard from him at all?'

'Not since this morning. He dumped us here about ten o'clock and went off. Said he was going to try at a few hotels, in case they . . . Where'd you get to, Anjie, all this time?'

'Searching for Liz,' I said vaguely. 'Same as everyone else.'

'I expect we're all making too much fuss. I mean . . . he wouldn't dare *do* anything, would he?'

'Of course not.' Hurriedly I added, 'Just the same, it's best if we get Liz away from his influence. She could land herself in trouble.'

An untypical silence from the other end indicated that Mum was cogitating. Presently she said, 'Shouldn't we notify the police, then?'

'Not yet. If we can find them ourselves, the whole thing can be settled without any fuss.'

'That's what Mr Joseph was saying. Dad reckons he's wrong.'

'How is Dad?'

'There again, I've not seen him since lunch. He went out.'

'Out?'

'With that look on his face that he gets sometimes. He's not been back.'

'Where was he making for?'

'I think he'd some idea of helping Mr Joseph call at the

hotels. Though seeing as we don't know which places Mr Joseph was trying and which he wasn't, I can't see he was going to do much good. But then he couldn't just sit here at home, twiddling his thumbs. He had to be doing something.'

'Yes. Well, Mum, you'd better stop around for the time being, anyhow. Liz might try to phone. I'll be in touch.'

'Where is it you're ringing from?'

'West London,' I said truthfully. Before she could insist that I spend the night at home, I went on, 'There's a number of places I have to try, so I'll hang up now and get cracking. Probably stay overnight in Town. 'Bye for the moment.'

Mum was still talking when I cut her off. Slumped against the side of the callbox, I tried to formulate a plan. When my brain withheld its co-operation, I did what I had always done at airports: I went and found a taxi and told the driver to take me into the city. In this case, to the West End. As we drove out to join the motorway I kept watch for Herbie's car: it was now nearly six o'clock and there had still been no sign of him when I left the arrivals hall. I couldn't help feeling that he had let me down.

Settled into his traffic lane, the driver addressed me across a shoulder. 'Anywhere in particular, lady?'

I reached a sudden decision. 'Make it the Cosmopole, will you?'

The reception clerk's scrutiny was impersonal.

'Just for the one night, madam?'

His thumb slid down the page. On impulse I said, 'The penthouse suite overlooking the Park . . . that's not available, I suppose?'

His appraisal became careful, taking in my solitary hand-case. 'We've had the pleasure of accommodating you before?'

'Some while back.'

'Delighted to welcome you again, madam. Suite Two is occupied, I'm afraid. Suite Five . . . would that do instead? No view of the Park, but a good sweep across London.'

'Fine. I'll settle for that.'

'You have some luggage outside?'

'No. I travel light.'

Having signed Mrs Jameson of Reigate into the register, I followed the porter to the lift, responding mechanically to his remarks concerning the English climate as we ascended. While he was unlocking the door to Suite Five, I glanced down the corridor. The door to Suite Two, formerly occupied by superstar Anjie Browne, presented an inscrutable face from a distance of twenty yards. Inside the suite, I let the porter go through the fussy motions of arranging my hand-case in the exact centre of the luggage stand and swishing curtains together, before handing him a tip of a magnitude that would have aroused comment in Las Vegas. He took it without a flicker.

'Thank you very much, ma'am. Will there be anything else?'

'Just a small matter. Can you, by any chance, tell me who's in Suite Two?'

He said with butlerian gravity, 'I'll instigate a few enquiries, ma'am. And call back.'

When he had gone, I sat on the arm of a basket-chair and asked myself what had prompted the query. Logic? Intuition? A stubborn refusal to ignore a possibility? Four years is a brief life for a marriage, but it had been enough to give me a dusting of insight into the mechanism that made Terry tick; the eccentricities of its design. If Terry felt that there might be a poetic irony in the installation of himself and Anjie Browne's sister inside rooms recently inhabited at vast expense by Anjie Browne, there was nothing in his make-up that would deter him from the venture: indeed, every working part would insist that he embarked upon it. Desperate as I now was for sleep, I knew that none would be possible until the check had been made.

Presently there was a discreet rap on the door. I dragged myself across. The porter spoke in a deferential murmur.

'There's a married couple in Suite Two, ma'am. Booked in as Colonel and Mrs Filbright of California, USA.'

'Thank you,' I said. 'I'm much obliged to you.'

Coiling a fist about his second gratuity, he padded away. I closed the door, stood motionless with my spine against the panels.

Filbright of California. The choice of name, to say nothing of military rank, was typical of the O'Malley sense of humour. Filbright had been the maiden name of his mother. And it was supposed to have been a colonel in the US Army who was responsible for the unwanted birth of Terry. The lack of enthusiasm created by the infant's arrival was something that its adult version had never wearied of explaining to me; and that had lost all interest for me after the third repetition. Suddenly, my interest was quickened to flashpoint. I sat down again to think it through.

Had he *wanted* me to track them down? So that on his own ground, with Liz at his side, he could dictate terms? Impractical or not, such a strategy would appeal to him.

The next move was up to me.

Twenty minutes limped past while I tried to assess the probabilities. Could I seize the initiative? How would Liz react? My brain circled. I needed help, and none was to hand. To a greater degree than ever before, I was on my own, forced to fight my way from a base of exhaustion towards an objective blanketed by dense fog. I stood, sat again, rose a second time, impelled myself to the door, let myself out. For seconds on end I stood in the quiet corridor, telling myself to proceed. The distant clash of a lift door provided the impetus I needed. With a jerk, I was moving. I was facing the door to Suite Two. Tapping its woodwork. Smartly. Three times.

The absence of a response was somehow a relief. For the moment, anyhow, it lifted responsibility from my shoulders. From habit, I tried the door-handle: it dropped under my weight. The door swung inwards.

Off-balance, I was carried into the room. Pulling up, I stared around.

Nobody was there. Every light was on: the door to the bedroom stood wide open. The heating seemed to be at full blast. Unthinkingly I pushed the door to the corridor so that it closed behind me. The thud of contact made me jump. It caused no other disturbance.

Although there were obvious signs that the place was in use, at first I recognized nothing. Had I slipped up badly? At any moment, a genuine Colonel and Mrs Filbright of California might erupt from the bedroom to demand what the hell I thought I was doing. Then I noticed the suit-case.

It stood, hasps unfastened, on a hard-backed chair next to the couch. The last time I had seen it was in room 17 at The Beeches. The sight of it made my vitals lurch. From the centre of the room, to which I had advanced, there were partial views of bedroom and connecting bathroom. I coughed. By now it seemed unquestionable that I was alone; and yet . . . I took in a difficult breath.

'Liz? Terry?'

Small, important details pressed their attentions upon me. The magazine for teenagers, folded on the writing desk. Holding it down, a feminine hairbrush, gilt-backed. Partly beneath the desk, a pair of slender, wedge-heeled shoes, unmarked, patently new. Nearby, propped against the base of the wall, a plastic carrier bore the Debenham's label: from its neck protruded an end of what looked like folded silk pyjamas in a Polythene wrapping. As I started to move across to investigate more closely, something beyond the open bedroom door caught my eye.

It lay by itself on the deep-pile mauve carpeting: a single shoe, modest in size, ornate in design, but unmistakably masculine. On its side, as though it had been dropped. Or kicked.

There was one other sign of disorder. The brass lampstand, I could see as I approached the doorway, lay horizontally across the polished surface of the dressing table, its bulb shattered, the flex in coils on the floor beneath.

Someone had been careless. It began to look as though a hurried departure had occurred, which in turn would suggest something else: that my arrival had been spotted and that the subsequent half-hour delay of hesitation had been exploited. Terry had no wish, then, to meet me head-on at this stage. He was keeping me guessing. Wondering, perhaps, whether he was already on his way, with a package, to the offices of the *Sunday World* and Nigel Moorforth; or had long since arrived to cast the die. Or whether he had other plans. Toying with me. Terry to the fingertips. And Liz? Where did she slot in?

One way or another, obviously they had left. I went through into the bedroom.

Terry's eyes were open and fixed upon me, but he made no movement of recognition. This, initially, I took to be a part of his psychological programme: then the answer came to me. He was drunk. Too often I had seen him like that, spreadeagled on a bed, pupils bulging, paralysis locking his limbs. It was like a quick flip backwards in time. Next to his head, the bed-cover was stained; the colour looked darker than whisky. A liqueur of some kind, perhaps. On a jag, Terry wasn't particular. I walked around the bed to find the bottle.

From there, I had an unimpeded view of the top of his skull.

Back in the main room, lifting the receiver, I felt calm. Again, it was like a scene I had played often: meticulously rehearsed, smooth-flowing, certain of respectful attention from an unseen audience that knew it was witnessing a classic. The lines came readily.

'Could I please speak to the manager?' No problem with the voice. Low, controlled, distinct. 'There's been an accident. I think somebody's dead.'

CHAPTER XIX

'LET ME GET this absolutely straight,' requested the Chief Superintendent. 'You booked into the hotel in disguise, and under another name . . .'

'To avoid publicity.'

'You knew Mr O'Malley was here?'

'Why else would I have come?'

'And you wanted to "have it out with him".' The flesh encircling his eyes puckered in perplexity. 'Was it necessary to book this entire suite to do that?'

'As I've said, I intended staying the night, whatever happened. I felt too tired to travel back to Hampshire this evening.'

Chief Superintendent Kaynes – he had spelt it out to me – tossed a glance in the direction of his inspector, who fielded it deftly. The plain message needed no spelling out. Each of them took another look around the suite's main room, as though evaluating its appointments, before Kaynes, urbane as ever, returned to me.

'So then, you called upon Mr O'Malley and proceeded to, um, put your case?'

'Try to clarify matters. Yes.'

'Something you'd had one or two previous shots at?'

'A number.'

'He'd been pestering you?'

I nodded. Kaynes frowned again. 'But there you were, filming down in Hampshire: and here he was, staying in a Park Lane hotel. With another woman.'

'Up until a few days ago, he was in Hampshire with us.

Coming here with someone else – that was just showing off. Another way of getting at me.'

'All right. You followed him here, then, to try to thrash things out.' Kaynes pondered. 'Where was his other young lady at the time?'

'He said she'd walked out on him. Which didn't astound me.'

'So when you turned up, he was alone?'

'Yes. Changing to go out.'

'And you talked?'

'We spoke.'

'But you got nowhere?'

'With Terry, there was never anywhere to get. As far as he was concerned, I still belonged to him and always would. He made that very plain.'

'While you, for your part, wanted nothing more to do with him?'

'I'd said so – consistently. In private and in public. The Press have carried stories about it.'

'The chat columns,' Kaynes said solemnly, 'don't entirely escape the notice of the police, Miss Browne.'

Adjusting his position on the luggage stand which he was employing as a seat, he folded his arms, rested his head against the wall. 'So what then?'

'As I told you, I lost my temper. We both did.'

'Who lost theirs first?'

'I wasn't making notes at the time,' I said coldly. 'All I know is, our voices started to rise, as they generally did when we went through the farce of discussing things, until finally . . . It's a bit hazy, to be honest. Terry . . . O'Malley slapped my face: I remember that. It made me dizzy. I had the impression he was coming at me.'

'And was he?'

'I can't say. Not for certain. He was definitely on his feet. He had a shoe in one hand – '

'Which hand?'

'His right,' I said without hesitation. 'He was clutching it by the heel. From the way he was standing, I concluded he was about to hurl it at me. It wouldn't have been the first time. I stepped back a few paces and bumped up against the dressing table. Something on it started rocking, so I automatically grabbed at it.'

'What was it?'

'The lampstand. That brass thing without a shade.'

'Tell me what happened then.' There was a sing-song quality to Kaynes's voice. His eyes were half-shut; he was rocking himself gently.

'Well . . . I had it in my hand. My right hand. I must have looked menacing or something – anyhow he leapt at me, intending to snatch it away presumably, but in a fright I brought it across and as luck would have it I caught him fair and square. He was coming forward at the time, so of course the momentum . . .'

The Chief Superintendent said non-committally, 'And then?'

'I think I must have panicked altogether. I lashed out again, and then I saw the blood. That was after he'd fallen back across the bed. I stood staring at him for a while . . . I don't know how long. Then I tried for a closer look at him, but I couldn't. I guessed he was badly hurt. I dropped the lampstand, I think. Back on the dressing table. The next thing I remember is phoning for the manager. Then you came.'

Kaynes waited a few moments, as though expecting more. At length he nodded, opened his eyes.

'That's how it was. I see.'

'I never intended to kill him,' I said. 'The incident just . . . evolved. Out of nothing. I'm still in a daze about it.'

He gave me an agreeable smile. 'What wouldn't I give for as lucid an account as that from all my dazed clients.'

From the basket-chair, the creakings terminated as the inspector completed his shorthand notes. The room became silent.

'It accords,' Kaynes added conversationally, 'quite well with the scene of the, um, occurrence as we found it.'

The observation seemed to invite no comeback. I stayed unmoving in my armchair. My brain felt clear, vigilant.

'I wonder,' he mused, 'just what did become of Mr O'Malley's lady friend.'

'Perhaps she got tired of being pushed around.'

'He was the pushing type, your husband?'

'My ex-husband,' I corrected him. 'Let's say he liked his own way.'

Kaynes handed me another of his neutral looks. Presently he said, 'And we all know what that can mean. In an instance like this, the departure of someone who was so very fond of his own way might not necessarily arouse a great depth of emotion.'

I echoed his reasonable tone. 'There's no secret about it, Superintendent. Ask anybody. What with his childish demands and his persistence, he was starting to add up to a bit of a problem . . . so naturally, in a way I'm not sorry. To be rid of it, I mean. But death's another matter. I never wanted that.'

Rising a little stiffly, Kaynes trod through the carpet to join his inspector. He carried too much weight, I noticed. A well-cut suit could do no more than its best. Inclining himself with a hand noisily upon the back of the basket-chair, he murmured briefly. The inspector, a hollow-cheeked man in his early thirties with a habit of jerking his neck at disconcerting moments, flipped through some sheets of his notepad, murmured a few words back. Kaynes nodded. He looked across at me.

'Now here I'm in a slight difficulty. According to our information, you've been heard recently to voice exactly that desire.'

'Oh – the odd remark, maybe. The kind of thing every-one comes out with. Not to be taken literally.'

'*I wish he were dead. I really do.* I'm quoting,' Kaynes informed me, 'from a statement made to us half an hour ago by a staff member of this hotel. He says he overheard you say it in conversation with a friend during dinner here the Sunday before last.'

'My recollection of the wording is, *I wish he would die.* Not that it's important. I might have said something of the kind, yes. Haven't you, ever, about someone?'

'From the bell-hop,' he continued, 'who helps to attend to the needs of guests on this floor, we also have a statement. To the effect that about that time – possibly the same evening – he was bringing drinks to Suite Three when he heard sounds of an altercation from Suite Two. Then the door opened and Mr O'Malley came out. Your voice was heard to say, quite vigorously: *You cause any trouble and you'll be sorry. I'm warning you.* That,' Kaynes added without any change of emphasis, 'is understood to be an accurate replay of your words. Our informant swears by them.'

'Well, he's probably right. Terry was being particularly bothersome that evening. There's no knowing what I might have come out with.'

'Are you in the habit of expressing yourself so frankly?'

I spread my hands. 'Aren't most of us? At times? People in my profession, especially. We tend to speak our minds.'

'So it was in your mind?'

'Of course . . . in a way. A hypothetical way.'

The inspector's neck gave a twitch of particular violence. Kaynes stared at the carpet.

'Hypothetical or not, the remarks I've quoted do seem to have been the prelude to an actual event.'

'Unhappily, yes.'

The basket-chair protested under resettlement. Removing his hand from its back, Kaynes wandered across to the door to adopt an attitude of meditation, his back to the room. I busied my mind with an assessment of his age. Late forties, had been my first impression. Suddenly he looked older. The sag of the shoulders suggested more than half a century of experience, not all of it enriching. Still facing the door, he said, 'Is there anything we can fetch you, Miss Browne? Some refreshment? You've been helping us a fair time.'

After he had left the suite, the inspector and I ignored one another for a while. He seemed engrossed in his notes. At last I stood up.

'Mind if I have the TV on?'

'No, Miss Browne,' he said politely. 'That's quite all right.'

The ten o'clock news was well into its stride. A Middle East coup was threatening Western interests. In the States, prominent Republicans were urging decisive though unspecified action upon the President. A snatch of recorded interview with the leading hawk, Governor Mason, accompanied his picture on screen. I glanced away. A knockdown was one thing: kicks in the ribs as I lay gasping were something else. The inspector was watching the screen without expression. The voice of the newscaster returned. I looked back.

'Here at home, police are investigating the death at a London hotel of Terence O'Malley, the American star of such films as *Devil's Witness* and *Riders of the Dawn*. Earlier this evening, Mr O'Malley's body was discovered in a penthouse suite of the Cosmopole in Park Lane; he'd apparently received head injuries. A few minutes ago, a woman was understood to be still helping the police with their enquiries. Mr O'Malley's former wife, screen star Anjelica Browne, walked off the set of her new film two days ago after – '

Sound and vision were snapped off. The inspector returned lopingly to his basket-chair. Presently he caught my eye.

'There won't be anything fresh. At this stage.'

His neck twitched.

I leaned back into the cushions. 'If it's my feelings you're trying to protect, please don't trouble.'

He said nothing. I wanted urgently to avert a resumption of the silence. 'It's only natural for the media to take an interest. Terry was a big name . . . at one time. And anything affecting me is news, whether I like it or not. I expect the lobby downstairs is full of Pressmen.'

'It is,' he acknowledged.

'So what are they being told?'

'The essentials.'

'You're so close. You'd keep sealed lips if your grand-mother was being attacked by a . . .'

I slurred to a halt. It wasn't the optimum moment for antagonizing anybody. Gulping down the words, I substituted others. 'Not that I don't appreciate the reasons. You have to wait until the . . . until your en-quiries are complete. I do see that. But how long is it going to take?'

'That's for the Chief Superintendent to decide.'

'I really don't see why I have to be kept here like a prisoner.'

'From your own point of view, it's best that you stay out of reach for the time being.' A pause. 'Do you wish to contact your solicitor?'

The notion of contacting anyone had not occurred to me. My concentration had been at full stretch. The inspector's query opened up new lines of thought. After some hesitation I shook my head.

'There's only one person I'd really like to be in touch with. And I've no idea where he is.'

The door opened to readmit Kaynes, pursued by a uniformed constable holding a tray which, at his superior's signal, he lowered tenderly on to a small table. The tray held coffee and sandwiches. There were three cups. The constable retired, closing the door in silence, firmly. Kaynes reclaimed the luggage stand.

'Can I ask you to do the honours, Miss Browne?'

From the coffee-pot, I filled the three cups. I held up the cream-jug: both men nodded. Collecting their mixtures, the inspector handed one to his chief, with a sandwich, before falling upon his own share with a voraciousness that suggested unavoidable abstinence in the course of the previous twelve hours. Eyeing my cup with sudden abhorrence, I left it alone and once more sat back, trying not to look at either of them but acutely aware of the furtive chewing and sipping sounds associated with the civilized intake of nourishment that can deliver the listening outsider to the doors of distraction. My grip was starting to slip. I had passed beyond fatigue to an area of absolute calm, the eye of the hurricane; now, approaching the turbulence on the other side, I felt the tightening of apprehension; to surmount this new ordeal I should have to pillage reserves whose extent was an unknown factor. As though aware of this, the Chief Superintendent ate and drank with deliberation. Finishing one sandwich, he began on another. Between mouthfuls, coffee went down in tiny audible surges. He dabbed his lips fussily with a handkerchief. Dusted breadcrumbs from his lap. Stooped, at last, to deposit his cup and saucer on the carpet. It sank into the pile; from the saucer's rim a sepia stain leaked into the fabric. I was watching its progress when he spoke.

'I feel, you know, you've not been entirely frank with us.'

'In what way?' I asked.

'In most ways that are relevant.' With a finger, he worked surreptitiously at something wedged between his teeth. 'Let's take an example. According to you, it was half an hour or so after booking in here before you went along to see Mr O'Malley. Right?'

'About that.'

He regarded me broodingly. 'I think it was earlier. Much earlier. I think you came up here, incognito, *before* booking in. Had the scuffle with O'Malley, knocked him cold, and *then* presented yourself downstairs at reception to book a suite, pretending you'd just arrived.'

I shook my head with a pitying sadness. 'How could I have managed that? And supposing I had, what difference would it make?'

'It would make the vital difference of two or three hours. Which is the additional time, my surgeon tells me, that O'Malley had been dead.'

'Utter nonsense. I only landed at Heathrow just before five. You can check.'

'We're doing so.'

'Then how could I have had the row with Terry earlier?'

'Just what I ask myself.'

'Your surgeon could be wrong. Room temperature and suchlike can affect the symptoms, can't they?'

His brows arched, as though in faint applause. 'Perfectly true. I'm sure the surgeon will have borne those things in mind.'

'What are you saying, then? That I'm lying? What on earth would be the point of that?'

'One can only speculate,' he said composedly. 'I'm bound to say, Miss Browne, you've been most forthcoming about the incident itself. Why would you want to mislead us as to the time it occurred?'

He sat looking at me with the self-possession of a man who knew all the answers. Swiftly I cross-tracked.

'You're certainly on the ball. All right. I didn't want to make it seem premeditated. I did get here earlier, in fact. I came straight from the airport, arrived here about five-thirty and saw Terry by arrangement. I'd phoned him from the States.'

Kaynes's eyes glazed over. 'So the bust-up happened . . .?'

'Almost immediately. Then I rather lost my head. I couldn't think what to do. I thought I'd be accused of murder. So, to give myself time to think, I went back down to the lobby and showed myself at reception as if I'd just arrived and hadn't – '

'As Mrs Jameson?'

'Pardon? Oh yes. I'd kept the wig on the whole time. After I'd booked in, I was shown up here. That's when I spent nearly an hour thinking matters over before deciding that the only course was to raise the alarm and tell the truth.'

'It didn't occur to you simply to walk away and leave his death an unsolvable mystery?'

'No, it didn't. For one thing, I felt I had to go back and make sure he really was . . . gone. For another, I knew I could never get away with it. Fingerprints and everything. I'm pretty dumb about all that.'

'When you went back, you examined him closely?'

'No need. There was so much blood. And the way he was lying . . .'

'You'd seen a corpse before?'

I shook my head.

Kaynes waited while the inspector scratched and rustled his way to the end of his note. 'Tell me, Miss Browne. What made you take this hasty flip to Los Angeles?'

'Private business.'

He regarded me blandly. 'Having to do with Mr O'Malley, possibly?'

'It was, in fact. I needed to check with my lawyer that our divorce really was valid in most places. Terry was casting doubt.'

'Wouldn't a phone call to your lawyer have been enough?'

'I wanted to talk it right through with him. There were a number of related matters we had to discuss.'

'What was the verdict?'

'Verdict? Oh . . . he assured me the divorce was in order. And that Terry's lawyers were aware of it.'

Detaching himself from the luggage stand, Kaynes embarked upon a meditative amble to the centre of the room. Halting there, he pivoted.

'I'd have thought, in that case, you'd hardly have needed to come back here for a meeting with your in- disputably former husband to tell him what he already knew.'

'I was anxious for him to be quite clear on the point.'

'So that he'd stop harassing you?'

'Quite.'

'But the clarification became a stand-up fight. What led to that?'

I sighed deeply. 'How does one trace these things back? Terry was an incredible mixture – hot-tempered and also mulish. He didn't believe, or wouldn't, that the legal boys were right. He didn't honestly care. All that weighed with him was his craving to have me back.'

'So the more you tried to reason . . .'

'The madder he got.'

'Until finally he launched himself at you. And you checked his progress with the help of the lampstand.'

'Right.'

Kaynes whistled soundlessly for a moment. 'Must have been a lucky blow. Unlucky, rather. To catch him like that.'

'He came at me so fast, I barely had to move my arm. He sort of ran into it.'

'And staggered back? Which was when you hit him again?'

I nodded. 'Reflex action. Couldn't stop myself.'

Kaynes came over to peer into my cup. 'You've not drunk anything, Miss Browne.'

'I can't.' I looked up at him. 'May we wrap this up now? I'm exhausted. I can't take any more. Whatever you're going to charge me with, for God's sake get it over and let me sleep.'

'There won't be a charge,' he said thoughtfully, 'at this stage.'

My muscles tautened. 'What do you mean?'

'I mean, Miss Browne, that the only accusation I could bring against you right this minute is one of wasting police time. For two hours or more, you've had us on a length of string. Nothing you've told us even begins to add up. The timing's all wrong; and for your information, Mr O'Malley was struck once – from behind.' He stood gazing down at me. His voice and manner hardened. 'You didn't kill your ex-husband, Miss Browne. Who did?'

CHAPTER XX

A RAP ON the door, the insertion of the uniformed constable's earnest head, broke up the muttered debate between Kaynes and the inspector which I had been observing in a state of apathy. The constable said, 'Sir . . .'

Kaynes went across. After a moment he nodded; the constable withdrew. Kaynes turned to address me.

'Friend of yours is here. Want to see him?'

'Who?'

'Your producer. Mr Joseph. He can come up if you like.'

I moved my shoulders. 'He might as well.'

Kaynes lifted the phone. 'Ask Mr Joseph to step up, would you?'

While we waited, they studied me covertly. Perhaps my reaction, or lack of one, perplexed them as much as it did me. At Herbie's appearance, under the watchful aegis of the constable, they drifted tactfully to the far end of the room to resume, ostensibly, their dialogue. Arms outstretched, Herbie advanced over the carpet.

'Honey . . .'

I didn't get up. Rocking to a standstill, he glared around suspiciously. 'They been working you over?'

The expressions of the two detectives hit me suddenly. I broke into weak laughter. Relief struggled with concern in Herbie's manner. 'No offence to anybody, but I figured – '

'Sit down, Herbie, for heaven's sake. Let me talk to someone on a level. Bring the footstool over. That's it. I don't know whether I'm coming or going . . . What happened to you? I waited at the airport but you never showed up.'

'Anjie, I'm sorry. I could kick myself. Guess I underrated your weekend traffic problem. Got snarled up good and static along the freeway – '

'The M4?'

'With symbols like that, they should stick to Intelligence. To be fair, there'd been some kind of an accident that was blocking the highway. So there I was, stuck, and not a callbox in sight. Just had to sit there, sweating and swearing, and hope you'd wait. Finally made the airport around six-fifteen, by which time . . . It was my fault. I should've left sooner.'

'Don't be silly. You couldn't have foreseen that. I might have waited. What did you do?'

'Made a call or two, couldn't trace you, so grabbed a sandwich and hi-tailed it back into town. Figured you might head for the Mayfair place – '

'I'd forgotten it existed.' My obtuseness startled me.

'That's not so surprising. You'd other things on your mind. Anyway, that's where I've been . . . and it's where I saw the TV newscast that told me what had happened. So here I am. What's the set-up, Angel? A mugging?'

I stared at him, estimating the possibility. Kaynes stepped forward.

'The matter's under investigation, Mr Joseph.'

'Sure. But let me tell you something.' Herbie jabbed a truculent forefinger. 'Miss Browne here had nothing to do with it.'

'We know she didn't kill him,' Kaynes said meekly.

Herbie sagged. 'Then what's she doing, shut up here with you?'

'There's no question of incarceration. She'd taken this suite for the night, so it seemed sensible for her to stay. You saw the mob of newsmen in the lobby.'

A grunt of semi-assent came from Herbie. 'Is she in line for more questioning?'

'Not at present.'

'Then why not leave the poor kid to get some rest?'

'We were on the point of doing so,' Kaynes said courteously, 'when you showed up. You're producing

Miss Browne's current film, Mr Joseph, do I understand?'

'You do. When can we get back to it?'

'You knew, obviously, about Miss Browne's trip to California and back. You'd arranged to meet her at Heathrow?'

'Only I got held up.'

'On arrival there, did you check that her flight had landed on time?'

'I did, and it had.'

Kaynes gave a satisfied jerk of the head. As though reminded of his own affliction, the inspector, behind him, twitched his neck. Addressing me, the chief superintendent said, 'We'll be off now, the inspector and I: but we'd like to speak to you again in the morning. Think carefully about things, won't you?'

His grey eyes drilled into mine. With a gesture to his assistant he stepped towards the door. 'By the way, I'm leaving a constable outside, but you needn't read too much into that. It's merely to protect your privacy.'

'Okay, honey – now what goes on?'

'Oh Herbie. I'm terrified about Liz.'

'Huh?'

'She was here – with Terry. Now she's gone. What do *you* think happened?'

'Christ, Anjie. A kid of fifteen?'

'If he was trying anything on?'

'She wouldn't have had the strength . . .'

'In desperation, she might. She's well-built. He could have panicked her into striking out.'

Herbie rubbed his jaw. 'Fairly ham-fisted of him, wasn't it? She was under his spell, I thought. Did he have to resort to the rough stuff?'

'I know what Terry can be like.' I was silent for a moment, remembering: then shook my head convulsively. '*Could* be like. I can't get used to the idea that he's . . .'

'Solves a few problems, at least,' said Herbie, bleakly

realistic. 'Was it you found the body, Anjie?'

'Yes.'

'Any sign of the negatives?'

'I only had time for a quick look. I suppose it was the shock. Like an idiot, I phoned for the manager without stopping to think. Before he came, I did go through Terry's pockets and a few drawers and closets – there wasn't anything. That's secondary just now. It's Liz.'

'Did you call your parents?'

'Up to now I haven't dared. The Superintendent seems to know I'm trying to shield someone . . . if he'd heard me enquiring about Liz, that would really have blown it. I'll try now.'

'No, honey.' Herbie held me back. 'They're sure to have a tap on the switchboard. Why don't I do it from outside?'

'Would you? And then come back and tell me if she's home?'

'Sure I will. If they'll let me.' He encircled me with a comforting arm. 'I'll get word to you somehow.'

I relaxed against him. For a few moments we stood together in an intimate stillness, united like brother and sister at a time of stress. Or father and daughter . . . I drew away from him. 'Have you seen or heard anything of Dad?'

'Your father?' Herbie was a little thrown.

'He was supposed to be making enquiries at some of the London hotels. Same as you.'

Herbie wagged his head. 'I've not run into him. Not since I dropped them off at their home this morning.'

'He may be back there by now. Which hotels did you try, Herbie?'

'A whole bunch,' he said vaguely. 'Smaller kind, mostly. I figured – wrongly, it seems – that O'Malley wouldn't steer for anything too much in the spotlight. I certainly never gave a thought to the Cosmopole.'

'Go and make that call, Herbie, will you?'

With a pecking kiss to the side of my head, he made for

the door. 'Don't worry,' he said, reaching it. 'Your sister couldn't have been involved. I have this feeling.' Giving me a pensive look, he let himself out.

Although it posed as Chief Superintendent Kaynes, it was not long before I came to realize that the approaching figure was Terry. The mincing quality of his step was the giveaway. And the smile.

I spoke to my limbs. *Unlock* . . . My position remained the same. The shape looming above me raised its right hand. Reaching the ceiling, it stayed there effortlessly, knuckles rapping the plaster in a series of echoing claps. Disintegration commenced. Huge chunks detached themselves, fell away, showered towards me. To avoid them, I tried to topple sideways. The rapping came again.

I stared numbly at an unfamiliar wall. In the centre of it hung a picture: a nineteenth-century view of Piccadilly Circus, all hansom cabs and long-gowned women in hats. In the half-light through the drawn curtains I couldn't see the detail, but I knew it was there: I had studied it while undressing the night before. Using it to obliterate thought. Now I used it to unfreeze my sinews. Presently I was able to jerk back the covers, stagger out of bed. Wrapping myself in my coat, I groped across to the connecting door and fumbled it open.

'Anjie . . . love!'

Mum's embrace as I reached the main room was full-blooded. Coming on top of the short-windedness caused by insufficient sleep and the nightmare, it took the stuffing out of me so that we half-collapsed against the basket-chair, which keeled creakingly under the load. Across her shoulder I met the anxious gaze of Herbie, encased in a padded jacket and with a pink tip to his nose. He was clutching newspapers.

'Sorry to fetch you up, honey. Would have let you sleep on, only your mother was getting kind of . . .'

'What time is it?' The aridity of my mouth got in the way of the syllables.

'Turned seven,' said Herbie, interpreting heroically. 'I knew you needed all the rest you could get, but your mother's been sitting in my car for an hour already, and she – '

'Oh Mum. Why didn't you come up?'

'We wasn't sure if they'd let us.' She let me lower her the rest of the way into the basket-chair; on arrival, she made dabbing motions at her hair and clothing. 'But the officer said it was all right, so . . .'

'Kaynes was around,' Herbie explained, 'a little while back. Time of death's been definitely established, he says. Which lets you out, Angel: no question. But he wants you to stick around for the moment.'

'I'm not going anywhere.' I looked at them in turn. 'Lizzie . . .?'

'She's back,' Mum announced, swamping Herbie's gruffer 'She showed up.'

'What time did she – '

'Soon after you rung yesterday, they come in. Her and Dad.'

'He found her, then?' The questions were being forced out of me. I was afraid of the replies I might get.

'Ran into her, more like. See, he'd got this idea in his head they might make for the Cosmopole, seeing as Liz has had this place on the brain ever since that piece about you in the *Sunday World*. So he was in the right place at the right time.'

'He was smarter than me,' Herbie said ruefully from beside the telephone. 'Honey, you want coffee?'

'Tea and toast, thanks. For both of us.' He lifted the receiver and I returned to Mum. 'So Dad found her here?'

'Well, not exactly. He showed her photo to the man at the desk, and he said he'd seen somebody like her belting through to the street about twenty minutes before. Dad goes haring out – '

'What time would this have been?'

Mum frowned. 'Why'd you keep asking that? I wouldn't know the exact time, love. Four-ish, I should think. You'd have to ask Dad. So anyway, off he goes to look for her, and as luck would have it, just as he's crossing by the subway at Marble Arch, there she is, coming out of the Ladies'. All upset and beside herself. Practically hysterical, she was.'

'Why?' I said faintly.

'Dad was half an hour getting her calmed down enough to talk straight. First they sit on a seat on the island up top: then he takes her into a coffee bar, one of them Wimpy places, and finally he gets it out of her. Apparently, Terry booked 'em in here late yesterday morning, and at first everything in the garden was lovely. Lunch in the Grill Room, and somebody come up and said how he liked Terry's old films, and Liz was the centre of attention and it was all marvellous. Then they went off back to their room, like, and evidently,' Mum said delicately, with a glance towards Herbie on the phone, 'that's when he started Trying it On with her . . . you know. Getting a bit demanding. I don't know what else she expected, silly girl. Whatever it was, she didn't much care for his style. So she tried telling him.'

My heart pounded. 'What was his reaction to that?'

'Well apparently, in the end, he gives her a slap round the face. And she locks herself in the toilet.'

'Then what?'

'After a bit she peeped out and he was lying sprawled on the bed . . . so she tiptoed over to the door and let herself out. She thinks he probably saw her go, but he didn't try to do nothing about it. She went straight down and out into the street. In a right state, she was. Didn't know if she'd be welcomed at home. Soppy thing. So she hid in the Ladies' at Marble Arch while she was making her mind up what to do. Then she bumped into Dad.'

Herbie separated himself from the phone. 'Tea's coming right up,' he told us. Retiring to a distant chair, he launched an investigation of the *Sunday Telegraph*.

I said, 'Why hadn't Dad contacted you by the time I called from the airport?'

'The airport, love?'

'I called there,' I said hastily, 'for a snack.'

'Well, it's like I told you. First he had to calm Lizzie down, then get her story out of her. Then persuade her to go back home with him. Time he got to a phone, it was turned five. Then it was out of order. So he gave up, and they took the Tube. Got in soon after six.'

I thought for a minute. 'When did you hear about the . . . accident?'

'Not till Mr Joseph rang last night. We'd been chewing things over with Liz, see – we'd not had the telly on nor anything. So it come as quite a shock. I wanted to get straight over to see you, only Mr Joseph said you'd be asleep and it'd be better to wait till morning. So I did.'

In the depths of the basket-chair she looked small but resolute, clasping her best handbag to her lap. I stooped and kissed her.

'Thanks, Mum.' Casually I added, 'Liz all right when she got back?'

'Oh yes. She had the sense not to give in to him.'

'I mean, she wasn't . . . the slap didn't hurt her?'

'Just her pride,' Mum said crisply.

'Where is she now?'

'At home. With Dad. We reckoned she could have a quiet morning with him, like, while I come over with Mr Joseph to see how you were.'

I stood looking at her. 'Not had a very peaceful three days, have you?' I said at last. 'Sorry, Mum. Things went a bit haywire.'

'You've not done that well yourself,' she pointed out. 'Whatever you might've thought of Terry, you can't have wanted . . . Who was it, Anjie, d'you think? Some yobbo, after his money?'

Her eyes, questioning, a little scared, searched mine. I turned towards Herbie.

'Before we discuss it any more, I'll freshen up and get some clothes on. What do the papers say?'

Silently he showed me the *Observer*'s front page. The

lead item was the Middle East furore: despite this, Terry's demise had captured double-column treatment down-page beneath a full-face picture of him on the right. *Star's Hotel Death: Riddle of 'Mrs Jameson'* was the headline above story and photograph. Scanning it only briefly, I made for the bedroom. 'Save some tea for me,' I told them, and closed the connecting door.

When I re-emerged, Kaynes was with them. A cup at his lips. Well-mannered appreciation showed in the look he threw over me. Herbie was the one who spoke.

'Honey, the Superintendent says there's no call for you to stop on here if you have other plans.'

'But,' Kaynes put in, 'we'd like to be able to reach you, Miss Browne, if need be.'

'I'll be at my parents' home for today. If that's all right?' I added, addressing Mum. The message seemed lost on her, but she gave the right reply.

''Course it is, love. Come back and have a good rest.'

Kaynes observed us both. 'Pretty close, the Brown family set-up, didn't I read somewhere?'

I said, 'Did you?'

'Um. *Modern Madam*, was it?' He stood frowning into the cup. 'I believe that was the one. Did a feature on you just lately. My wife read bits out.'

'I hope you enjoyed it. All right for me to go, then?'

'I'll call the manager,' he said helpfully.

I froze. 'The manager? What for?'

Herbie stepped forward. 'They're still cluttering the lobby, Angel. The Press boys. They're damn certain it's you that's up here. So we thought – '

'I can wear my Mrs Jameson wig.'

'The manager's plan,' Kaynes said slowly, 'seems an improvement on that. He can take you down in the service lift and out by a rear exit. There's a car waiting.'

'I left my own car outside the front entrance,' Herbie explained. 'Kind of a decoy.'

'You've been recognized?' I asked.

'You bet.' He fingered his tie. 'Which is one reason

they're so goddam positive who else is up here.'

'Nice,' I said, 'to be news. Occasionally. All right: one way or another, let's get out of here.'

While we waited for the manager I collected my suitcase, which Herbie took from me with a proprietorial air. Trying not to make it sound like a challenge, I said to Kaynes, 'Do you have any leads, at all?'

He smiled, the enigmatic slight smile of the eternal cop. 'Cherchez la femme, seems our best bet.'

'You've already found her – and ruled her out,' I reminded him.

'The other one,' he said imperturbably. 'She who ran out on him.'

By an effort of will I avoided glancing at either Herbie or Mum. 'Have you a description?'

'Several.' Kaynes said it seriously.

'Do they synchronize?'

'In many respects. Particularly as regards age. She was young, it appears. Extremely so. And another thing,' he added reflectively as he went to the door in answer to a double tap, 'at least two of our informants were agreed on.'

'What was that?'

'According to them, the young lady in question had been pictured recently in the Press. Closely adjacent to Mr O'Malley at the Savoy. On that occasion, she was described as your sister. Of course,' he observed, with fingers on the door handle, 'witnesses can make mistakes and they frequently do – but these two were ready to swear to it. So what I was wondering . . .' He paused diffidently. 'Would you mind terribly if we shared the transport to West Ham?'

CHAPTER XXI

INSIDE THE NARROW hallway, Mum took charge.

'Will you go into the Front Room, Mr Kaynes?' She was pale, but possessed. 'I'll just fetch Liz. Won't keep you a moment.'

We stood about the tiny, stripe-papered room, our eyes meeting briefly and skidding off. The nylon-tufted carpet gave off an odd scent. Kaynes stood at ease. The inspector took up a supported stance against the top of the stone fireplace. I still didn't know his name.

Herbie said expansively, 'So this'd be a typical English home . . .'

Nobody paid attention. Trying hard to feel grateful to him, I experienced only a kind of impatience; the same as in the car, when he had taken one of my hands protectively inside one of his. After a few seconds he had relinquished it, and since then there had been no physical contact between us. Now, I sent him a quick, artificial smile which he met blankly. He was out of his depth.

Liz entered. She looked childishly cute, vulnerable in a smock dress with her hair flowing. She gave each of us a flicker of a glance before countering with uplifted head the scrutiny of the Chief Superintendent, who looked and sounded friendly.

'Hallo, Liz.'

'H'llo,' she said guardedly.

Both Mum and Dad stood behind her, adding to the crush. Mum's pallor was counterpoint to Dad's moist flush. On the sagging lapel of his grey woollen waistcoat there was a brown stain – tea, coffee or chocolate – which normally would have been sponged out. His left hand was on Liz's left shoulder.

'You know,' Kaynes asked her, 'the reason I'm here?'

She kept her gaze level. 'Mr O'Malley?'

'That's it. There's a strong probability, Liz, that you were one of the last to see him alive.'

Liz chewed her lower lip. 'I left him about quarter to four. He was all right then.'

'From what your mother's told me on the way here, I gather he was lying on the bed at the time.'

'He was. He was resting.'

'You hadn't . . . laid hands on him? In any way?'

'Me? Laid hands on *him*?'

Kaynes regarded her in silence. With a glance at Dad, she added more soberly, 'I never touched him. Well, only to shove him off – when he tried to get fresh.'

'How did he take that?'

'Wasn't much he could do about it. I got away to the bathroom and bolted myself in.'

'How long did you stay there?'

Liz shrugged. 'Quarter of an hour. Twenty minutes. He kept on at me to come out, but he never tugged at the handle or anything. In the end he went and lay on the bed.'

'And then what?'

'I pulled the door open a bit. See what he was up to.'

'Weren't you afraid he'd make another grab at you?'

'The bed was a long way from the bathroom door. There'd have been time to lock it again.'

Kaynes was looking puzzled. 'How could you have known he was on the bed?'

'It creaked. Every time you got on or off.'

'I see. You'd managed to discover that much about it?'

Liz went bright pink. Mum said indignantly, 'She had a lie-down before lunch. They'd been traipsing round the shops and she was tired. Lizzie's told us – '

Kaynes lifted a placatory hand. 'Let her tell me, then. I only want to get at the truth. Right, Liz . . . you peeped out. Did he get up, off the bed?'

'No. He looked like he was asleep. Dozing. I reckoned he might be pretending, but anyway I took a chance – I was cheesed off with that bathroom. I crept out and he never took any notice. Just went on lying there, sort of staring at the ceiling. So I tiptoed through to the other room and let meself out.'

'Not stopping for your things?'

'All I had was a carrier. I'd forgotten about it.'

'You just wanted to get away?'

'Wouldn't you have?'

Kaynes seemed disinclined to debate this proposition. 'You were scared of him, by this time?'

Dad spoke up unexpectedly. 'That's a leading question, Superintendent.'

Kaynes remained unruffled. 'Perfectly reasonable one, I'd have thought. You've said your daughter was in "a bit of a state" when you came across her.'

'Upset.'

'Semi-hysterical . . . according to your wife.'

'I wasn't,' Liz affirmed huffily. 'Just het-up.'

'As a result of Mr O'Malley's slap on the face?'

'There was more to it than that. Ever since lunch, he'd been trying it on.'

Kaynes surveyed her. 'You seem a sensible girl, Liz. You're fifteen, and I should say mentally quite mature for your age. When you went off with Mr O'Malley, what exactly were you expecting?'

She looked at the carpet. I spoke into the silence.

'Really, you know, it was a gesture of defiance. Towards me. I'd tried to warn Liz off him, you see. I knew . . . I guessed he was just using her to get at me.'

He nodded slightly. 'So it was bravado on her part – and manipulation on his?'

'Something like that.'

Alongside me, Herbie stirred. 'I'll vouch for that, Superintendent.'

I wished he would stay out of it. Kaynes in any case ignored him. His attention returned to Liz, who once more was meeting his gaze.

'Tell me this, Liz. Having let yourself out of the suite, which way did you go?'

She looked bemused. 'Back downstairs.'

'I mean, did you actually use the staircase? Or a lift?'

'I wasn't stopping by one of them lifts. I went down the stairs.'

'Now: did you see anybody? In the corridor, coming up in a lift, on the staircase? Anybody at all?'

Liz's nose wrinkled. 'Not as I can remember . . .'

'You've a reasonably good memory for detail. You've described a lot already. Tell me some more.'

She looked at him appealingly. 'After I left, it's a bit muddled.'

'Earlier, then. Your emergence from the bathroom. First you peeped out . . . right? Mr O'Malley was on the bed. You wanted to get clear.'

Liz nodded.

Kaynes eyed the ceiling. 'You've said you tiptoed out of the bedroom and he took no notice. Just let you go past. Without doing a thing about it?'

Her face was blank. I said, 'Knowing Terry, I can easily visualize – '

'Let your sister answer, please. I want to have it clear.'

'I don't see how much clearer it could be.'

'To me, it's not terribly plain. One moment he's rampaging after your sister: the next, he's letting her slip away. It doesn't add up.'

'It would if you'd known my husband. He was like a child – moody and inconsistent. Once it dawned on him that Liz wasn't having anything, he'd quite likely give up.' Seeing Kaynes's scepticism, I added futilely, 'It would be typical of Terry to sink back on the bed and drift into some fantasy about the dear dead days beyond recall. He lived in a world of his own.'

In the renewed silence that followed, the Chief Superintendent's eyes switched from Liz to Mum, whose sustaining arm was about her waist. From there, they travelled on to come to rest upon the glistening countenance of Dad, whose colour was now at an unprecedented peak. For a while, Kaynes dwelt upon it broodingly. From the fireplace, the inspector observed.

At last Kaynes spoke again, with a gentle courtesy.

'I take it, Mr Brown, there's no doubt in your own mind that it was Marble Arch where you *first* bumped into your daughter?'

Dad's voice was low and steady. 'I don't quite see what you're getting at. I know my London.'

'I wasn't suggesting otherwise.'

'Then what are you implying?'

Kaynes scratched at an ear. 'You showed Liz's photo, I understand, to the reception clerk at the Cosmopole, who told you he'd just seen her leaving.'

'Correct.'

'We've spoken to that clerk. He agrees that this did happen. What he wasn't able to confirm is that you then went out directly in pursuit.'

I took a pace forward. 'Now look here – '

'The reason he can't confirm it,' Kaynes continued relentlessly, 'is that, immediately afterwards, he was surrounded by a large party of guests – medical specialists – who'd just completed a two-day conference at the hotel and wanted their accounts. Therefore he can't say for certain whether you, Mr Brown, headed for the street again or . . . elsewhere.'

Perspiration gleamed on Dad's skin. 'I went straight out,' he said quietly, 'at the double. I wanted to find Elizabeth.'

'Of course you did. You were exceedingly worried about her. Anxious for her to be separated from Mr O'Malley.'

'I'm not disputing it.'

'So what I'm wondering is whether you may have felt it to be a good opportunity – Liz being out of the way – for a few words alone with the gentleman, perhaps with a view to ensuring – '

I couldn't contain myself. 'You're not serious? My father had just been told that Liz had left. What else would he do but dash after her?'

'Your father,' Kaynes said calmly, 'had also been informed of the floor and suite number that the couple were occupying. The clerk, it seems, parted with the information in exchange for a contribution to a charity of his choice. Or are you disputing *that*, Mr Brown?'

All eyes were upon Dad. He took a laborious breath and seemed to grow bigger. The dampness about his forehead remained visible, but when he spoke his voice was firm.

'No. I don't deny it.'

Kaynes looked a little startled. Manifestly he had been drawing a bow at a venture, and had scored a lucky hit. I said warningly, 'Dad – be careful . . .'

A flap of a hand shook some shirt-cuff into view from beneath the sleeve of the waistcoat. Administering a reassuring pat to Mum, who was gaping at him, he stepped closer to the detective.

'I did grease the clerk's palm. When he recognized Elizabeth from the photo and said she'd just left, he was positive she'd been alone. From which it seemed safe to assume that Mr O'Malley was still inside the hotel. So I paid for that additional bit of information.'

This number of consecutive sentences from Dad was a revelation. Only Herbie, who was unacquainted with his character, reacted audibly. He rounded upon Kaynes with a snort.

'What does this prove? Mr Brown discovered the suite number . . . so? It told him what he wanted to know: that O'Malley was still safely installed near the roof where he could do the least harm. That's all it amounted to.' He made a sign to Dad, a leave-it-there gesture.

Dad took no heed. 'It amounted to more than that,' he told the Chief Superintendent. 'I did go on up to the suite.'

A gasp came from Mum. I saw her actually buckle slightly at the knees. My brain went on a brief retirement, refusing to produce anything that might prevent Dad from digging his own grave. Already he was shovelling aside more earth.

'That time of afternoon, hardly anyone was around. I
went up in the lift. Nobody saw me. Elizabeth had left the
door to the suite ajar – I just walked in. I could see Mr
O'Malley on the bed in the other room.'

Liz's face wore an odd expression. She seemed puzzled.

'I went through. He jumped up and came at me, asking
what I'd done with Elizabeth. He sounded unbalanced,'
Dad said on a note of apology. 'I gave him a push, told
him to cool off. Instead, he took a swing at me, so I
grabbed the lampstand and jabbed it at him. The end of
it caught him rather heavily. On the head.'

Dad thought for a moment. 'That's when he fell back
on the bed. I simply took it that I'd knocked him cold. I
didn't hang about. I left him there and went back out of
the hotel to find Elizabeth. I never realized he was dead.
I'm very sorry about it.'

I became aware of the inspector's ballpen racing
across his notepad. For at least half a minute after the
conclusion of Dad's measured recital, it went on scurrying,
supplying a scratchy accompaniment to the turmoil inside
my head. Far from assembling the objections to Dad's
preposterous story, my brain was feverishly lining up and
placing before me the supporting factors. The look on his
face as I had told him about Terry. His tenacious loyalty
to his offspring in the teeth of any threat. An onslaught
upon a molester in a park. Relative to manslaughter, a
slim array of considerations . . . but abruptly I knew that
what he had described was something of which he would
have been capable. And Mum, I could see, knew it too.
Only Liz continued to look perplexed.

Kaynes was putting questions in a monotone. 'Following this, you went and found your daughter at Marble
Arch, as you said?'

'Quite right.'

'When did you first learn of Mr O'Malley's death?'

'Mr Joseph telephoned us. Fairly late last night.'

'Why did he phone? Just to tell you about that?'

'And Anjelica's involvement, of course. Also to ask after Elizabeth.'

'The news concerning Mr O'Malley must have come as a shock to you.'

'Naturally.'

'No doubt you realized that Liz would almost certainly be a prime suspect?'

'Only if she was identified. I thought, with luck she'd remain anonymous and I could keep my mouth shut. It hasn't worked out like that.'

'Indeed it hasn't,' Kaynes agreed heavily. 'You've wasted a great deal of our time, Mr Brown. Anything else you'd like to say just now?'

'I wouldn't bother with that, Superintendent.'

The rasp of Herbie's voice in the confined space was startling. Attention switched to him. Gingerly he manoeuvred his bulk to bring himself into a position facing Kaynes, who was steadily being driven to the centre of the room. 'Not,' Herbie continued, 'unless you want that waste of time perpetuated. As I imagine you don't.'

Kaynes eyed him a little coldly. 'You've something to contribute, Mr Joseph?'

'Sure. A question. May I?' Taking silence for consent, Herbie swivelled. 'Mr Brown: you've been frank and helpful thus far. Can you throw light on this one? O'Malley, you say, was on the bed when you entered the suite. Did you notice at that time what he was wearing?'

Dad looked fixedly at nothing. 'He was fully dressed, I think. I didn't take much notice.'

'What mostly interested you was that he was there at all?'

'Exactly.'

Kaynes stirred restively. 'Mr Joseph, if you've – '

'One other question. Can you be positive, Mr Brown, that at the time you first entered, nobody was standing concealed in the closet next to the connecting door?'

I stared at him. Kaynes fired a glance at the inspector,

who was peering frowningly past his notepad as though trying to recall something. Liz seemed about to speak. Dad, however, got in first.

'No, of course I can't. But I've no reason to suppose there was.'

Satisfied, Herbie leaned back against a tall chair which spun under his weight. He finished up flush to the wall, his posture not deficient in dignity. He addressed the Chief Superintendent.

'I guess that about does it.'

Kaynes favoured him with a thin-lipped survey. 'Does what, precisely?'

'Proves my thesis. The absurdity of this story of Mr Brown's. There's no closet next to that door, Superintendent: it doesn't exist. Anyone who'd been inside the suite would know that. Furthermore, from the main room – as I know from personal experience – it's totally impossible to see the bed inside the bedroom or anyone on it, whether the connecting door's open or not.'

'Neither point,' Kaynes assured him, 'had escaped me.'

'That's good. Makes my task easier.'

'And what is it you see as your task?'

'Preventing a miscarriage of justice.' Liberating his hands, Herbie spread them in the way that I had so often seen him do it while expounding a point to a technician on set. 'By my reckoning, it's time we called a halt to this performance between Mr Brown and his daughter and got right down to basics.'

'Performance?' Kaynes formulated the word as though testing it for length, breadth and quality.

'This family protection charade.' Herbie spoke with some impatience. 'All credit to Mr Brown here, he wants to shoulder the blame – that's natural. But his account just doesn't measure up. I've shown that, I hope. He's concocted it from what I told him on the phone last night and what he's read in the Press this morning . . . but it falls down on crucial points.' Herbie paused to take in breath. He had turned a little pale. 'I don't doubt,

Superintendent, you'd have arrived at the same conclusion in due course: but cutting a few corners never did any harm. Assuming that you're halfway convinced he wasn't responsible, it simplifies my job of informing you who is.'

Kaynes sent a lift of the eyebrows to his inspector, impassively taking notes at the fireplace. 'Needless to say, we welcome any help we can get. If Mr Brown didn't do it, who did, in your opinion?'

'Me,' Herbie said simply. 'I put O'Malley out of circulation.'

CHAPTER XXII

THE CUISINE OF Verucci's Steak House in Knightsbridge set a towering standard, surpassed only by the discretion of its service, fully as obtrusive as late-night mood music played at minimum volume in the house next door. Solid double-glazing saw to it that the traffic outside passed in a whisper. Everything was muted, velvet-padded; even the clink of the china was duller than average, as though soundproofing had been fired into the glazing. The place was ideal for a quiet talk. If one felt like talking.

'According to this,' said Denny, making a heroic attempt, 'the cops are disposed to accept Herbie's account of what happened.'

He had the *Daily Mirror* in front of him. It was one of a bundle of dailies he had brought in. I rippled the untasted wine in my glass.

'It's still manslaughter.'

'Suspended sentence. At most.'

'One can't be sure.'

Folding the newspaper carefully, he returned it to the stack and bent an uninterested gaze upon the mixed grill coagulating on his plate before eyeing me again. 'With the legal firepower Herbie can whistle up, one can be moderately certain.'

'A lot still depends on judge and jury. What if they don't buy his story that Terry came at him like a maniac? He could get a year or two inside.'

'That's assuming things at their bleakest.'

'You're forgetting something,' I said.

'What's that?'

'The publicity. What's going to happen about *Furnace*?'

The apparent materialism of my remark didn't deceive Denny. He knew what I meant. He pulled a scoffing face. 'No threat to Herbie's dream, I'd say. At least, not from the public acceptance angle. As long as the film gets made, they'll trek along to see it . . . the more so, if there's notoriety surrounding it.' His tone was so convincing that I knew he was putting it on. 'The only danger I can see,' he added, 'is that it might *not* get made. For one reason or another.'

There was no need for him to elaborate. I stared out at a passing bus. Most of its occupants stared right back at me, with the dull, unquestioning, unhoping coddishness of those trapped in the time/space vacuum of public transport; if they saw me at all, no recognition was involved, since in addition to the wig I was shielded by glasses with frames of such enormity that Denny, on encountering me at Waterloo, had enquired what I had done with the rest of the bicycle, extracting from me the first smile for several days and inciting me to wonder whether I might be falling for him. It was a little early to decide. I knew only that the sight of him approaching across the station concourse – in response to my telephone call to The Beeches, he had taken an early train – had been infinitely consoling, in contrast to the trapped feeling I had experienced at home in Eastern Gardens the previous day after Herbie's removal for further questioning. The combined relief and sympathy of Mum and Dad had been hard to bear. As soon as possible, I had escaped to spend the night incognito at a small hotel in Hampstead where I had tried, without much success, to catch up on lost sleep and to devise ways of helping Herbie out. The effort, in each case, had left me spent, with an underlying feeling of black despair which for the time being was robbing me of the power to reach decisions.

Presently I said, 'It's all my fault.'

Denny said nothing. When I looked back at him, his expression was receptive and neutral. I touched his arm with a hand. 'As my co-star – I hope – you're entitled to know something of the background. Herbie was trying to get Terry off my back.'

'That much is apparent.' He tapped the newsprint at his elbow.

'But what the newspapers are suggesting is simply that Terry was pestering me to go back to him, and ruining the shooting of *Furnace* in the process. Which is true enough as far as it goes . . .'

'Only it doesn't go far enough?'

I looked him in the eye. 'There were some incriminating documents. That's why I was so helpless.'

Denny made a half-comprehending movement of the head. He asked no direct questions. He merely said, 'And it's all right now?'

I looked down at the wineglass. 'I'm not sure.'

No opportunity had arisen for a private talk with Herbie. Following his brief court appearance that morning and his remand on bail, he had vanished. Anxious to avoid the Press, I had kept clear of the hearing, subsequently telephoning Herbie's Mayfair retreat to be told by a lugubrious Wally Parsons, who had hurried from Hampshire to handle the Press inquisition, that Herbie was temporarily in hiding and would be in touch later, and that everything was fine and I wasn't to worry. Regarding his exact whereabouts, Wally was evasive. I thought it possible that he had returned to The Beeches, although he had not arrived there by the time Denny left. I planned to put in another call to Mrs Emmerson after lunch.

Everything was fine and I wasn't to worry. What did this convey? That Herbie had found nothing among

Terry's effects? Or that, whatever he had found, he had disposed of?

The first possibility was hardly a reassurance. If nothing had been found, it could mean that it was elsewhere. Ticking quietly, waiting to explode.

Wherever I looked, blackness scowled back at me. In one direction there was Herbie, who in a mood of bone-headed chivalry had killed for me. In another there was my professional future, disintegrating on a set near Winchester. In all directions there was the watching world, sucking its lips in anticipation of the juiciest morsel to come its way for months. Not a chink of light, any-where.

'If you feel like a good cry,' said Denny's voice, 'don't mind me. Or our fellow-lunchers. They're much too well-bred to notice.'

'I'm bloody well not going to put it to the test.' Accept-ing the handkerchief he offered, I blew my nose ferociously, unseating the spectacles and having to jam them back into place. Through their monstrous circumferences, I gazed at him across the table. 'Oh God, Denny. I'm not going to crack up, am I?'

'If I were you,' he advised, 'I shouldn't. It's never worth the fuss. Anyway, Dilys should be along soon. She said she'd be here in time for coffee.'

'You're a couple of stalwarts.'

'Frankly, love, we'd both sooner be here than mooning around The Beeches, kicking Mother Emmerson's menials to warm our feet. Besides, you need some feminine comfort. I'm doing my best, for God's sake, but the touch is clumsy.'

'I'm willing to put up with it.'

Our eyes met and locked. His battered good looks, coupled with the gentleness of his handling of me, had my emotions on the alert; I felt vulnerable, and therefore doubly cautious. I had stumbled like this before. And with Denny there was an extra dimension to consider. Instinct and observation had already informed me that he was somebody different, self-sufficient, a loner; a shell of easy friendliness covering a rind of thoughtfulness which, in turn, concealed the toughest of independent kernels on which it would be easy to break one's teeth. Up to a point, Denny would always have time for his fellow-mortals; and beyond that point he would always be inaccessible. In that moment, I saw it as clearly as though it had been inked in block capitals across his forehead. Which was the reason that I freed my gaze after a second or two and re-directed it at the traffic stream outside, studying it intently as if the answer to all my problems might lie somewhere in the midst of its ever-varying patterns rather than in the unspoken half-promise of a sympathetic but alien soul. My next remark was inconsequential.

'What if Herbie turns up on set this afternoon? Expecting to find some action?'

'He'll be ranting to himself,' Denny said cheerfully. 'Roger M. chucked the towel in yesterday. Not another foot of film, he foamed to an assemblage of hirelings, until the dust has finally settled – more than settled, been hosed out of sight. Must admit, I could see his point.'

'For once, so can I. He must be wondering what kind of crew he's got himself involved with. Killers, neurotics . . .'

Denny spluttered suddenly into his water-glass.

'Shouldn't we be making the film of the film-making? The screenplay could hardly be improved on. Sorry, I'm not meaning to laugh, it's not funny, not funny at all . . .'

He was doubled over the table and I was smiling wanly when Dilys entered the restaurant. The sight of her, as always, gave a lift to my spirits, elevating them from nought feet to a height of inches. On arrival she stooped and gave me a kiss: something she hadn't done before. I clung to her arm.

'Hi, Dilly. Welcome to the wake.'

'How's it going, kid?' She sat between us, throwing Denny a mystified glance as he struggled to compose himself. 'Seen anything of Herbie?'

'No. He might be on his way back to Winchester. Wally doesn't seem to know, or he's not saying. I'm ringing the hotel presently.'

'He *must* have been loco,' Dilys said with conviction. 'Okay, so he wanted his leading lady left undisturbed so he could shoot his masterwork . . . that's a reason for mayhem?'

'It was an accident.'

'So was Nagasaki . . . if you care to look at it that way. Got any plans, Anjie? I mean, are you stopping here in town for a while? You're clear, I'm assuming, so far as the law's concerned?'

'I've really no idea. I wasn't at the court hearing this morning, because of the newshawks waiting to swoop, so I didn't even see Herbie, let alone speak to him . . . and I've only talked on the phone to Inspector Paulson. At least I've found out his name. He said they'd probably be wanting to interview me again and would I hold myself available . . . what does that mean? At the end of a telephone? He didn't say. And I forgot to ask. Think I should call him again?'

'If they want you,' Dilys affirmed, 'they'll find you. So I wouldn't bother too much holding yourself any place. You two had coffee?'

'Not yet. We were waiting for you to – '

'If you girls will excuse me,' said Denny, rising, 'I have to honour my agent with a visit, and now seems as meddlesome a time as any. I'll be a couple of hours. Where shall we link up again?'

'Depends,' said Dilys, consulting me with a glance, 'what course of action Anjie fixes on for the next twenty-four hours.'

We arranged a rendezvous at the Mayfair headquarters. Wally Parsons might still be there, and if he wasn't there was a ground-floor lobby in which one could sit and wait. On the heels of Denny's departure, Dilys gave me a quizzical look.

'Now why would he want to be seeing his agent?'

'To discuss other parts?' I suggested realistically. 'He has to look after himself. Let's face it, Dilys: the fires of *Furnace* are pretty damped down at the moment.'

'Oh, come on. We'll all be back in the action before you can shout *blackmail*.'

The waiter arrived with coffee. When he had withdrawn, I slid my cup across to Dilys, who was handling the jug. 'What made you say that?' I asked.

'Say what, honey?'

'Back in action before . . .'

'I don't recall what I said.'

'Blackmail.'

She looked vague. 'I don't know what made me fix on that. Thinking of Miriam, I guess. She wallows in emotional blackmail, doesn't she?'

'I suppose she does, in a way. I hadn't thought of it like that. My God, Dilys, what are we doing, discussing the niceties of fiction? Haven't we enough hard fact on our hands?'

'Sure, but you need to take a rest from it now and then. You look peaky,' said Dilys, examining me closely. 'Candidly, honey, you look like you could be wiping your feet on the doormat of a breakdown. What gives? Grief for Terry on the rebound? You were frantic to be rid of him, I thought.'

'Not this way.'

'You have to admit, it's an effective way.' She eyed me ingenuously across the rim of her cup. 'If that sounds direct, it was meant to. What use was Terry O'Malley, to himself or anyone? He was falling apart. You said so yourself. And as he came to pieces, the sharp bits were stabbing everyone around. You especially. We all knew that. Herbie knew it. Why else did he ferret the guy out? He wanted a showdown. Not with that specific result, maybe, but since it happened – well, as I said, it has the stamp of finality.' She took a gulp of coffee, came up gasping. 'And after all, it was chiefly Terry's own fault. He got violent. Basically, Herbie was just defending himself, wasn't he?'

'That's what I don't understand.' I glanced at the headlines across the *Mirror* abandoned by Denny. 'Terry was never a violent type – that is, not with other men. He was too yellow. He might have slapped Liz's face, but to go at Herbie in that way . . . I just don't see it.'

'People behave out of character sometimes.'

'And that's another thing. Why did Herbie leave it so late to come clean? He must have known that Liz would be prime suspect, right from the start. Why wait until she was practically in irons and Dad was inventing his head off to drag the blame on to himself?'

'That's what happened?'

I gave her an outline of events. Listening seriously, she poured more coffee for us both; I had drunk mine without noticing what I was doing. She managed to spill some over the unused cutlery. Same old Dilys. Accident-prone in a small way. It was a relief to know that some things, at least, didn't alter. Replacing the jug with a wince at its weight, she said, 'My, what a mix-up. You certainly did go through the mangle, Anjie.'

'So you can see,' I pointed out, 'it was a fairly last-minute thing, and that's not like him. Before this, if somebody had asked me what Herbie would do if he found he'd killed a man in self-defence, I'd have had no hesitation in saying he'd go straight to the police.'

'But you have to bear in mind the circumstances.'

'Especially in those circumstances.'

Dilys shook her head. 'It's the old story. Panic and impulse.'

'Impulse,' I repeated bitterly. 'The cause of half our troubles.'

In a series of decisive movements she signalled the waiter, gathered her belongings, stood up. 'Come on, honey. You need a change of scene. We've an hour or two on our hands. Why don't you show me a few blocks of your home town?'

Taking Dilys at her word, the taxi driver let the world go by. The weather was unstable, bursts of sunlight alternating with deep-purple depressions. During the bright spells, London looked shoddy, like old wallpaper under a naked bulb; when the sky closed over, it looked like the end of all things. Halfway across Vauxhall Bridge, Dilys turned her attention to the evening newspaper she had bought. I stared out across the river.

Presently she said, 'You're down-page now, Anjie. The Arabs are back among the headlines.'

I said listlessly, 'They're never gone for long.'

'Looks serious. Things are really hotting up out there.'

She read for some moments. 'Boy, do they need a good kick in the pants. If we can just get some strong action . . .'

'Who's going to provide that?'

'We do have a Presidential election this year, honey.'

Coming off the bridge, the driver turned right towards Battersea, following instructions to cruise in the river region. Dilys, with a glance or two at the surroundings, read on to the foot of the report.

'This guy Mason . . . He has the right ideas, A to Z. It's people like him we want handling our interests.'

I swallowed. 'You buy the Republican ticket, don't you, Dilly?'

'All the way.'

Recrossing the river via Battersea Bridge, we turned right again along Chelsea Embankment. I said apathetically, 'We seem to be travelling in circles.'

Dilys nodded. 'Know something, Anjie?'

'What?'

'That's exactly what you're in mortal danger of doing. For years to come.'

I returned my gaze to her. 'What are you on about?'

'I'm talking about you,' she said calmly, 'and Governor Mason.'

Instead of exploding from my lungs, the breath left

gradually as the implications of what she had said came at me in waves. By the time I wanted to speak, I couldn't. I had to restock from scratch. Finally I managed a few words.

'What do you know about it?'

Producing cigarettes and a lighter, she offered the pack perfunctorily – she knew I had never been imprisoned by the habit – before lighting up. Sitting back, she puffed smoke at the glass partition.

'No cause to stampede, honey. Your small secret's safe with me.'

'But how – '

'You want the full story?' She flicked ash. 'The works?'

I nodded dumbly.

'I'll keep it as concise as I can.' With a glance at the driver, she lowered her voice. 'The point I want you to bear in mind, first of all, is this. We want Mason inside the White House. It's what we've been working for since – '

' "We"?'

She sent me a lop-sided smile. 'You knew I took an interest in politics. What you maybe didn't know is the position held by my father. Mason's front man. Directly responsible for selling him to the American people. That surprise you?'

'Of course it does. You never said.'

'Nobody ever asked. Anyway he prefers to keep a low profile. I do myself. And I'm involved with the Mason bandwagon right down to the axles.' She tapped the cigarette. 'Which, honey, is where you come in.'

My voice sounded dead. 'Who else knows?'

She counted off on her fingers. 'The Governor. My old man. Plus myself. Nobody else, Anjie.'

Breathing remained a struggle. 'Let me try to work it out. Mason's running for President. He's the one with the upright image, the *family* candidate – so one breath of scandal would blow him away. But five years ago . . .' I glanced at her sharply. 'Mason bought those photos back.'

'Some.'

'That's right. Is Chief Jansen putting the screws on him again?'

We were passing through Sloane Square and a sudden rain squall. Umbrellas had mushroomed. Moisture spiked the cab's windows.

Tapping away more ash, Dilys ground it underfoot. 'When a person becomes Presidential material,' she remarked, 'he's apt to find himself in a different league. Any mud that's slung, he has to be sure it can't stick. Not any.'

She exhaled smoke. 'In regard to the Mildendorf affair, obviously he was on tricky ground. Which is where my old man came into the picture.'

'To sound out Jansen?'

'More than that. Mason gave him the job of safeguarding the entire position. Anyone around with a possible axe to grind was to be squared off. Regardless of expense.'

Dilys eyed me cynically. 'Normal practice, honey. In this instance, numerically speaking, it didn't seem to entail too much. Aside from Mildendorf himself – and he pegged out in jail from a coronary, two years back – only two other members of the blackmail syndicate were in on names, details.'

'So what did your father do?'

'He squared them both. After they get parole, long as they keep their mouths shut, they'll be looked after.'

'Nice for them.'

'Justice,' Dilys observed, 'is a relative term.' She brooded briefly. 'So that was great. It left just the one loophole.'

'Chief Jansen.'

'Two loopholes. Jansen, sure. And Terry.'

I stared at her. 'How far back was this?'

'Six, eight months. When you and Terry were still supposedly in cahoots. By the time we realized he could be crossing us – '

'Wait . . . wait a bit.' I rested my forehead in a palm.

'At what stage did Terry come into it?'

'When he offered to buy back the rest of the photos from Jansen for us.'

'Terry *offered*?'

'Sure. He contacted us at the start of Mason's campaign. Said he happened to know that Jansen was still clutching some dynamite material. Suggested he acted as middleman in buying it back.'

'Didn't it occur to anyone that if I'd known there were still some prints to be bought back from Jansen, I'd have done it myself?'

'Naturally. But Terry's explanation was that you didn't know. Furthermore, that he didn't want you to. He was out to protect your peace of mind. You thought the matter had been cleared up years ago: Terry knew that all he'd done was pay Jansen a relatively modest amount for his silence. And that Jansen might get to thinking it was *too* modest when he came to realize he had potentially President-busting goodies locked away in his personal safe. To us, it made sense.'

'So you actually took Terry up on his offer?'

Dilys's tone became defensive. 'Terry had already dealt once with Jansen . . .'

'So had Mason.'

'Through an intermediary. This was merely swapping one for another – and, on the face of it, one that was more dependable.'

'Dependable!' My voice carried to the driver, whose neck stiffened.

'As far as anyone knew,' Dilys insisted in an undertone, 'you and Terry were the marriage of the century. The scandal sheets hadn't even begun to whisper. The way Dad figured it, Terry would want that remaining material destroyed, for your sake, just as badly as we did.'

I spent long moments coming to grips with what she was telling me.

'Terry, then, was handed a hundred thousand dollars to offer to Jansen?'

'A hundred and fifty thousand.'

I breathed out. 'That explains a lot.'

We were back in Knightsbridge. In the absence of a command, the driver took us into Kensington Road and continued to wave traffic on. The downpour was still hammering the gutters. People sheltering beneath awnings glared hopefully as we chuntered past, two people hogging a cab and bound for nowhere. In other circumstances, it would have bothered me.

'When did it dawn on you,' I asked, 'that Terry wasn't playing straight?'

'Pretty early on. We got wind from one of our sources that Jansen had paid a hundred grand – not a hundred and fifty – into his bank account. This didn't surprise us to that extent, but it did make us take a closer look at what we'd got out of the deal. And the chief thing to strike us was that although Terry had handed over a packet of prints, there weren't that many of them . . . and no negatives. According to Terry, Jansen had told him the negs had been destroyed, but we'd only his word for that.'

Dilys stabbed the butt of her cigarette into the ash receptacle. 'Eventually, Dad made direct contact with Jansen. He confirmed he'd sold prints *and* negs back to Terry, and he specified the number of each that should have been in the package. We knew then that Terry had held some back.'

'So then it dawned on you that Terry's motives might have been different from those he was making out?'

'You can't blame us entirely, honey. Up until the final break, you'd hugged your marital problems to yourself. Nobody imagined you'd be walking out on Terry . . . till it happened.'

'But when it did, the thought occurred to you that he might conceivably use the stuff he'd bought – with Mason's money – to put pressure on me?'

'It wasn't too hard to draw conclusions. So . . .' Dilys drew breath. 'When Terry followed you across to England, the baby landed plumb in my lap.'

'Why yours?'

'Because I'd a reason to be here. Plus, nobody knew of my connection with politics – Terry least of all. If there existed an obvious choice for the job of retrieving those prints, it was Dilys Meridew, I guess.'

We were skirting Kensington Gardens, heading for Lancaster Gate. Ahead, a figure in a blue track-suit loped across the tarmac to vault the railings and make for the trees. In his wake jogged a second figure in bright red, who earned an admonishing toot from the cabbie. I followed the progress of the two runners until they were lost to view.

'Couldn't you have let me know?'

'I thought about that. On balance, it seemed like a good idea not to affect your reaction to Terry's approach. While he was concentrating on you, I figured I might get the chance to find out where he was keeping the stuff and take it off him.'

'But you had no luck?'

She shook her head. 'Not for a while.'

I was casting back, recalling a few things. 'Did you purposely travel from London to Winchester on the same train as he did?'

'Most things I did at the time,' she said dryly, 'were custom-built. Like you, I'd gone in for some corny camouflage . . . headscarf and glasses. When I saw Terry head for the buffet car, I slipped into his compartment to examine his handcase. It wasn't locked, and needless to say there was no package. All I got was a damaged hand when I tried to rush things and the case fell back on me from the rack.'

'He was hardly likely to have left the stuff in there.'

'I had to at least try. The surest bet was that he'd carry them around on his person. If he wanted to really put the skids under you, he'd have needed to show you some solid piece of evidence, sooner or later.'

I glanced away. 'That night we came back from Jon Templar's to find Terry waiting . . .'

'There are two doors,' Dilys said composedly, 'to that Residents' Lounge. One's kept permanently locked, but that doesn't make it soundproof. I stayed on to listen.'

She pressed my arm. 'Forgive me, honey – but I was on your side, remember. From your conversation, I gathered he'd shown you a print or two, but this still didn't tell me where the rest were being kept. Later, when the chance came up, I searched his room . . .'

'So did I.'

'No kidding? Well, I guess we were both going through the motions. Frankly, I was running out of ideas. Then came the . . .'

She broke off. 'Hey look, the sky's cleared right across. How about a stroll, Anjie, through the Park? This rattle-trap's making my ears buzz.' She rapped the glass. 'Set us down here, will you?'

CHAPTER XXIII

ALREADY, THE footway puddles were starting to steam in the heat of the sun. Moisture plopped from branches. Out of the sodden grass arose a faint hiss, like a sigh of relief. Hyde Park on a treacherous April day was the place to be clear of the crowds.

Picking up an empty beer-can, Dilys dropped it into a litter bin. 'Why don't people take care of places? I was saying: that brawl at the studios was followed by your take-off for LA and Herbie's dash back to London with your folks . . . all of which left me sort of stranded up a blind alley. I couldn't be positive what you were aiming to do back in the States – though I guessed. As for Terry and your kid sister, Herbie was obviously in full cry after them. I decided to join the pack.'

'How could you hope to find them?'

'Psychology, honey. Travelling up, I tried putting myself in Terry's shoes. In his place, where would I head for? The answer kind of blinked at me like a neon sign . . . the Cosmopole.'

'Why?'

'Because you'd stayed there yourself, a week or two back. So Terry, being Terry, would have to show he could do the same, right?'

'You must have made a study of his mentality.'

'All you need to know,' said Dilys, brushing water-drops from her sleeve, 'is a little about children. Anyway, I got to the Cosmopole around two-thirty, and before I could even talk to a reception clerk, I spotted them. Hand in hand, coming out of the Grill Room and making for the elevator. They didn't see me. The minute they started up, I went across and kept track of the floor numbers. They travelled all the way to the top.'

Through the trees, the surface of the Serpentine sent up a sparkle. By tacit consent we turned towards the water with its boathouses, its gently-heaving craft, its air of springtide virginity. A man was exercising his black labrador, hurling a stick into the ripples: swimming out, the dog would collect it and paddle back to the shore, tail active, legs taut for a repeat performance. Obliging him, the man made leisurely progress in the Park Lane direction. The pair of them had the lake virtually to themselves.

'Sometimes,' I said irrelevantly, 'I wish I was a swimmer.' We walked a little distance. 'Go on, Dilys. Tell me what you did then.'

'Well, I felt kind of conspicuous there in the lobby. I went and had coffee in one of the lounges while I tried to figure something out. If I charged right up, I might be interrupting something. If I waited, they might check out, jazz off some place for the evening – anything. I must have sat there half an hour, trying to make a decision. Then all of a sudden it was made for me. I saw Liz leaving.'

'By herself?'

'And upset. One of the desk clerks threw her a look as she ran out, I noticed. She had her coat on but no baggage with her: just her purse. I waited a while in case Terry came skittering after her. Then I took the elevator.'

'To the top floor?'

'Penthouse level. When I got there, I was stuck again: which suite was theirs? I remembered you mentioning that yours had overlooked the Park, and there were three that seemed to be on that side . . . numbers two, four and six. I figured it wasn't improbable that Terry would ask for the one you'd occupied – part of his thumb-to-nose attitude – so the first one I tried was number two. As it turned out, the door was ajar. Liz hadn't stopped to fasten it, I guess. Instead of knocking, I took a chance and shoved it open. And there he was. Lounging back in his shirtcuffs, watching the television.'

'In the main room?'

'Why, yes.'

I made mental calculations. 'This must have been somewhere between three-thirty and four. Was he surprised to see you?'

'Apathetic. A cheese-straw would have been livelier. I said "Hi" and he gave a kind of a grunt; then I asked about Liz and he said, "She took off." Then I went the whole way and told him why I was there.'

'What did he say to that?'

'Barely a word. I made it clear we wanted all the prints and negatives, not just a selection . . . he nodded, like as if he was bone-weary or something, dragged himself out of the chair, went to his jacket, felt around a bit and brought out this package. Sort of an oilcloth pouch. He lobbed it across at me. "Take the damn things," he said, "they're no use to me. Nothing's any use. Get them out of my sight, for Christ's sake, and leave me alone." '

Out in the centre of the lake, a solitary rowing boat was being propelled with a rhythmic earnestness from left to right, either by a woman or a long-haired man. She or he had sole claim to the expanse; it was early in the season for pleasure-boating. In the abrupt enveloping warmth, the activity looked enticing. I stood still for a few moments, watching.

'You mean he just handed them over? Like that?'

Dilys shrugged. 'He seemed sort of . . . crushed.'

'Had he been drinking?'

'Not so that it showed.' She, too, was following the boat's course. Presently she added, 'Maybe it was Liz walking out on him like that.'

'And he let you have the package?' I asked the question because I wanted to hear the answer again, in plain words, distinct, unambiguous.

She put a palm on my shoulder. 'That's right, honey. I wish I could show it you, but I handed it over personally to my old man just this morning. He flew in from Washington to take delivery.'

'What will he do with it?'

'Take it straight back to the Governor. He'll be on his way right now. There wasn't time to contact you first. So I'm doing the next best thing. I'm telling you about it.'

I turned my body to face her. 'You don't know, Dilly, what it means to me.'

'Honey, I can imagine. Uncertainty's a killer. This is why I had to set your mind at rest . . . on that aspect, at least.' She looked at me shrewdly. 'You've been thinking maybe the prints might show up some other place – a city desk in Fleet Street, for instance?'

'The thought had rubbed against me.' A weak laugh escaped from my throat. Then a new fear struck. 'Look, I don't want to flog the point, but you don't think he could have been playing with you, even then? Knowing his vicious sense of humour – '

Dilys was shaking her head. 'You mean, keeping some back? Not if I know human nature . . . which I do. I tell you, that guy was on the floor. Stuffing whacked out of him. After throwing me the packet he slopped through to the bedroom and spread himself full-length on the bed and went in for some pretty intensive examination of the ceiling. If he was putting it on, my name's Amelia Witherspoon.'

'I'm convinced. Did you stay long?'

'You're fooling. I switched off the television for him and came out. Left him to it.'

'About what time was this?'

'Oh, let's see . . . I couldn't have been inside there more than three, four minutes. Quarter before four, latest.'

The individual in the rowing boat reached the café terrace at the east end of the lake, circled and started back.

'Dilys, listen. If Terry was like that when you left, and he'd given you the photos – why did Herbie have a fight with him shortly after?'

'I've been thinking about that.'

She frowned past me at the water. 'Theoretically it doesn't add up . . . and yet I don't know. Look at it this way. Soon after I've quit the hotel, Herbie arrives, finds out somehow from a desk clerk that Liz and Terry are booked in, heads directly for the suite and finds Terry there alone, sunk in misery on the bed. Demands the photos. Terry says, quite truthfully, he doesn't have them any more – only Herbie doesn't believe him. Figures he's stalling. So he tries a little persuasion.'

Recalling what Herbie had said, I nodded slowly. 'And Terry hits back?'

'Yellow or not, most men would react in some way, wouldn't they? One thing could have led to another. Terry could have got fighting mad, until finally Herbie grabbed at the . . . Then afterwards, he'd hunt around for any trace of a package, but what would he find? Nothing. It was already with me.'

A wooden seat nearby was drying in the sun. Walking over to it, I flicked away the excess moisture and sat uncaringly. After a brief hesitation, Dilys joined me. We stared across the lake. Presently she touched my sleeve.

'Don't let it eat at you, kid. Herbie'll be fine.'

'How can we be sure?'

'Look. Herb Joseph's a global name. What motive could he have had for killing a washed-up ex-movie star on purpose? All he went there for was to warn Terry off harassing you while you were trying to make a picture. That's what he'll tell the court.'

'They might think it's motive enough.'

'Balderdash.'

'I wish I could share your confidence.'

'You can . . . if you think about it. Great heaven, Anjie,' she said with energy, 'British justice is world-famous. Everyone's allowed one mistake. That's the way it's going to be with Herbie.'

'I'll do my best to believe you.'

'And remember. On your own account you've nothing more to worry about. Both you and the Governor can rest easy. No more fear of the lid blowing off.'

I rested my head on her shoulder. The faint scent of soft leather came from her jacket. I sighed. 'What an idiot I was.'

'We all do dumb things. You've more than made up for it since.'

'I'm so *tired.*'

'You need to relax. Tell you what, Anjie . . .'

'What?'

'Why don't we take a dabble across the water? With this sun, we'd be golden-baked inside of ten minutes, I bet.'

I looked up. The sky was still a deep blue. 'Okay,' I said. 'As long as you're the oarslady '

The boathouse attendant pushed us off, then forgot us. While Dilys found her rhythm we progressed in a series of surges and creaking rowlocks. Leaning back on the cushioned stern seat, I half-closed my eyes, feeling the sun drill into my flesh and bone. The quacking of ducks at the water's edge dwindled to a remote mutter.

Things were going to work out. I settled back further, breathing deeply, untensing my limbs. 'Not such a bad notion of yours, Dilly.'

The skin of my nose was frying. I didn't care. Removing the giant spectacles, I put my head back, positioned my face to meet the sun's glare full-on. I stretched my legs, planted both feet against an angled plank. Slackness crept into my muscles.

And I started to think.

'Dilys . . .'

'What, honey?'

'I've been wondering. About Herbie.'

'Sure you have.'

'Something puzzling.'

She rested the oars so that we glided, then drifted to a bobbing stop. Resignedly she said, 'Tell.'

'Sorry to harp, but . . .' I shaded my eyes to peer at her. 'It's just that I've been trying to use my imagination. And I keep coming back to the same thing.'

'What's that?'

'How tall would you say Terry was?'

She gazed at me blankly. 'A little shorter than me. Why?'

'And how was he built?'

'Slim. Despite all that liquor he – '

'That's it. He wasn't very large. Herbie's six feet tall, burly and active. If it came to a fight between them, why did Herbie need to grab a lampstand to defend himself?'

Dilys pondered. At last she said, 'You don't think maybe this is something we should leave to Herbie's lawyer to find his way around?'

I sat up. 'You're not implying it *wasn't* self-defence?'

'Now don't get mad. Facts have to be faced. If there was – '

'He never meant to attack Terry. Not Herbie.'

With a shake of the head, Dilys started to row again. I continued talking, partly to myself.

'He'd have had the strength to get Terry into some sort of stranglehold, try to *choke* the truth out of him. But to smash at him with a lump of brass? Where did he think that would get him?'

'Aren't you forgetting something, kid?' Dilys asked quietly.

'What?'

'Herbie's feelings for you.'

I felt myself flush. 'That's ridiculous. He's never been that far gone.'

'Don't fool yourself.' She adjusted course with an oar. 'Maybe I shouldn't be saying it, but it's been studio talk for quite a while. You didn't know?'

'I suppose I did . . . up to a point. But affection and – and concern,' I said stubbornly, 'don't necessarily turn a man into a homicidal maniac. Perhaps I'm wrong. Herbie could have needed the lampstand. Terry might have gone berserk.'

'He'd have had to,' Dilys observed, 'to kind of dash himself against a blunt instrument that way, then rebound back on to the bed.'

I gazed at her. 'That's *right*. Otherwise he'd have simply dropped to the floor. Wouldn't he?'

'I guess he would.'

'Unless Herbie actually carried the lampstand over to the bed and hit him with it there.'

'He could have done, at that. The cord . . .'

She broke off to put weight upon the left-hand oar. Glancing across a shoulder, I saw that she was getting us in line with the centre span of the bridge, still some distance ahead of us. On the farther side of the lake, a couple of resolute ice-breakers were bathing from the Lido. Nobody else was in sight.

I trailed some fingers in the frigid water. For a time, neither of us spoke. When Dilys again stopped rowing, a second glance showed me the bridge looming above us: through the centre arch, the stretch of lake beyond looked inviting, but chains half-submerged in the water made it unreachable. Resting the oars, Dilys peered. Her cheeks were pink from exertion and the sun.

'That must be some vista when the leaves are full out. Shame we can't get through.'

The boat settled to a cradle-rock, giving out low grunts. I twisted in my seat to observe the tantalizing keyhole view. The scene made a shallow impression; I wasn't really seeing it. Presently I said, 'Dilys . . . I wish you'd finish that sentence.'

When I turned back, she was regarding me uncomprehendingly. 'What sentence?'

'Something about the lampstand cord.'

The dullness spread to her posture. 'Honey, if it was about to signify anything, I've lost it.'

'I'll make a guess, then. You were going to say, the cord was plenty long enough for the lampstand to reach the bed.'

She rumpled her hair. 'I was?'

'And therefore, Terry could have been hit with it while he was *on* the bed. I go along with that.' I met her quizzical eyes. 'But how did you know?'

'How'd I know what?'

'The length of the cord. What made you take that much notice of it?'

Abstractedly she dipped a blade, correcting the boat's tendency to bump the bridge's stonework. Reshipping the oar, she sat gazing past me. The sun dived behind a small cloud that had rushed from nowhere. The instant its rays were obscured, the temperature plunged. I shivered.

Dilys peeped at me with a faint smile. 'I could say, I sized it up while he was handing me the package.'

'You didn't go into the bedroom.' My voice seemed to boom from the stone vault above us. 'He threw you the package in the main room. Then you left. You said so yourself.'

After some reflection, she leaned forward.

'Anjie, listen a moment. I'm sure you'd be the first to agree, we're living in dangerous times. In the Mid-East right now there's a very dicey situation; cries out for firm handling. There's trouble in Africa, Asia, South America.

The whole damn world's in a turmoil. The way it's sorted out is going to affect everybody, from here to Melbourne. The future of the human race.' She paused. 'I want you to see things in proportion.'

'Herbie never went near that bedroom. He was never at the Cosmopole.'

'We steer the right man into the hot seat, he can start right in tackling the basics. He gets squeezed out – for whatever reason – and we're in big trouble. All of us that believe in democratic freedom. You do see that?'

'Terry never gave you those prints. You took them off him – after you'd killed him. And now you're leaving Herbie to take the rap.'

'Come on, honey.' Her tone was kindly. 'I've said already, Herbie hasn't a thing to worry about, any more than you have. He'll get off with self-defence and a suspended term.'

I gaped at her. 'And if he doesn't?'

'So what?' Her voice had deepened slightly. 'He can mark it up as his contribution to Western security. Herbie's a patriot. He'd be glad to know he'd done something on account of his home team.'

'My God, Dilys. You make it sound like a college ball-game. Herbie's taken the blame for a killing that he thinks my father or Liz may have committed . . . it could blight the rest of his life. Doesn't that mean anything to you?'

'The future of mankind means more.'

The reasonableness of her intonation was making me question my own sanity. Convulsively I shook my head. 'This isn't happening. You're not saying these things.'

'But for your pigheadedness, I wouldn't need to be. Anjie, it's ridiculous. I didn't have to tell you about it, did I? You didn't have to know I'd ever been to the Cosmopole or gotten my hands on the evidence.'

'Then why – '

'I told you for the obvious reason. To put your mind at rest. Stop you panicking. The way you were talking, you sounded capable of asking the police whether anything

was found on Terry, whether Herbie had told them anything . . . all kinds of nonsense. Instead of leaving it as it
stands: a routine case of assault on a guy who was making
a nuisance of himself over a woman. Let it stay that way,
kid. Tidier all round.'

I stared at her incredulously. 'Set my mind at *rest*?'

In exasperation she blew out her cheeks. 'Look . . . I
didn't go there with the intention of knocking Terry off.
To be entirely frank, I was planning to use some feminine
wiles. Having seen Liz make off, I figured it might be a
good time to catch him on the bounce. Only it didn't pan
out that way. He wasn't looking for a consoling touch.
Not from me, at least. He was sprawled on that bed in a
cold fury . . . I might as well have gone to work on a
starving python. So, I fell back on the direct approach.'

'The direct – '

'A cash offer,' she said impatiently. 'I had to try
everything. Naturally, he wasn't interested. He already
had fifty grand; it was you he wanted. In fact, my approach seemed to infuriate him. He went crazy. Shouted
at me to get the hell out of his bedroom – honestly, honey,
for a minute there I was scared. But I stayed right where
I was, because I didn't want to give up that easily . . . and
that's when he came at me. So I grabbed the first thing,
which happened to be the lampstand. I just meant to
put him out for a while, so I could search his belongings. I
never meant him to die.'

The words sounded remorseful. And yet it was merely a
recital of regrettable events; an incident in a business
transaction. Dilys sat assessing me, observing the effect of
her unassailable logic.

I waited until I could speak audibly. 'The package was
in his inside pocket?'

'Sewn up. I had to cut the lining with a pair of nail
scissors. I doubt if the cops noticed anything; it just looked
like a frayed pocket opening when I'd done.'

'Did the package hold prints, or . . .?'

'Negs too. The works.'

I sagged a little in my seat.

'Well . . . at least we now have the full story. You'd better row us back, Dilys.'

She made no move towards the oars.

'Something still on your mind?'

'No, nothing. All straight now.'

'You'll leave it there?' she persisted. 'No more hysterics?'

'I promise not to get hysterical. Row us back.'

A sly look crawled into her features. 'What happens when we reach dry land?'

Apart from ourselves, this end of the lake remained a sequestered backwater. No indication of human activity came from either shoreline. The two bathers from the Lido had evidently retired to towel down, and as though its work could be considered accomplished, the sun had ducked back behind a violet veil that was drawing itself across the heavens, like a shutter blotting out a roof-panel. Branches stirred in a sudden gust. About and beneath us, the lake-water chopped uneasily.

'Come on, Dilys. Let's get moving.'

'We're better off here, I guess, for a while.'

'I don't like it here.' I looked up at the stonework. 'It's dismal.'

'You'd sooner we got drenched on the way back?'

'We must have had over the hour.'

She chuckled softly. 'Come in, number thirteen, your time is up . . . Tell me something, Anjie. You weren't possibly thinking of making a call when you got back? To your detective buddy, Mr Kaynes, for example?'

'He's no buddy of mine.'

'How about a straight answer, kid?'

Again the boat's prow nosed the buttress. The fingers of Dilys's right hand alighted upon the grip of an oar, rested there, failed to clench. Appearing to watch them, she eyed me from beneath her lashes.

Animatedly, to the ripples, I said, 'Why don't we row

back now, meet up with Denny, then get the train to Winchester? Whether Herbie's there or not, we could start work again. Take our minds off things. What do you say?'

The lashes fluttered. She said nothing.

'If you're tired, I'll take a spell with the oars. I've always wanted to. Let's swap seats. It's terrific here on the cushions. Really restful. I don't mind some exercise – actually, it's what I need. As long as you'll put up with me catching a few crabs.' My laugh echoed synthetically in the ceiling of the arch. Like crude counterpoint, a clap of thunder reverberated over London. I said, 'Hear that? We'll have to make a dash for it. As I step across, you slide into my seat. Ready, Dilly?'

Her head wagged with a kind of regretful contempt.

'Sorry to have to be the one to tell you this, Anjie, but as an actress you still have a whole heap to learn.'

Coolly deliberate, she pushed down with her right hand on the grip of the oar and swung the blade towards me.

Although I saw it coming, there was nothing I could do. I was programmed to the exact pace of the action. Synchronized with the projector. *Tom and Jerry*. Rampant cat with nuclear projectile. The mouse, though, invariably triumphed. Fragmented, vaporized, destroyed . . . he always turned up in the next scene. The oar-blade wavered, shot back to hit the water.

The rowlock's swivel had reached its limit, or jammed. Dilys made no fuss. Without haste she brought across her left hand, calmly lifted the oar clear of its housing.

I found words. 'Dilys, don't be stupid . . .'

She was on her feet. 'It's not me.'

The oar swept round in a scything movement.

Watching it start to come, I knew the truth. It stood out as plainly as though a book for the near-sighted, full of captioned diagrams in black ink, had been opened under my nose. Dilys, I saw from her eyes, knew that I knew. There had been no approach to Terry. No cash offer. No snatching at the lampstand as he went for her.

An image flashed across my brain: Dilys at the lunch-
table in Verucci's Steak House, wincing as she handled
a coffee-jug, nursing the hand which she had wrenched
while swinging the brasswork cold-bloodedly from behind
as her oblivious victim sat on the bed-edge, bending over to
pull on a shoe. A means to a necessary end. Just another
final solution. Because of that injured tendon, she now
needed both hands to deliver the latest instrument of
expediency. No problem. Her balance was good: dedica-
tion works marvels on the cerebral nerve-centre. And she
knew where to place her feet.

With both arms upflung, I felt the impact, felt and
heard the exodus of breath from my lungs.

I hung on. Dilys was trying to retract the oar, poise it for
a second blow; my weight balked her. She gave it a
strong tug, dragging me from the seat so that I tripped
over the footrest to sprawl along the boat's keel. Bilge-
water lapped into my mouth. I heard Dilys's shout.

'Help! Somebody help me!'

I retained a grasp of the oar. She was twisting it this
way and that, fighting for possession: keeping up her shrill
calls for assistance. The rocking of the craft was making me
dizzy. She began treading across the keel-struts towards
me, allowing the oar to pass through the crooks of her
arms. I tried a hard push upon the blade. The result it
achieved was to send it harmlessly away from me until it
fetched up against her leading elbow. She was within a
yard of me. Her eyes were open very wide.

'You're the one,' she told me brightly, 'that's being
stupid.'

The pitching of the boat returned me in a heap to the
stern seat as I scrambled up. Bilge-water strangled the
shout in my throat. Dilys halted. Stooping, she carefully
laid the oar lengthwise inside the gunwale before reseating
herself with a hand on each rowlock.

'Help me!' she screamed, rocking vigorously from side
to side.

The boat obeyed her movements. I went with the boat.

A last-second grab kept me aboard, only to be sent the opposite way, slithering across woodwork to confront the murk of water a foot from my nose. Somehow I held on. All my strength went into resisting the oscillations; there was nothing left for shouting with.

I didn't feel myself go. All I was aware of was a cranial explosion, pursued instantly by a violent abusage of nose, throat and chest; a dragging of limbs; utter blackness. I seemed to be on my head in treacle. The cold got through to me. A clamping gelidity, mind-numbing, sinew-paralysing . . . the termination of existence. I was spinning, a body impotent in space. Briefly, I saw daylight. The lake surface, vast and grey, level with my chin: for a split-second it beckoned mockingly before sliding upwards.

Before it closed over me, there was time to glimpse the whirl of the oar. Once more it was coming at me, with all the mindless insistence of an August wasp. The arm that I tried to raise, to flick it away, was held down by wool and fibre, defeated by density: the thrashing of my legs accelerated my descent. As I sank, I was jerked to one side.

Cloudily puzzled at the effect of the blow, I started to resist until a second wrench turned me on to my back. Again I could see the sky. I looked for Dilys. If she was there, towering above me, taking aim, there was nothing to be done. Even as I panted, fought for breath, futility roared at me. I was a floating target, spreadeagled for dispatch. Drifting. Or rather, making headway to the rear: I was on tow. Now I could see nothing. Water popped in my ears. The travelling motion was an improvement on the floundering one; for the moment, I was content to settle for it.

'Stay relaxed. You'll be okay.'

I kept my limbs still, wondering why Dilys's voice had become a man's. It came from somewhere behind. Water spots peppered my upturned face. They were dropping from the ceiling. The plasterwork was purple and charcoal, sadly in need of attention. Mum would have to get busy with her brush.

'She'll be fine.'

I might be, I thought, if people would stop lowering half-ton weights on to my shoulder-blades. The reflection was interrupted while I coughed out water. I wanted to retch, snatch breath, cough, clear my throat, all in the space of a micro-second. The weights, relentless, went on pressing down. Feebly I flapped a hand.

'She'll do, Paul.'

Under my chin, rain beat up from the sloping asphalt. One thing: there was no way I could become wetter than I was. The thought amused me. In all the gasping and heaving I was having to accommodate, mirth struggled for a place.

'How about the other one?'

I listened vainly for a reply. Hiccups shook me from neck to thighs: when the spasms had passed, I rolled myself over, peered up at a face.

'You'll be fine,' it assured me.

His vocabulary seemed one-track. Also he was pop-eyed. My internal giggles forced a way out.

Disapproval marched into his face. Trying to control myself, I noted that he was bare to the waist: below that, blue tracksuit trousers clung wetly to lean legs. He said with some severity, 'Your friend – '

A hiss came from somewhere. Turning my head, I saw his companion, crouched nearby, attired likewise in the lower half of running gear: scarlet, with white piping. Both of them seemed to be in their thirties. Hair dripped over their faces.

Helped by the blue one's arm, I got myself into a sitting position. 'She tried to kill me,' I announced.

They exchanged looks.

I tried to add something, but laughter seized me again. A stinging slap across the face put an end to that. True to convention, I wept copiously for half a minute. When I had calmed down, the blue one supporting me said on a prim note: 'Maybe you should be choosier about your boating partners.'

'Where is she?'

'You should be under cover. Steve, you take her legs . . .'

'I'm all right.' I shook them off. 'What happened? Did she get away?'

After a pause, the scarlet one said, 'We really must get you out of this torrent – you'll be ripe for double pneumonia. My colleague's car – '

'Please tell me.'

A few yards out from the bank. the outline of the rowing boat was discernible through the do .npour. It was empty and adrift. Climbing groggily to my knees, I saw something else closer to the bridge: a formless heap at the water's edge. Paul and Steve tried ineffectually to block the view.

Conceding failure, Steve said apologetically, 'I did what I could . . . but she'd had it anyway. Smashed her head against the bridge, I reckon, as she went in.'

As though intent on demonstrating that nothing was being left to chance, Paul said conscientiously, 'Kiss of life, Steve?'

'Nope.'

'Why not?'

'You try it,' muttered his friend, 'on someone who's bashed her brains out.' Rising abruptly, he vaulted some railings to vanish up a bank into bushes.

Paul gazed after him for a moment.

'You know,' he said earnestly, turning back to me, 'it's lucky for you we happened to be around. We don't normally jog this way.' He glanced towards the bushes. 'Don't worry about him. He'll be – '

'Don't tell me,' I interceded. 'Steve's going to be fine. *Everything's* going to turn out just great.'

A renewal of coughing brought tears back to my eyes. Wrapping an arm about me, Paul steered me along the footpath towards the slope that led upwards to the road.

CHAPTER XXIV

AND NOW – ANJIE THE AUTHOR?

CREAM SLICES AND I, unhappily, don't get along. Anjie Browne's metabolism is obviously different. When I met her for tea this week, not only did she accept one of the Imperial's sloshiest confections: she ate it, too. Sliver by sliver.

Watching its disappearance with respect, I reminded its equally delectable eliminator that sixteen months had elapsed since our last meeting. On that occasion, she was here to make a film. What was the purpose of her trip this time?

'To see my family,' she told me, 'and look up a few old friends.' She took a lingering bite. 'Also,' she added, 'for a rest. Which won't last long, I might add. I'm due back in Hollywood next week to start on another picture for Herb Joseph.'

I said it looked as though relaxation agreed with her. She concurred.

'Mind you, I've been playing a lot of badminton. This house I've taken in Highgate Village has its own court. And I've a neighbour who's as keen as I am. Very handy. Come over some time – I'll give you a work-out.'

If there was a private swimming pool as well, I hedged, I might be tempted. Anjie said there wasn't. 'Swimming's not exactly my thing. I can exist without it.'

Ever tactful, I made no comment. But Anjie Browne, superstar, is nothing if not a forthright East Londoner at heart. She looked me straight in the eye.

'I know what you're thinking. It's because I almost drowned in the Serpentine last year. But that has nothing to do with it. In fact, since then I've learnt to swim . . . well, it seemed scatty not to, didn't it? But as to being *fond*

of the water . . . On the whole, I much prefer dry ground.
A solid footing.'

And was this, I ventured, something that she now had?
Her smile knocked me back a yard.

'Yes, thank you. I know where I stand. I've come to
terms with myself.'

No regrets about making that costly disaster, *Furnace of
the Mind*?

She thought about it. 'Regrets? That's a harsh word.
It taught me something. I think everyone involved with
the project learned a lesson of some kind. Mine was: it
doesn't pay to step out of your class. Materially, artistically, or any other way.'

More pondering. A cogitative nibble at the cream slice.
'About the time *Furnace* came along, I suppose I was
getting fairly choked off with the kind of image I had. I
wanted to prove – to myself and the world – that I could
rise above it. I know; it's an old, weary story. Nearly as
trite as Just Good Friends. But *Furnace* really did seem to
represent an escape hatch.' Her lovely eyes met mine for
a rueful moment. 'Looking back now, I can see . . . I
think most people can. It was a frightful miscalculation.'

And Herb Joseph, I enquired delicately. Could he see
it?

A throaty chuckle. 'Herbie was the first to surrender.
He blamed himself for the whole shambles. Only of course
it wasn't just him. Roger Mayhew, for instance . . . he's a
marvellous director, I've still the greatest respect for him
– this latest thing he's just done with Graham Forde,
Whirlwind, is the tops – but as far as *Furnace* was concerned,
I think he saw it at a different point on the spectrum to
several of us . . . in fact, most people seemed to have their
own ideas about how it should be done . . . so we never got
co-ordinated. As for the author . . .' A reminiscent smile.
'Jon Templar was truly nice and philosophical about the
entire thing. We're still great pals, incidentally, he and
his wife and I. I've been along to see them again. I think
he came to appreciate – as most of us did in the end – that

Furnace is an incredibly elusive sort of book to try to put on screen. The narrative style . . . I don't know. It has a shading that doesn't quite show up.'

Another bite. 'At least, it didn't in our version. Someone else might have a more successful stab. I hope so. I'd love to see a motion picture that did it justice.'

Possibly, I hinted, the storyline needed, to put it bluntly, more action?

'You might be right. Anyway, if it's action you're looking for, the film I made directly afterwards, back in Hollywood, ought to be right up your street. On release here shortly. *Stampede*. It's me in my original style, only more so. Herbie's expecting big things of it. It's done well in the States, and we're hoping it'll appeal just as keenly to British audiences.'

From which, I remarked, the deduction seemed to be that Joseph Films were not exactly headed for extinction.

'The publicity,' she said dryly, 'from all the furore last year didn't seem to do any irreparable harm.'

A middle-aged female admirer paused at our table to gush. She was countered with charm, handed an autographed menu, sent away happy. Then Anjie Browne, with a total lack of self-consciousness, returned to her cream slice.

My next question was phrased with care.

Last year's furore, as she called it, could hardly have been a help in the making of *Furnace*. Without it, might the outcome have been different?

Her headshake was decisive. 'Not a scrap. I'm no dramatic actress – never will be.'

After some contemplative munches she added: 'My kid sister, Liz – now she could be another story. She's just made a big hit in a local amateur production of *The Chalk Garden*. And she'll be starting at drama school soon. She's mad about the stage. I think she'll make it, too. Though I say it myself, she's not bad.'

She did her best to keep the pride out of her voice. A close-knit family, the Browns of West Ham. The Thespian accomplishments of sixteen-year-old Elizabeth, one feels, are apt to take pride of place with her celebrated sister, to the exclusion if necessary of her own concerns. Just the same, I felt I should ask.

What view did she now take of the medium-term future?

'A placid one, I hope,' she said after a pause. 'By that, I mean I'm not looking for another *Furnace* to turn up . . . as I said, I've come to terms with my limitations. But I am hoping to diversify a little.' She peeped at me severely. 'You won't laugh if I tell you?'

I gave a solemn pledge. She said, 'I'm writing a book.'

Feeling no urge to laugh, I made no comment. With a mixture of defensiveness and defiance, she went on: 'I suppose you'd call it autobiographical. Anyway it's based on some of my experiences. Probably no publisher will look at it, but that doesn't bother me. I'm just enjoying the challenge.'

Those famous, flecked-blue eyes strafed me again. 'I can tell what you're thinking. Oh no – not another celluloid celebrity diving into print . . . I can promise you this, I shan't be hiring a ghost-writer. Every syllable will be mine. So if it comes out a mess, at least it'll be my own mess and nobody else's.'

I disclaimed any insinuation to the contrary. 'Would you describe it as a novel?'

She giggled. 'I'd describe it as indescribable. The readers had better decide – if they ever get the chance to see it. I half-wish I hadn't mentioned it to you.'

Was she asking me to treat the information as off-the-record?

'No,' she said, suddenly serious. 'I don't mind people knowing. If they're not interested, it doesn't matter. And if they are . . .' She doodled on the back of another menu. 'It might get 'em intrigued, mightn't it?'

Indeed it might, I agreed. Especially if the book threw light upon certain things that at present remained somewhat obscure.

'What things?' she enquired innocently.

Such as, for example, last year's Serpentine drama to which she had already referred.

'What more is there to know about that?'

'I was hoping you might tell me.'

'But it all came out at the time. Dilys Meridew killed Terry (*screen swashbuckler Terence O'Malley*) because he'd given her the brush-off and was trying to get back with me – via a member of my family. And then she had a shot at disposing of me because I'd guessed she did it. End of screenplay.'

But it had been suggested in some quarters that the background to the event was less uncomplicated than this.

She studied me with the same wholesome innocence. 'Suggestions of that kind aren't uncommon.'

True, I murmured. But sometimes they rested on a firmer base. For example, where did producer Herb Joseph come in?

'Herbie.' Her voice held the affection of a favoured niece. 'He was just trying to help out. There was a time – briefly – when he really had got hold of the idea that some-body close to me might have put Terry out of the way. So he stepped in to take the blame.'

More than a little quixotic, surely?

'I thought it was marvellous of him,' she said, un-affectedly. 'I'll never forget what he did. I'm only thank-ful that, as it turned out, he was able to prove he was elsewhere at the crucial time. Though I think it would have been all right, anyhow. That witness came forward – the hotel waiter who saw Dilys sitting in the lounge twenty minutes before Terry's death. Plus the fact that my two lake rescuers actually caught a glimpse of Dilys hammering at me with an oar before she swung herself overboard and hit her head on the bridge. I mean, at the time of that incident, Terry was already dead. Even allowing for jealousy, why would she have taken the risk – unless there was something she had to have kept hidden?'

Fair question, I conceded.

My hesitancy must have shown. 'I know,' she added impatiently. 'Lots of innuendo was drifting around at the time. It was even hinted that the boot might have been on the other foot – I was the one attacking her. Big names were supposed to have been involved in some way. Cloaks and daggers to the far horizon.' She smiled. 'Now that would make a story.'

'And will it?'

'You'll have to wait and see, won't you?' she said playfully. 'Like everybody else.'

On the last occasion we had met, I reminded her, I had asked her about a visit paid to me at the *Sunday World* offices by her ex-husband. Without being specific, he had led me to understand that he was in possession of documents whose publication could well be harmful to her. That was just a few days before his sudden death.

She nodded. 'I remember.'

Had she nothing now to add to this?

The last of the cream slice vanished. It all seemed to have travelled down pretty harmlessly. So had my questions. The survey I was receiving from Anjelica Browne was as winsome, as guileless as any she has ever beamed at a male recipient on a film studio set: and in the transmission of these, as most of us know, she has few equals.

'Not now,' she said.

CHAPTER XXV

'HI, ANGEL.' Herbie sounded medium-buoyant. 'It's all fixed. Shooting starts next week. That suit you?'

'I'm afraid not.' There was silence in California. 'But seeing it's you, Herbie, I'll try to show up.'

'You don't have proper respect,' he said reproachfully, 'for my cardiac murmur.'

'Sorry. Just testing the deadness of my pan.' I cleared

my throat. 'Oh, incidentally. I'll be bringing somebody.'

His response was quick, a shade hearty. 'Denny's filming in Yugoslavia, I thought?'

'He is. It's not Denny, it's Adrian.' Silence. 'You remember. Roger Mayhew's assistant on *Furnace*. Adrian Allister. We bumped into one another again, a few weeks back. At a party.'

'Oh sure. Nice guy. Quiet, as I recall. Also talented. Latest documentary of his just landed a PDI Award in New York . . . you knew that. Look forward to seeing you both, honey. We'll take in a celebration dinner at Carlino's, the three of us. Consider it a date.'

'Thanks, Herbie.' I gulped. 'See you in a couple of days' time.'

'Take care.'

It was a little absurd, I told myself as I hung up, to be biting back tears when I felt on top of the world.

My Beverley Hills house, lately acquired, was a good place in which to unwind. We used it as a base while I showed Adrian the sights of Los Angeles. For two days, anonymous, unpestered, we enjoyed ourselves. During a late breakfast on our third morning I was watching him spread honey on his toast when the telephone bleeped.

The voice was faintly guttural. 'Is this Miss Anjelica Browne, the screen actress? Miss Browne, my name is Sven Lundstrom. I've the honour to be the West Coast representative of Fullerton Publications of New York. Possibly you'll have heard of Fullerton Publications?'

'Didn't they bring out *Long Time Riding* a few months back?'

'You have it.' The voice perked up. 'Miss Browne, I'll get right to the point. We learn that you're in the midst of a work of literature at the present time. Is our information correct?'

'I suppose you read that in one of the newspapers.'

'The reports are inaccurate?'

'Not exactly. I am trying to write a book.'

'We'd be *very* interested to see it.'

'It's nowhere near finished.'

'No matter. We'd appreciate a first look at the manuscript when it's completed to your satisfaction. Meantime, we'd be happy to offer an appropriate sum to secure an option on the rights to publish. One hundred thousand dollars.'

I glanced through the arched opening at Adrian, reflectively chewing in the adjoining room. 'I'd need to think about that.'

'Please do.' He repeated his name and gave me a number. 'Call me any time. I hope you'll give serious consideration to our proposal.'

'What makes you think I wouldn't? Thanks for calling, Mr Lundstrom. I'll be in touch.'

I stood for a few seconds alongside the telephone before returning to the breakfast table. Adrian smiled up at me with his eyes.

'Somebody after your memoirs?'

'Fullerton's of New York.'

He sat up. 'They're big, aren't they? Will you accept their offer?'

'I said I'd think about it.'

His look became quizzical.

I sat down. 'From an apprentice writer, that must sound pretty arrogant. But it's not that I want to quibble over terms. It's just that I'm not quite sure . . .'

'Whether you want anything published at all?'

'Right,' I said gratefully.

I pondered for a while. 'One problem is, the book's not written yet. Not started, even. Just a few notes. I'll probably make a hash of it. Then what?'

'You can do it.'

'Time. That's another thing. Can I possibly get enough? Writing a book, the way I want to do it, takes an eternity. I've got commitments. After this next film for Herbie – '

'Is it me you're trying to convince? Or are you doing

your best to talk yourself out of the idea?'

I met his glance. 'I think you're getting to know me.'

Taking up his reading glasses, he polished them attentively with a serviette.

'One more avuncular question: then I'm through. Assuming you do get down to this opus . . . is it likely to include any eye-popping revelations?'

'That,' I said slowly, collecting plates, 'is part of what I have to think about.'

From Herbie's penthouse suite on the 38th floor, the view was fabulous. Con-cientiously, everyone at the party was ignoring it.

'Having fun, you two?' Herbie clapped Adrian's shoulder. 'Did Anjie tell you, we have a dinner date? Carlino's, next Wednesday. But first . . .' He gestured ruefully at the pack. 'First we have to do things the Hollywood way.'

Adrian gave his understanding smile. I said, 'If it helps sell *Typhoon* to the columnists, it's worth every hangover – right, Herbie?'

'Anjie's a good kid,' he informed Adrian. 'Hates the razzamatazz, but hides her feelings for the sake of the corporation.'

For an instant, as our eyes met, he was having difficulty in camouflaging his own. Then the smile was back. 'Honey, I almost forgot. Some guy was asking for you. Special request for an interview – some Washington paper, I gathered. Feel like talking to him? You don't have to.'

I twitched my chin at Adrian. 'I don't have to . . . stammers he, tears coursing down both cheeks. Where is he, Herbie?'

'Out on the terrace. Excuse us a few minutes, Adrian old buddy? She'll not be long.'

Steering me between bodies, he said, 'That young man'll be good for you, Angel.'

I made my reply light. 'I'm hoping not to do him any lasting damage.'

We reached the sliding doors; he pointed an elbow. 'That's him.'

The man surveying the lights of the city from a corner of the terrace wall turned at our approach. He was slim, soberly-suited, reticent in manner. Around forty, I decided. Herbie introduced him as Wilbert Franklin, before excusing himself. 'I have a party,' he explained, 'to jolly along. See you later, Angel.' He returned inside.

Wilbert Franklin regarded me in silence. I tried to exude radiance. 'Terrific view, isn't it?'

There seemed no risk of his coming back with a smart double-entendre, and in fact all that he said was 'Extremely.' He said it with abstraction. His gaze remained static.

I said, 'I understand you'd like an interview. Shall we sit over there?'

He looked round at the spot I was indicating, but made no move. 'Or perhaps,' I said, swallowing irritation, 'you'd prefer to go back inside – though it's rather a crush.'

He seemed to be weighing me up. The annoyance inside me threatened to bubble over. I managed a laugh. 'Look, I don't want to crowd you, but I do have other demands on my time. If there are some questions you want to – '

'Just one question.' His voice was confident but low. 'I'd like to ask whether you have any objection to leaving this party with me for a while . . . shall we say, approximately twenty minutes? No longer.'

I stared; laughed again. 'Is this a legpull of some kind?'

His head jerked, once. 'No gag intended, Miss Browne. And you've nothing to fear, let me assure you. I sincerely would appreciate your consent to accompanying me to the basement garage of this building where we have a car waiting. You'll be back here inside of half an hour.'

I examined him hard. 'Are you police?'

Another jerk of the head. 'Emphatically not.'

I cast a look around. The few other guests scattered

about the terrace were taking no notice of us. 'Then
either this is a very clumsy kidnap attempt or it's a stunt.
Are we being recorded? I'm sure Mr Joseph wouldn't like
it if – '

'No recording,' he said patiently. 'This couldn't be a
more private matter.' He paused. 'As a former acquaintance of Miss Dilys Meridew, you're in a good position to
appreciate that.'

'What did you say?'

He knew I hadn't misheard. With an unnerving mute
self-assurance, he stood waiting. A clutch of possible
reactions thudded through my brain, yielding finally to
the one utterance that seemed to make any sense. 'Half an
hour?'

'At the end of that time, you'll be right back here.'

'I can't even guess what this is about . . . but on that
understanding, I'll come. I must have a quick word with
my – '

'Tell him you're going to the powder room.'

I expelled some breath. 'Okay.'

A couple of minutes later he was waiting for me at the
elevator. Silently he pressed open the doors, stood back to
allow me in. We glided to the basement garage, and
stepped out. Side by side, we waited at the edge of a
vacant bay under harsh white lighting.

The parallels with a screen thriller were too patent to
be ignored. I said sardonically, 'When does the car pull
out to drive straight at us?'

On cue, a saloon with tinted windows appeared in a
hush of tyres and motor and braked opposite us; at the
same instant the front passenger door swung open. Wilbert
Franklin motioned politely. With a shrug, I ducked into
the seat. Waiting until I was settled, he eased the door
back into place. Ghostlike, the car took off, leaving him
standing there.

'My apologies, Miss Browne, for interrupting the
party.'

The line, too, was pure Bogart. The voice wasn't. I

peered through the gloom. The man at the wheel seemed to be elderly. 'The one thing I'm certain of at this moment,' I told his profile, 'is that I don't know you from Adam. What's this all in aid of?'

Now that I was committed, I was cursing my own gullibility. It seemed to me that I had fallen for the hoariest of tricks. The fact that he offered no reply, however, was due apparently to the fierceness of his concentration upon the hazards of the ramp. Achieving street level, he wheeled the car to the right and set it gliding in the downtown direction, keeping slavishly to the nearside and not exceeding thirty. In the radiance from the street, I saw that he was somewhere in reach of his mid-sixties and possessed a strong, cynical mouth above a jutting chin. His hair, white but still thick, was swept neatly back. His nose was straight. While driving, he divided his attention evenly between the road ahead and the car's mirror. He would have served as the model for an instructional film on roadcraft techniques. When he had reached top gear, he said conversationally, 'Mr Franklin had instructions not to take no for an answer if he could help it. Did you take much persuading?'

'What would you consider a lot?'

'Oh . . .' Breath buzzed between his teeth. 'Everyone has his own ideas on that, I guess. I'll assume you came readily. For which I'm grateful.'

'It's not your gratitude I want. It's an explanation. Where are we going?'

'Just around a few blocks.'

'What for?'

'So we can talk. If the nature of this operation seems excessively cloak-and-dagger, Miss Browne, then I can only apologize. I had to speak with you. Incognito. Ordinarily I'd have waited for some more civilized opportunity, but since there seemed to us to be an element of urgency . . . Do you have any idea what I'm referring to?'

'Joseph Films don't hire me for my mind-reading.'

He frowned slightly. 'All you showbiz personalities . . . They teach you this sort of talk? The mechanized wisecrack, I guess you might call it.' Brooding briefly, he added, 'Not that Washington's so different, in its fashion.'

'Washington,' I repeated slowly.

'A community with a language all its own. Then again, the newspapers: they seem to develop a brand of expression peculiar to themselves. Which brings me to the matter in hand.'

'That's something of a relief.'

He continued unperturbed. 'It concerns your . . . literary ambitions, Miss Browne.'

'Oh? You've been hearing about those?'

'Reading about them. Finding them intriguing.'

He eased the car right at an intersection. Conscious of a lessening of tension, I said, 'You're not a publisher, by any chance?'

'No, I'm not.' He spoke like a benevolent course-leader volunteering information at the behest of an inquisitive but favoured student. 'I do have to admit, however, this is one book I'm interested in.'

'It doesn't even exist yet.'

Intent upon the scene beyond the windscreen, he nodded. 'I was hoping you might say that.'

We travelled to the next intersection, which he crossed with due caution. On our left, a couple of cars slid past; he slowed further to accommodate them. The nature and extent of his vigilance bordered upon the ludicrous.

'I've drunk a little champagne,' I acknowledged. 'It may be that my brain isn't bang up to the mark. Would you mind talking down to it? First you say you're interested, then you say . . . I don't get it.'

He frowned again, this time more intensely.

'Dilys always described you as a young woman of exceptional intelligence. Which is certainly the impression you convey.'

Eighty or a hundred yards ahead, a pedestrian showed signs of starting to think about stepping into the road. The car's progress became a crawl. Headlamp beams flashed. If a siren didn't wail, I had the feeling that it was only because of a deficiency in the vehicle's equipment in this respect. As we passed, the pedestrian waved ironically, bawled something. He was ignored. The car picked up a little pace.

I said, 'You didn't see fit to introduce yourself. But since I'm so bright, perhaps I ought to draw my own conclusions.' I studied what I could see of him under the fitful illuminations. 'Dilys told me quite a lot about you, Mr Meridew.'

'We got on well,' he said without emotion. 'Had a good understanding. That whole London affair . . . awful. I trust, Miss Browne, you're fully recovered from your ordeal?'

'Look, I don't know what to say. Dilys was a friend of mine, an absolute bosom pal until – '

He lifted a hand from the wheel. 'Save it,' he said mildly. 'What's past is gone. She can't be brought back. I won't say I don't miss her. Sure, I miss her.' Changing gear with scrupulous movements, he leaned rather than turned the car into a corner, established it in its new direction along a minor street, gave attention to an adjustment of the speed. 'Tended to count on her overmuch, maybe. But then, she *was* damned efficient. Regardless of the finale, she did a good job that time. We'd like the result to stand.'

My brain was adapting, like the car, to a new rate of revolutions per minute. Until I had it smoothly at tickover, I was saying nothing.

'Which probably explains why, on reading newspaper accounts of fat offers by New York publishers for personal revelations by Hollywood screen celebrities . . . we do have this tendency to get a little flurried.'

'I see.'

'You do?' He kept his gaze fixedly ahead.

'I don't think Dilys was wildly off the mark about my intelligence.'

'Neither do I. So now we come to the tricky part.'

'You want me to give you an outline of what it is I'm planning to write?'

'We'd prefer that you gave an undertaking to write nothing whatever.'

'I'm afraid I couldn't do that.'

'What seems to be the obstacle?'

I examined his outline. 'The obstacle, as you term it, is simply that I refuse to do anything of the kind. My adult life, Mr Meridew, has been swayed and dominated quite enough as it is. I'm not standing for any more.'

His sigh sounded calculated. 'Okay. How much?'

My laughter was real. 'You can't think it's a question of money? I've more than I can ever hope to handle.'

'So,' he said quietly, after an interval, 'it's an ego-trip?'

'Call it what you like. I'd sooner describe it as something I must do. Putting the record straight.'

'You appreciate, the record features others in addition to yourself.'

'I'm only too aware of that.'

He was silent for a quarter of a mile.

'A verbal assurance, then. That you won't – '

'I'm making no promises of any kind.'

Presently he began to speak with a more measured cadence; although the pitch of his voice remained the same, it seemed to gain in timbre. I was reminded of Dilys when she was talking on the Serpentine.

'Miss Browne, may I put something to you? We have, at this present time, a firm hand at the helm of the American ship of state . . . if you'll accept a somewhat florid analogy. The benefits are self-evident. Before long – assuming that all goes well, and with one notable exception there's small reason why they shouldn't – those benefits will collect into an irresistible flood that will cleanse and purify the lifeblood not merely of the United States institution but of the entire Western hemisphere. It just needs time. Time for the antibodies to get to work, start pounding back at those bugs that are trying to eat their way inside. Now wouldn't you agree: anything – any single thing – liable to impede this course of events should be overruled and swept aside in the cosmic interest?'

'Very eloquent,' I said coldly. 'These benefits you're talking about . . . I can't truthfully say I find them so glaring. And if I did, it wouldn't make a jot of difference. What I decide to do or not do is my own affair.'

'You have a fine career behind and ahead of you. For the sake of a questionable excursion into what might be labelled a dubious form of literature – '

'It's hardly an excursion. I'm thinking of making it my goal. Just between ourselves, Mr Meridew, I've had far more than too much of Hollywood; it's only a matter of personal loyalty keeping me here at all.'

'Is that so?' He said it half to himself.

'It is so. And now I'd be obliged if you'd drive us back into that garage and let me out so that I can rejoin the party. The people I was with will be wondering what's happened.'

The illuminated garage-sign showed ahead to our right. Without a word, he steered to the head of the ramp and, with the same precautions that he had displayed throughout, took us underground. Halting the car opposite the elevator doors, he secured the handbrake before reaching across me to rest his fingers on the door-release. Instead of activating it, he stayed in that position. His face was a foot from mine.

'When I decided to make contact with you, Miss Browne, I figured I might have something of a task on my hands. But my assumption at that time was that I'd be talking to a screen star who was toying with the idea of dabbling in some profitable reminiscences. I didn't realize I'd be dealing with a would-be professional authoress to whom screen antics have become, to put it bluntly, a bore. That's a new situation. One we shall have to evaluate.'

He was silent for a few seconds, his breath fanning my face, not unpleasantly.

'Before I say anything more: are you still declining to consent to modify this project or abandon it?'

'I'm declining to say, one way or another.' My own breath was a little short; partly from anger. 'I haven't yet decided what I shall be doing. What form my writings might take. When I do, I shall simply go ahead: nobody's going to dictate to me.' I paused. 'And you can tell that to the President, next time you're licking his boots.'

The door-release clicked under his fingers.

'Good night, Miss Browne. Enjoy the rest of the party. Oh . . . and you will watch your step? Planet Earth can be a dangerous place to dwell. Every thinking person knows that.'

Adrian was waiting patiently where I had left him.

'Thought you'd walked out on us. Herbie's been looking for you. How did the interview go? Give all the right replies?'

'From where I was sitting . . . I think so.' I held his thin arm. 'Can we slip away, do you think? I'll phone Herbie tomorrow.'

'If you've had enough.' He looked faintly surprised, but relieved. 'Feeling tired, darling?'

'Just anxious for a good night's sleep.' I led the way to the nearest exit, waving to anyone who glanced across to notice. 'I'd like to be super-fresh tomorrow. There's a book I'm hoping to make a start on.'